FARADAY'S MIRROR

Book One

Through the Looking Glass

Scott Davis Howard

FARADAY'S MIRROR

Book One
Through the Looking Glass

Scott Davis Howard

PJPF Press
The Piedmont Journal of Poetry & Fiction

www.pjpfpress.com

This story is a work of fiction. Names, characters, businesses, places, events and incidents are the products of the author's imagination, from European history, mythology, and are used in a fictitious manner. Any resemblance to actual persons, living or dead, or actual events is coincidental.

ISBN: 978-0-578-73322-7

Cover design by Virginia Saunders

(www.VirginiaSaunders.com)

To my brothers, Lauren and Eric, and to my sons, Marshall and Alden,
without any of whom I wouldn't be the man I am today.

PROLOGUE
February 1996

Chief Aldrich set his coffee down beside the strobing lights and leaned against his cruiser. He pushed up his cap and scratched his coarse hair. Steam rose into the frigid air from his cup and from the wreckage of the Oakes' family home, especially where Mansfield stood in the shallow cellar-hole, raking the ash in search of human remains.

Thirty-two hours had passed since the catastrophic fire torched the house; only a skeleton of charred beams now stood. The Plymouth Fire Department was long gone, and Charles and Felicity Oakes had been relocated to the Econo Lodge off Daniel Webster Highway, where they were—hopefully—getting some sleep and beginning to cope with the tragedy of losing their home and children.

Aldrich focused his gaze on the outstretched glove of Officer Partlow in front of him. It held a Ziploc bag full of blackened teeth from the mouth of a large canine.

"So, you found the remains of . . ." he glanced down at a yellow notepad on his clipboard, inked over with handwritten information about the family and house, "the German shepherd, but still no trace of the boys?"

"Nothin', Chief," Partlow replied, giving a terse shake of his head. "Not a speck. No bones. No teeth. Nothin'. Don't think they're in there, to tell you the truth."

"Then where?"

Partlow shrugged, "Beats me."

Aldrich nodded, noncommittally. "Keep looking."

"Well, Chief, you know we already been through this wreckage three times," the officer said, rubbing the bristly auburn ends of his mustache with nervous fingers. "Not lazy times, neither. We done that archeology grid pattern you asked us to. We're being," he thought for a moment, "meticulous."

The old man met his gaze with cold eyes until Partlow mumbled, "Yeah, we'll go through it again, just to be sure." He turned, picking his way back to the steaming rubble. He took up a thin-tined rake, stepped over the blackened concrete foundation, and shook his head at his partner.

Bud Aldrich had been on the Plymouth police force for nearly 40 years and served as Chief for over a decade. He'd broken up a heroin ring, taken a bullet during a domestic dispute call, ticketed an acting governor for DUI, and yet this might be the most difficult case of his career. Aldrich liked answers, and he had none.

He flipped through the glossy pictures under the pad on his clipboard. The two-story clapboard house had caught and burned like kindling, faster than any fifteen-year-old home had a right to, what with federal fire-safety regulations. The cause wasn't electrical or connected to the kitchen or furnace—it was chemical and centrally located, as if someone had fire-bombed the place from the inside. Analysis of beam-ash showed that the napalm-like accelerant wasn't gasoline, kerosene, or butane. It had the chemists down in Concord stumped.

Arson, the word stung in his mind. He'd called an arson investigator yesterday, talked it all through. The man and his accelerant detection canine would arrive within the hour. The Chief prepared himself for a lecture on the ways in which his men had disturbed the crime scene while looking for bodies.

Aldrich glanced at his watch. He opened the door of his cruiser, tossed his clipboard and the bag of teeth onto the seat, picked up his coffee, and took a sip. Who, he thought, starts a fire in an upstairs hallway? What could be the motive? Similar fires had been set by homeowners for insurance money, but the Oakes weren't in debt. They had no wealth to speak of, maybe $9,000 in the bank and a bit more than that locked away in retirement accounts—not enough for ransom. The family was well-liked, too, members of a local church and Scout troop, charitable with their time and money. They homeschooled their kids, so there wasn't any high school drama.

Racial terrorism? It was an election year. Political tension was high. Felicity Oakes was black and the boys were mixed, but this was New England, and a college-town at that. It was an accepting place. To Aldrich's knowledge, they hadn't seen a hate crime in 50 years. What about drugs? The Irish Mob? He couldn't discount it. The family had come up from Boston.

He stared at the ruined home, forcing himself to reconsider some of the ugly possibilities. Perhaps the boys set the fire to mask their own flight? To where? Why? Could they have wanted their parents dead? He shook his head. There just wasn't enough data to make those kinds of grisly calculations, and as a small-town cop, he hated them.

He closed the door of his cruiser, grunted, and set off around the yard again, his boots crunching the frozen mud. The heat of the flames and hose-water had combined to melt and saturate the yard, which re-froze overnight. Crisply iced footprints of firefighters crisscrossed ruts from the wheels of the engines. It was all jumbled, but Aldrich couldn't find evidence that anyone had approached the house or left it. No prints went off into the woods beyond the ring of activity.

A wider search had uncovered little—no discarded fuel containers or evidence of vehicles parked along the road. Neighbors had nothing suspicious to report, and Rick Hubbard, diagonally across the street, had been tinkering with a snowmobile in his garage—its door wide open—at the time of the fire . . .

So, where were the boys?

Bud Aldrich cracked the knuckles in his right hand, popping them one after another. A raven scolded him from a hemlock tree. He scowled up, partially at the bird and partially at God. He had no answers, not even a lead, and unless the arson investigator turned up something he'd missed, he'd have to admit it to the parents soon.

Chapter One
The Fatal Slapshot

Three Months Earlier:

Like so many wonderful and tragic things, it all started by mistake. Byron C. Oakes, the fourteen-year-old phenom, gripped his hockey stick and wove in and out of a laundry-pile obstacle course, dodging, spinning, and sliding with ease. Puck-handling a worn-out tennis ball and trying to avoid his dog, Harald (who eyed it with more than a passing interest), Byron halted and took a slapshot. It clunked off the water heater at a crazy angle, ricocheting from a cluttered knick-knack shelf before bouncing down the hall, Harald in hot pursuit.

In fairness, Byron was a *defensive* phenom—the second best player on his travel team, but obviously not yet an excellent marksman, not with a ball, anyway.

On the shelf, a jade elephant toppled into a pewter frame, which tottered for a moment, half over the edge, before dropping to the linoleum with a crunch.

"Fudge sundae!" Byron swore through gritted teeth. He'd gotten in the habit of avoiding more robust cuss-words because his mom had excellent hearing.

"What was *that?*" a stern female voice carried down the stairs. She knew how to say it with just the right amount of understated threat.

"Nothing, Mom! Just practicing hockey," he lied. "I hit the water heater." Well, sort of a half-lie.

His ever-cheerful shepherd returned, ears erect, and dropped the unrepentant ball at his feet.

Byron kicked it back down the hall and bent to pick up the frame. It wasn't as bad as he'd feared. The glass had cracked into three long, jagged shards instead of shattering into a million bits. It'd be pretty easy to clean up. Taking a dirty shirt from the laundry, he placed the frame and shards in it, careful to avoid cutting his fingers. He'd bring it to his brother and see what his options were.

Replace the glass?

Hide it and feign ignorance?

Fess up?

Cole was older. He'd know what to do.

Harald returned again. The ball dropped, leaving a ring of saliva.

Ignoring it, Byron padded across the floor and up the stairs, silent in his socks.

Harald watched him go, whined, scooped up the ball between his teeth, and followed, his nails tapping happily and his tail wagging.

Now upstairs, Byron turned into Cole's room and shut the door. His older brother was sitting on a beat-up swivel chair, hunched over the exposed guts of a desktop computer, soldering iron in hand and headphones over his ears. Despite the sunshine outside, he had the shade drawn, and a bright lamp shone on his work. The room smelled like burning electrics, soccer cleats, and model glue.

"Hey, nerd," Byron began, "help me out here."

He got no response, so he repeated himself, using his brother's name this time.

"One minute, jock," Cole replied, pulling the headphones off and letting them rest around his neck. *Green Day's* "Welcome to Paradise" carried thinly across the room. He picked up a paper schematic and cross-referenced a detail from it with his work. "I've almost brought this dead processor back to life."

Harald whined and thumped outside the door.

"Oh, alright," Byron grumbled, opening it for the dog. Harald waggled both his tail and his butt, scooped up the ball, and padded into the room, repeatedly nudging Byron's hand with his snout. Again Byron closed the door—an *Apollo 13* poster of the *Saturn 5* rocket, mid-launch, covered its inside, its corners curling around pushpins—and turned back toward his brother.

Colton Augustine Oakes was a genius, at least Byron believed so. Maybe some wouldn't be inclined to agree, judging from his old, threadbare *Zelda* tee shirt and the various posters on the wall: *Stargate, The X-Files, Army of Darkness, The Terminator,* and the cover art for Rush's *2112* album, but Cole knew almost everything about science, math, and especially computers. Not surprising, considering their mom had been a computer science major at MIT. Yet, Cole wasn't like one of those TV nerds. Sure, he scored in the highest stanine on IQ tests, he didn't understand mundane things like cooking or laundry very well, and he'd outgrown his pants again, so he showed altogether too much sock, but he played excellent midfield in soccer and swam competitively. Cole was an extrovert, too, good with people and easy in conversation. And he was a wiz at video games. He'd won everything they'd owned or borrowed for the *Nintendo*, *SNES*, and *SEGA*.

Still tinkering with the computer, Colton continued ignoring Byron. His brother didn't like it.

"Hey," Byron whined, "I said help me out here." He dropped the dirty tee shirt on Cole's table. It made an intriguing muffled scraping sound. Cole looked up from his soldering iron and removed his safety glasses. He had his dad's blue eyes under his tangled mop of dark hair.

"What's that?"

"I busted a picture," Byron shrugged unapologetically. "Take a look."

Cole's adept brown fingers unfolded the shirt. "That old one from downstairs?"

"Yep. You think we can replace the glass? Or maybe take it out and put it back up? They might not notice."

Cole removed the shards, looking for the first time with seriousness at the photo. In splotchy black and white, it displayed five somber men in suits. They all posed around a table in a gaudy room. On the tabletop sat a machine. It was a film projector or something. A guy in the back, whom he recognized as his ancestor—Charles something, his dad was named after him—held a telegraph-tapper thing.

"Was everyone back then so boring?" Byron asked, studying the dignified expressions on the faces.

"Nope. Pictures just took a long time to expose—like a minute, I think. They had to stand still that long. Hard to hold a smile because even a twitch would leave the mouth blurry. Anyway, I think this is a lithograph, not a photograph."

"A what?"

"Never mind. It looks like the frame might be damaged," Cole said, noting that one of the corners of the silver metal seemed to be coming apart. "Let me take out the pic and see." He turned it over and removed the mildewed backing. "Hola," he said, fidgeting with it. "What's this?" Between the cardboard and the image hid some folded papers. He handed the frame to Byron and began withdrawing them, carefully. They were yellowed and thin, like Bible pages, and brittle.

Byron took out the photo—lithograph, he corrected—then flipped it over. Signatures scrawled across the back, one for each man on the front. Their cursive scripts presented difficulty, especially because Byron was dyslexic, but he thought he could make them out: Michael Faraday, Thomas Huxley, Charles Wheatstone, David Brewster, and John Tyndall. He cleared the area in front of Cole's desktop computer and moved a platoon of half-painted plastic miniatures—*Legionaries of Death,* he thought they were called, skull-headed cyborg warriors from some tabletop strategy game—and swung the giant clamp-mounted magnifying glass aside. He bent his arm around paints and brushes and tapped the mouse. Nothing happened. The screen-saver continued to build a 3D labyrinth of multi-colored sewer pipes. He picked up the mouse and shook it, sliding his thumb underneath to roll the track-ball. The monitor sprang to life, the computer's internal fan whirred, and Byron pulled up *Encarta*, the *Microsoft* encyclopedia.

Five minutes passed. Tinny music from the headphones played "Pulling Teeth" and "Basket Case." Cole remained caught up with whatever he'd discovered. Byron typed each of the names into the search bar.

The first guy, Faraday, was a world-famous scientist. He'd discovered electromagnetism and done all kinds of experiments with electricity and chemistry. Huxley was a biologist involved with Charles Darwin and the theory of evolution—he seemed like a big deal. The third person, Wheatstone, had been a major inventor. He'd come up with something called the electric telegraph, 3D glasses, some kind of science clock, and a bridge. He also helped lay the transatlantic cable. By the last two names Byron's head hurt and he'd lost patience with reading, but a skim of the entries showed that one did some work with optics and the other with infrared and radiation. A bunch of brainiacs, clearly.

"Which one is Dad's . . . um . . . great grandfather?" he calculated.

"I think it's double-great grandfather," Cole replied absently. "Charles something."

"Wheatstone?"

"Yeah, I think."

"He invented the electric telegraph and 3D goggles."

"Really?" Cole looked up.

"Yeah. Pretty cool."

"Well, wait until you get a look at this," he waved the paper. "It wasn't all he invented."

Chapter Two
A Very Victorian Warning

"Read it, jock," Cole used the playful insult again and handed a page over. "Careful, it's old."

Byron took it gingerly into his hands, sighed, and began to read. It took time because it'd been written in a cramped, odd cursive with some shorthand notations:

1 October, 1875 — Paris, France.

I, Sir Charles Wheatstone, being of sound mind—if no longer body—here do commit to paper the theory & plans of the Faraday Mirror, imagined by Michael Faraday & made reality through his collaboration w/ Babbage, Lovelace, & myself. As the last remaining creator of the device, at least on this side, my duty is to record our scientific discovery in such a way that it might be recreated, so those having traveled through may be recalled, & so that the greatest work of this generation's greatest minds will not be lost to posterity.

"Ugh," Byron complained. "Didn't they have typewriters in 1875?"

"Don't think so," Cole replied, his own gaze unwavering upon a sheet covered with drawings, equations, and figures.

Byron rubbed his eyes before returning to his page:

It is clear to me that Queen Victoria wishes this knowledge to die with me. I am, admittedly, ill & my doctors do not expect me to recover. Her Majesty has told me to expect her ambassador, who is tasked to collect & destroy the plans, on Wednesday next, & I am to gather them in one place so this may be the more easily accomplished. I shall, of course, comply, but not before making this copy & hiding it among my personal effects.

To you who have found it, I encourage caution. This knowledge is forbidden, like the apple to Eve, & like the apple it may bring you more harm than joy. The Mirror is a powerful invention that opens a gateway to another world, one that we had, of late, jokingly christened 'Wonderland,' but whose secrets can be both wonderful & terrible.

Yet, despite the warnings of old men & old books, do not doubt that knowledge is always more a blessing than a curse. Certainly, the last fifty years, if they have taught us nothing else, have underscored that fact.

Here Byron stopped reading. "How long is this thing?" he asked, flipping it over and seeing the thin-lettered script trail down the back page. "Ugh," he groaned.

"Never mind that," Cole said, his eyes wide with wonder. "I think I can build this."

"What? Seriously? No."

"Yeah," he replied. "Those old guys made it in what?" he squinted at the notation on the page, "1837—that's like 150 years ago. They had to invent the materials, they had trouble generating a stable flow of electricity, they couldn't figure how to insulate the wires without disrupting the effect, and they had difficulty with complex mathematical calculations. We can buy all this stuff over the telephone and have it shipped here. Heck, we can even plug it right into the wall when we're finished."

"What about the math? Can you do that?"

"The math?" Cole snorted. "I don't have to. If I type in the equations, my computer can calculate the answers almost immediately. Babbage and Lovelace had to *invent* a machine to do it. I mean it, Byron, we can do this."

"Okay, but should we?" Byron asked, rubbing a hand over his cropped black hair.

"Look," Cole answered, "I'm seventeen years old. Sure, I'm homeschooled and I aced the SATs. Sure, I run a successful computer repair business out of my bedroom. Sure, I can design a fully functioning website for a local auto dealer and teach their guy how to add and remove cars from it. But you know what I can't do?"

"What?"

"Get into Harvard." He pulled a rejection letter off his pegboard and waved it in front of Byron's face. He was becoming animated.

"But you can go to Plymouth State for free. Free, Cole. Dad works there. Faculty scholarship. And you got accepted to UNH and MIT."

Cole scoffed. "Plymouth State is a backwater compared to UNH, UNH is a backwater compared to MIT, and MIT is a backwater compared to Harvard. Going to Plymouth would be like sailing on a puddle instead of the ocean."

"Yeah, *your* opinion. And we don't have the money to send you to Harvard, anyway," Byron muttered. He planned to go to Plymouth to play hockey and he didn't much care for the way Cole talked about it.

"You sound like Mom. Now we won't need the money. Don't you see? This invention will get me into Harvard and it will make us millions. We can both go wherever we want. We can pay for better medicine for Mom—I'm talking about cutting-edge stuff. I'm not clowning, Byron, this will set us up for life—all of us. We just have to build it."

"Okay, where?" Always the practical one, Byron was a Boy Scout.

"Right here," Cole gestured around his room. He was not so practical. He, for example, preferred playing in *Magic: The Gathering* tournaments during his weekends.

"And when Mom tells you to clean your room?"

"Oh, good point." Cole admitted, despondent.

"I got it," Byron said. "We build it here but keep it in the tub." Their two rooms were connected by a bathroom. Their tub had both a constant drip and a leak around the drain, advertised by an ugly yellow stain on the laundry room ceiling below. Their parents weren't particularly handy, so the water had been shut off to the tub for almost five years. In consequence, they showered in their parents' bath, a source of conflict with their mom. "We keep the curtain closed anyway. No one would look."

He knew this from personal experience. He'd once hidden the 'teacher's edition' of his homeschool math book there for three months. It was really a rather funny story, he thought. Unlike Cole, he struggled with math, and pre-algebra was the worst, so while his mom answered the phone, he swiped her book and stashed it in the tub. He'd 'work' on his math in his room, often flipping through comic books or playing *F-Zero* with the volume on mute, and then scribbling in the answers behind the bathroom's locked door in a few short minutes before presenting it to his mother. Then she actually had to do the math herself to check his work. He got a chuckle out of that.

Byron was crafty, though, always intentionally getting enough wrong so as not to arouse her suspicions. When it became clear that she'd started to suspect (he fully realized she was smarter than he was), he waited until midnight and then slid the book under the couch, along with some of the dust bunnies from beneath his bed. It worked pretty well, unless you consider the fact that he bombed the math section of his 7th grade CAT test, and she never caught on. To be fair, he'd learned his lesson: the easy-way-out is empty, and he did feel guilty about it. He wouldn't do it again . . . at least not with a math book, but maybe with a science experiment . . .

"It could work," Cole admitted.

"Okay. That's settled," Byron concluded. "How do we pay for it?"

"Honestly, I think I already can. I've been repairing computers for three years, I made some money by designing that website for Granite State Used Imports, and I lifeguard down at Newfound every summer. I've got close to $3,000 in my joint checking account with Dad. It's supposed to be for college—heck, this *is* for college. How much've you got?"

"Not that much," Byron shrugged. "I keep most of my Christmas and birthday money, and I shovel Mrs. Rayner's driveway, and mow her lawn. And thankfully, I don't have a miniature addiction to upkeep," he waggled a skeletal legionnaire at his brother. Cole crossed his arms and raised an eyebrow.

"How much have you got?" he repeated.

"Maybe $800?" Byron frowned. "But it's in a savings account. I can't just go and take it out. Dad's on it with me, too."

"Yeah," Cole agreed. "But he never checks it. We'll just have to intercept the statements from the mailbox for a month or two."

A knock on the bedroom door startled them both. Harald barked and their mom's muffled voice came through the billowing flames of the *Saturn 5*. "Byron, we're going to be late. Hurry up and get your hockey stuff. We're out the door in 12 minutes."

Chapter Three
Plans on Ice

Byron stared out the window of the Jeep Cherokee. He shivered. The heater wasn't exactly young—it would start warming up about the time they arrived at the Plymouth State Ice Arena, and it squeaked. His mom had the radio tuned to the local pop station. Alanis Morissette's "Ironic" fuzzed from the speakers.

Outside, the frigid New Hampshire scenery shone in picturesque sunshine. Driving north on Route 3 near the Pemigewasset River—you had to give it to New Hampshire, he thought, where they named towns for England, mountains for US Presidents, and rivers for mispronunciations of Abenaki words—frost crusted over everything. Light sparkled off snow and icicles. Yet, his mind wasn't on the music, the drive, or on his upcoming practice. He thought only about the mirror.

Where would it lead? How did it work? It sounded more like magic than science. But, he mused, that's how most science must seem to those who don't understand it. A computer was basically magic to him, but not to Cole.

"How are you coming with your reading?" his mom cut in. "You need me to stop by the library to check out another book on tape or lecture?" She always hounded him about schoolwork.

"I, um, just finished that one about the Franklin Expedition," he responded, tearing his gaze away from the river and his mind away from the letter.

"Oh yeah?"

"Yeah, creepy stuff. Their ships—fun fact: they were named *Terror* and *Chaos*," he interrupted himself, "prophetic, I guess. Anyway, the ships froze into the ice; the crew got poisoned from lead in their canned food, then they got scurvy, went crazy, and even ate each other."

"Yuck. When was that?"

"1840s, Victorian era."

"If it was as cold up there as it is here," she took one hand from the steering wheel and blew some warmth into it, "maybe the weather drove them to it. "What do you want to read next?"

"Um," he thought for a minute. "Maybe *Alice in Wonderland.* Isn't there one called *Through the Looking Glass* or something?"

"There is . . ." she trailed off and glanced at him suspiciously. "But I didn't think you liked fiction—especially not *old* fiction. What happened to history?"

"I dunno," he said as they drove into town, passing a Texaco station and the fire department. Little electric wreaths and candy canes hung from the telephone poles. Christmas was only a week away. "Maybe you're right. I'm kinda sold on Victorian disasters lately. I guess I'll look for something on the retreat from Kabul or the battle of Islandlwana."

She groaned. "You and your father. *Alice in Wonderland*," she said, then turned to him, "How is a raven like a writing desk?"

"What?"

"It's an infamous riddle that has no answer. Comes from the book."

"Uh, okay," he replied. "But why ask a riddle with no answer?"

"Nothing in Wonderland makes sense."

"Not much here makes sense, either," he mused.

"Are you talking about your math problems or the nightly news?" She chuckled.

"Either? Both?" He shrugged.

Looking at his mother, her laughter and the smile on her face, he thought, someone might not know she was sick. He didn't know much about Lupus—he preferred ignorance to the anxiety of knowledge—but he knew the disease meant her body slowly tore itself apart from the inside. Her immune system attacked her organs and her skin. She took a lot of medicine, and most of it made her sick. The rest made her grumpy. She had good days, like today, and she had bad days when she didn't do much more than get out of bed. The bad days would get worse; he knew how sickness worked. Thankfully, she'd found a job where she could use her brains from home to make some money, something to do with operating systems, modems, and troubleshooting—those were the words she always used on the phone, anyway.

His mom's full name was Felicity Asante Oakes, and her grandparents moved to the US from Ghana, back in the late 1940s when the British still claimed it and called it the Gold Coast. In Byron's opinion Gold Coast sounded cooler than Ghana, anyway; it brought forth images of the wealth of medieval Mali and Mansa Musa, richest guy in the history of the whole world—and he was black. Secretly, Byron thought his mother the most beautiful person he'd ever met, but a teenager doesn't tell his mom that kind of thing. Her skin, where the Lupus wasn't scarring it, shimmered. One night, as a joke, she, Byron, and Cole had pulled brown colored pencils from the box to decide how to best describe themselves. She was proudly mocha, he claimed walnut, and Cole, the lightest of the three, dubbed himself caramel, though even that label seemed a shade dark. Their father, of course, was a pasty shade of pinkish plaster, very little changed from his English ancestors. He made an ironic observation about comparing skin to food and cannibalism, then observed wryly, after picking up a pencil he expected would be labelled "peach" and finding it to be "flesh," that his skin-tone could only be rightly described as "raw pork fat."

They passed the movie theater and turned across the bridge onto Holderness Road.

"*Jumanji*" his mom read the sign. "You wanna go? I kinda like Robin Williams. He's funny and seems like a nice, caring guy."

"Dunno," Byron replied as they pulled into the arena lot. "What's it about?"

"I only heard secondhand, from Charlotte Taylor, because they filmed it over in Keene, where her sister lives. It's set in New Hampshire. I guess a brother and sister find some old Victorian board game that's magic and when they play, it sucks them in, or something." She smirked. "Come to think of it, seems right up your alley—we'll go Wednesday night, after your dad's grades are due."

The Jeep came to a squealing stop, packed snow crunching under the wheels. Byron just gaped at her, his mouth open. That plotline sounded oddly prophetic.

"Alright," his mom urged. "Out with you. "

"Okay, I'm going," he grunted, opening the door and wrestling with his hockey duffel. Breath steamed from his mouth.

"I have to run by Hannaford to get some groceries," she said, turning off the radio. "I'll be back before you're done. You want anything while I'm there?"

"Uh," he thought for a second. "Get some Sour Patch Kids to sneak into the theater, oh and a Powerade or Gatorade, I guess. Orange?"

She nodded and he shut the door.

Byron cut across the arena ice, his skates slicing the surface and sending him sliding along. There was freedom in the speed, in the lack of resistance. Cool air blew through the wire cross-hatching of his facemask. He smiled. Even so, his mind didn't focus on the here and now; it remained at home with Cole, still on the mirror. If they finished it, he wondered, how would they test it? How would they reveal it to the world? To the government? Or maybe they'd sell it to a billionaire like Bill Gates? Or that old guy uh . . . Buffett? Was his name Jimmy or Warren? He could never remember. He made a cut, sending white spray flying. As for the mirror, he worried, would it endanger them? Should they build it at all?

Byron recursively returned to the letter. "So those having travelled through may be recalled," Wheatstone had written. That meant Englishmen had been sent to the other side 150 years ago. Why hadn't they come home? What happened to the original mirror? He had a lot of questions, and he didn't really know where to find the answers.

It was Saturday and until the first game of the season, Saturday was scrimmage day, so his practice passed in a blur. Oddly, in both video games and sports, Byron always played better when preoccupied, his body on autopilot, reacting on instinct instead of conscious thought. He played lights-out, limiting the starting offense to two shots, and no scores, but he barely registered it, and he certainly didn't notice his mom come in toward the end of practice and sit in the stands, cradling a coffee for warmth.

Reflexes and hand-eye coordination were Byron's specialty. He could knock a puck out of mid-air and make complicated moves to and with it before his opponents could react. Sometimes, his dad joked, it felt like he could slow time to make an impossible play. But, like all parents, he exaggerated his son's abilities.

"What got into you today?" his mom asked as he hefted his duffel into the back seat.

"What do you mean?"

"You scrimmaged like it was a game—like you were in a championship."

"Uh, thanks," he replied. "I guess I was just in the zone. You know, like I am with the cello sometimes. Most days I'm trash, when I'm still trying to read the piece, but sometimes I get the feel of it and it goes alright."

"You were better than alright. Play like that all season and you'll win your division, maybe even the state." From his mom, that was high praise; she'd been a college lacrosse and basketball player—a four-year starter. She swore lacrosse and hockey had a lot in common, and she was certainly right. Byron had learned as much about the game, its motions, and how to defend from her as he had from his father, who'd actually played hockey in high school, and with whom he sat and watched every Bruins and Sabres game.

"I'm a grinder, Mom," he reminded her with a grin. "Only grinder's moms and teammates notice them." He closed the door and buckled his seatbelt. She started the engine.

"A grinder?" she raised an eyebrow. "Enlighten me."

"A grinder. You know, the guy who works hard, plays hard, goes hard . . . checks hard. I'm good against the fast break and on the boards. I'm not going to score the goals."

"Oh," she laughed. "I thought you called that guy the enforcer."

"Heck no," he protested. "Westie's our enforcer. He's got twenty pounds and a foot on me. He can't skate, but boy can he put a hit on a guy. And none of us care if he rides the pine in the penalty box."

As she pulled out of the lot, he changed the subject. "Mom, do you believe in other dimensions? You know, like parallel universes or alternate realities."

"Yeah, certainly." She was a Trekkie from way back, so he shouldn't have been surprised by her quick reply. "Why do you ask?"

"Just curious," he adjusted the vent. "Do you think they can ever touch, or, you know, overlap? Like with a wormhole or something?"

She smiled. "Want to escape this reality?" she asked. He didn't answer. "Anyway, you're fourteen, and this is astrophysics stuff, so I don't really expect you to get it, but I love black holes. I imagine a 'singularity,' that incredibly dense marble at the bottom of a black hole, is like a doorway between dimensions, a point at which they all merge." Her voice became dreamy, "but in order to get through it, you'd have to be crushed down smaller than a period at the end of a sentence."

"Ouch," he grimaced. "And yeah," he admitted. "I don't get it. I always thought they were sort of bottomless pits, sucking everything in."

"Well, they're that, too. Listen, if I could explain black holes," she shrugged, "I'd have a cool job like Carl Sagan or Bill Nye. As it is, I'm just happy *I* can understand them. Maybe add Stephen Hawking's *A Brief History of Time* to your reading list. It's pretty good. They probably have it on tape at the library." She reached over and rubbed his head, then changed the subject. "Speaking of black holes, spaghettification, and bottomless pits, though, pasta's for dinner," she announced, gesturing to the grocery bags in the back. "And garlic bread. Oh," she reached for the cupholder, "I almost forgot." She handed him an orange Gatorade.

He smiled, appreciatively.

"Thanks."

CHAPTER FOUR
Jumanji

Byron and his parents exited the theater into the freezing December night alongside a crowd of happy moviegoers. Everyone chattered about the film and about Christmas in general. The wreaths and candy canes hanging from the electric poles twinkled with lights, bathing the street in a happy holiday glow, and the theater played carols on its PA system. As they walked away, the doors closed, muffling Elvis's "I'll be Home for Christmas."

Byron glanced up at the stars in the clear black sky. He exhaled a column of steam and licked his chapped lips. Kicking a clump of frozen slush down the sidewalk, he considered the strange parallels between the film and his life. Two siblings found a magic game from the late 1800s. Excited and curious, they tried it, resulting in a dangerous adventure that they were lucky to survive. The ice-ball skittered against the snowbank, bounced off, and spun out onto a slick of black ice. Byron chewed his lip, considering opening up to his mom and dad about the mirror.

"I give it a one and a half thumbs up," his dad said, interrupting Byron's musing. "Decent plot, solid acting. I just can't buy all the computer graphics. They weren't quite at *Jurassic Park* level; you know? Maybe it's because I know how a lion should move, but I can't say the same about a velociraptor, so I can suspend disbelief better on the dinosaur."

"Agreed," said Byron, "on all counts."

His father, Charles Oakes—he loved the name because it had 'snootie,' 'regular,' and 'blue collar' versions: Charles-Charlie-and-Chuck—was the American stereotype for a dad: overweight, balding, constantly cracking terrible puns and jokes, but kind-hearted, hardworking, and always there for his family. He only differed from other dads in his level of education.

Charlie grew up in upstate New York, went to college at Hamilton, and pursued a doctorate in history at the University of Massachusetts. He met Felicity in Boston. They married, intending to live and work together in the city. But then she'd been diagnosed with Lupus and Plymouth State sent him his only tenure track job offer.

They'd thought about trying to relocate since then, to be closer to Felicity's family in Maryland, but the university provided good medical benefits, so they'd stayed. The comparatively remote location bothered Cole and his mom, but Byron and his father rather liked it.

"Too bad Cole wouldn't come with us," Felicity sighed, watching the ground. She gripped her husband's arm as they crossed the ice patch. Byron took two swift steps and slid across it on his forward momentum. "I don't know why he's become such a hermit," she continued. "He needs more social time. I mean, he's an extrovert like you, Charlie."

"He's doing swimming every day—it's a team sport," Byron interjected, "and he uses AIM to talk to his friends. He's always got messages chiming in on his computer; it's constant. Even at home he's more social than I am, Mom."

"How about," his father chimed in, "we talk about the Oakes who actually went to the movie, instead of those who stayed home?" He turned to Byron. "What was your favorite part, fella?"

"I liked the cop," he replied, then quoted from the scene where the police cruiser was eaten by an enormous carnivorous plant: "FINE! *Take* it!" He giggled.

"Me too," Felicity added. "And I like that the actor who played the dad also played the hunter. That was clever."

"Yeah," Byron agreed, "that was pretty fun."

"Are you kidding me?" Charlie dropped his wife's arm and threw his hands in the air in a display of outrage. "Don't you think that sets a bad precedent for dads everywhere? I mean, A) that guy was unreasonable and encouraged his son to be violent, conformist, and macho. We've got enough of that in this world as it is. And B) he ends up hunting his son, planning to murder him with some kind of futuristic repeating elephant rifle?" He sighed. "It paints dads in the wrong light entirely."

"It's just a movie, honey," Felicity soothed, patting his arm. "Don't read into it."

"True," Charlie agreed, "and I'm overreacting on purpose to prove a point, but," he wagged a finger at Byron, "if you ever get sucked into some kind of magic jungle in a board game—far-fetched, I know—you'd better believe I'd come hunting you: to SAVE you, though, not to kill you."

"Thanks. That means a lot."

"I suppose," Charlie sighed, "I should be grateful that the dad was at least physically fit and competent. I'm *real* tired of comedies featuring dads who are just Homer Simpsons. Fat, stupid, incompetent fathers married to beautiful, intelligent women they don't deserve . . . where are the role-models these days?"

Felicity groaned. "Remind me *not* to take you to the movies next time. You over-analyze *everything*. You sure you shouldn't be teaching English?" They'd reached the Jeep and she unlocked Byron's door before shifting her key to her own. "No wonder," she said over the hood at Charlie, a twinkle in her eye, "you're against the unthinking, unreflective male stereotype."

"Hey," he got in at the same time she did, "I'm an anti-stereotype. Remind me, who's cooking our Christmas dinner?"

"Oh," her eyes widened, "and are you going to wrap the presents this year, too?"

There was a pause. Charlie inserted his key and started the engine.

"I thought so," Felicity smirked. "I'm hungry," she changed the subject. "If Cole was here, I'd suggest pizza."

"Who needs that nerd to eat pizza?" Byron prompted. "More for me."

Felicity sighed. "I wish you'd stop calling him that."

"When he quits calling me jock, I'll lighten up on the nerd," Byron replied. "Besides, I think it boosts his ego."

"As if jock doesn't boost yours?"

"How about Wendy's?" Charlie interrupted. "It's faster."

"Sure, Wendy's is fine," Felicity sighed again. "It's just that Cole will be off to college in a year and I feel like he's already gone some days, like all the fun family days are behind us. He's always busy with that business of his. You know," she glanced at Charlie, "I think he's becoming a workaholic."

"Then extrovert or not, he's more like your brother, Bruce, than he is like me," Charlie said. "No one's lining up to call me a workaholic. I graded my last exam this morning. I'm on vacation." He glanced at Byron. "Speaking of which, I hear Fox Pond is frozen solid. Want to go skating on natural ice tomorrow?"

"Sure," Byron agreed. "As long as you don't make any 'thin ice' puns."

"Deal," Charlie nodded. "And we'll force Cole to go with us." They bumped through a pothole into the Wendy's lot and pulled up to the drive-thru behind a rusted 1980s Chevrolet pickup with only one working taillight.

"What I liked about the movie," Felicity added, "was that it was set in New Hampshire. You know, they filmed it in Keene."

Charlie made eye contact with his son in the rear-view mirror. "I bet the town was real *keen* to sign that movie deal." He winked.

Byron groaned. "You know, it's only a couple miles home from here," he said. "I think I can walk."

Thankfully, the Chevrolet pulled through at that moment. Charlie rolled down his window, and a barely-intelligible teenage voice buzzed from the speaker: "Welcome to Wendy's, home of Dave's Triple, what can I get you?"

Chapter Five
Christmas

Christmas at the Oakes' house came and went with a familiar rhythm. As Byron and Cole got older, they no longer woke at the crack of dawn and pressured their parents for presents. Now nearing 18, Cole generally slept in, and gifts didn't get exchanged until he was up, so Byron didn't see the point in racing out of bed, either. He still woke up early, but instead of going downstairs, he switched on his Nintendo and played some *Star Fox*. He made it all the way to level seven before he got sucked into Venom's mouth and chewed up. Game Over.

He dropped the controller and crawled out of his knitted blankets, pulling on a pair of thick socks and a Plymouth State hoodie before padding down into the kitchen. His dad was already bustling around, getting together various elements of the upcoming meal. He wore a stained apron covered in a busy poinsettia pattern. He'd stolen it from his mom the last time they'd gone to Tupper Lake for Christmas, when she was battling cancer. Charlie had worn it to cook for every holiday since, Byron thought as a sort of tribute to her memory. His father waved an oven-mitted hand at Byron as he entered.

The soundtrack to "White Christmas" played from the tape deck that they'd mounted under the cupboards. A box of donuts sat open on the table, their Christmas morning tradition. Byron picked up a chocolate glazed and walked to the sliding glass door. It hadn't snowed overnight, but it was a frigid morning. The thermometer on the back deck had an icicle hanging from it and read -5 degrees Fahrenheit. The kitchen was hot, though, and the mouth-watering aroma of turkey was already permeating the room.

"Haven't you started the bird a little early, Dad?" Byron poured himself a cup of coffee, a habit he'd picked up to make it through early-morning hockey practices.

"I got a 25-pounder this year," his father answered, proudly. "Stuffed it to the gills. It's going to take five hours to bake, minimum. Had to get it in the oven by 8 AM." Byron shook his head and selected a maple-frosted. He shuffled into the living room to gaze at the pile of presents under the tree. His mom sat curled up in the armchair by the window, bleary eyed, nestling her coffee between her hands and chest.

"Morning, Mom. Merry Christmas."

"Mmm," she grunted, taking a sip. "You, too." She set her coffee down and reached for yesterday's newspaper, flipping through to the page with the crossword puzzle and Sudoku.

They sat in silence for a minute or two.

"Talking wolf, according to Lewis?" she asked, looking over the top of the paper. "Six letters."

"Lewis?"

"The *Chronicles of Narnia.* You read those, right?"

"Um, yeah," Byron replied, knitting his brows. "Fenris, I think." She nodded and her pencil worked on the paper. "You got the funnies in there?"

"Yeah," she thumbed through it and handed Byron the comic page.

"Thanks," he skimmed, looking for his favorite: *Calvin and Hobbes.* It was Christmas, and he was hoping for a new snowman massacre. He tried not to be discouraged that the strip was ending on December 31st.

Through the wall, he heard the hiss of water from the bathroom. Someone was in the shower. He leaned over to make sure his dad was still in the kitchen.

"Cole's up," he announced.

Four hours later, the family gathered around the kitchen table for their feast. As usual, Charlie had out-done himself. He'd loaded the table with steaming side dishes: squash, corn, rice, yams, two kinds of cranberry sauce, gravy, stuffing, and dinner rolls.

Byron sat in a chair, a bit self-conscious because he had his new hockey skates strapped tightly to his feet. He'd have to wear them for six to twelve hours to mold them to his foot shape, so he'd started early. He and his dad planned to watch *Gettysburg* (his present from the boys) that afternoon. With a run time of 271 minutes, it would go a long way toward reaching that six-hour goal. The new skates' best feature was a Kevlar toe. All Byron's old ones were steel-toed, and that steel got cold. He hoped that this new design would keep his feet a little warmer and provide the same protection. After all, if Kevlar could stop a bullet, he mused, it should be able to stop a puck. Behind him, against the wall, rested his new composite-shaft hockey stick, a glossy black Bauer.

Across the table, Cole perused an instruction manual. His uncle had sent him an Iomega Zip Drive and five disks with a 100 Megabyte capacity each. He'd practically lost his mind with excitement when he opened it. In addition, his parents got him a Nokia phone and a new, highly acclaimed PC game called *Command and Conquer*, and it was this manual that he read while their dad transferred the bird from the stove to the table.

"Did you know this game includes live action video cutscenes with professional actors?" he asked. "It's going to be like *playing* a movie."

Their mom stood in the corner, recording the arrival of the turkey on her brand-new digital camcorder. The thing was state-of-the-art and incredibly expensive—way out of their budget, but Felicity's brother was making a killing with his tech company down in D.C., and ever since he found out that his sister had Lupus, he tended to spoil her with extravagant gifts. She said it was just restitution for the way he'd treated her when they were kids.

She zoomed in on the pies, narrating as she went: "Christmas, 1995, at the Oakes' house. You're looking at dessert. I may not be much of a cook, but I sure can bake."

"That's because baking's a science, not an art," Charlie called over his shoulder.

"Let's not listen to him," Felicity continued, panning to the table to record her sons. "There are the boys, ready to eat," she narrated. "Cole just got his acceptance letter from Columbia this week. Next year at this time, he's going to be home from college. And Byron's hockey team is looking to make a run for the championship this season."

The boys studiously avoided looking at the camera. Cole flipped a page in his instruction manual.

"They're both getting so big," Felicity continued. "Cole, I think you're cultivating some fuzz there on your upper-lip."

"Jeez, Mom," Cole complained.

Felicity chuckled. "I remember when you fit on Santa's lap. Either of you have anything to say for posterity? Anything more than 'Jeez, Mom?'"

"Yeah, I'm glad my *peach-fuzz* made it into posterity," Cole complained. "Why don't you give me the camera and let me immortalize you for a bit?"

"Mmm, mmm. Oh my, will you look at that bird," Felicity ignored her son and turned to follow the turkey as Charlie lowered it onto the table. "How big is it this year, Charlie?"

"Twenty-five pounds," he glowed, "and browned to perfection. Who's hungry?"

Felicity put away the camera, Charlie cut the bird, and they heaped their plates.

Before tucking into the feast though, Felicity called for grace. "Thank you, Lord, for food, family, fellowship, and a roof over our heads on this cold, cold winter's day. We've got a lot of blessings heaped around us here, and we know it. Amen."

"Amen," they echoed.

As Byron dipped a bit of breast-meat into a pool of gravy he'd crafted inside his sticky rice, his dad added,

"I think it bears repeating to be thankful for family today. Not just that we're all here, sharing this moment, but that we all love each other, and that we all get along. I know it sounds corny, but not all families can say that. Your mom and I have done all we can to craft a house that is a home for you two, and now that you're nearing the age when you're getting ready to leave it," he looked directly at Cole, "we want you to know that you can always think of our house as home. Remember, too, that blood is thicker than money, thicker than politics, thicker than distance. How about a toast to that?" he asked.

Felicity raised her wine. "Yes, your father's right" she said through a mouthful of rice. She and Charlie clinked glasses. Then they turned to do the same with the boys, who raised cups of cider. "To home and to family," Felicity said.

They drank.

"You sure you have enough food?" Charlie asked, noting that Felicity's plate was comparatively empty.

"Yeah," she sighed. "I didn't want to say anything after you put in all this work, but I'm not feeling particularly great this afternoon."

Charlie nodded. "Probably the stress. Christmas is stressful. No matter," he added with forced cheer. "It'll all reheat well. We'll be eating turkey for days."

"To days of turkey," Byron added, lifting his glass again. He had a knack for smoothing over awkward moments. They all drank another toast.

"Hey," Felicity reminded, "you boys have to call your Nana and

Tata Asante this afternoon, and no forgetting Grampa Oakes, either. It's a family day, whether they're here with us or not."

"Yes, Mom." Cole agreed.

"Sure thing," Byron seconded. "Can do."

"I'll call Bruce this afternoon. You going to call Jack?" Felicity asked Charlie. He stopped his fork halfway to his mouth and set it down on his plate.

"Maybe. I know I should, but I don't want to talk about the government shutdown or the second amendment and the federal ban on assault rifles. It'll just be a way to ruin Christmas with another argument."

"I get it," Felicity said while the boys focused studiously on their food, "but like you said, blood is thicker than distance or politics. He's your brother. You've only got one."

"Yeah," Charlie sighed. "I'll think about it. Who needs gravy?"

"I do," Byron answered, sending down his plate.

They all ate for nearly two minutes in total silence

"So, Cole" Felicity finally asked, "you've been pretty busy with some kind of project recently. Want to tell us about it?"

He paused and looked over at Byron, swallowing his bite of yam. "Yeah, I'm, uh, building a computer for a client. Pretty high-tech stuff." He picked up a forkful of stuffing and slid it through gravy. "I don't want to bore you with the details, though."

"Wow," his mom looked impressed. "Is it a local commission or something from over the Web?"

"Long distance," Cole answered.

"Make sure the check clears before you send it off," his dad warned. "Computers are expensive—I don't want you to get scammed." Cole nodded, taking another bite.

"How long will you be working on it?" Felicity asked.

"A month at least," he replied through a mouthful of food.

"You going to show it to us when you finish? Before you send it off?"

"Absolutely," Cole agreed. "I'd be proud to."

That evening Byron entered Cole's room to find him chatting

on AIM. "That lie you told mom at dinner, about building a computer . . ."

"What about it?" Cole asked.

"Are you really cool with lying to them? For months?"

Cole's computer chimed an incoming message. He read it before answering. "I'm not a big fan of lies, but this has to be secret. You know they won't let us make it if they know about it."

Byron noted that Cole had said "us," when he usually referred to the mirror as his—singular—creation. He was trying to manipulate Byron, bargain for his silence. He needed him as a co-conspirator.

"And, I wasn't kidding about showing them the mirror when it's finished and working," Cole went on. "We're going to ask for forgiveness, here, not permission." He typed and sent another message.

"Who are you talking to, anyway?" Byron asked, glancing over his brother's shoulder and changing the subject.

"Melissa French," he answered after a moment of hesitation.

"You two dating yet? You write her about every night."

"Nah, just friends," Cole replied, a little too nonchalantly.

"Bullet-ship!" Byron exclaimed, again converting his cuss-word into an acceptable form. "Admit it—you've been into her for months."

"So what," Cole answered, grinning as he received another message. "She's unavailable."

"What do you two nerds talk about, anyway? Science?"

"Heh, mostly," Cole half-laughed, half-sighed. "We both like computers. Sometimes she helps me troubleshoot repairs."

"She still dating what's-his-name?"

"Andy Weathersby?" Cole was typing again. "Yeah."

"She's too smart for him, though. He's not in her league, mentally."

"Yeah, but he's a nice guy," Cole answered. "I mean, he's the goalie and captain on my soccer team, and he volunteers with the ambulance squad after school. He'll be an EMT when he turns 18. How do I compete with that?"

Byron shook his head and started toward the bathroom that connected their rooms. Another incoming message dinged over his shoulder. He looked back and added, "I think you're being dumb."

"How so?"

"Well," he turned, "it seems to me that you're filling a need for this girl—uh, Melissa. She needs intelligent conversation in her life? You give it to her. Now, she doesn't need to get it from her boyfriend, 'cause she's got you. She's sitting pretty, 100% fulfilled. He gives her the romance and you give her the smarts. You? You're pining and yearning over there without her."

"Your point?" Cole asked.

"Unless you stop giving her intellectual interaction, she's never going to realize that she needs it or that Andy can't give it to her. If you sat with Mom occasionally and watched her romance movies, you'd know that."

"Look," Cole's face darkened, "we're *just* friends, alright? I'm not going to hold my 'intellect' ransom to break them up. That's just weird, okay?"

"Suit yourself," Byron shrugged. "Just seems like a smart strategy to me."

"Yeah, well," another message chimed in, "there are some things that you shouldn't be strategic about. You've got to draw the line somewhere, and for me it's at manipulating the people I like."

"Yeah, except for mom and dad," Byron added, lobbing a parting shot. "Don't worry, though; the mirror secret is safe with me. Hey," he paused and put a genuine smile on his face. "Sorry about that. Your love life is none of my business. Merry Christmas."

"Merry Christmas to you, too," Cole replied. His computer chimed, and he turned back to the screen.

Chapter Six
Montage

The next weeks passed quickly. Colton pored over the plans, making lists of necessities, programming his formulas into the computer, shopping using the World Wide Web and his cellular phone, and recording it all in a private journal on his *PersonaLink* "cloud" drive. He told his mom he'd be receiving some shipments for the computer he was building. Soon enough, the boxes started arriving. Cole spent days in his room, barricaded by his door and headphones, only coming out for swim practice, cereal, peanut butter sandwiches, and dinner. He'd always had a tendency toward obsession.

Byron, lacking the mechanical and mathematical competence of his brother, began distracting his parents as much as possible, and since he knew that no distraction could be as engrossing to his mother as schoolwork, or to his father as hockey, he threw himself into his studies and practices with total abandon.

He requested his mom's help and attention with math and science. He asked for a unit on herbs and plants, something he knew she was unprepared to teach, so she would have to spend time learning and preparing on her own to be able to assist him. Besides, he figured he could use the unit to help earn both his Plant Science and Gardening merit badges for Scouts. He was going to earn Eagle, eventually. He promised himself that. Next, he enlisted his mother's aid in the writing of a compare and contrast paper concerning the two Victorian military disasters at Islandlwana and Kabul, even declaring he would give a ten-minute presentation of the paper to enhance his public-speaking skills. The research was fascinating, so listening to the books and watching the documentaries didn't feel like too much effort on his part. In both cases, outmatched local populations used surprise and deceit to overwhelm the much better-equipped, trained, and disciplined British troops. Honestly, the idea that South African Zulu tribesmen armed with short-spears and cowhide shields could defeat nearly 2,000 British regulars armed with cannon and Martini-Henry rifles inspired him. He even checked out a couple of print books and struggled through the pertinent chapters. His paper was mediocre, but the presentation was good enough that he gave an encore performance for his father, who was (after all) a history professor. His dad said it compared favorably with the work done by most of his freshmen. He then suggested they have a movie night to watch an old film called *Zulu*.

To further distract his father, he asked for assistance passing the puck, watching game film, and studying NHL and college hockey games. They even started playing one of his Christmas presents, *NHL 96*, together on the Super Nintendo. His dad couldn't make a move with the controller without moving it and his whole body in the intended direction. It was pretty hilarious in Byron's opinion. Even playing as the Redwings against the woeful Oilers, Charlie couldn't compete. At practice, Byron increased his effort and found his team, the Wildcats, undefeated as January came to a close. The games every Saturday, especially the away games, gave Cole plenty of undisturbed time to work. And the upcoming travel tournament at Norwich University's Taylor Arena would allow Cole a weekend for the finishing touches.

Finally, he spent some time with his dad going through maps and guidebooks, planning their summer trip. This year the family intended to head out west to Yellowstone and Glacier national parks in Montana. It was the most ambitious trip they'd planned. Over the past three years they'd been to the Adirondacks in New York, Acadia in Maine, and to Nova Scotia. The planning for this one was an order of magnitude more complex, and Byron used that excuse to involve his father, and frequently his mother, in preparations.

To be fair, all of this hard work and eagerness would have been more than a little fishy to his mom—she *always* knew—if he hadn't done plenty of bad things to offset it. In fact, whenever his mom said anything about checking on Cole or giving him chores, Byron would find an ingenious way to bring the focus back to himself. He broke a lamp, burned some toast (it was pretty awesome—flames actually licked out of the toaster), dropped an open milk jug in the middle of the kitchen floor, and chewed up a living room curtain in the spinning brush of their vacuum, to name a few.

In the interim, the mirror grew by leaps and bounds. Cole miniaturized it some to save on expenses and to reduce the power-consumption of the device. A series of copper-wire-wrapped three-foot diameter loops, like four stacked hula-hoops, formed the basis of the machine. The cores of these loops were made from an iron-nickel-cobalt magnetic alloy. He also purchased transistors, resistors, capacitors, circuit boards, microchip, and even a hard-drive. Two orange power cords hung off the back end. The mirror would plug into two outlets at once. The science of it all was more than Byron could comprehend, but Cole assured him it would work—better, he thought, than the original. So far, it had cost over $3,200 to assemble. Byron had a recurrent dread that they'd plug it in, switch it on, and the whole thing would fry, literally sending their savings up in smoke.

Chapter Seven
Gameday

The weekend of the hockey tournament, Byron broke his arm and Cole finished the mirror. The first event happened during a semifinal match against the Bennington Minutemen. Up 1-0 in the second period, Byron put on a one-man-show on defense. He knocked pucks out of the air, robbed the attackers—he even nutmegged their best player, stealing the puck off his stick, sending it between his legs, and carrying it up the far side of the rink. However, trying to dig the puck out of the back corner, Byron got slammed into the boards. He initially thought the snap he heard came from his hockey stick breaking, but when he looked down and saw his intact composite-shaft stick, then started to register the searing pain in his arm, he knew something had gone terribly wrong.

One trip to the ER at Central Vermont Hospital, two X-rays, a set bone, a fiberglass cast, and a prescription for painkillers later, they were on their way home with the classic rock blaring from the radio. In the back seat, Byron made a call to a teammate on his mom's Nokia and found that they'd been defeated 4-2.

"Well, we lost the semis," he announced.

His dad turned down the radio, then putting on a fake Canadian accent, said into the mirror, "Ookes endured ah season-ending injury, eh, and withoot him, it woos ah season-ending injury for his team, too, eh? EH?" his dad persisted. "What are yoo thinkin' aboot back there?"

"Quit it," Byron complained.

"Hey, cheer up, fella—you've now got proof that your team can't make it without you. You're not just a grinder—you're a star."

This was supposed to make him feel better, but ironically Byron felt embarrassed by it. As an introvert, he didn't much care for attention. He'd rather blend into the background. He had to admit, though, that in a paradoxical sort of way he did want to be a star, not for the fame—no—but because he liked to see his work pay off. He wanted to be the hardest working, most respected, and best. He was both gratified and humiliated by any public recognition.

"I think I might go back to the old wood-handled stick," Byron said, looking at his cast.

"Why?" his dad asked.

Byron smiled sheepishly. "I think the composite is stronger than my skeleton. I'd rather have a broken stick than this:" he held up his cast.

The phone, still in Byron's lap, rang. It was Cole.

"Hello?"

Byron?

"Yeah, it's me, the jock. I broke my arm," he offered.

Ouch. You okay? Still at the hospital?

"Yeah, I'm fine, and nope, we're on our way home."

I finished. It's done, he said.

"You plug it in yet?"

Yeah, Cole lowered his voice, *but stop saying suspicious things. Mom and dad are hearing your side of the conversation.*

"Oh, right." Byron agreed.

The mirror is sort of opaque-reflective, bright blue-green and hums like a giant fluorescent light. It's real magnetic, too. Pulled down the curtain rod.

"Huh?" Byron answered, feigning noninterest.

I can see a forest scene on the other side. I'm going to throw a ball through, see what happens.

"No. Wait for me."

How long?

"An hour. We're nearly across the river."

A long pause; Cole sighed. *Okay,* he finally answered. *But how am I supposed to resist?*

"I dunno," Byron quipped, "Maybe paint some more of your skull-faced miniatures, or—" he snorted, "—or go into my room and try to find another alternate ending on *Chrono Trigger*. We still haven't won it with Magus."

You're suggesting, he could hear the amusement in his brother's tone, *that to pass the time before testing my electrical portal, I play a video game about a malfunctioning electrical portal that sent a young man and his friends on a time-hopping adventure?*

"Yep, sure am."

Okay, he chuckled. *Great. Can do. Tell dad to step on it. If you're not here in an hour, I leave you no guarantees.*

"I'll try. See you soon."

Bye.

Byron turned off the phone and handed it back to his mom.

"How's Cole?"

"He's good. Bored. Wants us to get home."

"Did he finally finish that computer project he was working on?"

"Dunno," Byron lied. "He didn't say."

From the front seat, his dad made a comment about 'classic' rock somehow becoming the music from his teenage years, and then began to turn the radio back up, but then his mom continued talking. This was a regular occurrence. Charlie rolled his eyes in the mirror and good-naturedly lowered the volume.

"How's your arm feel now, sweetie?" Byron's mom asked.

"Hurts."

"You feeling up to some lunch?"

"You bet," he replied. "Let's go someplace with a drive-thru." The problem with his dad and driving was that he always took some windy back way to avoid traffic. Sure, this convoluted country route cut 20 miles off the trip, but it was full of frost-heaves, potholes, slow "Farm Use Only" pickups that blew nauseating exhaust, and it lacked any meaningful restaurants or rest areas. Despite its seemingly *direct* route on the map, the back-way would take a full fifteen minutes longer to complete than the *roundabout* interstate option.

"We're driving through Fairlee and Orford," his mom said. "There's gotta be something."

'Something' ended up being donuts. Two chocolate crullers, a hot mocha, and a Boston cream later, they were on their way again, bumping along Route 25A and listening to his mom lecture his dad about the need to take his early-stage diabetes more seriously: this, as he drank an iced "coffee" that was 65% sugar and heavy cream.

Finally, after the interminable trip, they pulled off of River Road into their driveway. They passed the two white oak saplings and the painted slate sign, adorned with acorns and declaring: "Oakes' Oaks," a joke of his father's—apparently in England the houses used to have names instead of numbers and he'd always been jealous. The gray clapboards of the siding mirrored the gray overcast of the New Hampshire sky. Byron swung his creaking door open, inhaling the coniferous aroma of the nearby woods, hemlocks. The sun warmed his skin, 38 degrees on the first weekend in February. The layer of frozen mud under the gravel driveway had melted. Harald barked down from the upstairs window.

"Go on inside, I'll get your stuff," his dad ordered.

Cole met him at the door, headphones around his neck. Byron waved his injured arm.

"Son of a—," Cole remarked (rather than replacing cuss words as his brother did, Cole handled the problem by omitting them entirely). "What happened?"

"Checked and wrecked. Broken arm."

"Radius or Ulna?"

"Ulna," Byron answered. "Two and a half inches from the elbow."

Harald bounded down the stairs, turned the corner, scraping his nails ineffectually on the hardwood, and nearly bowled Byron over.

"Okay, Okay. It's good to see you, too," he laughed, ruffling the shepherd's hair with his good hand while the dog licked his pants—probably for donut crumbs. "How's the mirror?"

Before Cole could answer, their mom and dad bustled through the door, burdened with hockey equipment and talking over each other. Then, the story of Byron's injury was requested and reenacted. A good ten minutes passed before his mother began rooting through the refrigerator, fretting over dinner.

"I hate these weekend tournaments," she complained. "The week's going to start tomorrow, and I haven't even been to the grocery store."

"Why don't I drive you?" his dad offered. "The kids will be alright at home for a couple hours"

She looked doubtfully at Byron's arm. "How's it feeling?"

"*Fine, Mom*," he replied with exasperation.

"You know you can have more medicine at 2:15."

"I know."

"I think they'll be fine," Charlie said.

"We'll be perfect, Mom," Cole cut in. "I'm here. I have my license. If anything goes wrong, I'll call. Promise."

"Hey," their father cut in, "I'm thinking of stopping by Blockbuster on my way home. Anything you want me to rent?"

"Yeah," Byron said, "I kind of want to watch *Stargate* again." He thought for a moment, "Or that cartoon series, *Gargoyles*. I missed a couple episodes last season."

"What about you?" Charlie turned to Cole.

"See if *Apollo 13* is out on video yet, oh, and I've heard that *Interview with a Vampire* is pretty great, too. Get that, will you?"

After a few more moments of fretting over Byron, Felicity and her husband left, taking the Jeep up to Hannaford for the week's grocery trip.

"Finally," Cole sighed. "Let's go." And he led the way upstairs.

Chapter Eight
Mirror, Mirror in the Tub

As they entered Byron's room, he noted that everything metal which wasn't attached to the walls or floor had been removed from the bathroom and sat in a disheveled pile. The curtain rod—now bent—leaned against the wall.

"They didn't put any screws or a plate in your arm?" Cole asked.

"Nope. It was a clean break. Why?"

"I didn't want the mirror to yank them out or anything. It's only magnetic from the outside, but it's pretty strong. All of the forces on the inside cancel each other out."

"Did you decide how we're going to test it?"

Cole shooed Harald out of the room. The dog whimpered from the hall and his claws slid down the door. "I'm going to start by throwing some things through it, then try using mom's digital camcorder."

"Wait, the one Uncle Bruce gave her for Christmas? That's like $2,000."

"Have to," answered. "The old one uses magnetic tape and the mirror would wipe the recording." Cole opened the door to the bathroom; Byron followed him in, so distracted by what he saw that he didn't really hear his brother's explanation—something technical about how the magnetic polarity captures the video signal on the tape, but how a digital camera records in binary code. His attention focused on the mirror, which sat upright in the tub. Turned off at the moment, the wire-wrapped loops coiled like a long, thin snake, trailing two orange power cords and a coaxial cable, all of which passed through the door into Cole's room. A bulky mechanism attached to the bottom of the loops, exposing electronic parts and some circuit boards.

"Are you even listening?" Cole interrupted his observations.

"Uh, sorry. Shouldn't you enclose that electric stuff?" Byron asked, gesturing at the base.

"I'll get to that," Cole replied. "No point in sealing it all up if I need to access it. Besides, if I enclose it, I'll have to add a cooling fan. Let's make sure it works first." He sighed. "Anyway, I was saying the camcorder and other more modern technology should be pretty much unaffected by the magnetic field. Anything digital has a magnet inside, of course, and while it nears and passes through the field, the recording may distort or disrupt, but once through and far enough from the field, it should return to normal operation."

"Got it. Are we going to plug it in or what?"

Cole laughed, bending to pick up the two cords, one much longer than the other. "I plug the short one in here, wait five seconds for the effect to run evenly through the coils, then plug in the second one into my wall—the rooms are on different circuits, different fuses—to double the power input. Otherwise, I'd have had to rewire the wall and use a dryer outlet. Anyway," he coughed self-consciously, "a few seconds after they're both plugged in, the coils will harmonize and the mirror should be functioning."

"What's with the coaxial cable?"

"My desktop is running data on the effect in the other room. I'm thinking of recording a video, for release *after* we've gone public."

"Okay," Byron replied, concerned about the idea of 'going public,' but too excited to see the mirror work to care much.

Cole plugged the short cord into the wall then disappeared through the door. His slightly muffled voice carried through the opening, "You may feel a bit weird when this turns on. I sure did."

The coils hummed, like electricity passing through an old fluorescent bulb, but deeper in pitch. Without any other sound or indication, a small blue hole, the size of a jelly-jar lid, appeared in the middle of the loops. Its edges rippled like water as it expanded in concentric spirals until it filled the central opening from edge to edge. It flickered, a translucent cyan disc.

Byron felt light-headed; his fingers and toes tingled, like they were asleep. He leaned back against the sink.

"Woah."

"Yeah," Cole agreed, returning from his room. "I'm calling it the Faraday Effect. Near as I can figure, it's caused by the magnet pulling on the iron in your blood. It takes a few moments for your heart to compensate."

As his pulse increased and his body stabilized, Byron leaned closer to examine the mirror. It was true that he could see his own image and that of the bathroom in the surface, yet they were translucent. They flickered in and out and rippled like a reflection on a puddle in the summer sun. Through this surface he could see depth, a scene of reeds like those around the edge of a brook or pond, and in the distance, trees and a white-capped mountain, beautiful as a postcard from Colorado or Montana, but tossed by a wind he couldn't feel.

"Cole?" Byron's tone changed.

"Yeah."

"This image is wrong. I mean, I feel like looking through a window in a wall, but the window looks up out of a pond or stream into the sky, or something—like it's a skylight. It's like gravity's sideways over there."

"I noted that," Cole said. "To me it feels like the orientation of the place is perpendicular to here. I bet if you crawled through the mirror head-first, you'd be standing upright on the other side. I've decided to call it a perpendicular dimension."

"But what does that even mean?"

"You've got me," Cole replied, "but it sounds pretty awesome. I've got a way with words, right?"

"Okay, Shakespeare, so what now?"

"Well, I want to throw a ball through. I figure I'll throw it straight in, and it should come out the other side traveling up, then it should fall right back through the mirror. But hold on," he said. "Would you mind filming me first?"

Byron stood in the bathroom doorway, a few steps back from the magnetic effect, holding up his mother's camcorder.

Cole looked into the camera. "I just want to have this recorded," he said, "to show that I did it. What you see before you," he gestured to the portal, "is the first working example of a Faraday Mirror built since the Victorian age. My name is Colton Oakes and the person doing the recording is my brother, Byron . . ." he went on for about three minutes, delving into some of the technical aspects of the mirror, but eventually picked up a tennis ball and tossed it through the portal. After an awkward few seconds, it fell right back through and arced down as it adjusted to the Earth's gravity again. It bounced around the bottom of the tub.

"Why was there a delay?" Byron asked, lowering the camera.

"Yeah, it's strange, how long it took to fall back," Cole mused. "Maybe gravity is weaker on the other side. The ball would fly farther and fall slower."

Byron stopped the recording, and they took turns with the ball four more times, until a bad throw landed it on the other side permanently, beyond the effect of the mirror.

"Houston, we have a problem," Cole chuckled. "Now we'll send the camcorder through." The two moved to his room, where the brand-new digital camcorder sat on Cole's bed.

"How are we going to get it through the mirror without going ourselves?" Byron asked.

"Tie a rope to it and gently toss it," Cole answered. "Then we can, uh, maybe drag it back?" He heard how crazy it sounded and shrugged. "I guess I didn't really think that through enough."

"Yeah, that's just nuts. What if it lands on a rock? Or in the water? I mean, it does seem like we're looking up out of a pond. Mom would kill us—it's hers."

"Ok, so what's your plan then, Einstein?" Cole sounded a bit sulky.

Byron thought for a moment. "Is aluminum magnetic?"

"Not really, but it can, technically, become a little magnetized. Why?"

"Well, Dad's roof-rake is made of aluminum. We could lash the camera to it and send it through until it's a couple stories up, then we could rotate it and see what we're dealing with."

"And you call me the genius," Cole said with admiration, clapping Byron on the back.

Chapter Nine
Portal Lag

They took a quick trip to the garage. Like every garage, it smelled of cardboard, mildew, and gasoline. Their family van, a nine-year-old powder-blue Dodge Caravan with fake wood paneling around the middle—not as reliable as the 4WD Jeep in the winter—occupied the space, but above it, resting on a pair of wooden pegs, sat the roof-rake. A two-story aluminum pole topped with a flat shovel, like an oversized garden hoe, the rake was easy to take down, disassemble, and carry upstairs. It was pretty simple, too, to affix the camera to the shovel end. Lashing proved difficult, so they ended up using three feet of duct tape instead. Then they snapped the pole back together. The pole went well out of the bathroom door into Cole's room, but they could manage the angle to send it through the portal. They pushed the red RECORD button and advanced into the room, both holding the handle. Once through, they slowly rotated the rake 360 degrees, then withdrew it from the mirror.

Cole hooked the camera up to the desktop monitor and they both watched with eagerness as he pushed PLAY. They saw the bathroom, the portal, then, as Cole predicted, the image distorted and became blurry and difficult to decipher. A few seconds later, the scenery came into focus, a brook in a meadow surrounded by birch and conifer forest and bordered by large mountain peaks in the distance: a breathtaking scene illuminated by a setting (or rising) sun. Then it swiveled at an almost dizzying speed and the camera withdrew.

"What the?" Cole began.

"Was that sped up? What's wrong with the camera?"

Cole looked at it carefully. "Nothing. Nothing at all."

"So . . . ?"

"Let's do it again," Cole said. "I have an idea, but we'll have to test it. This time we rotate it really, really slowly."

Again they sent the camera through the mirror.

"I want the rotation to take a full two minutes," Cole said. "I'm going to time it." He looked at his watch. "Okay. Start."

This time when they watched the recording, the view swiveled at a reasonable speed, though still much faster than they'd actually spun the camera.

When it finished, Byron spoke first. "That was like half a minute."

"Just about 25 seconds," Cole confirmed.

"What does it mean?"

"That time runs slower on the other side, I think. Given the differential, it's about five times slower."

"How can that be?"

"I dunno. It explains the delay with the ball, too. We threw it and it took too long to fall back through the portal. It wasn't gravity, it was time."

"Ok," Byron nodded. "So now what? One of us goes through?"

"No, absolutely not," Cole said. "Mom would kill us if something happened."

Harald whined from outside the door and scratched again. Cole looked in that direction and his eyes lit up.

"No," Byron said. "Absolutely not, you can't send Harald."

"Why not?" Cole asked.

"If it's too dangerous for me, it's too dangerous for him," Byron said. "At least I understand the risk. He's just a dog."

"He doesn't have to stay long," Cole said. "We throw a ball through; he gets it and comes right back. We can test our theory, too. I'll sync my watch with my wall clock, then I'll put it on his collar, and we can see what time it is when he gets back. It'll be just like *Back to the Future*."

"What if he doesn't get back? What if the forces kill him?"

"Look, we have Wheatstone's letter. People went through 150 years ago and returned. Why should this be any different?" He opened the hallway door and Harald waggled into the room.

"But what if he can't find the portal or if he's scared to jump through? What if he runs off into the woods or something?"

"He loves fetch," Cole said. "He'll come right back."

"Hold on," Byron said. He ran out, returning a few moments later with a peanut butter jar and a knife. He cut the duct tape with the knife and wrenched the camcorder off the roof-rake. "We'll do it, but if he's not back in one minute, I'm slathering this thing with PB and sending it through. He'll come for that."

"A minute is too short. Over there that would be just 12 seconds. Better give him three minutes." Cole synced his watch with his clock and looped it around Harald's collar. Byron gave the shepherd a hug and a kiss while Cole dug another tennis ball out from under his bed.

"Hey, Harald!" Cole said, shaking the dust from the ball. The dog's eyes moved with his hand, glued to the fuzzy yellow toy. "Ooh look, a ball! You want the ball? You going to get the ball?" He held it out of Harald's reach and the dog barked, his tail wagging out of control—in a circle rather than back and forth.

"Sit!" Byron commanded.

Harald sat, his almond-colored eyes glittering and his tail sweeping the carpet. His whole butt waggled.

"Fetch," Cole yelled, then tossed the ball into the mirror at an angle such that it wouldn't come right back through the hole. Harald bounded after it and leaped through the portal, disappearing from the bathroom. Cole and Byron looked at each other, the former's face showing a thrill of excitement and the latter's creases of anxiety. Byron counted the seconds, nervous for Harald, his senses keyed up for any sound or change from the mirror.

Two minutes elapsed. Neither brother spoke.

The deep thrum of a motor vehicle and the sound of crunching gravel came through the wall from outside. Their parents had returned.

Cole's eyes bulged. "Oh no!"

But then Harald bounded back through the mirror, two balls—the one Cole threw and the one Byron had lost—lodged firmly in his mouth. Byron enfolded him in his arms, laughing. Harald dropped the balls and licked his face.

The front door thumped. "Cole, get down here and give us a hand with these bags," their dad shouted up the stairs.

"Okay," Cole said, "be right there!" He bent to pull his watch off Harald's collar and held it up to the wall. "Over half a minute slow," he announced with a smile, then headed for the hallway. "Unplug that thing," he said through the door. "Then come downstairs because I'm sure Mom wants to ask you how your arm's feeling."

That night before going to bed, the boys had a conversation which would change their lives forever.

"So," Cole came into Byron's room and sat on his brother's bed as he fought Lavos on his TV screen, "it's obvious the next logical step is for one of us to go through."

"Yeah," Byron agreed. "After dinner while mom told me to nap, I put together my scout pack. Tent, sleeping roll, hatchet, knife, first-aid kit, flint, matches—"

"No one is talking about an expedition here. In fact, I've been thinking about it, and I imagine we can get about two hours undisturbed in the daytime and more at night. Two hours on this side is barely a half hour over there," he replied. We can treat it like a moon landing, collect samples, run experiments, that kind of thing. Film it, too. You won't need a tent, though."

"Scout motto is 'Be prepared,'" Byron replied, still focused on the screen. "What if the power went out or the mirror broke? Speaking of which," he continued, "I'm the one who has to go through. You have to stay here and watch the machine. I couldn't fix it if there was a problem." One of Byron's characters died. Two remained.

"I get your point," Cole responded. "And I think, too, we have to do some more testing before you go through."

"What kind of testing?"

"Well, durability testing, for one. We know the mirror works, but we've never had it on for more than an hour. What if it burns out? What if it can't handle a long duration of being powered up? It gets pretty hot, after all. And then there are other questions, like is the portal location stable? I mean, what if the portal were to travel on the other side? You'd be lost forever."

"So what do we do?" Byron asked.

"We run the machine all night and run data, directly to the desktop, so we can check on it tomorrow. I've already changed the smoke detector batteries and placed it in the bathroom in case it overheats."

"You're making me nervous."

"Nothing's going to happen, but like you say, it's always better to be prepared." He smiled. "If it runs all night without failure, we'll treat tomorrow like a documentary. You interview me, I'll interview you, we'll reproduce our experiments, then you can go through, film some stuff, collect samples, and—I dunno—plant an American flag or something. Then we'll talk about who to send it to." He laughed.

A second character crumpled on the screen, leaving the red-haired Chrono standing alone against the final boss.

"Use Luminare," Cole advised, finally drawn into the game.

"Not enough MP. Got to go with Frenzy," Byron replied. It didn't work. Lavos chewed Chrono up and spit him out. The end-scene began to play, Lavos screamed his otherworldly keening scream, the camera zoomed out to show the dying world, and the words *But . . . the future refused to change* lingered as it faded from view.

"Cole," Byron asked, putting down his controller, "don't you think we should tell Mom and Dad?"

"Tomorrow," Cole said. "Tomorrow night, after dinner."

Chapter Ten
Midnight Visitor

Byron woke up, sweating. He had the oddest sensation that he was being watched and felt sure he'd been dreaming about it. His broken arm throbbed. "Ugh," he groaned, reaching his good hand out to the bedside table for his digital clock to make sure he could take more pain meds. The time read 12:13 AM. He could hear AIM chimes from across the bathroom. Cole was still awake.

"Good day to you, sir!" a cheerful, high-pitched, British-accented voice called from the foot of his bed. Byron dropped his pills, spilled his water, and sat bolt-upright. The empty glass rolled off the table and thumped onto the carpet.

When his bleary eyes finally focused, Byron saw (bathed in cyan light that the mirror emitted from the bathroom) a small, stylish man sitting cross-legged on the foot of his bed. The man was a foot tall and chubby. About forty years old, he had a clean-shaven face, wore a blue vest, brown pants, and a pointed red hat. His eyes twinkled and a smile played on his lips. His miniature hands were folded on his lap.

"You scared me," Byron said. "Do you come from in there?" He asked, gesturing at the bathroom and already knowing the answer.

"Aye, indeed, certainly so," the man replied.

"What are you?"

"Ahh, humans and their so, so rudely-phrased questions," the man answered, pursing his lips. "He couldn't ask *who* I am. No, he asks *what* kind of *thing* is this?" After sharply inhaling and breathing slowly out his nose, he continued, "Your kind has myriad names for my kind. I have been called fairy, brownie, elf, redcaps, gnome, and even leprechaun; though," he now chuckled, "each name wrongly refers to a different phase in my astonishingly long physical development. Just now, however, I am inclined to prefer 'elf' as it is generally the term you people apply to benevolent and attractive members of my species. And, as I am quite attractive," here he caressed his protruding belly, "and tend, at least at this particular moment, toward kindliness, that seems most fitting to me."

"Uh, okay," Byron struggled to wrap his mind around this. "My name's Byron. What's yours?"

"Your sadly simple language cannot hope to properly pronounce it."

"Try me."

"*Payndyrztyrr*," he drawled.

Byron opened his mouth to repeat it, then licked his lips, hesitating. "Ok, so you're right," he conceded. "What do you want me to call you, then?"

"Most Britons call me Poindexter. It's a butchering of a beautiful name, but I'll answer to it."

"Wait," Byron's mind fully awoke. "Did you say Britons? You've got an English accent!"

"Accent? *Me*?" Poindexter laughed in a slightly mocking way. "I speak The Queen's English, and I speak it far better than you, I might add. Accent," he scoffed in disbelief.

"How? You're an elf from another world. Who taught you?"

"I was taught by the esteemed Douglas Sterling, himself. It's a bloody simple language if you ask me, and, for your information, you're the one with an *accent*."

"Douglas who?"

"You aren't one of the smart Brits, are you?"

Byron frowned. These taunts about his language ability and intelligence were hitting a bit too close to home. 'You try being a dyslexic younger brother living with a genius,' he thought with some bitterness. Instead he asked, "If you're a lepre—ah, an elf—then can you do magic?"

Poindexter disappeared from the foot of the bed with a faint popping sound and reappeared next to Byron's ear. He whispered, "Yes," then appeared again at the foot of the bed.

"Cool," Byron said, impressed. "But why are you here? I mean, I'm going from what I've heard in stories, but I don't have any shoes to fix, or dresses to repair, I'm too young to have a firstborn for you to steal," at this the elf's eyes flashed dangerously. Byron tried to recover his tact. "And it's winter so we don't have a garden, a toadstool, or a rainbow . . . ah, Christmas has come and gone, too. Do I have to solve some kind of a riddle or something?"

"Ooh, riddles!" Poindexter clapped his tiny hands, the danger leaving his eyes. "How I do adore them!" And he began one on the spot:

She leaps from the sky
But she never does die.
She flees from a hill
And she never stands still
Unless she catches cold
And then she's so bold,
To change her skin tone
And crack a great stone.

"Uh, that's a pretty tricky one," Byron replied, thinking carefully, repeating the words in his head and forming them silently with his lips.

"Take your time." Poindexter patted his chest and fumbled in his pockets until he found what he searched for: a white clay pipe and a pouch of herbs. He stuffed it, lit it up, and began to puff out small, curling whorls of smoke that smelled like parsley and licorice. "Take your time," he repeated, half to himself.

By now, though, Byron started to figure it out. "Oh yeah! It's water, right?"

"Very good, human boy. Now try your best on me."

"Um," his mind blanked, but then he remembered an earlier conversation with his mom. "Okay. Why is a raven like a writing desk?" he asked.

"Ah-ha! I've been asked that before. The story from which it comes is very popular where I'm from, and," he blew out a large ring of smoke which floated toward the ceiling, "the simple answer is, it's not. A raven, in fact, is *nothing* like a writing desk." Poindexter's face got thoughtful, "Though I admit I have tried to find a commonality, even one based in pun. All I can conclude is that if your English was an intelligent language, they'd both," he chuckled, "begin with R, and that one produces a lot of meaningless noise, while the other produces much meaningful silence."

The door at the other end of the bathroom opened and Cole poked his head through, headphones around his neck. "You talking to me, Byron?" he yawned. Then, coughing, "What's that smell?"

"No," Byron answered, "I'm talking to Poindexter here. He's an elf from the other side and he's smoking a pipe."

While Poindexter continued talking, as if he hadn't just been interrupted, Cole crept in, mouth agape, and sat gently on the bed.

"The part of the riddle that always bothers me" Poindexter said, "is the 'why?'" He took a pull on his pipe. "'How' seems the proper way to frame the question. '*How* is a raven like a writing desk?' but" he pointed at Cole with the long stem of his pipe, "it begins with a 'why.' Why?"

"Poindexter," Byron cut in, "I'd like to introduce my brother, Colton."

"Oh, a pleasure, I'm sure," Poindexter replied, giving a cursory nod at Cole.

Cole looked at Byron and mouthed "alright?"

Byron nodded.

"He's the firstborn," Poindexter observed, winking at Byron. "I can always tell."

"Excuse me, sir," Cole cut in, "but may I ask a question?"

Poindexter cleared his throat and looked up at Cole. "Certainly, young man. Go right ahead."

"You came through my mirror?"

"I traveled through that glowing hole, yes."

"From where?"

"The stream by the woods. I could see the light in it, and as I was being stalked by a dangerous barghest, traveling to your world felt like an intelligent alternative to an immediate, fiery death."

"A barghest?" Byron asked.

"Oh yes, large black dog, strong, swift, crafty. Very dangerous. Scary, too. They regularly eat elves. I believe you British sometimes call them hellhounds."

Both Byron and Cole turned to the bathroom, blue light still glowing out the door. Fear shone in their faces. They'd been so concerned with their plans to travel through that they hadn't fully considered the dangers present on the other side.

Poindexter laughed again. "Oh, you needn't worry. Barghests detest water, so the chances that it shall willingly jump into your pool are slim, very slim indeed. I imagine we're quite safe here."

"Even so," Byron cautioned, "maybe we should shut off the mirror."

"And trap me here?" Poindexter asked. "I warn you; I shall not stand for that. I can make it hard, very hard, on you if you do." His expression and demeanor markedly chilled.

"Then," Cole began, glancing at Byron, "perhaps you should go home before we disconnect the power?"

"My dear boy," Poindexter replied, coolly, "I fully intend to do so, just as soon as I'm sure the barghest has moved on. Just a quarter hour more, I'm sure."

Cole sighed, then changed the subject, edging slowly toward the bathroom door, "What do you call your homeland?"

"Home," Poindexter winked, mirthful again. "Elves, my young man, though sometimes territorial, are not insufferable nationalists like you British. We're what you would call anarchists. We don't have a 'land' to name. Though, you people do certainly have your names for our world: Fairyland, Avalon, and Wonderland are all in use; some have even called it Aelfheim. I prefer Aelfheim, when forced to make the choice."

"And are there a lot of, um, other beings like you over there?" Byron asked.

Again Poindexter laughed. "Like me? No. There is but one of me—a pity, to be sure. But you mean elves? Oh my, yes! Elves, gnomes, goblins, trolls, giants, dwarves, talking owls, fire wyrms—more types of beings than I have the patience to name, but lots of people too, just like you."

Cole and Byron exchanged a look, but before either could speak, a sudden thumping and scraping came from the tub and a deep growl sounded from the bathroom.

"Well, it's been pleasant to chat," Poindexter said in a worried voice, then vanished with a faint pop.

Out from the bathroom door stalked a large dog, in form like a Doberman: big chest, lower and thinner haunches, narrow face and erect ears, these sticking up like devil's horns. Its fur glistened, jet black, but where a Doberman would have been brown—around the mouth, under the chest, and on the paws—this dog had blood-red fur. Smoke curled from its mouth through gaps in its black, bared teeth, and its eyes flashed red, tracking infrared-like lines across the thin smoke whorls left by Poindexter's pipe.

Cole retreated to the bedside. Byron looked in terror at his brother. "Fudge sundae!" he whispered.

Chapter Eleven
Through the Looking Glass

The barghest growled again, clearly scanning the room for signs of Poindexter.

"There's a knife and a hatchet in my Scout bag," Byron whispered. "With my arm I'm no good. I'll make a break for the hall. You come out through your room and surprise it."

Cole clearly wanted to protest, but just nodded instead.

Without warning, Byron faked right and then went left. At his motion, the barghest twisted its head, opened its jaws and belched forth a spout of liquid fire. It missed by centimeters, dousing the bed. The sheets erupted in flames. Byron reached the door, wrenched it open and burst into the hall, the barghest in pursuit. Cole bent, scooped up Byron's frame backpack and sprinted through the bathroom and into his room, fumbling with the snaps to release the hatchet.

Byron pounded down the hall toward the stairs. A jet of liquid flame splashed against the wall beside him, dribbling down toward the carpet. A particle hit him in the shoulder, singeing a round, black hole in his tee shirt and burning his skin. The barghest howled; the chilling sound reverberated from the hallway walls. Then the smoke alarm activated, an ear splitting, shrill shriek.

The barghest shrunk back, momentarily, at the sound, then gathered itself and sprang, landing on Byron's back and knocking him prone, his face shoved into the carpet. Pain shot up his arm from the break and down from the claws scratching at his shoulders. But more barking could already be heard, this coming from downstairs.

Harald charged up steps and into the hallway, bowling the barghest over. The two dogs fought fiercely, growling, barking, circling, and biting. Their jaws snapped in anger and saliva flew, the barghest's sizzling into steam as it splattered the walls.

Byron backed away and Cole burst out of his room into the hallway, a hatchet in his right hand, and an inverted knife in his left.

Harald, slightly larger than the barghest, caught his adversary by the throat and began to shake it, tearing its flesh. In retaliation, the barghest shot out a gout of fire. Because Harald throttled it, the flames spewed everywhere, igniting the ceiling and both walls, arching down and setting Harald's fur alight. The German shepherd whimpered, surprised. Harald released the barghest and retreated in obvious pain, rolling to put out the flames, but only spreading them further. Byron ran for a towel to put out his dog's fur. The upstairs now clouded with visible smoke.

The barghest stood and shook, drips of molten blood spraying from its wounds. Cole, not waiting for the creature to make the first move, launched himself at it. The creature dodged the hatchet, but in so doing, plunged itself onto the knife. It whimpered, lunging the other way. Cole kicked it in the ribs, knocking it against the wall, and with a violent effort, brought the hatchet down square on its glowing red eye. Two more vicious stabs with the knife finished the thing.

Looking down at his handiwork, Cole felt equal parts horrified and proud, but the feeling didn't last. Blood poured from the creature's wounds like molten lava, incinerating the carpet and torching the walls. It dripped down like acid through the floor and into the guest room below. A wall of flame erupted between them and the only staircase. Then the floor around the corpse caved in, crashing into the basement and making it impossible to jump.

Byron finished patting out the fire on Harald, then grabbed at his brother's arm. "We have to get out of here!" he coughed, screaming to be heard over the blaring smoke detector and crackling flames.

Their father stood on the stairs now, his arm held up to shield him from the flames. "Come on!" He shouted, gesturing emphatically toward the stairs and squinting through the smoke. "Now!"

"We'll never make it," Cole returned, shaking his head. "I'll get him out, Dad, promise!"

He and Byron retreated into his room and closed the door.

"Let's jump out the window!" Cole said, but realized the bulky air conditioner was still screwed in place, so he turned toward Byron's room. It blazed with an impassable inferno. Flames were everywhere. The door to the hallway began to burn, real fire blackening and curling the printed fire on the *Saturn 5* poster. Smoke clouded their vision and their eyes watered.

"We'll die here," Byron coughed. "Let's go through the mirror!"

"It'll burn up. We won't come back," Cole replied, all color draining from his smoke-stained face.

"Better that than death," Byron concluded. "And we've got to go *now*—the electricity won't hold up." He ran to Cole's closet, grabbed a handful of sweatshirts and jeans and threw them over his cast; then he clutched up a pair of sneakers and sandals and ran for the bathroom.

Cole shouldered the backpack, grabbed a water bottle from his desk, and followed. The two lunged through the portal, followed by their loyal dog. Four seconds later, the power cut off to the room and the portal went dark. One minute after that, flames engulfed the area. The sirens of the Plymouth fire trucks rolling up the hill outside could be heard over the crackle of flames and the weakening whine of the melting smoke-detector, but no one was there to notice.

Chapter Twelve
Hunter-Gatherers

The two brothers collapsed on the edge of the stream, coughing, hacking. Harald limped over to the water and took a drink, then he too flopped down in the grass, licking his wounds. Cole glanced down at his mud-spattered pajamas and back at the stream in time to see the cyan glow fading from the water.

"Oh, boys" a familiarly accented voice said from nearby, "I'm truly sorry to see it turn out this way, I am indeed." Poindexter sat on a stone, his face solemn.

"This is your fault," Byron said, unable to contain his anger. "If you hadn't led that *thing* to us, we'd be happily asleep right now." He balled his fist and took a step toward the elf.

"No," Cole interjected, laying a hand on his brother's shoulder before Byron could pick a fight. He coughed and spat, smoke still in his lungs. "This is my fault. I built the mirror. I left it on. I trapped us here. I burned down the house. I wanted to be famous and successful, to go to Harvard. This one's on me." He swallowed. "You think Mom and Dad got out?" He stared at the water flowing down the stream, listening to it gurgle as it passed over and around protruding rocks. Silence hung in the air between them. A cheerful twitter of birdsong eventually broke it.

"In my extensive experience," Poindexter observed, "the ideas of blame and fault are weaknesses of the human mind. Blame doesn't matter once the deed is done, unless vengeance is required. It is, as they say, as it is, and the sooner you align yourselves with reality, the more obvious shall your paths become." He cracked his tiny knuckles. "Nevertheless, you two young people have done the world a very great service: you have saved *my* life. I am in your debt, and an elf does not take such a debt lightly. Three times, I shall help you in your need, for we fairy-folk repay our debts with interest."

"Can you use your magic to get us home?" Byron asked.

Poindexter shook his head. "Sadly, I do not yet possess such power. I hope to one day, though. We, you see, live for millennia and the eldest of our race possess very great powers indeed. I, however, have only counted a few centuries of life to date."

"Where are we?"

"Next to the stream, by the woods, in the twilight shadow of the mountains," he answered, unhelpfully. "And I am afraid I must leave you."

"What?" Byron clenched a fist. "You're the only person we know here. How can you just leave?"

"Like this," he answered, and with the same faint popping sound he vanished.

Byron gazed blankly at the vacant stone for a few moments, then made the decision to follow the elf's advice. It was what it was, and if they hoped to survive here, they had work to do. He pushed down his panic and sorrow and decided to take charge.

"Hey, Cole," he said. His brother still stared longingly into the stream. "Help me out here. We've got to inventory our supplies and decide what to do. I don't know the direction, so I can't tell what time of day it is—either sunrise or sunset—and the sky's cloudless, so we don't have to set up camp yet, but we've got decisions to make."

Cole rubbed his eyes and stood. "Alright." It was clear that he'd been crying, but Byron pretended not to notice. "And it's evening," Cole observed. "Poindexter said we're in the *twilight* shadow of the mountain. Assuming an east-west solar trajectory, that's east," he gestured away from the mountains, "and that's west," he pointed back.

Byron nodded, realizing they were going to have to accept a great deal on faith in the coming hours, if this place even had hours.

They laid out their belongings in the grass. Both wore soot-stained tee shirts and damp flannel pajama bottoms, so their first order of business was to change. Byron had brought four pair of Cole's jeans and two sweatshirts through with him: Plymouth State Panthers and Team USA Swimming. He took the former. It felt somewhere around 60 degrees Fahrenheit, and windy, so the sweatshirts were necessary. They also had a pair of sneakers and Velcro-strap sandals, both two sizes too large for Byron. They didn't have socks, but the sandals would strap tight, so Byron chose those.

Aside from that, their inventory included: one tent, one sleeping bag, 50 feet of thin nylon rope, a small first-aid kit with Band-Aids, aspirin, Neosporin, and a wrap, one folding knife, one Swiss-Army knife, one hatchet, three fishing hooks, a red and white bobber, a spool of fishing line, a whistle, a small metal pot, a folding bowl and plate set, bug spray, sunscreen, a clear plastic poncho, a hand-crank flashlight, a box of matches, a flint, a compass, a bag of zip ties, a box of brown-sugar and cinnamon Pop-Tarts, a canteen, a water bottle, a bag of teriyaki beef jerky, and a pack of spearmint gum.

"It could be worse," Byron said as they made their assessment. "We can make it for a while on this. I don't want to eat our food, though, until it's necessary." He looked at the sky. "So it's evening, then. What do you want to do?"

Cole thought for a minute. "I think we should stay here for a few days, in case the fire wasn't so bad and Mom and Dad . . ." he had to stop to gather himself. "In case they can get the mirror working. I think each day here should be about five days there, assuming a 24 hour cycle—I'll measure it on my watch tomorrow. So, maybe we should stay three days to be sure."

"Sounds good," Byron replied. "You set up the tent in a flat place where the ground is dry. Then collect firewood and build a fire pit—we'll need a lot of dry wood—all different sizes. It's best to clip the lower branches off a standing conifer. They'll be dry. Take the hatchet and Harald with you and I'll take the whistle and knife with me. I'm going to make a fishing pole and see what I can catch in this stream."

Cole nodded, amused to be taking orders from his little brother, but Byron was a Scout and he knew the outdoors.

"Maybe Poindexter will come back," he suggested, hopefully.

The elf did not come, and the night didn't, either. Rather than set, the twilight glow simply slipped slowly, arching counterclockwise along the landscape from the direction they'd reckoned as west toward the south. High above their heads a few bright stars could be seen poking through the indigo sky. Despite the strange perpetual twilight, the hours passed uneventfully for the boys. Byron caught two decent-sized fish that he was reasonably sure were rainbow trout, and thanks to his mom's recent lessons, he recognized many plants along the riverbank, willows, oaks, and some yellow birches as well. Deciduous trees became less common farther from the water and were replaced by fir and pine. Cattails clumped in pools along the bank. He smelled a crisp note of mint at one point, and he even thought he spotted a blueberry bush, but decided it wasn't safe to risk it.

Sitting with Cole and Harald next to the campfire later and eating fish (Harald got the heads, tails, and skins—not enough for him, really, but it would do for now), Byron could almost fool himself into believing they were on a camping trip somewhere in Franconia Notch

State Park. He leaned back and gazed at the few visible stars. They looked familiar enough, but he didn't recognize a single constellation. The fire crackled.

"You'd think, if he could just vanish like that, Poindexter should have been able to escape that barghest without coming to our house."

"Maybe he can't hide his smell," Byron offered. "Dogs have eyes, but their primary sense is smell, not vision." He ran a hand down Harald's back.

"Yeah, makes sense," Cole remarked. He swallowed and avoided Byron's eyes. "I'm real sorry about this, Byron" he gestured around them, "about the house and everything."

"Shut up already" Byron snapped. "Yeah, it's your fault, but I didn't stop you, did I? If you're just going to mope and cry all day, you're not going to be any use to me or yourself, so just shut up and get over it, will you?" He broke a stick and poked the end into the fire, stirring up the coals. "Besides, I'm the one who broke that picture in the first place."

Cole sighed, staring up at the twilit sky. The wood hissed and a pine log popped.

"You remember when we used to visit Grandma in New York?" Cole asked.

"Yeah," Byron replied, relaxing some of the tension in his shoulders. "Tupper Lake," he forced a smile, "closer to nowhere than Plymouth, New Hampshire, that's for sure."

"Five hours trapped in the car on twisting roads, only to arrive at a town with one traffic light and at a house so small we had to camp out in their backyard."

"You're right," Byron agreed. "It was just like this at sunset."

"Except you could hear Mom laughing. Grampa always made her laugh."

"He made everyone laugh. Remember how he woke us up one morning by playing *Reveille* through the tent door on a kazoo?"

They shared genuine grins. "Yeah," Cole said, "then we asked him what grandma planned for breakfast and he said, 'weasels.' Weasels! Who says that?"

They shared stories for a while, then decided that on the following day Cole would try to fish and Byron would collect berries and set some snares in the woods. Finally, they talked about the future.

"Ok, so," Cole said, "if the mirror doesn't turn back on in two days—in 48 hours, rather, and if Poindexter doesn't come back, what do we do?"

"The elf said there were people here. I think we have to find them."

"Where do we go? To the mountain? We might spot some trace of a town or village if we get high enough up."

"I don't think so," Byron replied. "In Scouts we always were told to stay put, but if no one knew where we'd gone, the best idea was to find water and follow it downstream. First, it gives us a water source. We don't want to leave that. Second, civilization always springs up around rivers, lakes, and coasts. And third, I can trust fishing to give us dinner. Speaking of which, you should fish upstream tomorrow—or after we sleep, whatever you want to call it—because we'll be moving downstream soon, and we don't want to deplete the food supply in that direction."

Cole nodded. "Makes sense. I'll give it my best, but you're the fisherman. Last time I went, all I caught was some lily pads and a tree branch" He stood up. "Well, I'm going to turn in. Should we bring Harald in or leave him out?"

"In," Byron replied. "I'll sleep better knowing he's listening."

CHAPTER THIRTEEN
Hunted-Gatherers

The hours passed uneventfully. Gathering food remained the only real problem. By the third day, the fish didn't bite, the snares sat empty, and they'd cleaned out the blueberry bushes—hunger had eventually changed Byron's mind on trying those. Even Harald became restless, loping off on forays of his own. So, when the sunset started its fourth full orbit around them, they laid out their tent and sleeping bag to dry (they'd been using it, unzipped, as a blanket) and ate some cold Pop Tarts. Once they broke camp and gathered everything, Cole shouldered the pack and they began their trek downstream, each munching a single piece of beef jerky.

At first, the going was pretty easy. They averaged probably twelve or fourteen miles in a ten-hour span. Byron fished before breakfast and also while Cole set up camp. The ground didn't reveal a single worm, but they caught grasshoppers and crickets as they walked and popped them inside the folding mess-kit for safekeeping. They worked well as bait. Meanwhile, the stream continued to get deeper and wider, and they caught bigger and more filling fish. Though well-fed, they were already getting sick of fish.

They'd seen some wildlife—a few deer and what looked like a grizzly across the stream—and a lot of birds, especially crows and ravens, but as of yet, no people. It was all surprisingly *normal.* While fishing, a few days into their journey, Byron felt sure he'd seen a brown-hatted elf beside the stream, but when he opened his mouth to call out, it vanished, leaving him to question whether it had been a figment of his imagination or not. They did, however, get a clear view of a strange predator toward the end of a daily hike.

"Get down!" Cole shouted, tackling his brother. A shadow darkened the grass, and Byron looked up to see what could only be described as a gryphon pass overhead. It cried out; a deep, resonant raptor-like roar echoed off the trees. The eagle-lion hybrid probably measured seven feet long in body, and twice that in wingspan. It curled both its front talons and rear paws while flying, steering through the use of wings and a fan of feathers splayed out at the end of its long, catlike tail.

Harald began to bark and growl. At the sound, a doe and two fawns bolted from the deep grass on the far side of the river, running toward the shelter of the trees. The gryphon changed flight angles and dove, catching one of the fawns in its talons and then raking it repeatedly with its rear claws.

Cole grabbed Harald by the collar, shushing him and dragging him away from the stream and toward the woods, where he sat on Cole's lap while he rubbed the dog's ears, whispering to him calmly. A few moments later, the gryphon took off, the limp fawn dangling from its talons, and disappeared over the forest toward the snow-capped mountains.

"Well," Cole joked, "that was comforting." He released Harald, who ran to the stream and swam across to sniff the area and lick up some spilled blood.

"Yeah," Byron nodded, flexing the fingers in his left hand. His arm didn't hurt much anymore and the cast itched.

"You'd better keep one eye on the sky while fishing." Cole brushed dog fur off his jeans. "And maybe I'd best try to set the tent up in the shadow of the woods."

"Agreed," Byron said, "because who knows how big that thing's hunting range is?"

"Or how big its appetite is."

Later, the river widened into a dark-watered swamp, surrounded by boggy marshland. They camped on a mossy flat under the trees and sat in the twilight watching a pair of bluish-white will-o'-the-wisps blink at each other across the swamp.

"You suppose they work like bug lights?" Cole asked, slapping at his arm. "You'd think here in fairyland there might be fewer pests. What kind of a wonderland is this if there are mosquitos?"

"Watch out that you don't slap a fairy by mistake," Byron joked. "They probably don't take kindly to that."

"Hold on," Cole chuckled. "Remember the giant bug light Dad bought for Grampa one year? It was like $200 and 120 watts."

"Oh, yeah," Byron chuckled. "And it shorted out in less than a week."

"Yeah," Cole really laughed now. "Because a bat flew into it."

"I felt bad for the bat," Byron admitted.

"Okay, okay, but imagine the sparks and the light! It must have been like a transistor blowing. And afterward, the bat must've been totally fried, like Luke Skywalker's uncle." Here he snorted and had to hold his breath for a moment. "Now, think about what you might accidentally kill with that thing here. We'd be lying in the tent and—BAM!—there'd be a huge white blast and maybe a high-pitched squeal, and Grampa would be like, 'got me another pixie, Grandma!'

Byron started getting in the spirit as well. He added (in imitation of his grandfather), "Serves those little monsters right—they were hexing my tomaters!"

"Now imagine the kind of light you'd need for a cockatrice or a harpy."

"Or a gryphon! You'd basically need a bug-lighthouse."

"And what about the fireworks when it made impact!"

The two had a good long laugh before bed and forgot their worries and problems for a few moments.

Not far into the next 10-hour march they found their first sign of civilization. Halfway around the swamp, in a murky conifer forest, they ran across a path that led from the woods down to the water's edge.

"This seems too well-used to be an animal trail," Byron observed, bending to examine it. He picked up some loose soil and rubbed it around in his fingers, emulating a knowledgeable tracker from the movies. As he felt the muddy soul squelch in his hand, he absently wondered why movie trackers always did this. To catch a scent like a wolf? To get a feel for the ground and how prints would best be made? It felt absurd.

"So what do we do now, Clint Eastwood?" Cole asked, mocking his stance. "Follow it?"

"I hate to lose the river" Byron answered, ignoring the jab. He squinted up into the sunlight and stood, brushing his hands on his pants. It felt like a Hollywood moment, but it was broken when Harald began to bark, the fur rising on his shoulders.

"Easy," Cole said, reaching for his collar.

Byron scanned the area toward which his dog barked and saw what had roused his attention. Through the forest, up on a hill, and straight along the path, stood a strange looking creature. It can perhaps best be described as a centaur, but instead of a horse's body, it had the body of a small goat. Coming off that, about the size of a child, was a torso that looked to Byron like it belonged to a goblin from *Labyrinth*—pinkish skin, wild hair, pointed ears, and an unpleasant expression. It had two curving horns sprouting from its temples and it held a small spear.

"What is that thing?" Byron asked aloud.

Harald broke free, sprinting up the path and barking madly. The goblin-goat-centaur turned and fled.

"Harald!" Cole yelled, chasing the dog up the path. "Come back!"

"Harald!" Byron screamed, following.

It was no use. The shepherd disappeared over the hill and into the shadowy forest. The two boys, winded, stopped running, and leaned on trees for support. They both called out to their dog again, then Cole turned to Byron, his speech interrupted as he gasped for breath.

"Now we're in trouble. This isn't a human path, and with our dog chasing it, that faun isn't going to be happy. What if there's more of them? A village or something? What if Harald kills it? We shouldn't follow this trail. Let's get back to the river."

"We can't just leave Harald," Byron replied, setting his face into a determined expression and beginning to walk farther along the trail. "Besides, that goat-man-thing looked too small to be dangerous."

"Sure," Cole replied, moving to keep up, "unless there are 20 of them. And it's called a faun."

"No," Byron didn't slow his pace, but he took on an argumentative tone. "A faun has two legs, like Mr. Tumnus. A centaur has four legs—this is more like a centaur."

"Semantics," Cole replied. "It's half goat, so in this nerd's book, it's a faun."

"Number of legs matters," Byron insisted, doggedly. "It's how we quantify living things: biped, quadruped, insect, spider, centipede, millipede."

"HARALD!" Cole yelled again, effectively ending the argument. Byron followed suit.

After about three minutes, Harald reappeared, cresting a rise and limping back along the trail, his physical demeanor one of weariness. Byron ran ahead and hugged him as he collapsed, panting. "You've got to stop doing this to us," he chided.

A small arrow protruded from Harald's shoulder. Byron pulled it out and Harald whimpered.

"You're okay, bud." Byron soothed, examining the wound. It wasn't deep, but it bled.

Cole took off his backpack. Digging in it for a few minutes, he pulled out the nylon rope and the Swiss-army knife. Cutting off about ten feet, he looped it through Harald's collar and tied it off. "There," he said, "that should take care of that."

"Do you smell smoke?" Byron asked. As he said it, he felt certain he heard the faint snapping reports of distant gunfire.

"What was that?" Cole asked. "Is that a gun?"

It sounded again, three more times, and they definitely smelled smoke. Both the sound and smell came from up the path.

"Guns means people, right?" Byron asked. "Probably the British Poindexter kept talking about."

"Let me think," Cole said. "The mirror was built in 1837," his eyes unfocused as he did mathematical calculations in his head. "It's 1996, so, roughly 150 years ago, but time here is five times slower than home, so . . . like 30 years?"

"You mean to tell me if the British are still here, they've only been here for 30 years?"

"Best guess, yeah."

"Then they're the closest to modern civilization we're likely to get."

"I'm thinking the same thing," Cole said. "Let's go." He shouldered the pack and walked along the path, toward the sounds. "Let's keep an eye out for those fauns," he said over his shoulder, "they're obviously armed."

Byron let the 'faun' stand, this time, but vowed to revisit the point with Cole later.

As they moved deeper into the woody hills, the sounds and smells of combat increased. Now, mixed with burning wood, they could clearly make out hints of gun smoke, the spent powder reminding them both of many Fourth of July holidays spent with their grandparents on the lake in New York, and of the time they'd gone to see a reenactment of Pickett's charge at Gettysburg.

The woods surrounding them had transitioned from swampy hemlock and cedar into a pine grove that reminded Byron of old New Hampshire forests. The moist ground sprouted moss and fern, and orange needles littered the forest floor, dotted with long, pitchy cones.

There wasn't a lot of cover, except behind tree trunks. He didn't think much more about it before his brother interrupted him.

"There's one of them!" Cole said.

Sure enough, a goblin-goat creature moved along the hill-line, limping away from them into the woods. Clearly, it'd suffered an injury to the hindquarters and it paid them no heed at all.

"You think they have a village up ahead and it's under attack?" Byron asked.

"That's exactly what I think," Cole replied. The pace of the gunfire ahead began to slacken.

"I think it's a bad idea to walk into a war zone."

"Me too, but I am definitely planning to sneak up on it and take a peek."

"You sure?" Byron raised his brows questioningly.

"Stay here if you want," Cole shrugged. "I'll be careful."

Cole edged up to the top of the rise, over which came the snaps and pops and wafting billows of smoke. He lay down parallel to a rotting trunk. After a moment of hesitation, Byron followed, leading Harald. They both snuck a glimpse down the other side.

"What the—? Are those . . . ?" Cole's mouth hung agape.

"Fudge sundae!" Byron whispered. "Skeletons."

Sure enough, down in the forest dell where diminutive wood and thatch huts burned and smoldered, pale-boned skeletons stalked back and forth, gleaming steel-headed spears in hand. With these, they skewered the wounded and dying goat-goblins. Each skeleton had a red cross painted across its cranium, red paint on white bone, like the flag of England.

At the far side of the village, gathering into a loose formation, stood seven red-coated British soldiers, complete with white campaign helmets and bayoneted rifles. One raised his gun and fired; a brief flash illuminated the twilight. Beside the soldiers, shifting his feet back and forth and holding a flag on a lance, stood a bugler. Rigid beside him, sabre in hand, a tall officer sat upon a dark horse.

The flag was the British Union Jack, England's red Cross of St. George superimposed over the white X of Scotland's St. Andrew's Cross, but instead of the traditional blue background, this flag flew on sable cloth.

"What do we do now?" Byron asked. "They've got skeletons, and that flag looks, I dunno, *evil* somehow. You want to just walk up and introduce ourselves?"

"I don't know," Cole whispered. "They're still our best bet at making another mirror and getting home, but—not going to lie—those skeletons creep me out."

"This reminds me too much of that poster mom wouldn't let you put up in your room. *Iron Maiden*. Remember? That skeletal British infantryman could give anyone nightmares."

"Yeah," Cole nodded soberly. "I put it up inside my closet. It's burned now, along with everything else."

Harald began a low growl, deep in his throat. Byron grabbed him by the collar and got in his face. "Shut up, bud!" he whispered, then rubbed Harald's ears to calm him.

"Um," Cole said, sounding worried. "One of them is headed this way."

Byron poked his head back over the log, and sure enough, a hollow-eyed skeleton had lifted its red-crossed skull and silently ascended the hill toward their position. Its spear gleamed dangerously in a stray sunbeam that pierced the canopy and smoke. Across the dell, a soldier took note, and pointed out the movement to his sergeant.

The boys looked at each other with a start, then fled at full sprint into the forest.

CHAPTER FOURTEEN
From the Ashes

"Ma'am," Chief Aldrich repeated patiently to Felicity, "The boys and me have been all over the wreckage of your place. I know it don't make sense, but let me lay it out for you again." The old policeman stretched his wrinkled hands across the motel room table. "We found the bones of a dog in the ashes, but no remains of your boys." He cleared his throat. "While it's true that bones can sometimes burn up in the flame—if it's hot enough—teeth don't, and there's no dental material in there, either, except a dog's teeth."

"But Charlie saw . . ." Byron's mom began.

"The cause of the fire is another thing," the chief continued. "It's not electrical. It's not related to the heating system or the oven. It's chemical. Some kind of chemical accelerant residue, like napalm, in the children's rooms and concentrated in the ash of the upstairs hallway. The chemists are still working on it."

"Then it was arson?" Charles asked. He stood behind his wife, his hand on her shoulder. "Who started it?"

"We don't know," the chief admitted. "I had an arson investigator out there yesterday. There are no foreign tracks heading into the property and none leading out. If it's arson, why the complex chemical starter when lighter fluid, gasoline, and kerosene are so cheap? If it's arson, too, we need a suspect and a motive. We have neither. Would anyone want to kidnap your boys? Do your boys have motive to run away?"

Byron's father looked at his wife. "No, to both questions."

She nodded her agreement.

"The bank tells me," the chief said, shuffling some papers, "that both boys have drained their accounts. What do you know about that?"

"It's news to me," Charles admitted. "But they weren't rich. No one commits arson for a couple thousand dollars."

Felicity blinked away tears. "Cole was working on a project for one of his business customers. He ordered a lot of stuff recently."

"I'll have to look into that," the chief said. "Maybe it was something explosive? An accident? Can I get copies of their latest statements? We'll check on his purchases and see if we can figure what he's been up to. Maybe he fell in with some bad folk on the internet. I'd like to access their emails. You know their passwords?"

"I know Byron's," Charles replied. "He uses it to write his grandfather in Maryland." Aldrich handed him a pen and he jotted it down for the chief in an open spot on his yellow notepad. "Anything else I can do, I will. Remember, Chief, I saw them upstairs in the fire and Cole swore he'd get Byron out."

The chief stood. "Look, I promise you we're doing everything we can and following every single lead. This case is puzzling—full of twists and dead ends. We won't quit until we have answers—even if we have to bring in the F.B.I." He held out his hand and Charles shook it.

"So," Felicity summed up, "If I'm hearing you right, Chief, you're telling me there's a chance—maybe a good chance—that my boys are alive, that my house was attacked, and that they've either been kidnapped or fled."

Chief Aldrich pushed his hat up on his white-haired forehead. "Ma'am," he said, collecting his clipboard, "we don't have enough evidence to support any such conclusion. But, if it helps, we can't disprove it, either."

After he left, Felicity and Charlie drove down to the bank, getting copies of the boys' account activity and cleared checks. Back in the hotel, Felicity sat at the table going through them page by page. Her husband finished Byron's account summary, walked to the sink, and poured himself a glass of water. After downing it like whiskey, he sat heavily on the creaking bed beneath a faded print of a sugar shack in autumn.

"You remember all that howling, barking, and growling from Harald?" Charlie asked. "Maybe someone did invade the house. We made it out moments after I saw Cole, though. I still don't see how anyone could have got them out of there faster, without us noticing . . ."

"Charlie," Felicity interrupted, clearly puzzled, "Cole has been buying a lot of weird stuff. Metal alloys, magnets, a lot of purchases from electrical suppliers. He was up to something, and it wasn't building a computer."

Charles tilted his head. "And Byron transferred all of his money to Cole's account."

"Let's go to the house. Maybe there's something there we missed."

"Yeah," Charles replied. "I think you're right."

But they never made it to their property. Halfway there, Felicity sat up straight in her seat.

"AT&T PersonaLink!"

"What?"

"Cole was really excited about it over the summer. He got it for his business—a Cloud Server. It saved your data offsite so if there was a fire or damage to your disk, you kept your data."

"A fire?"

"Yeah, that's how it was marketed. Safe offsite storage."

"So, you think . . ."

"There's a chance," Felicity replied. "A good one. Turn around. Let's go to the library. I need to access the web."

Charlie pulled a hasty u-turn.

"It's going to be password protected," he said. "You have any ideas?"

"Yeah, a few. But if all else fails, we call the company."

CHAPTER FIFTEEN
Breakfast with Champions

Byron and Cole fled back down the path toward the water, never daring to stop despite the reassurance that over their shoulders they could see nothing but trees. When they reached the swamp, they splashed off the trail, only stopping once they entered a thick tangle of conifer boughs and snaking vines.

"What are the English doing with skeletons?" Cole asked, stepping noisily up out of the muddy water onto a creaking snarl of twisted branches left by floodwaters.

"I don't know, but I don't like it," Byron replied, joining his brother. The boughs swayed around him as he bent double, breathing hard. Harald padded into ankle-deep mud at the end of his leash and flopped onto his side.

"My whole plan has been to hook up with them and build another portal." Cole rubbed a hand across his sweating face. "What do we do now?"

"I dunno," Byron offered. "But I tell you what: I'm not going to walk up to a squad of armed soldiers and undead. Bad idea. I've watched enough horror films to know that."

"Yeah . . ." Cole thought of the miniatures he'd been painting and shuddered.

A black-beaked raven landed on a nearby branch and cawed loudly. Byron shooed it away. "What about this," he said, "we keep on down the river and look for a British town? The civilians can't have changed that much. They won't want to see kids imprisoned or killed, right?"

"I hope not," Cole replied. Then his face lit up. "Hey, maybe skeletons are just the height of fairyland military technology—you know, like Apache helicopters or Abrams tanks. I mean, they're pretty scary, too. No kids would dare to walk up to a tank battalion in a war zone, either."

"Maybe," Byron replied, unconvinced. "Anyway, we'd better get moving. I don't like waiting here so close to those things. Look, I've got goosebumps." He showed Cole his arm, upon which the skin still prickled and the hairs stood up.

The rest of their daily march went strangely well. The swamp terminated in a series of large beaver dams and beyond those the water spilled again into a river and the terrain dried out. Eight hours later, Byron caught four trout, Cole set up the tent on a mossy flat under a stand of yellow birch trees, and they kindled a fire using bark peelings and a match. They sat beside the flames in the eternal twilight, gazing at the stars and eating their fill of fish. Even Harald had plenty.

"While fishing," Byron observed between mouthfuls of trout, "I kept seeing what I thought was a large dragonfly flitting between the reeds, until it landed on my pole." He paused for effect. "Turned out to be a fairy."

"What?"

"I'm not clowning you, a flesh-and-blood fairy. About three inches long and totally naked."

"What did she look like? Tinker Bell?"

Byron laughed. "Nope. This one seemed old—if she was a woman, I'd say she was eighty, but I don't know how to count in fairy-years. Her skin was all wrinkled and saggy and she looked kinda—I don't know—Mongolian, I guess, like Genghis Khan's grandma. But her wings were dragonfly wings, not butterfly wings."

"Did you talk to her?"

"No, and she didn't talk to me. She just winked and flew off."

"Leaving a trail of pixie dust?" Cole laughed.

"Shut up," Byron replied with a chuckle.

"Who would have ever thought this place existed," Cole said, fiddling with his Walkman. "And right across the mirror from our room the whole time . . ." but his tone changed as he spoke. "Byron, my batteries are dying. Music's warping. Last bit of charge, gone. I know it doesn't matter, but I listened for a moment before bed every day and it reminded me of . . ." he trailed off again, then stood abruptly. "Yeah, I think I'm going to get some more firewood," He ducked away from the fire into the gloom under the trees.

Byron sat for a few moments, staring at the dancing flames and rubbing Harald's fur. A wet branch hissed away in the flame, steaming moisture into the smoke. The last song he'd heard Cole listen to played in his head and he whispered the lyrics under his breath "Round Here," by the Counting Crows. He looked down at the cast on his arm and thought about riding in the Jeep with his Mom and Dad—about classic rock and Boston cream donuts, and about getting Cole's call that the mirror was finished. He stood and followed his brother. On the far side of the clearing, he found him crouched with his back toward the tent and his head against a birch trunk.

"It's okay, nerd," Byron said. "I mean it when I say I don't blame you."

"It's not okay," Cole said, turning and looking up, "and it's my fault—all of this. I just *had* to make that portal. I was greedy, and conceited, and . . ."

"And you accomplished an amazing task," Byron finished.

"I miss Mom and Dad," Cole said simply. He cradled his Walkman in his hands. "I know you said to shut up about it, but I miss our house and New Hampshire and America." He rubbed his eyes. "I'll never see them again, and you'll never see them either, and I can't help but sit here blaming myself. They probably think we're dead—they're probably sitting at home mourning us. Maybe they should be. Jesus, I'm the older one. I'm supposed to be strong."

Byron crouched down, picked up a twig and bent it in his fingers. "I miss them, too," he admitted. "If I could go back and change things, I would. But we're here now, and we can't go back—not by feeling sorry and not by wishing it so. So, maybe we shouldn't look back." He paused, then snapped the twig. "This will sound lame, but it's like my hockey coach says, 'Blame don't win games.'"

"Yeah, that line's corny as hell," Cole agreed. "Did it come straight from the script of *The Mighty Ducks?*"

"It's good advice, though," Byron insisted. "We're here and we've got to look forward if we're going to move forward."

"I guess," Cole ran a finger across the black buttons of his Walkman. "I've just never felt so useless. I don't know anything to help us here. I don't know how to be a woodsman. I don't know fairytales. I can't hunt, can't fight, can't even identify edible plants—all my learning, everything that made me exceptional at home, is pointless. Any of the knuckleheads that live up our road—any one of those guys that ride four-wheelers, hunt, shoot, and don't read—any of them would be better help to you than I am."

Byron smirked. "Welcome to my life, Colton Oakes. You think it's easy being a dyslexic kid in a world of books, papers, and tests? My *entire* life, I felt like you do now—and you know what I do about it?"

"What?"

"I deal with it. I grind. I work my ass off. You, Mom, Dad—you all know I'm smart. I know it too, deep down. I'm just a kind of smart that doesn't achieve real well in academics. I've got ambitions, though, so I work. I'm a grinder. When I grind, I get better. I have success." Byron threw away the bit of stick and reached to put a hand on Cole's shoulder. "Maybe in the short term," he said, "a guy like Rick Hubbard, Bob Donahue, or Uncle Jack would be a difference-maker here and now. But I know you, Colton Oakes." He stood. "You're a quick-study and a hard worker. You learn fast, you make connections. And I trust you. Give it a year and you'll be better adapted to this place than I am, guaranteed."

Harald padded over, dragging the leash behind him, and flopped down in Cole's lap, licking his hand.

"That sounds like one of dad's 'inspirational' speeches," Cole sniffed. He rubbed Harald's dirty fur. "A year here is five back home. Home. If we ever get back, could they forgive me? I burned down our house, Byron."

"They love you, Cole. They won't even think about blame if they get you back. Look," Byron said. "I'm going to bed. Stay out long enough to get your head right, but not too late. You whine enough for both of us without being overtired, and we've got a long walk ahead of us tomorrow." He considered the twilight in frustration, "If there's even such a thing as tomorrow here." Sighing, he turned toward the tent.

"Thanks, *Mom*," Cole replied, but from his tone Byron could tell his brother felt a bit better.

Byron woke to the throaty sound of a crow's cawing. Looking up against the green nylon of the tent, he saw the bird's three-toed feet shadowed against the dim light, walking along the fly above the mesh sunroof.

He reached a hand up, batted the fabric, and the bird flew away, its call joined by the caws of three or four others. He rolled over to see Cole still asleep next to him but sat up with a start when he didn't find Harald. Then he smelled . . . cooking meat? He strained his ears and over the noise of birds and the rolling current of the river, he could hear the sizzle of something suspiciously like bacon.

A desperate prayer that he'd been dreaming on a Scouting overnight flitted through his mind.

Sitting up and carefully pulling on the zipper, Byron swung his feet out of the tent and strapped on his sandals. A crow heckled him from low in a nearby branch. He wondered how Cole could manage to sleep through all of this racket, but his brother was never a morning person, and who knew how long he'd stayed up?

The bacon scent made his mouth water. Byron stood, looked over the tent, and to his great surprise locked eyes with a middle-aged man who hunched over their cookfire. The man's long, dark, unkempt hair was knotted in places. A short beard darkened his chin, about an inch long around his square jaw, but his upper-lip had been shaved clean. His skin shone brown, either naturally or tanned; Byron couldn't tell. His eyes smiled kindly, and a raven landed on his shoulder, cawing into his ear. The man reached out a dirty hand and patted Harald's head.

"What?" Byron's mouth dropped open. Yes, he acknowledged with astonishment, his "guard" dog—fearsome Harald—lay curled up at this stranger's feet.

The man cocked an eyebrow and then spoke. "Come," he said, his voice deep. He patted the earth near him. "Eat. Meat makes fast friends." He stroked Harald's fur again.

As Byron crossed warily, he assessed the man's appearance. The stranger was big and broad—six feet at least, though, squatting, it was hard to tell. A worn leather shirt clung just a bit too tightly to his chest. He had fringed leather pants and wore high boots. From a braided belt dangled a long knife and a hatchet, and next to him on the ground lay a discarded cloak and a sheathed sword.

A nervous whinny sounded behind him, and Byron glanced up to see a piebald horse grazing by the river. Against a nearby tree rested a saddle, a round wooden shield, saddlebags, a quiver of arrows, a rifle, and a large bundle of animal furs.

Harald stood as Byron approached, his tail wagging.

"Some guard you turned out to be," he scolded, thumping the dog's shoulder.

"Meat makes fast friends," the stranger repeated. He smiled, and withdrew the pan from the coals, flipping the bacon with a pair of sticks.

"My name is Byron, and this is Harald," Byron said, gesturing to the dog. "My brother is asleep"

"Was asleep," a voice came from inside the tent. "Is it safe or should I shoot him?"

Byron was thrown for a moment. They didn't have a gun, but he quickly puzzled out his brother's ruse.

"It seems safe enough," Byron called back. Cole emerged from the tent, his face wary.

"Call me Crowmane, as do all the British," the man said, completely unmoved by the threat of being shot. He gestured to the birch trees, upon which sat no fewer than a dozen crows. His accent sounded strange, not British exactly, but British in the same way a native South African or Indian might speak the language. It'd clearly been learned from the Victorians, Byron thought.

"Crowmane," Byron offered. "A strange name."

"In the clans," Crowmane replied, "Call we each other by child names until earns a man the name he wears. My child-name is Alain. My man-name is *Craeka-mune*—Crowmane in your tongue—because these follow me," he spread his arms to indicate the many crows and ravens perched in the trees around them.

The bacon popped in the pan, diverting everyone's attention for a moment.

"This wisdom is good," Crowmane continued instructionally, "for if a man is liar or thief, then may you know him by his name. Come, a man-name can at any time, so teaches it honesty, kindness, and courage, lest one be named liar, selfish, or coward."

"I guess that makes sense," Cole said, crouching to warm his hands at the fire. "But how do you know who belongs to which family?"

"Clan is family," Crowmane shrugged, then scowled. "Tell me, why look you both like *Lothka* but speak you both like British?"

"*Lothka*?" Byron asked.

"*Lothka*—we who are here," he gestured around, "in this, the land call, the British, Avalon."

"What?" Byron asked. "I didn't follow."

"Ah," Crowmane nodded. "Am yet young in speaking the Queen's English. But learning, it comes as time does." He thought for a moment. "In this land . . ." he paused, "that the British call Avalon."

"You're a native, then?" Cole asked.

"Born, I am, here."

Cole looked at Byron. "Their native language must be a VSO language, like Arabic or Celtic."

"VSO?" Byron asked.

"Verb-Subject-Object," Cole replied, matter-of-factly, "a language in which the verb comes first. You know, 'Fought I the battle,' or 'Ate I the bacon.'"

"Like you to learn speech in different tongues?" Crowmane asked.

"Oh yes," Byron replied, proud of his brother. "He already speaks three languages."

"Teach then, I shall, you." He pulled the bacon off the pan and lay it on a clean damp stone he'd fetched from the river. Reaching into the pouch next to him, he drew out three eggs and handed one to each boy, keeping one for himself. He began peeling it, tossing the shells into the fire.

As he followed suit, Cole asked, "What is your clan called, Crowmane?"

"Am clanless," Crowmane replied. "Gave up my clan when became I champion of the Illenthane."

"Illenthane?" Byron asked between bites of hard-boiled egg.

"Yes," Crowmane replied, "a wise teacher, a . . ." he paused, searching for a word, "sage from the mountaintop. Illenthane is clanless so may she aid the clans without favor, equally." He handed each boy two strips of bacon. "Eat."

"Champion," Byron cut in, "does that mean you're a warrior?"

"How many clans are there?" Cole asked at almost the same time.

"Am warrior," Crowmane replied, touching his breastbone. "And one clan is named for each god. Now, ask I questions. Answer clearly." He wiped his mouth on his sleeve. "Are you not British?"

"No," they answered in unison.

"We're American," Cole added.

"Come you from the British world?"

"It's not a British world anymore," Byron said.

"No?"

"The United Kingdom still exists," Cole added, helpfully, "but the British Empire has fallen."

"Came you through a mirror?"

"Yes," Cole replied. "I built it."

"You?"

"He's pretty smart," Byron explained.

"Where now is your mirror?"

"Destroyed. Burned up in a fire."

"Careful," Crowmane warned, "lest earn yourself the name liar."

"It's the truth," Cole cut in. "A barghest came through and burned it, we barely escaped alive."

"And," Byron added, "now we can't get home."

"Barghest?"

"A fire-breathing dog. Black and red fur."

"Ah, a *loatheehund*," he paused, thinking. "Did you kill it?" he asked, intentionally placing his subject and verb.

"Yes," Cole answered.

"You, too, are warriors and clanless, seems it to me," Crowmane chuckled. "So be it."

Byron nodded, savoring the crispy meat—it had been so long since he tasted something other than fish. He couldn't help a wave of nostalgia for pancake breakfasts.

"Your skin," Crowmane poked Byron's arm, "is not British. Are pale, like butter. Look you like *Lothka*," he held out his arm, noting the similarity in skin tone between himself and Byron.

"Yeah," Cole explained. "Our dad's skin came from England, but our mom's came from Africa, so we're lighter than her but darker than him." He hesitated, then admitted, "It makes it hard to find a place in America."

"Find, you will, a place here," he said simply. A shadow passed and they looked up to see the Gryphon pass, flying southwest. The horse whinnied, nervous. Crowmane stood. "Talking we can do when walking. Gather your things."

Chapter Sixteen
Light from the Cloud

I just want to have this recorded, Cole said into the camera, *to show that I did it. What you see before you,* he gestured to the portal, *is the first working example of a Faraday Mirror built since the Victorian age. My name is Colton Oakes and the person doing the recording is my brother, Byron—* Felicity hit PAUSE. This was the third time she and Charles had watched the video and seen the tennis ball fly in and drop back out. Tears paved twin paths down her cheeks.

They stared at the freeze-frame for a few moments, then Felicity clicked the mouse, closing the window. She scrolled through Cole's files, repeating the words "Thank you, thank you" under her breath. Her son had made high resolution scans of Wheatstone's letter and plans, which were legible, and he'd written an itemized purchase list and taken some notes as he assembled the mirror. He'd saved all of it there on the cloud. She thanked herself again for teaching him the scientific method and for getting him involved in computers. Using his online journal, she could—she hoped—recreate it.

"So," her husband said, determination in his voice. "We construct this mirror and go after them." He pushed back the library chair and stood, placing his hands on his wife's shoulders.

"Yes," Felicity agreed. "I know I can build this. We've got the money—the insurance check for the house. Let's drive down to Concord and buy an expensive laptop. Then I'll rush-deliver all the equipment and parts."

"Okay," Charles nodded. "And let's not rebuild the house. I'll buy a cheap trailer home and have it delivered to our property. It'll give you a place to work, and the portal should open near the original location."

"Okay," she wiped away a tear and smiled. "Charlie, can this work?"

"It has to," he said, lowering his voice and glancing around the library. It was nearly empty on a Tuesday afternoon. "How long will it take you to build?"

"If all the parts can be purchased and shipped—if nothing's backordered—and if I can figure out how it all works, and if I can work through the Lupus, a few months—two or three. But that's a lot of 'ifs.'" She bit her knuckle for a moment. "Four to six months may be more likely. It's April, so four months would put us in August, and six would put us in November." She ejected her disk from the computer and waved it at him. "I've saved the Word files. I'll need a Zip disk for the video and photos."

"We can do that at my office," Charlie offered as they left the building, "at the university."

"Tomorrow," Felicity opened the Jeep's door.

"So," Charles said, "I have time to get in physical shape and to get together a survival pack and plan, if I'm going through."

"Who will you take with you?" she asked. "You're not going alone." The unspoken fact that her Lupus made Felicity too ill to join him nearly killed her.

"We won't tell anyone outside the family." He started the engine. "You get the government or the police involved in this, and it will be taken away from us, out of our control. Those kinds of organizations move too slowly and methodically. I'll call Jack. He'll go with me."

Jackson Oakes was Charles' younger brother, an army vet with combat experience in Panama and Desert Storm who now worked as a lumberjack in Maine. The two used to be close; despite vast differences in education, life experiences, and political ideology, Jackson had been the best man at Charles' wedding. His idea of a bachelor party for his Ph.D. brother had been to get a bunch of their high school friends together at a paintball range and shoot each other all afternoon, then tell old stories around a bonfire with three cases of Old Milwaukee. But his toast at the wedding reception had been warm and heartfelt. He was a stereotypical upstate New Yorker, gruff on the outside and full of small-town prejudices, but kind-hearted and extremely loyal to those whom he knew and loved. The last time he and Charlie had seen each other had been three years ago—at a family reunion, where they'd parted, angry, after a fight about politics. They hadn't talked since.

"He's got a lot of useful skills," Charlie said, a bit defensively, "and I trust him."

Felicity nodded. She and Jackson had a turbulent relationship for many years, until the kids were born and they finally began to understand each other—shared unconditional love will have that effect, she realized. Still, tension existed between them; yet, she had to admit he was the logical choice. "Call him," she said. "And mail him a copy of the video. He won't fully believe you until he sees it."

"You'll need to stay here and keep the mirror open," Charles said.

"Before we get too caught up in the future," Felicity opened her door again. Charlie raised a questioning eyebrow, "let's start with the present. It's barely noon. We have time to get down to Concord and buy that computer. Maybe we can get a mobile home, too." She handed him her Nokia. "Switch with me. I'll drive. You talk."

Chapter Seventeen
Into the Woods

Byron looked nervously behind him as they hiked toward the mountains. He knew the river was his last tenuous path back to the mirror and his old life, but it shrank into the landscape behind him.

"What is the name of that river?" he asked, intending to commit it to memory.

"Called the *Wyrmhod*," Crowmane replied.

"Where are we going?" Cole looked ahead.

"*Yulc* clan lands," Crowmane replied. "Beyond the mountains." He gestured to the high snow-capped peaks.

"Is there a pass or do we actually climb over?" Byron assessed the height dubiously.

"A cleft in the rock, the *Byarj Bruu Balkir*. Pass we through it."

They walked in silence for about ten minutes, two boys, Crowmane, Harald, and the brown and white piebald horse. Crows followed them, cawing. Byron had considered not joining this stranger, refusing outright, but how do two lost, unarmed boys say no to a large man with a rifle and sword? But he'd been friendly, and the only offer of help to arrive since they crossed over. Byron and Cole had shared some questioning glances, and this was their joint—if silent—decision.

A black raven croaked and fluttered to Crowmane's shoulder.

"Which clan owns these lands?" Cole asked.

"These," Crowmane looked around at the tall dry grasses and conifer trees, displacing the raven, "are not clan lands. Long, long ago, were home to the *Rungt* clan, but were the *Rungt* defeated by the . . ." he searched for a word ". . . Necrologists."

"The what?" Byron asked.

"Necrologists," Crowmane shrugged, "control they the *Danath*—the dead—of this world."

"Oh, I get it. You must mean *Necromancers*." Cole said.

"The British here name them Necrologists. Called in our tongue *Danathskoti*. These are *Danath Byoth*, The Dead Lands, in consequence." He gestured to the empty land around them.

"But we haven't seen any dead, except with the British," Cole answered.

"Because the British and the *Danathskoti* are allies here."

"Why are the British here at all?" Byron asked. "What are they doing?"

Crowmane sighed. "Is a lot to know, and I am a poor teacher." He stopped walking and turned, pointing back to a line of dark hills. "There lies, beyond those hills, the sea of grass. Stretches, the grass, farther than the hawk can see, endlessly in all directions along the edge of the mountains. Hot, dry, and windy, is the sea. No water, no shade. Frozen, unforgiving in winter. Hunted by dragons, is not safe to cross, nor to live in. Through it, came the British. Shooting metal from their guns, drove they off the dragons. Biting shovels dug into land for metals and water. Their hands laid rails. Now cross they the sea of grass on fast, smoking ships of steel and wheels."

"Steam trains," Cole nodded. He shifted Harald's leash from one hand to the other.

"Here" Crowmane gestured around again, "find the British the *Danathskoti* and fight they a war."

"And the *Danathskoti* lost," Byron predicted.

"Lose must all to the British," Crowmane responded. "Like a machine for killing men, the red-coated army is more dangerous than dragons. But the *Danathskoti*, know they how to bring themselves back from the dead." He chuckled as if this were a joke. "See, do the *Danathskoti* the gleam of British rifles and know how many will be killed, so offer themselves to join the British and bring slain enemies back to serve as necroids. Eager, are the British for slaves. Now, come they across the sea of grass to build villages, gardens, and fortresses, and to dig great pits in search of ores or the black burning rocks, and the *Danath*—the necroids—and the rocks go back on the rails to serve the British."

"So there's coal in these hills," Cole nodded. "What about copper? A shining metal that turns green with age."

"Here, too." Crowmane nodded.

"Have the clans ever fought the British?" Byron asked.

"The *Yulc* clan," Crowmane answered. "Fought the British one battle, here in these hills, and faced defeat, but lost the British many and now fear the united clans, so have they not yet dared to cross the mountains."

"Byron," Cole said, excited. "If the British have coal and steam engines, and if they're mining copper out here, they may have electricity and foundries!" He slapped Byron's shoulder enthusiastically. "We may be able to build another mirror and get home."

"Yeah," Byron answered, a bit sarcastically, rubbing his shoulder, "all we have to do is introduce ourselves, ask them to take us across that steppe, become wealthy, invaluable, and trusted members of their society, and then ask them to donate the majority of their resources to our research. Easy-peasy."

"I'm not saying it would be easy," Cole replied, suddenly sullen.

They were in the forest now, under the shade of conifer boughs. Byron looked over at the horse, noting the variety of equipment slung across it.

"Crowmane," he asked, "May I see your rifle?"

"Yes," he replied, walking over to the horse and drawing it out of a leather holster. He handed it to Byron. "Careful," he said, "prepared, it is, to shoot."

"Loaded," Cole offered.

"Loaded," Crowmane nodded.

Impressed by the trust just placed in him, Byron took the gun, flipped it over, made sure he engaged the safety, and then examined it carefully. He was no rifle expert, but he'd seen enough pictures in his Victorian history research to be sure. It was an authentic Martini-Henry. It had the crown inspection stamp as well as the initials V.R.1.P. and a serial number of A14310. Further back an engraving read "Enfield" and a date: 1873. He looked again at the crown stamp and back to Crowmane.

"This is a military-issued rifle. How'd you get it?"

"From a dead soldier," he replied, unflinching.

"If you've got a rifle," Cole chimed in, "how come you need a bow?" he gestured to a quiver of gray-fletched arrows rattling against the horse.

"Can make arrows," Crowmane said. "Cannot make bullets, and the British don't sell them. Have only 12 left."

They passed out of the shadow of the pines into a grassy clearing. Byron shifted the rifle to one hand and wiped some sweat out of his eyes. They'd been ascending steeply and Crowmane set a fast pace. "What if I told you," he puffed between breaths, "that two times, in our world, British armies, armed with these rifles and with field artillery—cannon—were defeated by men like you, worse armed than you, even?"

"Then, ask, would I, how this could be accomplished," Crowmane replied, his eyes intent on Byron's face.

Byron opened his mouth to answer, but a thunderous eagle scream split the air and a shadow passed over like a low-flying aircraft. They ducked instinctively, then the horse screamed and toppled, and on top of it crouched the gryphon, talons tearing into its flanks. The horse rocked, flailing wildly to escape, but the gryphon only gripped it tighter. It bit deep into the horse's shoulder, then turned its beaked head and yellow eyes toward them and roared. Blood sprayed from the end of its beak to pepper the rocky ground.

Crowmane put both arms out and grabbed a boy in each hand. He backed away slowly and quietly, dragging them with him. Harald barked madly. In the shock, Cole had lost the leash. Too scared to attack, the dog stayed just out of range of the gryphon's bloody, yellow beak. The horse screamed again, and the gryphon bent to it, tearing and rending the flesh of its neck. The horse went limp. The crows flew hither and thither, cawing raucously.

"Have you one bullet in that gun," Crowmane said, slowly drawing his gleaming longsword from its sheath. "The rest are on the horse."

"And so is the food," Cole said.

"And the water," Byron added.

The gryphon flapped its wings, but the horse and gear were too heavy for it to carry off, so it folded them up and stalked around the dead horse, screeching at them, snapping its beak, and whipping its tail back and forth. It lunged at Harald, forcing the dog back, then turned toward Crowmane. Byron drew up the rifle and took careful aim down the steel barrel. Remembering the safety, he switched it off. Cole unsnapped the frame backpack and drew out the hatchet. He edged toward his dog and the leash dragging in the dirt.

Crowmane advanced, shouting in his native tongue: "*Reesa! Hymetal! Hymetal!*" and waving his blade.

The gryphon shrank back before him, until it curled directly atop the horse's corpse, hissing at him angrily. It hesitated, indecisive for a moment, as if it might take flight, but then it sprang.

Crowmane brought his blade down on its forearm with force, but its momentum bowled him over and he cried out in pain. The beast brought its head up and opened its yellow beak to strike.

Byron pulled the trigger. The crows all flew higher, screaming.

Byron fell backwards, and the gryphon roared, lurching to the side. Crowmane scrambled out of range, his left arm bleeding profusely.

The gryphon turned to Byron and advanced. Harald's growling and barking intensified. Cole started shouting. Byron scrabbled back, his broken arm tingling inside the cast. Either the recoil or the fall tweaked it. He shifted his grip on the rifle to use the butt end as a club if he needed to, and he rose to one knee. The Gryphon lunged and Byron swung. He clubbed it in the side of the head. It backed up but then lunged a second time. Byron fell again, holding it back with the rifle sandwiched in its beak. It struggled to bite him. Harald leaped at it, snapping at its legs. Crowmane stood unsteadily and lifted his sword. Cole lunged for the leash. The crows flew back and forth, jabbering.

And just at that moment, over the corpse of the fallen horse, vaulted a red-coated officer on a black stallion.

The stallion came to a halt and reared. Using his knees to steady his mount, the officer drew a well-oiled revolver from a holster on his belt, took careful aim, and fired. Shot after shot echoed in the clearing. Smoke blew from the revolver, and the gryphon shuddered again and again, screaming until the fifth and final bullet had driven into it. Then the officer discarded his pistol, drew a curved sabre, and leapt from his horse, landing gracefully on the dusty ground. He took three strides toward the wounded animal and made a surgical thrust, his arm raised and curved sword inverted, to stab the creature deep along the neck. The gryphon, already shuddering, gave a final muscular surge, then lay still.

The officer drew out a handkerchief, calmly wiped down his blade, sheathed it, then offered a hand to Byron.

"Lieutenant Arthur Rochester at your service," he said in an aristocratic English accent. "Are you hurt?"

"No," Byron said, "I'm fine—thank you—but Crowmane isn't." He gestured toward the injured warrior.

"Indeed," Rochester said, glancing toward Crowmane. "You travel with a native?"

"We met him at breakfast," Cole said, stepping forward. He held out his hand, "Colton Oakes. This is my brother, Byron." Rochester shook it—a good, firm handshake like his father always taught him to give.

"Strong English name, Oakes," Rochester nodded approvingly, "but your accents aren't exactly Oxfordshire."

"We're Americans," Cole replied. Harald sniffed at Rochester's hand and give a tentative tail-wag.

"Ah, Yanks. That is what they call you, yes?" Rochester smiled invitingly, his blue eyes twinkling. He removed his white campaign helmet and mopped his blond hair. "I was unaware that any of your descent were in these territories."

Byron left them and walked over to Crowmane, who gazed warily at Rochester while applying pressure to a series of parallel gashes on his left forearm. They were deep and Byron could see hints of bone at the bottom. Blood seeped through Crowmane's thick fingers. Clearly, it would require stitches.

"Let me tend to those," Byron said, trying to remember his first-aid classes from scouts. With lacerations and no help coming, they needed to apply even pressure and if the bleeding didn't stop—and it wouldn't—he'd need to sew them closed. He had a needle and thread in his pack, but wounds of this depth might do better with fishing line, he thought. They'd need to be sterilized, too. "Come with me," he ordered. He led the way toward their pack. Harald loped over, tail wagging. "Good boy," Byron smiled.

He opened his pack and rummaged through, removing the sewing needle, fishing line, first-aid kit, zip ties, and a pair of fleece pajama bottoms. He tied the line to the needle and opened an alcohol pad, rubbing it down. "This will hurt," he told Crowmane. "Sit here."

Crowmane sat. Cole and Rochester walked over to watch. Byron took up the needle and thread. He hesitated. "We need to clean this," he said. "Anyone have alcohol?"

"Will this do?" Rochester produced a silver flask from his breast pocket. "It's gin."

"It'll have to," Byron replied. "Thanks."

He carefully dribbled it into the wound, and Crowmane, who had all this time been eyeing Rochester with suspicion, grunted and closed his eyes. Byron then began to sew up the gashes with quick and measured motions.

"This won't heal pretty," he said, wincing as he worked. His fingers smeared alcohol and blood. "And you'll have to cut this line out when it heals, but it should heal." Byron felt incredibly nervous doing this work, and a bit nauseated, but he kept it together as best he could, covering his nerves with conversation. After sewing the wound, he used a pocket knife to cut a leg from the flannel pajama bottoms and tightly wrapped the arm Then he secured it snugly with three zip ties, trimming the ends with the knife.

Rochester bent down and with perfectly manicured fingers, picked up a discarded zip tie end from the ground, examining it. "What is this material?" he asked, genuinely interested.

"Plastic," Cole answered. "A petroleum derivative."

"Indeed? Yankee ingenuity, I suppose." As Rochester pocketed it, a noise from behind them drew their attention. A file of red coated soldiers strode out of the woods, marching at the double-quick and followed by a troop of red-crossed skeletons. "Ah," Rochester smiled. "If you'll excuse me." He strode over toward the leader, a brown-mustachioed and thickly sideburned man of about forty who wore stripes on his arm. "Sergeant," he said loudly, "Take these people into custody. Treat them kindly and with respect, if—*if*—" he repeated the word with emphasis, "they do as you tell them."

"Yes, Lieutenant, very good, sir." The sergeant moved toward them, followed by his men.

Rochester turned to look after them. "I'm sorry about this, chaps," he said, looking at Cole and resuming his conversational tone, "but you are in Her Majesty's lands without authorization, so I must take you back to Fort Douglas for questioning. I promise you safe conduct if you cooperate. I am a man of honor and shall keep to my word."

Crowmane stood, his hand on his sword hilt and his eyes defiant. The bulky sergeant stepped toward him.

"Now, sir, be kind enough to hand that over like a good gentleman," he said, polite, but with an edge of danger in his voice. He and Crowmane stared at each other pretty fixedly for a tense few moments before the native warrior wordlessly unbuckled and handed over his sword.

"Steven," Rochester said, turning to a small, brown-skinned man in a black bowler hat and gray suit who skulked in the shadows behind the skeletons. The man stepped forward. When he came into the light, the boys felt a thrill of fear run down their spines. His skin was worn and papery, and he looked about a thousand years old. Though facing Rochester, one of his yellowed, unblinking eyes moved independently to focus on Cole and Byron. Crowmane stiffened beside them.

"*Danathskoti,*" he hissed under his breath.

"Can you reanimate a gryphon?" Rochester asked, unfazed by the man's unnatural appearance and behavior.

The Necrologist cocked his head, like a buzzard in a tree considering a prime corpse, and rasped out a heavily accented reply: "No. It lacks the intelligence in life to be controlled in death."

Rochester nodded absently. "A pity," he said, then turned unconcernedly to his soldiers. "Brewster," he ordered. "Cut off its head and talons. We'll bring them back as gifts to the Lord Douglas, then dispose of the corpse. Hutchins," he faced another, "start a cookfire so we'll be ahead of the game when the baggage ponies arrive. Godfrey, go through their things and report to me. And James, butcher that horse. We'll have fresh meat this noon. And Sergeant?"

"Sir?" the sergeant answered, clicking his heels together in salute.

"Put a guard on that Crowmane chap. He makes me nervous."

The sergeant saluted and assigned a rifled guard with a fixed bayonet to stand watch near Crowmane, who sat cross legged at the base of a tree, his eyes closed and a pained, weary expression on his face. The rest of the soldiers went about their business, and soon the clearing bustled with activity.

Cole looked to Byron and raised his eyebrows. The thought passed clearly, but silently between them: What were they to do now?

CHAPTER EIGHTEEN
A Brief and Wondrous History of Faerie

Hours later, Byron, Cole, and Crowmane found themselves attached to the baggage train of Rochester's column. With two sections ahead of them and one behind, they marched along in the twilight gloom, mostly in silence. After a break for water and some dried meat, they resumed the march, but Cole—always the extrovert—couldn't handle the silence. After crossing the *Wyrmhod* for a second time, he turned to Byron and said, "My feet are blistering in these wet shoes, my thighs are chafing, and, clearly, I didn't get enough sleep. And these skeletons creep me out—I swear, they keep looking at me with those empty eyes. I'm not clowning; it's like they're staring through my soul. Talk to me. Keep my mind off it."

"Okay," Byron said, glancing over his shoulder at the skeletal contingent, "let's play a game. How about categories?"

Categories was a classic camp-game he often played with his Scouts friends while hiking. The premise was simple: each player named something from a specified category, until one accidentally repeated something that had been already named, or until a player could not think of an item from said category.

"Fine," Cole replied—they'd played this game before on car trips. "Breakfast cereals. Go."

"Frosted Flakes," Byron said.

"Sugar Smacks."

"Cocoa Pebbles."

"Cocoa Krispies."

"Rice Krispies."

"Corn Flakes."

"Honey Bunches of Oats."

"Cookie Crisp."

And it went on for a while like that, until they got to the less well-known and kid-friendly cereals. Five minutes later, they were winding down.

"Special K," Byron said.

"Grape Nuts."

"Eww. Okay, Bran Flakes."

"You already said that."

"Nuh-ah. I said Raisin Bran."

"They're the same thing," Cole complained.

"They aren't. Different name. Different box. Different cereal."

"Fine! Then, Apple Dapples!"

"What?!" Byron complained. "Apple Dapples are just Hannaford brand Apple Jacks."

"Different name. Different box," Cole repeated. "Different cereal."

"Ugh! You're impossible!" Byron groaned, setting his jaw and preparing himself for the off-brand version of the game just played, racking his mind not only for Hannaford off-brands, but for Shaw's and Price Chopper as well, when Crowmane interrupted.

"What are these things you keep saying?" The older man grumbled, apparently driven to the point of exasperation by their continued bickering.

"They're, uh," Cole sounded apologetic, "breakfast foods."

"Morning meals in our land," Byron agreed.

"Enough of this game. Tire I of it."

"Then why don't you tell us about the clans?" Cole suggested. "About the *Lothka*."

"What is it wish you to know?" he asked.

"I like mythology," Byron replied cheerfully. "Why not start from the beginning?"

"Is a lengthy tale," Crowmane warned.

"I gather that Fort Douglas is pretty far away," Cole replied. He kicked a pinecone and it trundled downhill.

"And it will give you a chance to work on your English," Byron added.

Crowmane grimaced. "Yes." He sighed and seemed to arrange his thoughts, preparing to tell a well-known story in a poorly understood language.

"In the beginning," he said, pausing to arrange his subjects and verbs, "Forge-goddess Ruelank hammered the outer-world flat from a molten ball she wrestled, red hot, from the forge. From that was hammered all that is. In the sky shine the sparks of hammer-strokes. Long, was her labor and to aid her, made she a polished shield, Fugin, and hung it opposite her forge to better reflect light when embers grew cool. This let her craft in the darkness."

"The sun, stars, and moon," Byron observed.

"But there's no day and no moon here," Cole protested. "It's been a week without a noon or a moon."

"So, did the people here originally come from Earth?" Byron asked.

"Oh," Cole's eyes lit up, "good question!"

Crowmane coughed, glowered them into silence, then resumed, haltingly, "Ruelank's first great forgework, after lands, sea, plants, and creatures, was Drakooth, first of dragons, made to watch over the world while Ruelank journeyed to the center of void, on the edge of abyss, to bargain for the souls of Woman and Man from the Great Father. Ferocious, Drakooth was made to protect the land like a great guard dog, but she was also first of Ruelank's creations to have a flaw. Overhasty to make Woman and Man, Rulank hammered into Drakooth fear and envy, ever the defects of dragons. Drakooth worried that Man and Woman would outgrow her in power. To prevent this, vomited she a deadly venom on Ruelank's anvil and hammer, so upon Forgemistress' return, when fashioned she new creations with her tools, would they not live. Hoped Drakooth to be the last of Ruelank's living creations."

"Your nouns are slipping," Cole chided when Crowmane paused. "People come first and actions second in English. Crowmane nodded and his narration resumed, slower but more coherent.

"So it happened that Ruelank returned from the edge of abyss with two souls in her sack and then forged Woman and Man on her anvil, but soon as their eyes saw the light from the forge, they rolled up into their skulls, and tongues hung limp from dead mouths. Slain, they were, by venom. Skillfully, Ruelank snatched their fleeing souls in her sack as they plunged toward abyss. Angry at Drakooth but unwilling to destroy such a masterwork of forge-skill, Ruelank decided to bury her alive at the base of the Tallest Mountain, where she might never trouble anyone again.

"Having done this, thought she then long to find a way to craft Woman and Man on her poisoned anvil without again watching them die. Having an idea, made she first Woman as an ungrown babe, and while slept a steppe tiger, slipped she the babe into the great cat's womb, where was it safe from the venom. Following this, crafted she Man the same way, and while slumbered a brown bear in a mountain cave, slipped she man into her womb. Thus were Woman and Man born into the world separate and nurtured by different mothers.

"*Men are from Mars, Women are from Venus*," Cole smirked, quoting the title of a self-help book his mom kept in the bathroom. "Your English is slipping again, though. Focus on those verbs—the action words. The thing is first, the action second. It's doing you good to talk."

"What happened next?" Byron asked, waving an arm to silence his brother.

Crowmane shrugged. "Woman and Man then had children and more children—generations. Forge-light shone on the world, and Ruelank smiled because all seemed well with her creation."

"But?" Byron prompted, "there's always a but."

Crowmane chuckled. "But," he said, "at the root of the Tallest Mountain, the dragon Drakooth found some metal from Ruelank's forge still glowing hot. Hammer blows under the earth shook the lands. There made Drakooth all manner of snakes and lizards that live and kill by poison. Her hammer blows birthed spiders and centipedes and scorpions as well—all attempts to create a companion. Finally, forged she a hulking steel serpent with iron claws and a beating heart of molten fire. Though it could not be her mate, she loved it like a mother, for she knew it could dig to the surface. For a time, hope was enough. Digging endlessly, the serpent tunneled while Drakooth schemed to steal Ruelank's hammer.

"When the serpent broke surface and opened the tunnel, all of Drakooth's foul brood boiled forth. Woman and Man were long dead from age, the slow-working effect of Drakooth's venom, still in our blood—age and time, ever the death of men—but their children, caught unaware, died in great numbers. Seeing this, Ruelank, grasped her sword, Heltchan, and shield, Fugin, and journeyed down to slay the serpent with iron claws, for it caused havoc among men.

"As Ruelank left, Drakooth snuck out from under the mountain, and flew to Ruelank's workshop, where used she the Forgemistress' hammer to forge herself a companion and mate.

"When slain was the steel serpent, Rulank heard Drakooth's hammering. Bounding back to her forge, overboiling with anger at Drakooth, intended Ruelank to slay her and put a final end to dragon mischief. However, when arrived, found she Drakooth shuddering in sorrow. Ruelank's heart unhardened. Mounted she Fugin on the wall and sheathed Heltchan. Ruelank banished Drakooth again, this time under the vast field of ice atop the lands, where there would be no iron to forge. Realize, Ruelank did not, however, that Drakooth made a mate—a small creation that the dragon had slipped, inside an egg, into her belly, where it would be safe.

"So for a time, was Drakooth locked under the ice, and tried Ruelank in vain to stamp out all of the poxes the dragon had left in the world. Taught she men and women to make weapons and armor and how to wage war against Drakooth's creations. Yet, fell Ruelank into sorrow, for seemed to her the outer world but a theater of affliction and torment. Finally, resolved that all the anguish of man could be laid at her feet, forged Ruelank the heavens, a blue crystal dome, laying it like a lid on the eight-cornered plate of land to forever separate the world from her forge and to prevent any more meddling.

"Meanwhile, deep in the ice, laid Drakooth her egg and hatched it into a child she named Drangdoo. The child wyrm, whose molten core never cooled from the forge before being locked in the egg, spewed fire rather than poison from a churning belly, though still dripped, his fangs, with it."

"Venom," Cole corrected. "You mean venom, not poison."

"Yeah," Byron chimed in. "Poison is something you eat, like a poisonous toad. Snakes inject venom."

Crowmane sighed. "Then did Drangdoo have the twin powers of fire and *venom*. Rejoice, this made Drakooth; for realized she that the heat of her child could surely melt the ice around them, and thus was an escape unlooked for. Hoping to challenge man and Ruelank for control of the land, mated then Drakooth with her own son."

"Ugh! Gross! Vomit! She had babies with her own son!" Byron made gagging noises.

"Yeah," Cole agreed, "pretty nasty, but maybe dragons don't follow the same evolutionary rules as humans. I mean, there are probably some insects or lizards on earth that do it too, and some animals are hermaphrodites."

"What's that mean again?" Byron asked.

"They reproduce by themselves."

"Oh, right—mom just taught me that in the plant unit. I guess some ferns can do that."

Crowmane cleared his throat. When they quieted, he resumed, "Together bred Drakooth and Drangdoo the monstrous race of dragons there in the ice. There made they the many kinds of wyrms to be found in the world. All of their brood vomit either fire or venom. Shapes and sizes, there are many, from smallest wriggling lesser-wyrms that slither as snakes in the dust, to large land-borne drakes, which may crawl upon legs but never fly, to winged wyverns that have only the wings that keep their snakelike forms aloft. Alone and above these lesser dragons are the full-blooded dragons, or greater-wyrms. Fearsome in the form of their mother and father, these are the strongest. Was only one dragon ever born greater than these, and ever has he been called the Great Wyrm, Dracdath, foul, black, and indomitable—but his is another story."

"Jeez," Cole whistled. "That dragon sounds like a boss."

"Shut up," Byron elbowed him. "Let the man talk. This is getting good."

"For many generations of men," Crowmane continued after an annoyed pause, "stayed the dragons in ice, laying eggs, breeding and building their forces until the time ripened. When the time came, gave Drakooth the command to melt the ice, and it was done in a moment. This formed the great sea and drowned many men and creatures. Then did the dragons come forth to battle, slaying men at will and glutting themselves upon the flesh of man-children.

"Seeing this, rage seized Ruelank at Drakooth's wickedness. Again took she up her sword, Heltchan, and shield, Fugin. Lifted she the dome and strode forth to finish Drakooth. Powerless against the fury of Ruelank, cowered Drakooth into a coil and begged for her life, but frenzied, lopped Ruelank off the dragon's head. Enraged by the death of their Great Mother, Drangdoo and all of his brood attacked Ruelank, filling her veins with venom and burning at her flesh, but was resistant to fire, the old forgemistress, and not made with a heart to be poisoned, so slew she nigh all of the dragons that attacked her, causing the few remaining to flee to the eight corners of the lands.

"Then, gazing about her at the smoking and poisoned ruin of her creation, hearing the tortured screams of wounded men and animals pierce the crackling hiss of boiling sap and fire devouring her forests, fell Ruelank into despair. In a fit of anguish, perhaps aided by the venom-fever, used she her own long, black hair to hang herself from the branches of the Tallest Tree, which reached nearly to the sky-dome."

He paused for effect. No one spoke for a few paces. Finally, he continued. "So passed Ruelank, the great forgemistress and All-Mother, from the earth. Then cooled the forge and red went the sky on the horizon, and fled, her soul, back to the center of void, at the edge of abyss, into the embrace of the Great Father."

"Hold up," Byron said after Crowmane finished, his eyes wide with amazement. "You're telling me your creation myth ends with the creator killing herself? Suicide? That's just brutal."

"Actually, I think it's Shakespearean," Cole added—he'd read *Hamlet*, *Macbeth, Othello*, and *Julius Caesar* as part of his homeschool education and could be pretty intellectual. "It's textbook tragedy," he explained: "Watch the tragic hero meet her self-inflicted doom."

"Comes all our woe from Ruelank's death," Crowmane replied. "Thus it is that we in the clans do not abide self-killing."

"So," Cole prodded, "that's all there is? That's the whole story?"

"There are many stories," Crowmane replied, "but ends this one with Ruelank's death and the slow cooling of the forge."

Byron shook his head again, "I still can't believe it ends that way."

"Talked, I have, to your British," Crowmane said, his tone offended. "Died your Christ no different. Knew he did, what would happen if stayed he in the city. Stayed he. Happened it as he foresaw."

"That's different," Byron replied. "That was a sacrifice made for others. It wasn't done in selfish despair. And Jesus was resurrected. He didn't stay dead."

"A god isn't killed," Crowmane insisted. "A god is too powerful for that. *Lets* he himself be killed. *Chooses* he the killing. Not so much different."

"It is to me," Byron replied, now grumpy.

"Calm down, Byron," Cole urged. "Don't hold his gods up to your standards. No one gets bent out of shape at the Greek gods, and look at all the crazy stuff Zeus got up to. I mean, infidelity, grudge-holding, murder, rage, jealousy, domestic abuse, mass-slaughter . . . he was a train-wreck. And this mythology is probably as fictional as that one."

"I guess," Byron shrugged, somewhat mollified.

"Besides," Cole concluded, showing a bit of his natural genius, "it doesn't matter so much what gods folks say they believe in—people are people and they're either good or evil. Plenty of Christians did terrible things—waged aggressive wars and held inquisitions, for example—in defense of a savior who was a neighbor-loving pacifist."

"Point taken," Byron replied. "Shut up already."

Chapter Nineteen
Thrift Store

"This certainly is their lucky day," Charlie nodded his head toward the Salvation Army sign. He stepped down to the cracked gray pavement from the cab of local U-Haul that they'd rented to furnish their newly-installed trailer home. "We're going to be buying out the place. We still need . . ." he paused, making a mental list, ". . . just about everything."

"Did you lock the back?" Felicity asked. "We've got the appliances and mattress in there, and Laconia's a busy place. Don't want to lose those."

"Yep," Charlie nodded, holding open the store's door for his wife. An electronic bell chimed. "How do you want to do this?"

"Let's start with the furniture. We'll want a couch and some chairs, a bed-frame, dresser, mirror, and a small table, maybe a nightstand. We'll do that together."

"Then we'll divide and conquer?"

"Yes," Felicity nodded. "After the furniture, you get what we need for the kitchen: silverware, plates—that kind of stuff. I'll try to get us some decent clothes. Remember the goal is to spend as little as possible while making the house functional."

"Function before form," Charlie followed her into the small furniture cluster. There were only two sofas on display. One was an overstuffed blue velvet monstrosity that had been worn threadbare in both corners. The other was a 1970s-era scratched wooden futon with an unsettling plaid cushion: cream, avocado, and orange. They looked at each other and shrugged.

"Futon it is," Charlie smirked. "Jack can sleep on it if he needs to." He sighed, grimacing again at the colors and then around the room at the worn 70s and 80s castoffs. "Our trailer is going to look like an episode of *Welcome Back Kotter*."

The armchair selection wasn't much better—they decided on an olive-green corduroy material, but in pretty good shape. Then they picked up a water-stained dresser that was missing a knob, a card table with three mismatched folding chairs, and a few lamps from different decades. Charlie enlisted the help of a 20-something employee, a student at PSU, to help him load the U-Haul. The elderly cashier kept a running tab of everything they carried out.

On his own after that, Charlie got a grocery cart and gathered necessities for the kitchen: pots and pans, cups and flatware, mugs, knives, spatulas, a dish rack, a toaster—the essentials. It only took about fifteen minutes to feel totally equipped. He parked the cart beside the register and went to look for Felicity.

She had her own cart loaded with gently used clothes, curtains, blankets, and towels.

"I'm not buying underwear here," she said over her shoulder. "I have to draw the line somewhere. We'll stop at K-Mart for that."

"Sure." He lifted up a flannel shirt and smiled. "You know, I'm glad that men's fashion is pretty stable. I mean, the collar's a bit wide, but I bet guys will still be wearing button-down flannels in 20 years."

"Yeah," Felicity agreed. "Women's, not so much though. I'm not going to be winning any fashion contests in these. I've taken just about everything my size, except dresses. Got a fair number of shirts that fit me in the Men's small section . . . Charlie?" She looked up to see that he wasn't listening, his gaze intent on an old framed oil painting set on a shelf above the clothes. It was a western scene: snow-capped mountains reflecting down on a clear, glacial lake, a bit grimy and dusty, but they could probably clean it up with some soap and water.

"Yeah, I'm here," Charlie shook his head, breaking his trance.

"You like that picture?" Felicity asked, taking it down from the shelf and giving it a closer look.

"Not really. I mean, yeah—I do—but it's just that . . ." he rubbed moisture from his eyes, "we were thinking about heading out west this summer to take the boys to Yellowstone and Glacier in Montana. I was just imagining a family trip that may never . . . well, you know."

Felicity put the picture in the cart. "I'm buying it and hanging it over our bed. Next summer when we've got them back, we'll go on *this* vacation together as a family. The painting will be our reminder—our rain check." Her jaw was set with determination.

"And that is why I love you," Charlie said and kissed her forehead.

Felicity sniffled, wiping her eyes now, too. "It's true that," she reached down and took Charlie's hand, "it's not real glamorous being married to a small-town college professor, but the summers are underrated. You *know* me and our boys in a way that a lot of fancy businessmen will never understand their families with their two piddly weeks a year. You spend two months with us—every day, all summer. The boys are lucky. I never had that with my dad."

"Me either," Charlie admitted.

She pulled a baseball cap off the shelf and set it on Charlie's head. "That'll do," she nodded, and shifted it into the cart. "You'll wear that hat in a picture in front of Old Faithful with Cole and Byron next summer. That's a promise."

He nodded.

"And I'm going to write my mom and dad. Write your father, too. We need some pictures of our boys to hang in the house. All of ours may have burned up, but they have some. "I think we can check out now." She wheeled off in the direction of the register.

Charlie stood for a moment, amazed by the strength of his wife, then followed in her wake.

CHAPTER TWENTY
A Fortress on a Hill

The next three solar orbits passed in much the same fashion for Cole and Byron—sore feet, tired legs, and conversation between the brothers and Crowmane, punctuated by occasional sightings of strange creatures. Rochester's column marched endlessly on, mostly at a slight downhill grade, through forest and foothills onto an undulating grassy plain, then into a wide valley between low, rounded, grassy mountains. They then passed through a pine forest, the upper branches of which were populated by brownies. The tiny humanoids moved like squirrels, leaping from branch to branch and climbing trunks. It was a welcome pleasure and distraction to watch them. Both boys smiled.

"Not so pleasant when shoot you with poisoned arrows," Crowmane observed, tartly.

At the end of their second march, they crossed a churning river on a stout log bridge and camped on the far side, where a few redcoats manned a squat garrison-house. From scraps of conversation he overheard in line for dinner—boiled meat and crackers—Byron gathered this was the only safe crossing for fifty miles in either direction. It had been built by the British for their campaign against the *Yulc* clan *Lothka.*

The final day's march passed through cultivated farmland. Large fields stood on both sides of the road, growing various crops—corn, wheat, oats, tobacco—all irrigated through a system of clay pipes. Log cabins dotted the landscape, and farmers in overalls and straw hats waved and smiled at the column as they passed. In one wide field, a large group of skeletons dug smallish potatoes and deposited them in an oxcart manned by a top-hatted Necrologist. In the distance ahead, a single plume of smoke could occasionally be seen curling into the rose-colored sky.

Left to themselves and trying to ignore their aching feet, Byron and Cole amused each other by singing songs (and singing them badly—neither had a great voice and Byron had a talent for mistaking lyrics). A lot of times, the songs ended abruptly or faded to spirited humming or air-guitar riffs, as the brothers realized neither of them could remember the whole verse. Nevertheless, the time passed more quickly, and their selection, mostly alternative rock, and the classic stuff their dad listened to, with a few Michael Jackson and James Brown hits sprinkled in, reminded them of family road trips in the minivan. As they rounded out a trio of songs, R.E.M.'s "Losing My Religion," Joan Jett's "I love Rock and Roll," and Charlie Daniels' "The Devil Went Down to Georgia," Crowmane interrupted.

"Do you know any song-stories of length?"

"You mean like epic poems?" Cole asked. He'd also read *The Odyssey*, *Beowulf*, and *Gilgamesh* as part of his English studies.

"Long stories of battle and bloodshed—deeds of valor done by gods and heroes. These are, say you, epic poems?"

"Yeah," Cole said. "They are, but we don't *know* any of them." He laughed out loud. "They're thousands of lines long—how can anyone be expected to remember so many words? I mean, now that there are books and movies, what would be the point?"

Byron snorted in agreement. "We've read them," he said. He'd listened to *The Odyssey* and actually read *Beowulf*. "We could tell you what happens, but we can't *sing* them."

"Singing just now, told you many thousands of lines," Crowmane shrugged, his tone of voice expressing an understated dislike of their songs, "and yet show you no signs of stopping."

"Huh," Cole responded thoughtfully, "I suppose we have."

"How's the arm?" Byron asked, changing the subject.

"Pains me," Crowmane replied. "But pain means life." He brought it to his nose and sniffed. "It has not sickened, nor have I. This is good."

"Do you know any songs of, uh, battle and bloodshed? Deeds of valor?" Cole asked, changing the subject back. "Um, *Lothka* songs?"

"Know many," Crowmane replied, "but in my own language. Loudly, sing I them at gatherings, feasts. Stories share the wisdom of the Illenthane."

"Sing us one," Byron urged. "We'd love to hear it, right Cole?"

"Yeah," Cole agreed, swatting at a horsefly that had been buzzing around his head for the past 20 minutes. He wrinkled his nose, too. He hadn't bathed in longer than he cared to remember, and he began to tire of the smell of his own sweat. At fourteen, Byron didn't yet stink like he did.

Crowmane nodded and then sang, but his rich, deep song might more properly be called a chant. The words were sonorous and flowed into each other, full of rhythms and alliteration but no obvious rhyme. Though they couldn't understand it, the two boys were spellbound—even Rochester slowed his horse to ride alongside and listen, his sabre jangling in its scabbard. The lieutenant smiled occasionally, as if he understood the meaning. After many uninterrupted minutes, he held up his hand, stopping Crowmane mid-stanza.

"I approve of your selection, *Lothka*," he nodded condescendingly. "*The Song of the Third Wyrmwar*, is the best of your native lays."

Crowmane glowered at him, grim faced.

"I have," Rochester offered a winning smile, "even made an English translation of the early verses. It remains a work in progress, though, I admit."

"You're a soldier *and* a scholar?" Cole asked.

"All effective officers must be both," Rochester explained. "We practice the arts of study and observation, for both apply to warfare. And to paraphrase the wise Chinaman Sun Tzu, to overcome a potential enemy, one must understand his culture. Besides," he shrugged, "one must have something to occupy one's thoughts on long marches."

"Sing us your translation," Byron urged. "I really do want to know what he said."

"I don't sing," Rochester pursed his lips, "except on Sundays in cathedral. But, if you like, I can tell it, as a poem."

Byron nodded vigorously. Cole, too, nodded, but with only half-hearted attention. He'd begun to focus on the nearing smoke plume, which curled up from over a rise ahead. He'd noticed a sparkle of what he assumed were steel rails cutting across the fields in the distance and suspected they were nearing a railroad crossing or depot.

"Mind you," Rochester warned, "it remains a work in progress. *Lothka* poetry is wild and erratic in rhyme and line, and it is alliterative—tied together by repeated sounds. The language structure is different as well. It doesn't convert very well into English. I always find myself having to choose between keeping the meaning and losing the sound or keeping the sound and losing the meaning. I fear that by trying to keep both, I really accomplish neither." Rochester smiled sadly. "In any case, this is what I've translated, and committed to memory thus far," he said. "It's funny that even here in this culture, epics begin with an invocation of the muses—storytelling gods. Greek

Homer did it, and Roman Virgil, Dante, and even our own Milton. It amuses me how much cultures—even across different times and worlds—are the same, despite their differences. Perhaps it says something about the essential oneness of humanity."

He paused to consider his observation, then cleared his throat and began:

"Sing loud! Sing long, Illen, sing through my lips!
A swordsman's song, drunk on blood and valor!
A sage's song, world-wise, old and worn with years!
A song of mourning, wending, bending, torn with tears.
A song of armies, of dragons, and of men,
Clad in gilt armor, glistening upon the ground,
Of helms flashing, faces stern, and eyes that burn,
Of banners flapping and horns blaring,
Of stallions stamping and wyrms glaring,
Of gods, immaculate, fearless in full array,
Of dragons' arrogant, invincible might,
Ordered for war, corps upon corps; horrific sight.

Beneath lofty Wyrmspine's rock-strewn ridgeline
Of sky-scratching granite, its ice-crown gold with light,
Bold warriors wait, shields toward the sun, backs to this sight.
Banners snap taut in a wailing west wind.
Hearts hammer a cadence beneath armored skin.
Calling forth courage, Faldan, godlike, sublime,
Urges them forward, to combat, to strife, to cheerfully greet
Wyrms with spear, sword, and knife–better off dead than alive in defeat.
A brave war-cry echoes. Horns thunder off peaks.
The army advances without further speech.

Across the brown plain, undaunted in sight
Of warriors in arms, boldly striding toward strife,
Rears Dracdath the mighty, a terror, glistening, black,
A writhing wyrm-horde awaits war at his back.
He hisses an order to begin the attack, and laughs,
Dripping venom that sizzles and sears, crisps the dead grass,
And steams into dirt. His words strike like spear-thrusts
That splinter wood shields, and all his horde hears
Him, and marks every word: "So, soldiers draw near,

Sun upon shields, feeling no fear. Leave not one alive
On this yellow-brown plain; instead pile corpses,
A mound of the slain, to rival that which Yulc built at Gulheme!"

The wyverns take flight, the lesser wyrms wriggle,
Blazing serpents stride forth, but the dragons delay,
Awaiting that moment when armies engage.
The bright lines of men form walls with their shields
With the clash of precision that well-trained men wield.
The scales of the wyverns show: red, bronze, and gold;
They wing through the air while wyrms slither beneath,
Each fire within longing to breach–a horrible gift only dragons bequeath.
Arrows arc high, spears fly afield, iron shields boom,
Battered by flame, and burning men gurgle their short-fated doom."

A high-pitched steam whistle peeped cheerily from beyond the hill. Rochester cleared his throat. "It appears that's all the time I have today. If you gentlemen will excuse me?" Without waiting for a response, he cantered forward toward the front of the column, his horse's hooves clattering on the dry ground.

Byron watched the receding red of his jacket. "Burning men gurgle their short-fated doom," he repeated, awe and revulsion in his voice. He turned toward Crowmane. "Was his translation accurate?" he asked.

"Yes, accurate," Crowmane grudgingly admitted and his eyes, too, followed Rochester, for the first time with a hint of respect.

"Wyrmspine's rock-strewn ridgeline" Cole quoted. "The Wyrmspine is clearly a mountain range. And you called the river where you met us *Wyrmhod*." He pointed at the distant snow-capped mountains lit now by a sunrise glow coming from away across the plain. "Are those?"

"Called the *Wyrmhretha* in our tongue. Wyrmspine in yours," Crowmane replied.

"So the battle took place here?" Byron asked.

"Not here," Crowmane said. "Stretch, the mountains, long. Many marches, there," he pointed ahead.

Byron nodded. He looked that way, imagining the sky filled with dragons, and a thrill went up his backbone. He broke into goosebumps.

They crested the rise, and below them, as Cole had predicted, the smoke rose from a steam train. It was a smallish train, not the kind one would expect to see in a western movie, but more of a home-made looking job. A cylindrical boiler attached to a narrow smokestack; four small wheels rested on the track in front, and a pair of large, powered wheels in back. These were painted red and spoked. The rail was of a narrow gage, thinner than any track Byron had ever seen. Five open wagons were hooked up behind the engine, each resting on two pair of small, spoked wheels. The engine smoked next to a whitewashed log station with a water tower and coal shed. The whistle tweeted again. Byron noted what looked like a telephone line running along the track on poles, following it off into the distance.

A puff of steam escaped the engine, and it lurched backward, away from them. Byron watched Rochester canter down the road and signal the engineer. A whoosh of bright white steam sounded and the engine stopped. Rochester signaled to the column, and they increased their pace—double-time.

It seemed they'd be traveling the rest of the way by train.

Seven bumpy, soot-stained hours later, they clattered into Sterling City. Fort Douglas loomed over the valley-town. Set on a rounded grass hump in the middle of a flat—to Byron it looked like too perfect a hill to be a naturally occurring—the fort consisted of two layers of defenses, an encircling log palisade about halfway up and buttressed with wooden towers, and a large rectangular brick-and-log construction seated atop the hill itself. The building had an odd architectural sense, a combination of some kind of Viking great-hall with a Chinese Buddhist temple, Byron thought. Built of red brick, the bottom story met the next at an overhanging, steeply slanted roof. This stopped partway up at a second story, constructed from thick logs and also roofed with a precipitous overhang. A square brick tower loomed over one end, topped with battlements. A pair of huge flags fluttered from a pole over the tower. On top flew the black-backed Union Jack, and under it, a crimson falcon on a white field.

The "city" itself looked like a frontier town: a long main street dotted with affluent shop faces, as well as some more notable buildings. A stone mill with a churning water-wheel jutted out over the river that ran by the station. At the other end of town, a pair of brick buildings, one two stories and one three, cast their shadows on the street. Each was backed with an enormous brick smokestack that belched out black clouds. Wires ran from the furthest of them along a series of poles to the fort on the hill and to the train station. Across the street from the factories squatted a one-story stone church with a tall steeple, topped with a copper crucifix. Behind these, the villagers' houses, small log and clay-brick hovels, fanned out in a haphazard pattern.

"Right, everyone off," ordered the sergeant with the sideburns, a man named Smythe, as the train clanged to a halt and released twin hissing billows of steam. Byron, Cole, Crowmane, and Harald all leapt from an iron running board to a wooden platform. Harald wagged his tail and nuzzled Byron's hand. A glance passed between Rochester, who was the first to disembark, and the sergeant, who gave a curt nod.

"You Oakes boys will come with me. Unfortunately, your animal cannot go where we're going. Shall I have one of my men take it to the kennels?"

"We can't leave Harald," Cole said, surprising himself because he'd always been the more aloof of the brothers. "He's saved our lives."

"Nevertheless, we shall be dining with Lord Douglas." He brushed soot from his shoulder, "and your pet is most certainly *not* invited."

"What about Crowmane?" Byron asked. "Can he watch Harald? They like each other well enough."

"I regret that it will not be possible to place them together."

"Why not?" Byron's eyes widened. "What are you going to do to Crowmane?"

"Crowmane," Rochester said the name with some distaste, "isn't your concern." He turned to Smythe, "Take the prisoner to the guardhouse. Place him there in a private cell. See to it."

"Yes, sir," Smyth replied, "very good, sir." He clicked his heels.

"Johnson," Rochester ordered, "Take the dog to the kennels. See to it that it's fed."

"Sir," Johnson nodded.

"Come along now," Rochester beckoned to the brothers, his tone commanding. "I shall tolerate neither arguments nor delays."

Chapter Twenty-One

Dinner, Somewhat Spooky

Byron and Cole entered the banquet chamber last of all Lord Douglas' dinner guests. Dressed in borrowed and uncomfortable shoes and clothes—starched white shirts with bulging neckties called "cravats," black dinner-coats with arms intentionally sewn short to show their stiff sleeve-cuffs, and pants with oddly high waists that belted nearly across their belly-buttons—they felt alien and adrift in a way they hadn't back in the woods with Crowmane.

The room, a long hall decorated with hanging Scottish tartans, landscape paintings, standing suits of foreign-looking armor, and mirrors, seemed like a museum or gallery. Above them, exposed beams arched across a high ceiling. From these dangled stout bronze chandeliers, all alight and glittering. The floor shone with polish, tiled in exquisitely cut slate flagstones, and a fire burned within a hearth and mantle recessed into a side wall. Tied to perches on either side of this were a pair of beautiful, hooded falcons. One fluttered its wings and shuffled its yellow, taloned feet.

In the middle of the floor shone a polished wood table, upon which lay a narrow linen cloth, dinner settings of blue-glazed china plates, sparkling crystal goblets, copper flatware, tall yellow candles, and a glistening silver centerpiece—an orb, set among fresh-cut fern and flowers.

Guests milled around the room, about a dozen in all, talking in groups of three and four. Most were male, wearing either black coats like the boys' or red army dress uniforms. There were also three women, two older matrons and one younger girl with dark hair. They wore dresses of patterned cloth that looked more akin to the simple designs favored by settlers in the American west than the fancy gowns of Victorian England. At the side of the room, his back straight against the wall and arms folded, hulked a broad-shouldered dark-skinned man in a red military coat and striped black pants. Remarkably tall and imposing, he stared forward, carefully impassive, an oversized sword buckled to his waist.

Behind the soft drone of conversation, music played, a Baroque tune coming from a piano-like harpsichord in the far corner of the room. Typical of that instrument, the sounds lacked depth, all coming at equal volume. Looking closely, Byron realized with a thrill of horror, that the talented musician was, in fact, a skeleton. Its bones swayed to a rhythm it certainly couldn't hear.

"I've heard that song before," Byron commented with wonder.

"Have you?" a familiar, aristocratic voice responded. The boys turned to see Lieutenant Rochester advancing, accompanied by an elderly and rather stout man in a red coat. The man had a black sash across his chest, studded with metals and military decorations. Rochester put a friendly hand on Cole's shoulder. "May I introduce Lord Douglas Sterling?"

The old man proffered a beefy hand, which Byron and Cole each took in turn. He wore clean white gloves and had a firm, cool grip. A large nose dominated his ruddy face and keen blue eyes peered out from behind it. A bushy, white, imperial moustache grew directly into his sideburns, but no beard covered his chin.

"These young gentlemen are Byron and Colton Oakes," Rochester said to his lord. He paused for a moment, then returned to his previous question. "You say you recognize this piece?" He prompted Byron, gesturing toward the harpsichord.

"I've got no memory for titles," Byron admitted, "but after playing his works, I'd bet good money it's Bach."

"Jolly good ear; indeed it is," Douglas smiled. "The second English Suite. Do you play, or are you simply—as they say—a connoisseur of the musical arts?"

"I play cello," Byron hesitated, then added, "sir."

"And you, lad, do you play as well?" Douglas turned to Cole.

"The piano, sir."

The old man nodded. "Capital. It does me good to hear that children of the old world still take an interest in the classical arts. I'll have you in to play for me sometime this week or next—not this minute, of course," he added with a hearty laugh. "You can play me something new. I tire of the repertoire of my musician."

"Can I ask," Byron said, "how a skeleton—obviously without ears—can play music?"

Douglas chuckled again. "Ah, yes. That would seem odd, I expect. The player spent his life as my court musician. His name was Wilhelm. When he died," he remarked conversationally, "naturally, I retained his services. He plays as well as ever, even if he can no longer enjoy it."

Byron's brow furrowed as he attempted to decipher from Douglas' inscrutable tone whether the word "naturally" referred to the way he died—of natural causes—or how logical it was to reanimate him. Probably the second, he decided. He stared at the player, and while he did so, the skull rotated to look at him—no, not at him, he realized, at Cole. The flawless playing didn't falter, but the hollow-eyed stare gave him a shiver.

"In fact, most of my servants are now necroids," Douglas continued. "It's undeniably cost-effective, and there are no petty squabbles between them, and no problems with *loyalty*. The household simply runs itself. I retain a living butler, of course. No one wants cold hands dressing him when he awakes." He chuckled, as if this were the most natural statement in the world, then lowered his voice to a conspiratorial level and changed the subject. "I have been told that you two are Yanks."

They nodded.

"That being the case," he winked, "I must ask you the question we all wish to know—what year is it now, on the other side?"

"It's 1996," Byron said.

"And who is King? How does the Empire?"

"Well, Elizabeth II is Queen, I think. And, as it turns out, the British Empire has collapsed. The United Kingdom still exists, of course, but it's pretty much limited to the British Isles."

"Indeed?" He gaped, astounded.

"Yes, sir," Cole cut in, tearing his gaze away from the skeleton. "A lot has happened since 1832. There have been two world wars, we've learned to fly, split the atom, travelled to the moon," his eyes brightened, "and next year we're going to put a rover on the surface of Mars." As he spoke, he noticed that the conversation in the room had hushed, and he made lingering eye contact with the young woman. Her dark hair, eyes, and features indicated that she was of Indian or Pakistani descent, and the deep butter-yellow of her dress perfectly framed her complexion. Her beauty affected him so much that he trailed off, stumbling to a halt, a lump in his throat.

Byron saved him, picking up where he left off. "The British Empire remained the most powerful force in the world until the 1920s or so, when the United States, Germany, and Russia began to overtake the U.K. in everything except naval power."

"Indeed?" Douglas interjected again, his tone one of guarded belief.

"Pardon me, did you say that humanity 'learned to fly?'" The young woman asked. She'd crossed the room toward them, uninvited, her black hair shimmering in the candlelight.

Douglas looked at her disapprovingly. Before Cole could answer, the old lord cleared his throat and introduced her, grudgingly. "Colton and Byron Oakes, may I present Miss Adhita Lovelace, daughter of my Indian orderly from my early campaigns in the Old World."

"Lovelace?" Cole asked, his eyebrows raising, "as in Ada Lovelace, the mother of computer technology, the first person to write an algorithm?"

"If you're talking about Ada Lovelace, the daughter of Lord Byron, the poet, then, yes," Douglas replied with a snort of derision. "Rather than burden their daughter with her father's family name, Singh, Adhita's parents chose to christen her with her mother's surname. A shrewd *political* move on their part, as the majority of Her Majesty's subjects treat half-castes with a certain natural disdain—"

"My mother," Adhita interrupted, "is in fact Ada Lovelace, and my father is Amarjai Singh, a servant of the Lord Douglas who journeyed with him through the mirror and has been here as long as anyone—"

"They've done rather well for themselves, too," Rochester cut in, politely taking Adhita's hand and inclining his head in greeting. He returned to Cole. "Amarjai is, despite our old-world prejudices, the current Governor-General of Avalon. No doubt partially due to the keen counsel and advice of his wife, the lovely Adhita's mother." He released her hand.

"Ada Lovelace is alive, then?" Cole asked, carefully scrutinizing the other two women, who were talking to a young soldier across the room. "My understanding was she died of fever in her 30s. Am I to take it she came through the mirror instead? Is she here?"

"Why, yes," Adhita answered. "She lives, but she resides with my father in Victoria City, on the far shore. I am here alone, a . . ." here she paused for a moment as if choosing the proper word, ". . . *guest* of the Lord Douglas and I do survive upon his generous hospitality."

"She is my ward," Douglas explained. "I am to her both guardian and godfather, holding her in trust and good faith for her parents until such time as they come to visit me and carry her away with them." A black-coated butler wearing a powdered wig arrived and whispered in Lord Douglas' ear. He cleared his throat to silence the room. He announced, "My steward informs me dinner is prepared. Shall we be seated?"

Each of them was shown to a place at the table. The Oakes brothers found themselves sitting on opposite sides, Byron next to Rochester, and Cole next to Adhita. As they sat, unwrapped their napkins, and placed them in their laps, the steward opened double doors at the far end of the hall, and a troop of skeletons marched in, carrying trays and tall decanters.

The platters, as it turned out, each contained several bowls of soup that were distributed among the guests by skeletal hands. Then the skeletons poured a yellow-gold liquid into each cup from crystal bottles. No one ate, so Byron self-consciously toyed with his spoon.

Once everyone was served (with the single exception, Byron noted, of Lord Douglas, who sat at the head of the table with nothing before him but empty cloth), the skeletons withdrew, closing the doors behind them. Lord Douglas then clapped his hands together three times. "Eat, by all means, eat, I implore you," he urged. Without hesitation, his guests fell upon the food.

Byron found the soup to be a cream-based fish and potato recipe, clearly made from the same river-trout species he and Cole had been eating for weeks. It was hearty, but not particularly appetizing. After a single bite, he reached for his glass.

"A pity," Rochester observed as Byron took a sip of the golden liquid, "that grapes do not grow here—our winters are too harsh, our light too thin, and our rains too sparse—but we do keep bees in a vast apiary and make a fine honey-wine. This, I believe," he raised his glass, "is two-year aged spring mead—primarily nectared on apple-blossoms. It's a delicacy, as most of our bees nectar on barley, wheat, and oats."

The wine had a cool honey flavor with subtle flowery and spiced tones. Byron nodded approvingly, feeling the strange sting of alcohol on his throat. He felt oddly guilty, even though the concept of a drinking age didn't exist in Avalon. He would, he warned himself, have to be careful not to take too much—especially inexperienced as he was. He couldn't afford to make a fool of himself on first impression.

"The Lord Douglas," Rochester continued, "has been raising bees on this land for over a decade, and the beekeepers and mazers—mead-makers—work together to nectar the hives on different flowers in different seasons. This allows an astounding variability in flavors of small-batch mead, quite like, I imagine, those of wines in the old world."

"How do you grow crops here if it's never daylight?" Byron asked, changing the subject. "And how do you tell time? You all talk in days and years, but what makes a day here, or a year?"

"Plants grow well enough, especially in the summer. During those months, you see, the entirety of the sun is very nearly over the horizon, so we have full-light for about a quarter of the year. It's autumn now, and the sun lowers into the horizon a bit more each day until the solstice, when it ebbs lowest and we see no trace of its fire, even over the plains. A day is, as you might have guessed, a cycle of the sun around the horizon. It's 21-and-a-half hours long, by the old-world measures. We've adapted the old-world calendar, too, keeping the twelve-month cycle and working to match the seasons. Most months have 23 days. I'll show you the one I keep in my office if you like."

"I would," Byron answered, "very much."

"We manage the days here in three shifts, each seven hours long. The first shift, the one we call morning, includes the odd half-hour. Most of the important business is transacted during first and second shifts. The second is called afternoon and third, evening. Most important people choose to sleep during evening shift."

"Which is it now?"

"Now? It's late afternoon, nearing 13 o'clock. After dinner, most of us will retire to sleep."

"Got it," Byron nodded, taking another sip of his mead.

Across the table, Cole and Adhita were sampling their soups. She reached over and touched his hand to get his attention. "Did you say, I meant to ask, that in the year 1996 we have learned to fly? You don't mean hot air balloons?"

Cole smiled, a faint blush darkening his cheeks. Probably no one could tell but Byron. "Yeah," he replied, "and not balloons. In fact, we learned far before the 1990s. The Wright brothers, two Ohio-born Americans, invented the first airplane in . . . oh, gosh, I don't know, 1902, or something. We've been flying for almost 100 years and now our aircraft can travel many times faster than the speed of sound. The SR-71 Blackbird, a high-speed jet aircraft, flew from New York City to London in under two hours.""

"How," she asked, wide-eyed, "is that even possible?"

"Do you have a pen or a pencil? No?" Cole sighed. "Well," he began, "the Wright brothers learned that wings should be shaped into something called an airfoil. Basically, a curved and angled wing can create upward thrust by the pressure-differential it creates as wind blows across it." He took her hand and molded it into an airfoil shape, showing her how the wind would flow above and below it, and why the differential caused lift. "The faster the wind," he explained, the greater the lift or upward thrust . . ." realizing that he was touching her hand, he lowered his eyes and blushed again. She was rapt at his words and oblivious to his discomfort, so he continued, neglecting both his soup and his wine.

Byron, however, had little interest in the technical aspects of flight, so he began to examine the room. His eyes fell upon the centerpiece. What had seemed to him before to be a simple orb was in fact a human skull, gilded with polished silver. He shuddered looking at it and a chill ran down his back. Large, round-cut amethysts filled the empty eye sockets, and the grinning teeth, too, had been replaced with sculpted amethyst stones. He felt that it looked at him, considering him personally. He turned to Rochester.

"Yes, I know," the lieutenant nodded, following his gaze, "grisly thing, isn't it?"

"What is it?" Byron asked.

"That," Rochester chuckled, "Is the skull of Syrinkeri, a sacred artifact of the *Danathskoti*, whom Lord Douglas conquered here thirteen years ago. Apparently, it's the head of their original high-priestess, a demigoddess. Her story is long and convoluted. Like any good myth, it involves a quest, physical intimacy, betrayals, and immortality. Anyway," he shrugged, the epaulettes on his shoulders swishing, "it's now a trophy of his lordship's. If you'll look around after dinner, you'll find he's fond of commemorating his victories." He gestured to the mantlepiece and the walls.

Byron's gaze roved around the room, noting swords, spears, flags, and armor on stands, and also that the pictures he initially took for landscapes actually were scenes of large-scale combat. Armies clashed across panoramic twilit vistas, amidst clouds of dust and rifle-smoke. Above the double-doors through which they'd entered, Byron noted for the first time, a mounted dragon head glaring down at them. It had blue scales and a pair of yellow-white horns.

"Is it a dragon?" he asked Rochester.

"A wyvern," Rochester swallowed, wiped his lips, and replied. "A particular breed of dragon, yes."

"Did Douglas kill it?"

"Indeed. It was the conclusion of one of his earliest adventures in Avalon. Ask him about it sometime. He loves to tell stories, especially those involving himself." He raised his glass in mock-toast and took a sip behind mirthful eyes.

The second course, also delivered by skeletons, turned out to be roasted goose and boiled potatoes with a cherry sauce. This was followed by a chilled maple custard garnished with huckleberries and walnuts. All and all, a very satisfying meal, one through which Cole and Adhita chattered on and on about science and physics, and which Byron found difficult to fill with conversation with Rochester. It certainly wasn't that he disliked the man, quite the contrary, but he didn't know what to say, and he felt like his incessant questioning had become an imposition. He could not resist asking one question though. As the meal progressed, Byron noted that Lord Douglas never ate any food. He refused to be served and instead engaged in constant conversation with his neighbors. Eventually, Byron felt compelled to ask Rochester why Douglas didn't eat.

"The truth is rather appalling," Rochester admitted. "About three years ago, the lord was poisoned, clearly an assassination attempt by his enemies, but after a few very tense days, he made a full recovery. It looked so bad at one point he had the priest in to read him the last rites—we're Catholic, you know. Now, since that time he has refused to eat before testing his food thoroughly, and never in company—and I, for one, cannot blame him in the slightest." Again he raised his glass and took a sip. After swallowing, he continued in lower tones: "It has, truth be told, made the old fellow rather paranoid." Here he gestured across the room at the tall soldier still leaning, cross-armed against the wall. "You see that man?"

Byron nodded. "Who is he?"

"Aquinas Justice, the Lord Douglas' bodyguard—or the blackguard as he's more often called."

"Blackguard?" Byron asked, aghast, taking in the man's glistening ebony skin. "Isn't that blatant, casual racism?"

"Pardon?"

"Racism—you know, judging someone because you assume negative things about their race—because they look different. Because he's black."

"But isn't he different? Isn't he black?" Rochester shrugged as if the observation didn't much matter. "In any case, I don't find it safe to assume anything about Aquinas Justice. He's too strong and has too much influence over Lord Douglas to be trifled with—power in both of the arenas that matter here. And," Rochester raised his eyebrows, "it is Justice himself who promotes that nickname. Perhaps he enjoys puns. Though, he rarely smiles, so I doubt it."

After a pause, in which Byron struggled to overcome a newfound distrust of Rochester, he asked, his tone noticeably less friendly than before, "Is he born here?" He noted Justice's dark complexion and familiar features. He would have bet money that Justice, or at least his family, came from Ghana.

"Before he came through? He lived in Jamaica, I believe. Came to England with the circus as a strong-man but ended up in Avalon. He's easily the best warrior in the province—killed 26 men, two ogres, and a mastodon in personal combat."

"A mastodon? One of those hairy elephants?" Byron evaluated Justice more carefully, but when the bodyguard shifted his stony gaze to meet his, he looked away.

"You should see the man in his fitted armor—an imposing sight, let me assure you, one to make any opponent weak in the knees," Rochester added offhandedly, gesturing with a dollop of custard on his spoon. He flashed an ingratiating smile, then ate the bite.

After the meal, the women retreated to a different location and the men remained to smoke, drink, and play cards. Pipes were lit; the skeletons replaced the wine with tumblers of gin; the harpsichordist exchanged Bach for Handel, and the discussions turned to politics. By listening carefully, Byron gathered that there were tensions between Douglas' mountain territories and the original colony on the coast, that Douglas was, if not preparing to annex *Yulc* clan land, then at least considering the idea carefully, and that the silver and copper mines were experiencing a production boom because of a change in workforce from humans to necroids and the establishment of a 21-hour workday.

Eventually, the men fell to playing cards. Rochester invited the boys to play a game called whist, but as the brothers didn't understand it, they settled for cribbage, a combination card and board game with pegs that the two used to play with their mother and grampa. It was a four-player game, so Rochester recruited Douglas to join them. It all looked very natural, but Byron had his suspicions that this pairing had been staged in advance. In any event, Byron and Cole were teamed together, and they played against Douglas and Rochester. They were trounced by the more experienced players.

Midway through the first game, though, Douglas broached a topic he'd clearly been waiting for since their earlier conversation. "So, I'm told you boys made a Faraday Mirror."

Cole nodded.

"Could you do it again?"

"I don't know," Cole replied, honestly. "There's a lot more difficulties on this side. Materials for one. I used an iron-nickel-cobalt alloy. Power's another. How do we get a large enough supply and a stable rate of flow? And then there's the math. I don't have any of my calculations with me here, or Faraday's plans. I'd be working from memory."

"There's an electrical factory at the bottom of the hill. We have an unlimited supply of copper and iron, and Adhita Lovelace is like her mother—a born mathematician and computational savant. Will that suffice you?"

"I'd be a clown," Cole said, cautiously, "to guarantee anything, but I can commit to doing my best to create a mirror for you."

"Capital! That's as fair an offer as I'm liable to receive, and I heredo accept," Douglas smiled. "I'm sure you are as eager as I am to leave this fantasy world behind and return to Earth. Oh," he sighed with heartfelt longing, "to once again see the moon, to *eat* a strawberry, to stand under a bright noon sun upon the earthy fields of Galloway and fill my lungs with the air of *home* . . . On the morrow, then, you and Adhita shall begin your preparations. Make me lists of what you require and I shall endeavor to supply your needs."

"Okay," Cole replied. He hesitated. "I cannot guarantee success, sir."

"No one can, my boy. No one can. All we are able to do is work our hardest."

Chapter Twenty-Two
Bond of Brothers

Charles looked out the window of the trailer for the fourteenth time in the past thirty minutes. Jack was on his way down from Maine, and his lifted 1989 Ford Bronco might pull in at any moment. He turned away from the vacant driveway and returned to the sink, picking up a plate and scrubbing off some crusted egg yolk with the rough end of the sponge. Behind him, electrical components, circuits, and cords littered the floor of the living area . Felicity had been busy for almost two months, familiarizing herself with the plans, making calculations, and assembling the mirror, and it was still in the early stages of construction. Parts were arriving in the mail every day.

He heard the toilet flush. Felicity came out from the bathroom, located halfway between the living area and bedroom. She wore one of his flannel shirts and sweatpants. Her hair stuck up wildly. She looked tired.

"Enjoying this luxury trailer life?"

"I'm beat," she admitted. "The Lupus."

"And the late nights," Charlie added, nodding. "You're the only one who can put that thing together." He gestured to the pile of electronics in the center of the floor. "You push yourself too hard and you'll get sick and be in the hospital. It will take more time to complete it then, not less."

"You know as well as I do that I don't have a choice." She sat on a low stool and picked up the Gateway computer, scrolling for the 10,000th time through the images of Wheatstone's letter. Her husband returned to the dishes in silence. The hiss of the tap, her typing, and his scrubbing brought a bit of a rhythm to the room.

The computer clattered to the floor. Charlie turned around. "You okay?"

"It's these damn hands." She held them out in front of her. It hurts to bend my fingers today—more than usual. My joints are swelling again. It's probably because I've been using them so much."

"It's not like we've been eating well, either," he replied, starting across the room to comfort her. But as he did so, Charlie heard the throaty rumble of a custom exhaust and the characteristic crunch of gravel under car tires from outside. "Jack," he said nervously.

Jack's Bronco looked unchanged since the last time Charlie had seen it, three years ago during the reunion at Tupper Lake. Two-toned, steel-gray up top and indigo on the bottom, with lifted suspension and over-large tires, it was a stereotypical macho-man machine, and it came to a stop at the top of the driveway, next to the Jeep, right beside the pile of blackened, twisted rubble and the overfull construction dumpster containing much of what used to be their home. The Bronco's engine pinged as it cooled. The door opened and Jack stepped out.

He was a younger, harder, and fitter version of Charlie. The differences were mostly cosmetic. Charlie's thinning hair fell a few inches too long, in need of a cut. His clean-shaven chin and reading glasses, pushed up on his head, contrasted with Jack's crew-cut and tightly trimmed beard. While Charles wore a button-down shirt and jeans, Jack had on an unbuttoned checkered shirt over a plain white tee and brown, patched Carhartts. He sported a camouflage baseball hat, fronted with a worn military-style patch: shield-shaped and yellow, with the embroidered words "Operation Desert Storm: I Smoke Camels, Baby!" His stance, too, showed more confidence than his brother's, verging on cockiness. He took in the wrecked house, dumpster, and three-room trailer in a series of quick head and eye motions.

They locked hands and shook, firm grips on both sides.

"Good to see you, Jack."

"Charlie," his brother nodded. "You, too, man." He put his hand on Charles' shoulder and nodded a second time. Their blue eyes searched one another and found what they expected: recognition, respect, love—family—the bond was still there. "I'm sorry to hear about the fire and the kids, I—" he hesitated, turned his gaze to the ground. "—I should've called."

"Yeah," Charlie agreed. "You should've. But you're here now." Jack looked back up. After a long second, Charlie released his brother's hand.

"Where's that pretty wife of yours?" Jack asked.

"I'm here," Felicity offered cautiously. "Come on in."

Jack looked the place over dubiously. "I don't think y'all have room for three in there, honey" he said. "I brought my tent and camp gear. If you two don't mind, I'll set her up out here. I'm just as comfortable outside as in—brought my cot. We'll all get a bit more privacy that way." He nodded at Charlie. "You got a flat, clean place where a guy can lay down a tarp? Someplace close enough for an extension cord?"

"Sure," Charlie said, moving toward the truck. "Let me help you."

"I'm ordering pizza for dinner," Felicity called as they walked away. "Anything you want?"

"Yeah," Jack said over his shoulder. "I'm a pepperoni and bacon guy. Stuffed crust. The greasier, the better."

An hour later, after setting up the tent, unpacking the car, and eating two large pizzas, the three of them sat in the living room around Felicity's work area. Charlie and Felicity reclined on the futon with the plaid cushion, the former's arm around the latter. Jack eased himself into the green armchair on the other side of the room. He had a large gray duffel at his feet, from which he disinterred guns and lined them up across the floor.

"Looks like the work is coming along," he said, conversationally, taking a sip from his bottle of beer.

"I'm getting there," Felicity agreed, eyeing the project, "slowly."

"If you didn't send the Zip disk of the video, I wouldn't have believed it," Jack said. "Had a helluva time finding a drive to play it on up in rural Maine." He pulled open the chamber on his Ruger P-series and looked inside. "I mean, here I am, looking straight at a, uh . . ."

"Faraday Mirror," Charlie supplied.

"Yeah, and I'm still not sure that I believe this is happening. It's June. I'm missing prime logging time, but family comes first, you know!"

"Do you really need all those?" Felicity asked, scowling at the guns.

"You wouldn't think so. Hell, I didn't think so," Jack admitted, "Not when I bought 'em. One gun's a matter of need. A personal arsenal?" he chuckled now, low and steady, "why, that's more of a luxury or an art purchase, like a Porsche or a big-screen TV, or so I always figured."

"But now?" Charles prompted.

"Now, seems like I'll be going to Narnia with you. Who knows what's over there—Goblins? Aliens? A Dragon? It's like some science fiction show." He bugged out his eyes and put on an Arnold Schwarzenegger voice "*If it bleeds, we can kill it!* Bet you dollars to donuts that whatever burned down your place came through that portal. You'd better believe if I'm going across, I'm gonna be the one *they* should fear. I'm going armed—to the teeth—and you are, too. What do ya have?"

"Me?" Charlie asked.

"Yeah, you. What have you got here?"

"Nothing," Charlie admitted. My Remington burned up with the house. And the kids' 22s."

"Don't worry, then, I gotcha covered." He gestured to a pair of AR-15 semiautomatic rifles he'd laid on the ground by his feet.

"Thanks," Charlie fiddled with the corner of his bottle's label.

"Weren't those banned last year?" Felicity asked, looking at the guns.

Jack shrugged. "Billy Clinton's law bans the *manufacture* and *sale* of new ones, yeah. I already had one. Bought the other on sale the day before the law went into effect. If ol' Billy wants them back, he can come get them," he smirked. "*Molon Labe.*"

Felicity collected the pizza boxes and took them into the kitchen.

"We'll have to get to the range, though," Jack continued, ignoring the tension in the room. "You got one here? I'm not taking you to Narnia all covered in rust—who knows how long it's been since you've shot a gun, now that you're a college teacher. I don't care how good you used to be. And we'll need to hit an Army-Navy for some surplus."

"Fine," Charlie replied, and took another sip from his bottle. "There's a surplus in Conway, and Bobby Donahue, up the road, has a range out behind his cabin. I can still shoot."

"We'll see about that," Jack replied, then changed the subject. "You lost weight," he observed. "Just grief, or you been training?"

"Both," Charlie admitted. "If I'm going after them, I have to be in shape."

"Good 'nough," Jack nodded. "We'll work on that, too."

"You still living with that woman in Bradley?"

Jack chuckled again. "Yeah."

"What was her name again," Felicity returned to sit beside Charlie, "Susan?" She cracked open a can of soda.

"Yeah—good memory. I still rent a room at her place for the winter—I'm out camping all summer, cutting timber. I made foreman last year."

"Ever plan to settle down, have a family?" Charlie asked.

"Guys like me don't have families," Jack answered, suddenly a bit sullen. "Y'all what I've got." He forced a smile and lifted his bottle. "To brothers."

"To brothers," Charlie nodded, lifting his as well.

Felicity watched them, thinking of her two boys and where they might be at that moment. "To brothers," she mouthed, and took a sip.

CHAPTER TWENTY-THREE

Avalon Montage

The next few weeks were both strange and dull for Byron. Cole and Adhita spent their hours together in a room Lord Douglas dubbed "the laboratory," located near the top of the brick tower. Obviously, they had plenty to discuss, lists to draw up, calculations to make, and work to complete. The task was wholly engrossing for both of them, but far less so to Byron, who didn't understand the complexities of the project.

If that wasn't bad enough, the two were also clearly enjoying each other's company—flirting, staring into each other's eyes, brushing hands whenever possible—falling in love, generally. Every teen movie and after-school special Byron had ever seen followed the same melodramatic trajectory: predictable and cliché. They just needed a sappy soundtrack and maybe a few floating heart special-effects. Byron knew Cole would inevitably fall for someone; he just didn't expect it to occur *here*. So much for Melissa French, he thought with a smirk.

Anyway, in consequence of their mutual affection, both Adhita and Cole began to ignore Byron's presence more and more, or even to see him as a nuisance. The only time he had real access to his brother was during third shift, in the evenings, within the room they shared down in the living quarters of the fortress.

For the first two days—orbits, as Rochester called them—Byron spent a lot of time with Cole and Adhita, being bored and ignored, but eventually he left to wander the area. First, he found the kennels and Harald. He talked the kennel-master into letting him walk his dog and used it as an excuse to explore the town. Sterling City was not a big place. A few miles in circumference, it fit his mental image of how a frontier town must have been in the west, like Dodge City or Cody, Wyoming. At the center, as a hub in a wheel, stood the train depot and telegraph office, a large building with a roundhouse, engine sheds, and storage warehouses. Spreading out from that were a number of local shops selling things from across the plain: needles, cloth, luxury goods, furniture, fancy foodstuffs, and the like. The town also included a barbershop, an inn, a restaurant and bar, a mill, a place called "Migsby's Solicitor's Office" (a lawyer, he thought), post office, chemist (pharmacy?), bank—the usual town buildings, in fact. Unusual, though was a "Necrologist Limited," a showroom where people could purchase various skeletons to work their farms or homes. Byron felt a little too creeped-out to enter, especially given the jerky head motion and slightly cross-eyed stare of the brown-hatted Necrologist sitting on the porch, and the way Harald growled at him, low-throated and tinged with fear.

"Your dog doesn't seem to like Thomas there very much," a young woman in a pale plum-colored cotton dress said, conversationally, as she stepped down the stairs from a neighboring building and into the street. Byron sized her up, concluding from her age and cheerful demeanor that she wasn't likely to be a threat.

"I trust my dog's instincts; I don't much like *Thomas* either," Byron admitted. "Honestly," he nodded toward the porch, "they all give me the creeps."

"There's a fair number of us who feel like you do," the woman said, gesturing for Byron to walk with her. "Being unnerved by walking corpses and their masters seems only natural to me. Still," she chuckled, "they can be useful at times."

"You ever talk to one?"

"To a Necrologist? Bless me, no. What would I say to one? Ask what it's like on the other side, I suppose?" She chuckled again.

"Aren't you curious," Byron asked.

"Certainly, but I'm not sure I want to know. Not from a Necrologist, anyway. They seem more likely to have visited hell than heaven." She drew herself up awkwardly, stopping near the end of the lane.

"Byron Oakes," Byron offered his hand. The woman grinned sheepishly, looking at the proffered hand. She hesitated, then took it.

"Alberta Otis. I'm the only female clerk at the foundry. My father's a foreman." She gestured over her shoulder at a large brick building with a smoke stack.

"I'm guessing that men and women don't shake hands here," he shrugged. "Sorry."

"No," she smiled. "They don't, as a rule."

"I'm a guest at the fort," Byron added. The woman seemed taken aback.

"My! Always an honor to meet a guest of the Lord Douglas."

"I'm just a kid," Byron said. "My brother's the real guest. He's sort of a traveling scientist, I suppose you'd say."

"Indeed? An older brother, no doubt. Well," Alberta seemed suddenly preoccupied. She cleared her throat. "I hate to run out on you, but I cannot be late for my shift."

She curtsied and turned away, leaving Byron in the middle of the street between a pair of looming brick facades. Both had tall, belching smokestacks and were alive with activity. The more imposing of the two was the foundry, into which Albert vanished through vast, open double-doors. At a glance, it seemed to be producing mostly hardware items—rails, screws, bolts, sheet metal and the like—but there were also rifle barrels, spearheads, bayonets, and cast brass field artillery stacked along one wall. The cavernous doors rang with hammer-blows and shouted orders.

The smaller building functioned as a power station, boiling river water to produce steam to generate electricity. A loud engine chugged inside and copper wires on poles ran to the train station and up to the fortress. This interested him, since he didn't think electrical wiring had been a common thing in Victorian times. Maybe, he considered, this world's intimate connections with Faraday, Lovelace, and science in general had influenced their society to be forward-thinking. Certainly the chandeliers in Douglas' greathall had some form of primitive incandescent bulbs.

In any case, he decided, he'd try and walk back by here in hopes of running into Alberta again. She seemed nice, and he liked knowing someone outside of Fort Douglas.

Another place Byron went on his own was the guardhouse, a clay-brick jail with iron-barred windows. Squat and with a flat roof, it'd been situated against the palisade wall on the side of the fortress facing the mountains. Crowmane paced back and forth inside, like a caged animal. To his horror, Byron discovered that the *Lothka* warrior had been accused of spying and of murdering a British soldier because he had a military-issued rifle in his possession. Both of these offenses carried very serious consequences.

"What's going to happen to you," Byron asked. He leaned against the wall outside the window, since he wasn't allowed past the front door by the redcoat standing guard there.

"Giving me a trial," Crowmane said, his face striped by shadows from the bars, a large hand curled around one in frustration. A crow cawed from the roof.

"When?"

He grunted. "Does it matter? Justice is not important to the British, only the appearance of justice. And, judgement here is made by the Lord Douglas."

"What will you do?" Byron asked, his eyes wide. "Can I get you a lawyer? There's one in town. Migsby, I think."

"Care I not for British law," Crowmane replied with a shrug. He brought his face close to the bars. "Convicted, that will be the result. Guilty, will they call me."

"Are you?" Byron asked.

A slight smile twitched across Crowmane's face. "Yes."

"You killed a soldier?"

"Many. Fought them on the field of battle with the *Yulc* clan."

"So, they find you guilty. What then?"

"Take me out, place my back to the wall, and . . ." he made a shooting motion. "Pop. Pop. Pop. Finished."

"Maybe I can break you out," Byron whispered.

"Then shoot you, too," Crowmane shrugged again. "Known is Douglas in the clan-lands. Respects he our ways and our laws—or says he does. To prove it, must he show it. Demanding a combat-trial is our way. Grant it, will he, think I. If shoots he the Champion of the Illenthane, will it create much ill-will in the clans, but if dies the champion in combat, then will the *Lothka* simply nod their heads and find another. This is our way. Reason is a quality that Douglas does possess."

"You're a champion, though," Byron observed hopefully. "You can win."

"Perhaps," Crowmane agreed, "but if must fight Justice, maybe not. No one has. Still, prefer I a sword-death to a gun-death. And, as say you, maybe win I."

Byron remembered the hulking form of Aquinas Justice leaning against the wall at the dinner. He swallowed uneasily.

On his way back to the laboratory tower, Byron passed another curious sight. Out training in the middle of the courtyard were a group of twelve boys around his age. They all wore strange uniforms over their clothes—sort of like ponchos hung over their heads and belted at the waist. These were white with a crimson falcon emblazoned on the front and back. They practiced swordplay with what looked like medieval-style longswords, though the blades had a slight curve, reminiscent of a katana or cavalry sabre. An older red-coated soldier walked between them, correcting their posture and commenting on the effectiveness of their tactics. The instructor spoke with an Irish brogue.

"Hot work out there today," an aristocratic voice observed from behind him. It was Rochester, who was also crossing the courtyard toward the tower. Byron matched pace with him as he passed.

"What are they doing?" he asked. "I mean, I know they're practicing fencing, or something, but why the uniforms? Who are they?"

"Oh," Rochester may have been smirking; Byron couldn't tell. "They're a pet project of the Lord Douglas. He calls them his *Young Squires*. He's training them to be knights—armored shock cavalry. It's an attempt to shift the odds against the champions of the *Lothka*."

"Will it work?"

"It isn't my place to criticize the decisions of my uncle," he said. "There is certainly a historical precedent. The *Lothka* are essentially a medieval army, and in Europe, from the fall of the Roman empire until the campaigns against Robert Bruce, no army lacking heavy cavalry ever claimed victory on the field of battle." He paused. "But, no. It won't work."

"Why not?"

"Two reasons, mostly. First, they take too long to train. Squires start training at age seven and become knights at 17. It's a ten-year commitment. Second, they'll be easy prey to rifle bullets. It shall be a waste of resources."

"But I thought the *Lothka* didn't have rifles.

"Officially, they don't," Rochester said, "but that Crowmane bloke had one, didn't he?" He sighed, "We *civilized* Englishmen often underestimate our enemies—that's our tragic flaw, you might say. We think they're savage because they look different and have different customs and accents. They are not. They are human, and the chief trait of the human is that he is cunning. It is only a matter of time before they've disassembled and copied our weapons and ammunition. The casings shall be hard for them, but they'll figure it out eventually. It may take ten more years . . ." he laughed. "In which case, they shall be just in time to gun down our knights."

As this conversation ended, they passed directly beside the squires. Byron watched their smooth, practiced motions, realizing that he lacked any skill for self-defense with a blade. "Could I learn to fight?" he asked Rochester.

"With a sword or gun?"

"I can shoot," Byron replied. "I'm a pretty good shot with a .22."

"A what?"

"A small caliber rifle. Your Martini-Henrys are .45 cal, I think. I wrote a report on them for school."

Rochester scratched his chin and nodded. "So, I am to assume that you want instruction with a blade?"

"I think so, yes."

"I'll talk to Lord Douglas about it. But in the interim, I'd be happy to give you a few pointers and maybe spar with you a bit. Tomorrow, perhaps around the nine-and-a-half hour?"

"Thanks," Byron said, smiling and offering his hand. They shook. He was preparing to ask Rochester about Crowmane and the trial, when Rochester pulled out a pocket watch and glanced at the time. Byron snatched a look at the watch face, noting that it ran from 0 to 21.5 on an outer band with 1-60 on the inner.

"If you'll excuse me . . ." the Lieutenant said, trailing off, then entered the building.

Byron turned to squint into the lurid orange light of Avalon's perpetual sunrise. Strange, he thought, how the light could vary so much in color as the sun moved around this world. He watched the practice for a few more minutes before passing through the door himself.

Later, after dinner in the greathall and a harpsichord performance by Cole (he'd played some John Williams—a piece he'd memorized for the New Year's recital), Byron prepared to tell Cole the news. Unfortunately, as soon as the door closed, Cole proceeded to chatter at him about Adhita. He droned on, telling stories from her childhood, quoting Adhita many times, and slipping in innumerable compliments about her intelligence, reliability, and competence. This lasted through their whole bedtime routine.

When Byron finally slid into his twin bed, the rough, air-dried woolen blankets against his skin, he turned to his brother, hoping to change the subject. They both talked at once.

"They're going to kill Crowmane," Byron said.

"Adhita taught me about magic today," Cole said at the same time.

"What?"

"What?"

"You first," Cole said. "I've been talking for a while."

"I said that they're going to kill Crowmane," Byron repeated. He explained the situation to his brother. Cole looked genuinely upset.

"What can we do?" he asked. "I'll be a character witness for him—you can, too."

"I don't think they'll care about character witnesses," Byron mumbled. "He's guilty. He told me so. He's going to ask for trial by combat, like in old fantasy movies."

"I don't think it's fantasy so much as medieval Europe," Cole replied. "Have you noticed," he gestured in the direction of the great hall, "how the Lord Douglas fancies himself to be a medieval lord reincarnated?"

Fancies himself? Byron noticed the phrase. Ugh, he thought, Cole even started to talk like Adhita and the Victorians.

"Look at this place," Cole continued, "Douglas has got a great hall with feasts. He's got hawks, hounds, suits of armor, a sword-wielding bodyguard—his nephew, Rochester, is even in charge of the army—that's feudal nepotism. Douglas thinks he's a medieval lord."

Byron nodded in agreement. "Yeah, and he's training squires to be knights—I saw them today. It's not medieval, though, it's *medievalism.* I came across it studying for my Victorian disasters report. They were fixated on the middle ages. Painters, musicians, writers, all of them were called pre-Raphaelites, I think. But so what? So Douglas wants to play at being a medieval lord?"

"So, maybe, if we understand him, we can manipulate him," Cole continued, "I'm just trying to observe everything I can."

"What can we do about Crowmane, though?" Byron prodded.

"Nothing," Cole said. "We don't have any power here. We can't change the justice system. You break him out, and like he says, you'll be an outlaw. Where would you go? You don't know the lay of the land, where to hide, how to survive—nothing. We'd never be able to make the mirror, either. We'd trap ourselves here forever. And I don't think we owe Crowmane our lives or our futures in exchange for some bacon, eggs, and stories. He's a grown man who's made his own choices. Let's do what we can through the legal system and hope for the best."

"That's not very inspiring," Byron said, rolling away from Cole. He felt frustrated and a bit betrayed.

"Nope," Cole admitted. "But if we want to be part of society here, we need to operate within its laws. We need to bank some goodwill if we want to receive goodwill from Douglas and his people. That's how society works. Karma." He rubbed his chin, which was beginning to grow a bit of fuzzy stubble. "Look, I don't want to stay *here* forever—just long enough to make the mirror. I want to get away from the skeletons—necroids," he corrected. "They freak me out. I feel like they stare at me as I pass in the corridor. Sometimes they turn their heads to watch me."

"Can't say I've noticed that," Byron lied, his tone sullen. "Maybe it's your imagination."

"Maybe," Cole replied, unconvinced.

"But Crowmane only got caught because he was helping us," Byron returned to his topic. "It's our fault he's in jail."

"Cole sighed. "You can't blame yourself for chance. He didn't come looking for us, and we were reluctant to go with him. He didn't have to stop at our tent." He hesitated. "To quote Poindexter, 'It is, as they say, what it is, and the sooner you square yourself with that fact, the sooner you can move on.'"

"How's the mirror coming?" Byron asked, changing the subject.

"Slowly," Cole said, thankful for the change. "We're gathering materials and trying to reconstruct the math. I had my computer do it all, and I cannot remember the formulas. It's taking some time."

Byron rolled back over. "How long until you finish?"

"Honestly? Months. Maybe a year." He sighed. "Things are a lot harder here."

"And you've got distractions."

"Adhita?"

"Yeah. How you can think about romance at a time like this, with the house burned down and us trapped here, is beyond me."

"It's not like I . . ." Cole hesitated, "like I do it on purpose. It's just sort of happening."

"Yeah, well, you're not doing anything to stop it either."

Cole sighed, struggling to frame a response. Byron took pity on him and spoke first.

"What were you saying earlier, when I told you about Crowmane? Something about magic?"

"Oh! I was talking to Adhita, and she started explaining magic to me."

"You mean like what Poindexter could do?" Byron named the elf who had gotten them into this mess with not a little frustration in his voice.

"Exactly. Except, it's not limited to fairytale creatures here. According to Adhita, at least one in four *Lothka* is born with some degree of ability. She doesn't have any magic and neither do we—nor do any of the Victorians—because we're all foreigners. Our world is mundane."

"What kind of magic?" Byron asked. "You mean, like, there are wizards wandering around Avalon?"

"Yeah, I guess. She thinks Merlin came from here and really existed. But, Adhita is a scientist at heart, so she's been working to categorize, understand, and label the magic, to identify its rules and how it operates. We had a long conversation about it. There's necromancy—power over the dead—we've seen that, but I guess there are people with powers of persuasion, powers over animals, over plants, abilities to move or control physical objects, and even limited control over time and space. They all bend the rules of physics."

"Do you believe her?" Byron asked.

"I don't want to," he rubbed his hand through his hair, "because the idea of magic is terrifying, especially if I can't do it, but given what I've seen since coming here, I don't see that I have a choice. Living with the British, feels pretty normal, but I imagine that things are strange out in the clan-lands."

"Do you suppose Crowmane has magic?"

"Yeah," Cole said, matter-of-factly. "He's got to be an animalist. Look at how the crows follow him and he can almost talk to them. Maybe he can even see out of their eyes or something. That's not normal."

Byron chuckled. "What is normal?"

"Good question," Cole agreed.

CHAPTER TWENTY-FOUR
Locomotives, Swordplay, and Monsters

Byron woke up after about seven hours of sleep, and once he'd finished a breakfast of oatmeal and honey with Cole, he decided to walk Harald. The two brothers split at the base of the tower, and after picking up his dog, Byron headed into town.

It was cool and breezy with high, white clouds scudding across the rose-tinted heavens. Because Byron struggled with Crowmane's plight and with Cole's "solution," he walked for a long time and at speed, using the exercise to clear his mind while hoping to find an answer. The practical and pragmatic parts of him rejected every rescue plan he concocted, but the empathic and honorable elements refused to give up. Frustrated, but well-exercised, he eventually turned back. On his return trip, after passing the foundry and not seeing Alberta, he stopped at the train depot, where men loaded a powerful locomotive for a trip across the steppe.

The engine was a hulking black behemoth with a huge boiler, mammoth pistons, and four drive wheels as tall as Byron's chest. It shone with black polish and red trim. A Union Jack with a traditional blue background was emblazoned on the side, and underneath it, the engine's name in sparkling golden letters: *Royale*. Smoke rose lazily from the stack into the air, only to be carried away by the mountain wind. An enormous coal tender sat behind the engine, attended by no less than three Sikh engineers.

Squatting in the shade of the depot and running his hand along Harald's flank, Byron watched the boxcars being loaded. The back three, next to the caboose, were filled with sacks of wheat flour, the next with heavy loads of refined copper, and the first three were packed with reanimated skeletons, pale white and glistening, perfectly cleaned of all their flesh, and possibly even waxed or lacquered. They were loaded carefully onboard by four silent, unnerving Necrologists in their traditional dark suits and hats. Beyond the boxcars were some flatbeds stacked with tall, straight pine timbers, and a trio of container cars filled with coal. At the very front, right before the coal tender, rested one passenger car, which remained empty.

"Wonder where it's heading," Byron mused to his dog, pulling a tuft of loose hair from beside Harald's tail, and watching it blow in the wind.

"She's headed all the way to Victoria City, on the coast." This answer came from a kindly-faced station attendant who happened to be passing by.

"Ever been?"

"Me? No sir—not since I travelled out," the man removed his visored cap and scratched his thinning blonde hair. "I'd jolly well like to, though, someday. Maybe retire back east with the missus."

"How long's the trip?"

"On the *Royale*? With stops? Six days."

"How much does it cost?"

The man chuckled. "Coming out here costs a pretty penny, to be sure, but going back is free. All you need is the permit signed by Lord Douglas. No one goes back without his say-so."

"How many people are going back this trip?"

"Why, none. No one's left Sterling City in over four months, leastways no one but Necrologists, and most of them come back after handing off their charges."

"But—" here Byron was interrupted.

"Now, I beg your pardon, child, but I do have a job to do—can't be answering questions into the afternoon. I wish you a good day." The attendant hustled over to the engine and began to talk to one of the engineers, a tall man with a light blue turban wrapping his head.

Byron glanced up at the sky and reminded himself of his training appointment with Rochester. He stood, stretched, and considered how best to itch his wrist under the cast. It had been a good while since they came through the portal. Three weeks, maybe four—he struggled to calculate old-world days here. It would soon be time to try to find a way to cut that cast off. He shrugged and started back up the hill toward the fortress, Harald in the lead and wagging his tail.

After returning his dog to the kennel (always a sad moment for him—Harald emitted a high-pitched whine, his tail drooped between his legs, and he had to be pushed through the door), Byron hoofed it over to the courtyard, hoping to beat Rochester there. He did not. The red-coated soldier waited for him, standing beside two swords leaning, point-downward, against the rough brick wall.

"Sorry I'm late," Byron said. "I was dropping Harald off at the kennels."

"And how is your animal? Well, I trust? The servants are giving it enough care?"

"Oh, yeah. Harald is fine, thanks." Byron shifted his gaze to the blades. "Are those real swords?"

"Yes," Rochester handed him one, "but they are blunted training swords. If the smith put an edge on this, it would slice you."

Byron nodded, feeling the dulled edge with his thumb. The sword felt lighter than he'd expected. He thought it would have the heft of a gallon of milk, but it was really closer in weight to a baseball bat, perhaps, maybe just a bit heavier than a goalie-stick.

"You've never used one before?" Rochester asked.

"No, sir," Byron replied. "But I'm athletic," he offered. "I play hockey. I'm pretty good."

"That Scottish game?" Rochester asked. "With the ball and clubs?"

"Golf? No!"

"No, not golf. Hockey—used to be called Shinty, I do believe. They have nets and they hit each other."

"Oh," suddenly it dawned on Byron, "no, not *field* hockey—that's a girl's sport in America—I play *ice* hockey, on skates."

"Hockey is a girl's sport in America?" Rochester laughed, incredulous. "Yankee girls must be fierce, truly something to behold. I played a game of hockey one time and left with many bruises and a broken rib. In any case, we're neglecting our studies in pleasantries. Time is always limited, especially for an officer," he observed, "which is, I suppose, why anything in this world has any value."

He held out the sword, instructionally. "First, you need to know about the weapon. All swords are in two primary parts: the blade and the hilt. The blade can be single edged or double-edged. It can be pointed for thrusting or curved for slashing. This is a traditional longsword. It's straight, double-edged, and only slightly pointed." He paused, waiting for Byron to acknowledge him.

"Got it."

"The hilt is composed of various bits, as well. Your sword has what's called a cross-guard. It's composed of two pinions. He gestured at the two protruding metal pieces that protected Byron's hand. "These come out perpendicularly where the hilt meets the blade. Beneath them is the grip or handle—in this case wrapped in leather—and the pommel, this round bit at the bottom. Its function is primarily to balance the weight of the blade. They're usually filled with lead. Some hilts have different kinds of guards, but they're all designed to protect the hand while being attractive. Form and function combined, you see."

"Got it," Byron said again. "Is this called a cross-guard because it crosses the blade? Or because it is at the point where the blade crosses into the hilt?"

"No," Rochester inverted his sword and held it up, handle in the air. "We have the crusaders to thank for this design. It looks like a cross."

Byron nodded. "Okay. So, how do I hold it, what should my stance be?"

Rochester instructed Byron for a few moments, showing him basic thrusts, attacks, and parries. He critiqued angles, stance, footwork, and gave some instruction. Following this, they did some slow-motion sparring and swordplay. Byron soaked up information like a sponge.

"Young man," Rochester smiled, "I'm bound to state that you show immense promise. Shall we take this sparring up a notch in difficulty? Attempt to hit me, and I'll try to strike you. Do not worry about hurting me—I'm an expert and the blades are dulled, in any case."

The two began an exchange of slashes, lunges and parries that increased in speed as the seconds ticked by. After about a dozen seconds of action, Rochester scored a tapping blow on Byron's cast.

"Very good," he said. "Again?"

Byron nodded and they began. This time Byron lasted about half a minute and came close to touching Rochester twice, before his opponent's blade drilled him in the chest, pushing him back and surely leaving a bruise.

"Sorry about that," Rochester apologized. "I made a stronger lunge than I intended. But that's a compliment to your natural talent. I actually have to try a bit, not a very common occurrence against a novice."

Byron flashed a smile. "I've had worse," he said, rubbing his chest, and then held up his left hand to show the cast. "Broken arm. Hockey."

Rochester smiled again. "I told you hockey is a dangerous sport. Shall we?" He raised his sword to a salute position and bowed slightly. Byron copied the motion.

The third series of thrusts and blows became even more intense than the others. Twice, Byron made incredible blocks, forcing Rochester to use all of his concentration. True, Byron wasn't yet good enough to score a hit on his opponent, but he focused more on defending himself than launching an attack—he was a defenseman, after all.

After a hitless bout that, by dueling standards, lasted a remarkable length, Rochester left himself open to a thrust. Byron tried to take advantage, but the gap in his defenses was just a ruse. As Byron lunged, Rochester sidestepped and slashed. Byron had no chance. He braced himself for the inevitable bruising across his exposed back.

And yet, time seemed to slow, to protract, and Byron dropped to a knee and brought up his blade—only just in time. The two swords clashed loudly and Rochester backed up, lowering his weapon.

"How did you do that?" he asked, all humor gone from his tone. "That was impossible."

"What?" Byron asked, standing. "I just blocked your shot."

"Yes, but no one can move that fast," Rochester said, a strange look in his eyes. "I had you right where I wanted you; there was no escape. I didn't falter. I should have struck you—rather hard, I'm bound to say—across the shoulder."

"I dunno," Byron admitted. "I saw it coming and blocked it. I had to move fast or I would have been hit."

Rochester shook it off. "Never mind," he said. "Certainly today we've made a good start on your education." He wiped some sweat from his forehead. "Clearly you've given me some exercise." He was obviously trying to bring the session to a conclusion, and his thoughts seemed suddenly distracted.

"Did I do something wrong?" Byron asked.

"No, no," Rochester reassured him. His eyes and thoughts refocused on the situation. "Being able to save your life is the point of training. In that, you did exactly what you should. Some instructors shall tell you that the sword is an offensive weapon, but they are wrong—dead wrong. Remember: the most important part of the fight isn't the thrust or the lunge, but the parry. Wait for the mistake. Stay alive and wait. That's how you win."

Byron nodded again. "When can we do this again?" he asked, accepting that the lesson was finished.

"I'm not sure," Rochester reached out to take Byron's blade.

"I'm a busy man. Perhaps, though, I can get you some training time with the squires? I can talk to Lord Douglas about it if you like."

"Please, I'd appreciate it," Byron replied. "I'd rather spar with you, of course, but if I'm going to live in this world, I'd better learn how to stay alive and be competent here."

"With your natural talent, you'll be more than competent," Rochester smiled. "Are you headed inside?"

"Yes."

"Walk with me."

They entered the cool lower story of the fortress. Their footfalls echoed off the brick walls.

"Have you seen Douglas' trophy room?" Rochester asked suddenly.

"You mean he has things that are *not* on display in the greathall?" Byron asked, surprised.

"Oh my, yes," Rochester smiled. "It's like a museum down there. Do you have a moment?"

"Sure, why not?"

"This way, if you please." The older man led him toward a staircase. He leaned the training swords against the wall before the first step. "The trophy room is in the first deep—one level down inside the mound, below the fortress."

The air down the stair felt cooler, even, than the bottom story of the tower. The light faded and oil lamps burned along the walls. Rochester removed one from its holder. Two skeletal necroids passed them by, heading upstairs. "It's always dark down here," Rochester noted as they turned a corner. "*Fuginfell*, the Necrologists called this place. It had been their headquarters during the war. Tunnels spiderweb all through this hill. It's an excellent location, so that's why my uncle built Fort Douglas atop it. Ah, here we are."

The "door" was just a purple cloth hanging from a rail. Rochester pushed it aside and they entered. "Hold on a moment, while I light the sconces." Rochester moved along the circular edge of the room with his lantern.

"This isn't very secure," Byron observed. "Isn't Douglas worried about anyone stealing his treasure?"

"Oh, you misunderstand," Rochester said over his shoulder. "This isn't a treasure room, but a *trophy* room. It's full of curiosities, mostly, and the majority of them are far too heavy for anyone to abscond with."

By now, enough light shone in the room for a strange suit of bronze-colored armor to capture Byron's attention. It stood seven feet tall with short arms and legs, by human standards. An armored tail came off the back, and the helmet looked like it'd been shaped for the head of a large water monitor or Komodo dragon. He inspected the intricate design work on the metal scales of the shirt. "What is this?"

"That?" Rochester came over, evidently finished lighting the room. "It's the suit of armor of a battle chieftain of the Qesh."

"The Qesh?"

"Draconian lizard men. They live in the jungles and build pyramidal temples. Our first great war here was with the Qesh. Before my time," he sighed.

Byron stepped back and scanned the room. It stretched maybe 150 feet in diameter and displayed many strange and curious objects—mostly remains of dead creatures. There were a number of human items, too—at least a dozen suits of armor and ceremonial looking costumes and masks. There was a rack of odd-looking weapons, as well. However, the monsters really drew his attention—a stuffed sabre-toothed tiger, the skeleton of some kind of 20 foot bipedal giant laid out on the floor, a wall of mounted monster heads (prominently featured among them, a very recognizable gryphon), and a bell-jar in which lay a mummified male pixie. Byron walked up to this and tapped it.

"Turns out," Rochester observed, "that pixies and elves don't reanimate. Douglas thinks that their spirits—their wills—are too strong to submit to control." He considered the trophy wall. "You see your gryphon there?"

"Yeah," Byron nodded.

"It's a formidable addition to the collection," Rochester nodded, "if I do say so myself."

Byron's attention was drawn to a hideous carapace hanging beside the gryphon head. It looked like a combination of an enormous dragonfly and scorpion with claws instead of pincers. His expression must have shown his revulsion.

"We call that the jabberwock," Rochester observed, "with jaws that bite and claws that catch. Its sting causes paralysis. Like a wasp, it'll carry your living body to a cave or hole and lay an egg inside it. Horrible creatures, but at least they're solitary."

Byron broke his gaze from the jabberwock and turned to a

large, white object in the rear of the room, hidden under a sheet. "What's this?"

"The head of Drothtauk, a wild dragon. The moisture down here is causing some damage, so Douglas had it covered with this tarpaulin. If you'll help me, we can remove it."

"Okay." The two slid off the sheet to reveal a terrifying yellow-scaled head that was longer than Byron was tall, and over which he could barely see, standing on his tiptoes. It smelled of formaldehyde, a preservative he recognized from Plymouth State's biology building. He let out a whistle of admiration, measuring the teeth with his hand—they were just longer than the distance from his outstretched thumb to the top of his middle finger. "This is more than twice the size of the head Douglas has mounted in the greathall."

"Yes," said Rochester. "Mounting this on a wall would, for obvious reasons, be . . . problematic. The blue one is the head of an immature wyvern. This came from a fully mature, full-blooded dragon. They killed it coming across the steppe; it attacked them while they were building the railroad."

Byron looked into its dead eye and shivered. "You can't reanimate dragons, either, I suppose."

"We don't know," Rochester shrugged. "We haven't killed one since the alliance." They pulled the cloth back over it. "I'm afraid that we're running out of time. I'll be late for my meal with Lord Douglas—bloody awkward lunch when I'm the only one eating," he chuckled.

"Okay," Byron replied, turning to head out.

"Wait while I blow out the tapers—they attract bugs, which in turn eat the artifacts." Rochester went around the room, blowing out candles in the sconces. Byron stepped up to one more curiosity to examine it. It was another insect carapace, this one enormous in length. Shaped like a centipede, it was probably a foot in diameter and forty feet long. He touched it—it felt like plastic. Like fingernails, he thought.

"Shall we?" Rochester called from the entryway. He held his lamp once again.

"Coming," Byron nodded, passing by the curtain. As he passed he noted a hairy mastodon-leg umbrella stand, filled with swords. "Why did you bring me here?"

"I thought it might interest you, that you might like it," Rochester answered, "and it seemed to me that it would behoove you to know what an uncivilized world awaits beyond the safety of our imperial domains. I often see you recoil at the sight of necroids. That is only natural, I assure you, but when you consider the alternatives, you may come to appreciate our way of life a bit more."

By now they had climbed the stairs out of the first deep and were walking down the brick-lined hallway of the fortress.

"As for me," Rochester continued, "I have become so used to necroids that I regard them in the same way that you might regard a table or a bit of furniture. With proximity comes indifference. As Chaucer so famously said, 'familiarity breeds contempt.'"

Byron only nodded and walked along in thought for a moment. "Lieutenant Rochester," he changed the topic, "what will become of Crowmane?"

"That *Lothka* chap we found you with?" He coughed slightly and then thought for a moment, considering no doubt whether to soften the blow. He decided not to. "He's to be put on trial for espionage and murder. He'll almost certainly be sentenced to death."

"What can I do to help him?"

"You can be a character witness at the trial," Rochester said. Here he stopped and turned to Byron, "but I don't want you to have false hope. I believe he is guilty and if so, he shall be punished. We have a lot of damning evidence."

"But," Byron began.

"There are no extenuating circumstances," Rochester cut in. "We live in a land ruled by law, and in order for law to create peace, it must be enforced. Sometimes that means a good man must pay the price for his lawless actions. So be it. Laws, as well as the might of our armies, keep our lands safe and civilized."

Rather than argue, a pointless endeavor, Byron simply followed Rochester out. They walked to the base of the tower. Here, the two split up, Byron heading up the stairs to Cole and Adhita, and Rochester down the hallway to his uncle.

"Thanks again for the lessons," Byron said at parting.

"It was my pleasure," Rochester responded.

CHAPTER TWENTY-FIVE
In Dracula's Castle

Byron opened the door into the lab to find Cole kissing Adhita, tenderly, like he was imitating some Hallmark movie his mom would watch during the holidays—*I Got a Husband for Christmas*, or *The Love of the Season*, or something suitably irritating. They made another one every year and his mom got suckered in, annually. Adhita sat on a table and Cole stood, facing her, with his arm around her back. Her hand caressed his cheek. She locked brown eyes with Byron over Cole's shoulder for a split second before disengaging.

"Eww! Gross!" Byron averted his eyes. He backed into the wall. "Is this how the mirror's getting made? *This* is the great collaboration you've been telling me about every night?"

Cole immediately backed off, blushing. He cleared his throat, sheepish. "Um," he fumbled for words.

"I thought this was a workplace. And I thought Victorians were big on propriety and chaperones and stuff like that!"

"Yeah, I um . . ." Cole stammered, rubbing the back of his head.

"Should I knock next time?" Byron regained his composure. He lowered his tone. "I didn't mean to interrupt, honest."

"Well, you did!" Adhita snapped. She'd evidently chosen to cover her embarrassment with anger.

"Give him a break," Cole said, soothing her. He reached out and self-consciously touched her sleeve. "He's only fourteen. I thought kissing was pretty gross then, and I bet you did, too."

She smiled. "Yes, I suppose that's true." She gazed back into Cole's eyes dreamily, "but not anymore."

Now Byron felt both sickened and patronized. That kind of comment took things a few steps too far. He turned on Cole.

"Look," he said. "We're both stuck here, and I know we need to make the best of it—you obviously are—but you're all I've got, and I don't need you turning on me because of *her*." He pointed at Adhita. "She's smart. I get it. She's pretty. Believe me, I get it. But what you need isn't a girlfriend. New Hampshire, America, and *home* is on the other side of that portal. Mom and Dad. Harvard. The future—*our* future. You get that, right? Right? And every twenty-four hours here is five days there. A year here? Five there. I know the days and months don't match up, exactly, so it's easy to lose count and forget. I guess I should remind you that Mom has Lupus. She may not have five spare years."

"Yeah," Cole said, suddenly quiet. "I get it." There was an awkward pause. "What'd you come up here for, anyway?"

"I was training with Rochester—sword fighting—and something happened."

"What?"

"Um, I blocked an attack that I couldn't have."

"What do you mean?"

"I mean, he had me dead to rights. I couldn't stop him—it was physically impossible, but I did it anyway."

Cole looked at him sideways, confusion on his face. "I don't—"

"You mean you used magic?" Adhita cut in.

"Maybe," Byron answered. "How's it work—magic?"

"Well," Adhita shrugged, and slipped down from the table. She wore a paisley patterned, periwinkle dress with full length sleeves—probably cotton. Her black hair fell down her back in a single braid, and a silver chain necklace with a lapis stone dangled around her long, thin neck. Even Byron had to admit that she was beautiful. She rubbed a tapered finger across her lips. "No one really knows how. It just sort of happens as an act of willpower. But you're from the old world. You shouldn't be able to do it. Tell me what happened, exactly."

"Well, he lured me into a lunge, like this," Byron demonstrated, "but he sidestepped and when I was out of position, brought down his blade, like this." Again, he made the motion. "I saw it out of the corner of my eye, and reacted—too late, I thought, but then he seemed to slow down, like a slow motion video."

"A what?"

"Never mind," Cole said. "I get it. Then what?"

"I dropped to one knee, lifted my blade, and blocked him." Again, he made the motion.

"Hmm," Adhita mused, "you're correct. Your motion would take far longer than his—three times as long, by my estimate. It's physically impossible. How did Rochester react?"

"He ended the lesson. He acted shocked and took a few minutes to, ah, rationalize, I guess, what he just saw."

"So," Cole said, leaning back on the table, "what does this mean?"

"Well, let's test a hypothesis," Adhita said, reaching for a pair of scissors from a nearby table. She also picked up a candle and started trimming the wick. "If I light this candle," she began . . .

"I don't see what that has to do with anything—" Cole interrupted, but without warning Adhita whipped around and threw the scissors at Byron. He stood only five feet away, and should have been stabbed, or at least hit, but somehow he caught them. He held them out to her. A smile appeared on her face. "—wait—you could have killed him!" Cole finished, aghast.

"Please be rational; those scissors were too small to *kill* him," Adhita soothed, this time stepping to Cole and placing a hand on his forearm, "but there had to be a real threat to force him to use it. Byron," she addressed him, "It seems that you are a Temporalist."

"A what now?"

"You have Temporal powers. I think you can slow time, briefly. It's a powerful ability. It can give you the edge in most combats, as you just showed. And it's rare."

"But how?"

"I don't know," she answered. "Is this new? Has it happened before? Before here?"

"I don't think—wait, yes. Yes, it has," Byron answered. "When I play hockey, sometimes I make impossible saves, like lunge out and knock a 70-mile-per-hour slapshot out of mid-air."

"He's right," Cole confirmed. "I've seen it, but I didn't believe in magic then."

"Okay, so, tell me your history again. You said your ancestor helped build the portal?"

"Yeah—Charles Wheatstone" Cole answered.

"Did he go through?"

"I didn't think so. His letter didn't say so."

"Are you suggesting that—" Byron began.

"—that he had an, um, dalliance on this side and that you and Cole are the descendants of his coupling with a native woman? Yes," Adhita confirmed. "It's the only thing that makes logical sense to me."

Byron sat down heavily in a hard-backed wooden chair. "Yeah," he confirmed. "It does. But 'dalliance?' That's a ten-dollar word."

"I'm sorry if my vocabulary is too *expensive* for your simple *American* tastes,"

"Don't paint all Americans with the same brush," Cole cut in.

Adhita pursed her lips in response. "Maybe," she offered, studying Cole for a moment, "making the mirror wasn't an accident—maybe you were fulfilling your heritage and destiny."

Cole nodded, his expression somber. "I didn't used to believe in destiny, either. Not sure I want to now—that's a lot of pressure to put on yourself."

Adhita paused to compose herself. She set her jaw and nodded twice. "Alright," she said, then looked from Byron to Cole. "I have some things to tell you." She crossed the room, opened the door, looked up and down the stairs, and closed it again. "I hadn't confided in you because, well, because I wasn't sure I fully trusted you. But now is the time, I think."

"Confide what?" Byron asked. "And you trusted him enough to romance him, but not enough to talk?"

"Attraction," she smirked, her eyes twinkling at Cole, "isn't the same thing as trust." She returned her gaze to Byron. "You may have gathered that I'm a prisoner here," she continued. "I never came to visit Lord Douglas. I am no one's ward. Douglas had me kidnapped. He's holding me here as a bargaining chip against my parents. They wanted to remove him as provincial magistrate because he was too aggressive. There's bad blood between them. He could not stand that a Sikh—a man who had been his servant and whom he thought of as his inferior—should be elected Governor General of the colony. Relations have deteriorated to the point where there isn't much communication at all between the mountains and the coast."

"How'd he kidnap you?" Cole asked.

"Justice did it. Almost five years ago. It was midsummer and I was out in the garden behind our house with my governess. She had me painting a scene of sun on the pond, when he came running out of the woods, knocked her down, gagged me, and dragged me off to his horse before anyone could stop him. It was terrifying." Adhita rubbed her eyes.

"But, couldn't you escape?" Byron asked.

"I've tried, three times," she admitted. "All failures. They always catch me. I cannot cross the steppe. Once I tried to hide on the train, but they telegraphed ahead, stopped it, searched it, and found me. Why do you think I'm so interested in the power of flight?"

Byron nodded.

"There's worse, too," she said. She lowered her voice to a whisper. "Douglas carved out this dominion by defeating the Necrologists."

"The *Danathskoti*," Cole added, using the native word.

"Yes," she nodded. "And since their defeat, he has incorporated them into the social structure here and commodified the dead—the necroids. He's getting rich off them, shifting the balance of wealth. Douglas sends the dead east as either automatons or slaves, depending on one's viewpoint. Doubtless, they are useful, and that too is part of the plan, to make them invaluable to Avalonian culture."

"But?" Cole prompted.

"But it is my belief that the Necrologists control Douglas, not the other way around. Three years ago Douglas almost died. He took to his bed and seemed to be poisoned."

"Yeah," Byron nodded. "Rochester told me about that at dinner when we first arrived."

"Since that time Douglas hasn't eaten in public. He always wears gloves. He no longer makes skin contact with anyone. Before then he'd always been an awkwardly touchy person, always with his fat hand on my shoulder or back." She shuddered slightly.

"So," Cole prompted, "the assassination attempt changed him?"

"I think he *was* assassinated," Adhita answered, bluntly. "I think he is dead, a complicated magical reanimation of the Necrologists. I think he's one of them, a necroid."

"Yeah, but" Byron said, "wouldn't he be all zombified and gross? Or skeletal? Or something?"

"Not necessarily," Adhita said. "The Necrologists are all dead. They just *look* alive, somehow. I touched one once—his skin felt like cold wax. Maybe there's some kind of embalming—like those books about old-world Egypt. I don't know, but more than once, I've caught Douglas following my movements with only one of his eyes, moving independently."

"Jeez," Cole exclaimed. "Then, we're inside Dracula's castle."

"Where's Simon Belmont when you need him," Byron cut in, humming the opening music to *Castlevania.*

"What?" Adhita asked.

"Dracula," Cole prompted, ignoring his brother's video game

reference, "a Victorian novel. It's about an undead vampire who comes to London, I think. I only watched the movie. You haven't read it?"

"It must have been written after the portal closed. Mother has a massive library."

"I wonder if Bram Stoker—the author—was ever on this side of the mirror? I'd look him up if I had access to *Encarta.*"

"What?" Adhita asked again.

"Never mind that." Byron brought them back to the topic at hand, "So, if Douglas is a . . . um, vampire, for lack of a better term, then you think the skeletons that are being sent to the coast as servants are really a secret army and he plans to attack?"

"I do," she confirmed. "I think there is a complicated plot in progress, and I don't fully understand it, but I'd be willing to bet that a necroid uprising is part of it, probably silently and in the dead of night."

"How do we know Douglas is undead?" Cole broke in. "Have you tested this hypothesis, too?"

"I haven't dared," Adhita replied. "If he finds out that I know, he can have me killed and made into a, as you say, vampire, too. I wasn't lying to you when I first met you. I only survive because of his hospitality. And so do you."

"I'll test it," Byron said. "I can't make the mirror, but I can be useful. How do I do it?"

"What?" Cole broke in. "No—it's too dangerous."

"How are you going to stop me?"

"I'll, ah . . . I'll . . ." he trailed off, realizing that he didn't have anything on Byron here. In the past he would have told his mother and father, but here they were on their own.

"Right," Byron confirmed. "So, how do I prove that he's a necroid?"

"His skin would be cold—room temperature," Adhita said. "But reaching up to touch his face would be a dead giveaway."

"Pun intended?" Byron asked, forcing a chuckle. "*Dead* giveaway."

"Also," Adhita mused, smiling, "he wouldn't feel pain. If you stabbed him, say with a knife or a fork, he'd barely notice and he wouldn't bleed."

"But he would notice?" Byron asked.

"It's hard to walk around with a fork sticking out of your leg and not draw attention," Cole said. "What we need is a pin or a needle.

Take it and drive it all the way into a beefy part of him—bicep, butt, or thigh. If he's alive, you'll find out real quick."

"Do you have one?" Byron asked Adhita.

"I have hair pins," she replied, "but they're all blunt. I don't make or repair my own clothes," she said, apologetically.

"They carry needles in the store downtown," Byron said. "I've seen them. Does anyone have any money?"

"No," Adhita said. "Douglas is no fool. If, when he's getting undressed at night, he finds a pin through his clothes and in the meat of his leg, he'll be curious. He'd send to the shop and ask about pins."

"And that will lead him to me," Byron concluded.

"Yes," Adhita said. "I will visit a friend, an elderly woman who lives in town and enjoys needlework. I can steal a pin from her with little difficulty. I'll pass it to you. We'll test the hypothesis, and then we'll know."

"And knowing is half the battle," Byron added, quoting one of his childhood T.V. shows.

Chapter Twenty-Six
G.I. Jack

The little bell above the door jingled as Charlie and Jack entered Conway's Army-Navy Surplus store, called "The Army Barracks." It was a long, squat one-story building, painted gray, and crammed full of shelves and racks. Admittedly, the store had far more hunting and combat knives on display than necessary. Almost everything else had camo print, and the place smelled of rubber, plastic, and gun oil.

"We're gonna need a lot of stuff," Jack said, walking past a case full of knives, taking a cart and the lead. "I hope you got a high credit score."

"I'm gold," Charlie responded, glibly. "Never missed a payment. Anyway, we've spent less than half of the insurance check for the house. We should be good."

"We got to be smart about this," Jack said. "We're a two-man team on a covert rescue mission."

"Covert?"

"It's always better not to be seen—that's a universal truth of military operations. We'll need camo. We'll need slings and holsters. The goal here is comfort and ease—we'll be doing a fair bit of walking. Boots, too. What do you think about night-vision? It was a game-changer in Iraq." He stopped, considering a display of compasses and other navigation tools.

"Those might not work," Charlie said, ignoring the night vision question. "Let's bring one, but who knows if there'll be a magnetic north, or even a sun and moon for that matter. No maps. No known constellations—unless it's a parallel universe or something—Felicity and I have talked this through. Navigation's going to be the hard part."

"If we think like the boys, maybe we'll find their trail."

"Agreed." Charlie dropped a compass and a pair of goggles into the cart. "That's what I'm hoping for, though it's already pretty cold. I don't want to just blunder about."

"It'll be tricky to balance mobility with preparedness, too," Jack observed. "Kevlar?" He stopped next to a display of $400 bullet-proof vests.

"How much do they weigh?"

Jack hefted one. "Ten, maybe twelve pounds?"

"Yeah, okay. Get two—extra large."

Jack put them in the cart, steering toward the camouflage jackets.

"Look, Jack," Charlie asked. "How much weight can a guy carry and still make 20 or more miles a day?"

"Average infantry kit is 65 pounds or so. Some guys carry more. When you add in water, rations, and ammo, it starts multiplying pretty quick. I knew a machine gunner once who carried 120 pounds into combat—more than half the guy's weight." His gaze unfocused for a moment. "That was a real firefight. Our Bradley hit a mine on dune-top and we had to scramble. We were exposed—no cover. Didn't lose anyone, but three guys lost limbs. Republican Guard didn't do as well as us, but not a man of them wouldn't rather have his right leg than a war story and a purple heart."

Charlie held a respectful silence. "So," he said after a moment, "how do we balance equipment with rations?"

"I've thought about that. We'll diversify so we don't double up on equipment—well, not much, anyway. We'll both have canteens, knives, and handguns. We'll each have an AR-15, but yours will be configured for accuracy at range and mine for rate of fire. Both'll use the same ammo, so we can mix and match. I'll take a machete. You take a hatchet. We'll share one set of night vision. We'll have to weigh it out and split it pretty even."

"How many days rations in MRE form can we carry?"

"We don't take MREs," Jack replied. "We take LRPs. Tastes worse—freeze-dried, dehydrated food—everything chews like jerky. After a week on them, you'll start dreaming of steak and eggs—but they're light and full of calories. They're what special ops carry, you know Seal Team Six, guys like that. If we do LRPs, we can carry a couple weeks' worth at least. If we go down to half-rations, maybe a month. Now, if your wife could make a mirror big enough to drive an ATV through, that would be a game-changer."

A smile suddenly creased Charlie's face. He slapped his brother in the chest with the back of his hand. "That's a great idea. But what if we go old-school? What was the first ATV?"

"Uh," Jack shrugged, "probably something by Jeep."

"No, moron, the first ATV was a donkey. Darius carried all his baggage on them in Persia. They were attached to Roman armies.

Heck, through the first world war most armies had baggage trains of pack animals."

"Ok, professor," Jack said, holding up both hands. "So?"

"So, a donkey is small—it'd fit. We could load it up, and those things eat anything. Feed wouldn't be a problem."

Jack laughed out loud. "Yeah, I suppose we could." He considered it for only a heartbeat, then nodded. "Let's do it."

Over an hour later and $3,000 poorer, the two left. Charlie thumbed through a "borrowed" phonebook in the passenger seat of the Bronco, writing down the numbers of farms from the yellow pages. Humid 80-degree July air blew through the small gap in the window and the exhaust rumbled like an old fighter plane. Funny, he thought, thumbing through the yellow-pages, how it was easier to find and buy guns and ammo than farm animals.

CHAPTER TWENTY-SEVEN
Waiting on Pins and Needles

A week and a half passed before Adhita could procure a needle for Byron. When she did, it turned out to be a sewing pin with a tiny, oblong, white glass bead for a head. It was longer than the pins Byron had seen before, too, and the thought of sticking it into the Lord Douglas made him extremely nervous. Nevertheless, he accepted it with a jaunty grace, cracking an anachronistic joke about pinning the tail on the donkey that only Cole understood.

In the interim, Rochester had been good to his word. He'd got Byron a spot training with the squires. It turned out that the old swordplay instructor with the Irish accent was named Campbell and seemed hard as steel. He resented having Byron thrust upon him, so for four daily sessions he made Byron's life hell. Every demonstration of a slash or parry involved Byron, who knew nothing and was easy to mock for his ignorance. He became a laughing stock. Every time Campbell outwitted him at swordplay, which was, in fact, *every* time, he struck hard, leaving a bruise. Worst of all, Campbell "fenced" with a wooden cane, and he still soundly thrashed Byron. And if that wasn't enough, he assigned Byron extra hours of practice after each session to "catch up." These left Byron's arm shaking, throbbing, and exhausted time after time.

However, Byron had been in contact sports since he turned four. He'd seen all kinds of coaches, lived through hard times and injuries, and he had actually been considering joining the marines at eighteen. He hadn't told his parents or even his brother about that—all that kept him from it was his desire to play college hockey. Byron had emotional strength, so he handled the mental challenge well, and his athleticism helped him excel. On day five, he even earned Campbell's respect by getting some difficult footwork right when students who had been studying for over a year still couldn't master it.

The approbation for this came in the form of a sound whack to the chest with a cane and the words, "I may make a swordsman of you yet, Yankee boy."

After that, he gained acceptance from the squires and was less singled out for periodic brutality. The training went smoothly each afternoon and Byron absorbed everything he could, leaving the training sessions bruised, aching, and drenched in sweat, but markedly improved. He also tried to hold his *Temporal* powers—as Adhita called them—in check during training, always choosing to take a blow rather than draw attention to himself.

One day the group had a surprise visit from Aquinas Justice, Douglas' personal champion and bodyguard. "The blackguard," whispered one of the squires, seeing him approach. The group of trainees buzzed with an electric excitement. The awe and fear with which Justice was viewed by the boys, and even by Campbell was something to behold. At six foot six, dark skinned, muscular, and athletic, Justice looked to Byron like an NFL linebacker—like Lawrence Taylor. He joined their formation and trained with them for a full hour, doing everything gracefully and to perfection despite his mammoth size. At the end, while Byron gasped for breath, Justice wasn't even winded and didn't show a bead of sweat. He must have sensed Byron's stare, because the two made eye contact for a lingering moment. Justice curled his lip—something between a smile and a snarl, tilted his head in recognition, and swaggered off, leaving no small impression on Byron or the rest of the squires.

Toward the end of the week, while Byron walked Harald, he heard drums, fifes, and bagpipes playing in the distance. Following the sound, he exited town, and crested a rise, to behold the amazing sight of a British army on the march, a brown dust cloud billowing off in its wake. He stepped from the road into the shade of a tall pine and watched with awe as the musicians and color guard marched up the road and passed in front of him, playing "Scotland the Brave," a tune he remembered from the pipers at the Highland Games at Loon Mountain back home. The musicians were followed by a cavalry troop, Byron estimated about 200 mounted soldiers with lances. They had black coats, strange square-topped hats, like graduation mortarboards, and from their lances fluttered small, forked white flags, each adorned with a red falcon.

Behind them marched, probably 1,500 dust-crusted red-coated infantry in white campaign helmets and black pants, followed by an artillery brigade of fourteen pieces of field cannon. This was trailed by a baggage train—carts of food and supplies, and behind all of that trudged the skeletal regiments, about twice as many necroids as soldiers, all armed with spears, all with red painted crosses on their foreheads. These, too, were broken up into infantry and cavalry regiments. The cavalry—maybe about 300 strong—was composed exclusively of reanimated goat-goblin creatures, the kind Byron had seen earlier. Their horned skulls seemed oddly demonic. Mixed among this extended column of undead were around 50 Necrologists in their brown and black suits and tall hats.

Of course, the pomp of the march hadn't gone unnoticed, and a number of townspeople had gathered near him to watch and cheer. Some of the women clearly had husbands, lovers, or sons among the soldiers, and they shouted names and waved kerchiefs, even though their loved ones could not show recognition.

"Oliver, my brother, is with the third battalion," a female voice said over Byron's shoulder. He looked back to see Alberta there, her blue eyes bright. "I saw you standing there and thought I would say hello."

"Hi," Byron replied. "Where's this army coming from?"

"It is Douglas' Legion," Alberta replied, "the Great Mountain Army. This is their station. They've been north, clearing off the goat-demons so they don't kill our cattle and steal our children. I feel safer having the men in town, though, and it will be nice to see Ollie again."

"It's a big army. How do you feed them all?"

"There is a vast tract of land to the north that is farmed by necroids: chickens, pigs, cattle, wheat, barley . . . all of it goes to the bakery and cannery for the soldiers."

"Do you need this many soldiers? It's got to be almost a quarter of the population of the city."

"There are a lot of necroids now. I don't think Douglas trusts them, and he wants to keep everyone safe. Our soldiers beat them once, and they can do it again at need, of we have enough of them. And the *Lothka* have been waiting for revenge for the beating we gave them in the mountains. If we look weak for a moment, my father says, they won't hesitate to wipe us out. We're the only thing standing between them and the coast, too. And I don't even want to think about the dragons."

"Oh," Byron replied. "I didn't consider dragons. How long will the troops be in town?"

"Who can tell? A month? Three?"

The army had filed by and the crowd began to follow it, Alberta included. Byron walked with her, asking questions and carrying on the conversation.

The following morning Adhita brought Byron the pin, and three days after that, Byron and Cole were scheduled to have a dinner with the Lord Douglas in his greathall. By now Byron knew what to expect—music, at least three courses, and strong mead, all served up by skeletons, and followed by parlor games and political discussion. The easiest time to stick Douglas, he figured, would be during cards. He could contrive to sit to the lord's left or right and then pin him under the table. Byron was right handed, so sitting at Douglas' left would be best.

In a way, though, the pin-sticking was a lose-lose scenario for Byron. If, as Adhita suspected, Douglas was a necroid, then there were two outcomes: one, he got away with it. Well, then he'd be playing cards at a table with a powerful undead and would be expected to act naturally, making no change in his behavior. That would be difficult enough. Outcome two in this scenario would end with his attempt being discovered. Who knows what would happen to him, then—especially with Justice in the room? And then, what if Douglas turned out to be alive and human? Well, then he would have stuck a powerful lord in the leg with a sharp pin. What would be his recourse? To stammer, '*Sorry, I thought you might be a necroid. False alarm. No worries.*' seemed entirely inadequate. He could, he supposed, throw Adhita under the bus, claiming it was all her idea. He didn't much like the prospect of being a snitch to save his skin, though. And he certainly didn't think Cole would take that well.

"You know, you don't have to do this," Cole said as they changed into their dinner clothes. "It's a pretty big risk, and the only reward is knowledge."

"Knowledge is power," Byron answered. "I'm doing it, but if he is a necroid—a *Danath*—what then? I mean, now he claims to want the mirror to go home. If he's dead, there's no going home for him. So, what does he want the portal for? To invade our world? He's certainly got the army to try it."

"Good points," Cole conceded.

"If Douglas is a necroid, you can't build the portal. We'll have to get out of here. But where? And how, with that army suddenly encamped outside of town?"

Cole shrugged noncommittally. "Maybe I could finish the portal, we could go through and then throw some kind of explosive back? Boom."

"Yeah, like you'd have explosives handy wherever we came out. They'd be through before we could blow it."

"Probably right." Cole tightened his cravat. He sat on the bed and began to lace up his shoes. "Let's wait until we know the result before we start planning our reaction, though. Who knows, the whole thing could be nothing." He ran his fingers through his curly hair, which made no measurable difference. "How do I look?"

"Like someone dressed up my brother in badly-fitting museum clothes," Byron answered, wrinkling his nose.

"Thanks," Cole laughed sarcastically. "Thanks a bunch."

CHAPTER TWENTY-EIGHT
Pin the Tail on the Zombie

Dinner went just as Byron expected, except that Rochester was absent, and in his place were a bunch of military officers in parade coats. Dinner consisted of potato soup, a duck-filled pastry dish, roast beef, and a mint custard, all served alongside honey mead. Skeletons delivered the food and cleaned up after each course. The harpsichordist played some Telemann and Vivaldi. Conversations were carried out across the table, all around the glistening silver skull centerpiece. Douglas didn't eat, and Justice leaned against the wall, scrutinizing everything. Byron sat between an elderly, overweight woman who smelled like licorice and moth balls and who treated him like a child, and a middle-aged army captain with a handlebar moustache who seemed much more interested in his meal and in stealing glances at the lady than in conversation. It was all barely tolerable, and Byron drank more than he should have, both because of his company and because of nerves.

He'd slid the pin into the cuff of his left sleeve, the glass pinhead touching the spot where his palm joined his wrist. All dinner it rubbed against him, reminding him of his task.

When the dessert was finally cleared and the card tables being set up, Byron got Cole and Adhita and moved toward Douglas and a group of fancy-looking officers. Unfortunately, Douglas and the senior military officers were already moving toward a table. Taking a chance on Victorian customs, Byron picked up a glass of mead and pressed on. Sure enough, when Douglas made eye contact with them, he felt obligated to introduce them.

"Ah," he cleared his corpulent throat, the flesh beneath his jaw jiggling unpleasantly, "gentlemen, you already know Miss Adhita Lovelace, but may I introduce my latest guests? These here are the Oakes brothers, Byron and Colton. They are Yankees from old New Hampshire, and are here assisting Miss Lovelace in her, ah, studies. And, boys," here he looked at Cole and gestured to the three soldiers near him, "may I introduce General Alexander, commander of the Great Mountain Army." He stopped to chuckle. "I always prefer to have an Alexander leading my army." The general, an older man with white whiskers, shifted his feet uncomfortably. He wasn't sure if he should laugh at a joke that he'd obviously heard many times before. Instead, he smiled and shook Cole's hand. When he turned to shake Byron's, Byron reached out in such a way that he knocked the full glass of mead from Alexander's hand to shatter on the stone floor. With everyone's attention drawn by the shattered glass and spilled liquid, he removed the pin from his cuff and slid it, gingerly at first and then with more force, into the meat of Douglas' posterior.

The pin sank in up to its glass head.

Douglas made no motion or reaction.

Byron gazed at the white pinhead snugged into the black fabric of Douglas' pants and pushed down a cold thrill of horror.

"I'm . . . I'm sorry," he stammered, snapping his gaze away and looking down at the smashed glass.

"Ha ha," laughed Alexander, "no problem, my boy. Happens not infrequently, I assure you. I may be a tactical genius, but I have never been a coordinated man."

The four men and two boys sidestepped away from the spill, as skeletons entered to clean it up, Douglas introduced the other two men, a Colonel Fitzwilliam, and a Doctor Lister. Fitzwilliam shook their hands, his fleshy palm reassuringly warm, but the Doctor did not, instead making a comment about communicable diseases spreading by handshake, and Byron wondered if he, too, was a necroid.

During the cards and conversation that followed, both Byron and Cole were abstracted, each thinking about their situation and next actions. Byron considered who might already be dead and reanimated. He thought of Aquinas Justice, how he'd practiced with them for an hour without breathing hard or sweating. He added him to the list of the dead. Rochester had a warm hand. He lived—at least he'd been alive when they last met. Could his absence tonight be because he was being converted? Byron sighed. This was getting more and more like some *Twilight Zone* episode. He flinched, thinking about the aptness of the title and the perpetual twilight outside.

Cole, on the other hand, found himself more concerned with the future. He scanned the room, noting all the officers and thinking about the Great Mountain Army encamped outside. How would he, Byron, and Adhita escape? What of their work could they take with them? He chanced a question with a nearby officer, the fat captain who'd sat by Byron at dinner.

"How long will the army be in town, do you think?"

"I'm not highly ranked enough to know for sure," the captain blustered, "but we're usually here for about a month or so. Long enough to resupply and plan another local campaign. But, between you and me," he leaned in conspiratorially, "the reality is it's long enough for the men to spend their back-pay in the local shops. Good for the economy, what?" he chuckled.

Cole nodded, wondering if they could pretend ignorance for a whole month.

"I prefer town to campaign," the captain continued, conversationally. "Good food, good conversation, attractive women," he winked at the old woman who smelled of licorice, "and there's plenty to entertain. I hear that tomorrow we're going to be treated to the trial of a spy. And after that, an execution by firing squad."

Byron's head snapped around at this news. "You mean Crowmane?"

"Indeed," the captain nodded, "I did not suspect that you children would be familiar with a known felon."

In response, Cole told the story of how they met, of their fight with the gryphon, and of how they were all saved by Rochester. He had a flair for the dramatic and the story drew the attention of more than one onlooker.

"I'm looking forward to getting my hands on that Rochester," the captain said as the story finished. "I hope he's assigned to my regiment, though he'll probably go to Swift's lancers." He nodded to another captain, this one in the black coat of the cavalry.

"Why isn't he already commanding a unit in the army?" Byron asked.

"Why, because his uncle wants to keep him close, of course," the captain answered. He leaned in again, lowering his voice, "some might call it nepotism, but one cannot put a price on *loyalty*." He sighed. "Wouldn't be surprised to see Rochester make captain, though, and 23, too. An obscene age to have that much rank, really. I was 44, you know."

Byron and Cole nodded. Shortly after, the women vacated the room, and the cigars and political talk emerged.

"Did you ever fight the necroids?" Cole asked the captain.

"Why yes, my boy, I did," the captain answered, standing straighter and thrusting his chest out with pride. He lit a cigar and picked up a glass of gin. "I was a first lieutenant with the 21st Foot: the

Royal North British Fusiliers. Proud regiment, that. Fought you Yanks at Ticonderoga and New Orleans. Took Bergen from Bonaparte, too."

"How were they as fighters?"

"Necroids? Oh my, fearless. Utterly fearless—marched straight into the teeth of our guns and cannon. Straight into our bloody teeth. Blasted them to smithereens, again and again—ground covered in so much bone it looked like snow, like a bloody Christmas morning— but they just kept coming. Disciplined, iron disciplined, the necroids, but stupid. Every battle had the same rhythm. They march straight at us and lose, and afterward walking across the bone-field was like treading on shells at the beach—a series of easy victories until their surrender."

"So, they're not really a threat?" Byron asked, drawn into the conversation.

"Oh, they're very much a threat," the captain replied, tapping ash off his cigar into a saucer and puffing out a lopsided smoke ring. "Even now," his gaze fell on the skeletal harpsichordist, "they're a threat. Pretty soon, we'll be like the Spartans here, outnumbered by our helots, always on the edge of revolt."

Cole understood the allusion. "What's the ratio at the moment?"

"Here?" the captain asked. "Probably one to one living to dead, but it's shifting all the time. On the coast, though, the ratio is still three or four to one in favor of the living. Trains can only cross the steppe so fast."

"I see," Byron nodded.

"Necroids and Necrologists have their flaws of course, the main one being that they cannot innovate. The dead can think, but they cannot learn. The tactics they know when they die are the tactics they must use forever. None of them had ever fought an army with artillery or rifles, so they marched straight into our bloody teeth to be cut down like so much wheat or grass. But despite that flaw, the necroids are a patient bunch. They don't age, you see, and they've already died, so they can wait—forever, if need be—to come back to power. We thumped them, soundly, and they're our servants, for now. For now, but mark my words: they're biding their time. They'll sit by, serve us, and wait, lifetimes if they have to, but if we ever weaken, they'll try to throw us off. Won't happen in my lifetime," he pointed with his cigar, "or yours, but it's coming. Mark my words, it's coming," he repeated, then downed the rest of his gin in one large gulp. A skeleton came by and refilled his cup. He eyed the necroid uneasily, then excused himself, moving across the room to talk with a group of younger officers.

Byron and Cole distracted themselves by listening in on the surrounding conversations. A lot of talk focused on if and when the army would march into *Lothka* territory. Many officers seemed to long for a chance at vengeance and reprisal against the *Yulc* clan from some unnamed offense or atrocity committed in the last war. The feeling in the room was that the Great Mountain Army was more than ready for the challenge and were eagerly looking forward to an extended campaign. Some officers were wondering if the provincial governor in Victoria City would ever give them permission to attack. A few were of the opinion that he would, but most were convinced that his petty feud with Douglas would stop operations and that, for the good of the empire, Douglas would eventually have to launch the attack himself. Byron wondered if it was for the good of the empire, for Douglas' reputation, or to secure a large increase in bodies for necroid production. It was strange to consider battle casualties as a potential resource.

As the conversation went on, the boys gathered that there was a significant Indian presence on the coast—the Victorians kept calling them Punjabis. Cole knew some of this history from his talks with Adhita and filled Byron in on what he'd heard. British Avalon had originally been founded as a paupers' colony. It was different from most penal or transportation colonies because it hadn't been populated by criminals, but by those in the slums or in debtor's prisons and workhouses. People came—mostly the Welsh, Irish, and Scots—to escape the crushing poverty and hopelessness of slum life. Early in the history of Avalon, the British government sent the 34th Bengal Fusiliers, a Sikh regiment, through the mirror to support the colony. The queen couldn't send a whole British regiment through without questions being asked, so she shipped one over from India. The delay almost proved fatal, as the Qesh, a group of draconian lizard-men, laid siege to the colony, but the time-delay allowed faster movement on the old-world side. The Bengal regiment came through at a pivotal moment, heroically crushed the Qesh army, and stabilized the colony, intermarrying with local women after the portal closed, and becoming the most important voting minority in Avalon. All in all, he concluded, there were probably fifteen or twenty thousand British on the coast. Nearly a quarter of them were of Indian descent.

The resulting political problem stemmed from a personal conflict between Adhita's father, the provincial Governor-General, and Douglas, but their conflict mirrored British prejudice against the Indian minority, and the two boys could hear that discrimination being voiced over strong drink and cigars. Men of Scottish, Welsh, and Irish heritage, who used to be reviled by the English, passed their mistreatment on to the Indians. Being occasional victims of such prejudice in America, it made the boys mad to hear it, and both had to bite their tongues.

"Why did they destroy the mirror?" Byron asked Cole. "Did Adhita tell you that?"

"Yeah," Cole replied. "I asked her. I guess because of the time differential it wasn't very lucrative to the Victorians in terms of resources or trade. And as it turns out that a wyvern flew through in 1874 and laid waste to a whole city block before they gunned it down. Apparently, the newspapers covered it up, claiming it was an explosion at the gas works and Queen Victoria had all the witnesses moved through the portal before closing it down, 'temporarily.' The mirror never turned back on."

"Yikes," Byron grimaced. "And I thought the barghest was bad."

The time wore on, feeling interminable to both brothers. Covering their growing fears and frustrations with small talk, Cole and Byron pretended polite interest and bided their time, gathering what information they could, until evening shift when they were able to return to their rooms.

CHAPTER TWENTY-NINE
A Bedtime Battle

"What are we going to do?" Byron asked. The door to their room was barely closed when he started talking. He leaned against it. Cole flopped down on his four-poster bed, massaging his forehead with a hand.

"What can we do?"

"Escape."

"How? To where?"

"I dunno—bust Crowmane out and get his help—he knows the area."

"We can't," Cole replied. "Even if we could break him out, how do we get past the army? And you want to flee from cavalry and undead who don't have to sleep? And they have hunting dogs—you've been to the kennels."

"Okay, then, we steal the train and go across the steppe." Byron sat on his bed for a moment, but then lunged up, pacing the room.

Cole remained calm. "I can't engineer a steam train—I know the physics, of course, but not the instrumentation, not the technicalities of how to work it—and there's the telegraph problem, like Adhita had before. They'll just call ahead and stop us."

"We *can't* just wait here."

"We *have* to," Cole sighed, rubbing his eyes. "Look, Douglas hasn't killed us yet, and I don't think he's going to. Adhita is still alive. He's *using* us. He needs us alive because like that captain said, the necroids can't innovate. If they want a portal, *living* people are going to have to invent it. We're safe, for the moment."

"Maybe you are," Byron snapped, "but I'm not. I'm not some great brain who can invent an interdimensional vortex. Believe me, they could bump me off any minute and not feel a pang of guilt."

Cole sighed, but didn't respond. He probably knew that what his brother said was true.

"And what about Crowmane?" Byron demanded. "We're just supposed to let him die?"

"Honestly, yeah," Cole said. "We can't help him. It's too

dangerous."

"I can't let the guy get tried and killed by a bunch of Victorian zombies. It's just not right."

"Things that aren't right happen every day."

"What's that MLK quote Mom hung on the wall in the schoolroom? 'Injustice anywhere is a threat to justice everywhere?' I can't remember the rest."

Cole's eyes focused on the white plaster above Byron's head as he imagined the downstairs room where their mom had taught them to read and write. "'We are caught in an inescapable network of mutuality, tied in a single garment of destiny. Whatever affects one directly affects all indirectly.'" He looked back to Byron as he finished. "They're nice, philosophical words, and I want to follow them, but they don't do us a bit of good if they get us killed."

"Okay, then, let's put philosophy aside. You have to admit that Crowmane's our only ticket out of here. We only know two kinds of people in this world: Crowmane and the zombie-lovers."

"And Adhita," Cole pointed out.

"Fine, and Adhita," Byron agreed. "When we bust out, we take your girlfriend with us."

"Thanks," Cole replied, "and she's not my girlfriend. Not yet."

"Ok, so, let's make a plan," Byron said. "How do we bust Crowmane out and get Harald and Adhita at the same time? How do we get onto the train? How do we cut the telegraph lines?"

"WE DON'T!" Cole exploded. "It's *literally* impossible to do that. We wait. We watch. We scheme. After the army leaves, we move—not before."

"But Crowmane will die."

"Why are you so damn loyal to a guy who fed us bacon and eggs once? I don't get it. It's not like he's Dad or Uncle Bruce or something!" Cole threw his arms over his head in frustration.

"He saved us from the gryphon."

"No, Rochester saved us from the gryphon."

"I'm going to rescue him," Bryon set his jaw.

"You'll do *nothing* of the kind," Cole said in his best impression of their mother's voice. He advanced on Byron, grabbed him by the shoulders and leaned in until their faces were inches apart. "We're brothers. We're in it together or not at all, and I'm not in on this one. Not now, anyway." He turned and walked away.

"Cole," Byron said, the passion leaving his voice.

"Yeah?"

"What did we get ourselves into?"

"A horror movie," Cole replied, sinking onto his bed, "a real one—like *Ghost Brigade*—not a stupid one like *Evil Dead III*, *Army of Darkness*."

"Hey," Byron forced a laugh, "You put that movie's poster up in your room. What's with the sudden judgment?"

"I liked it *for* its stupidity," Cole explained.

"I wish the solution was as simple as finding a Necronomicon," Byron said.

"And then saying the magic words," Cole chuckled.

"Yeah, yeah—I got 'em. I know your damn words," Byron giggled, quoting the movie, then immediately sobered. "But what are we going to do, Cole?"

"Go to bed" Cole replied, yawning. "Like Dad says, things always look better in the morning."

They blew out the oil lamp, but rather than sleep, Byron lay awake, planning a prison breakout that he'd attempt with or without his brother's help.

Chapter Thirty
Contra

Charlie, Felicity, and Jack walked side-by-side down the flat-tiled hallway of the Steeplegate Mall in Concord. Throngs of families with children, and groups of teens passed them by on both sides as they made their way around an island of well-manicured jungle vegetation—palms, bamboos, and bromeliads. They'd come to do some necessary shopping, and to get it all done at once. The mall had the best-stocked RadioShack in the area, and Felicity needed to spend some time in the store selecting circuitry components for the mirror. The muzak played Peter Gabriel behind the hum of passing conversations. Charlie watched a family with a pair of young boys heading toward the toy shop, bit his lip, and silently decided that they shouldn't have come on a Saturday.

"Preppy. Preppy. Hippie. Redneck. Grunge. Goth." Jack ticked off as they passed teenagers, noting their various styles. He slapped Charlie's arm to get his attention. "Hey, what do you think about goth girls? Creepy or attractive? My jury's still out."

"What? I'm married," Charlie answered. He glanced over his shoulder at the pale girl with raven hair, fishnet sleeves and shining black high-heeled boots—obviously a college student. "And she's what? Twenty, at most? C'mon, that's half our age."

"Hey," Jack defended himself. "I'm barely in my 30s, thank you, and I'm an attractive single vet—a real catch. And you didn't answer the question at all. Attractive or creepy?"

"Attractive," Felicity cut in, also looking back. "I mean, like anything, it can be overdone, but she's pretty tasteful. Her ensemble comes together. And besides, the whole theory of goth fashion is the desirability of difference. They're sick of being *normal*, so they make themselves abnormal. If you think she's dressing up for *you* or to attract men, you're crazy. She's dressing up for her—to feel like a more exciting person—to make her normal life more interesting. I'm sure she cares just about zero for your opinion on the matter, too. If she wants to go goth, good for her. Shut up about it and leave her alone."

Jack stood a moment, his mouth agape, then laughed. "Yep, you're right." He turned to his brother as the two of them increased their pace to catch Felicity. "Charlie," he said, "you know, the more time I spend here, the more I understand why you married this woman." It was the first genuine compliment he'd given her, and a tight smile creased Felicity's mouth.

"Stick around a while, and you might learn some things," she replied as they came abreast of the RadioShack. She stopped and kissed Charlie on the cheek. "I'll probably be around an hour." She handed him a short, handwritten list. "Walk on down to K-Mart and pick these up for me, will you? I'll be here when you get back."

"Can do," Charlie nodded. He glanced down the list and turned to Jack, but his brother was gone. "What the? Where?" he began. Felicity cut him off.

"He wandered into the arcade across the hall," she pointed. "Hope I didn't hurt his feelings, but he can be an ass sometimes. Go check on him, will you?" She turned and entered the store. Charlie stood for a moment, rubbing his chin, then he pocketed the list and went to find Jack.

The sign above the entrance read "TimeOut Arcade." It was a small hole-in-the-wall place with darkened lights and a laser pattern on the blue carpet, and it was crammed full of machines. Charlie passed two sit-down racing games with steering-wheels and handlebars, then glanced at *Rampage*, *Millipede*, and *Ultimate Final Fight*, as he zeroed in on Charlie, who stood behind a flashing machine watching a chubby middle-school kid play. The sounds of machine guns and grenades emanated from the game, alongside synthesized electronic music that could have come off the intro track of *Europe*'s "The Final Countdown." Charlie stopped beside Jack and looked up at the game's title.

"*Contra*, huh?"

"Yeah," Jack replied, keeping his voice low out of respect for the kid playing. "We had this one down at Fort Polk in Louisiana. Played it with the guys back before Panama. I'm pretty good—well, used to be. Won it on one coin once."

"What's it about?"

"Two guys—U.S. Marines—brothers, I think, a blonde one and one with dark hair—they get in a giant firefight with a bunch of commie bastards called the Red Falcons. But as it turns out, the Reds are being controlled by space aliens, and only two guys—um Bill and Lance, I think—can save humanity from enslavement and destruction.

Not much of a plot, really. It's all about jumping and shooting. It's kinda cool 'cause it's got both horizontal and vertical levels."

An explosion resonated on the screen and the words "Game Over" flashed. The kid released the controls and swore. He picked up his stack of tokens and turned, heading toward the racing machines.

"Wanna play?" Jack asked. "A full game is only about 15 minutes, start-to-finish. I'll spot you the quarters." He didn't wait for an answer, just walked toward a coin vending machine, taking out his wallet and inserting a five-dollar bill. A clatter of tokens fell into the slot.

"Since I'm buying, I get to be the Schwarzenegger-looking guy. You can be the one that's basically John Rambo." He stacked the tokens on the machine, took two, and slid them into the slot. The scoreboard appeared and the music started. The machine prompted for a one or two player game, and Charlie reached for the tokens.

"I'm going to go through your stock pretty fast," he said. "I'm not a gamer. Never played this before."

"Then my job will be to keep you alive, *Lance*," Jack joked. "Stay behind me and keep your head down and you'll be alright."

But the first gun emplacement took Charlie out. "Sorry," he winced, as he slipped a coin into the slot to revive his character. Lance dropped out of the sky into the firefight again and was almost immediately slain by a charging Red who Kamakazied himself into the character. Charlie grabbed another coin.

"Jesus," Jack laughed, "will ya try not to die more than about 20 times—we don't have unlimited tokens."

Charlie died five more times in the first level, but he started to get the hang of it soon enough. At this point he was fighting with a blue and red laser cannon and Jack had some kind of four-shot-spread gun. They were mowing down everything in sight.

"Not a lot like a real firefight," Jack admitted, ducking and blasting a turret. Charlie jumped, avoiding a slow-moving bullet. "First off, in real life the guy behind you can't fire through his friends. Second, the baddies don't tend to mindlessly charge your guns—not since Korea, anyway. Though, I take it that Mogadishu was a bit like this in '93." He obliterated another wave of Reds.

"How many you been in?" Charlie lasered a sniper off his brother's 2:00.

"Firefights?"

"Yeah."

"Six, maybe seven where there was real incoming fire." He shrugged, "More, if you count the times we annihilated enemy positions without meaningful retaliation." They entered a base and the view shifted to vertical. A rolling cylinder covered in spikes came down the screen and Jack jumped it. Charlie was crushed and reached for another coin. "They're scary as shit. I felt the wind of a burst of 39 millimeters go by my neck in Iraq. Air was hot. Bullets were hotter. The last one must've missed by the width of two hairs. Took a bit of shrapnel in the Kevlar once, too. Damn." He'd accidentally picked up a flamethrower, losing the quad-shot that he'd been using. He couldn't eliminate Reds as fast and the barrage of incoming bullets redoubled. Charlie's character crumpled to the ground again.

"I don't talk about it a lot," Jack added. "Try not to think about it, too. It gets to me sometimes at night, though, especially on hot nights. That's why I like Maine—not many hot nights."

They were at the second-level boss now. Jack's moves were inspired. He dodged, fired, dodged, jumped, fired, and kept alive despite a storm of incoming fire. Charlie died. There were four coins left.

"Yeah," Charlie filled the silence, "I've never shot a man or been shot at. My nightmares are family ones, usually involving Felicity or the kids. Byron fractured his skull when he was seven." He added a coin to the machine. "He was rollerblading in the parking lot at the university, jump-switched to backward and ran over an upturned bottle-cap. Came down hard on the back of his head. Blood was everywhere. He went unconscious for over a minute, eyes rolled up, seizing. Felt like a year. I thought I'd lost him. There are still bloodstains that never came out of the van's upholstery. Left a stain on my mind, too. Still wake up sweating over that one."

Jack only nodded. As they moved farther into the game, the difficulty was becoming more and more insane, but he still hadn't died. The middle school kid was standing beside them now, awe in his face as he watched Jack play. Charlie jumped to avoid a charging Red and ran into a bullet.

"Here, kid," he said, handing off his spot to the boy. "Jack I've got to go down to K-Mart to pick up some," he glanced at his list, "Pert-plus, coconut oil, Bic razors, and a bunch of other things. I'll be back in a bit."

Jack grunted in response.

The middle school boy died, and Jack said, "Welcome to the jungle, kid. You can play with me, but you'd better be using your own coins. I'm not a charity."

"Okay," the boy responded, shoving a chubby hand deep in his pocket and pulling out a fresh token.

Charlie walked back out into the mall. He strode alone, head down and chewing at his lip, along the happily buzzing strip full of busy families and laughing friends.

When he returned nearly 30 minutes later, toting seven plastic bags, he was astonished to find Jack and Felicity sitting together in an off-road race game, chasing one another down the Baja coast. He set the bags carefully on the carpet and watched for a moment. His wife was definitely in the lead and, apparently, was trash-talking Jack.

"Remind me again, which one of us drives a lifted Bronco, and which drives a minivan?"

Jack grunted, leaning to avoid a boulder. He rounded a corner at too high a speed, skidded off the track, and slowed in a dune. Gunning it, he overshot the track, hit a cactus and spun-out.

"I can't even see you in my rear-view," Felicity taunted. She downshifted, floored it, and flew over a hill, getting air before landing back on the track, passing the lead AI racer.

"How the hell are you so good at this?" Jack grimaced as he fell into fifth-place behind a purple pickup, whose cowboy-looking driver screamed 'Yee-haw!' as she blew by.

"Perhaps the better question is," Felicity asked, pulling across the finish line to artificial cheers, "how are you so bad at this? That's three in a row, soldier-boy. You owe me a twelve-pack." She stood, moving awkwardly to get out of the enclosed place. "Oh, hey," she acknowledged Charlie's presence. "How long you been here?"

"Long enough to see you kick my butt," Jack cut in stretching beside them. "That thing's not built for a grown man."

"About three minutes," Charlie answered his wife.

"Do they have a refrigerated row in K-Mart?" Jack asked. "I have to pay-up."

"Yeah. East side of the store."

"What do you want?" he asked Felicity. "Budweiser? Sam Adams?"

"Sunkist," she smirked. "I don't really drink—it doesn't mix well with my meds."

"Sunkist it is." He turned to Charlie, "You want anything?"

"Whatever you get is fine by me."

Jack left, chuckling to himself and muttering about Sunkist soda.

"How'd you beat him?" Charlie asked.

"Oh," Felicity smiled. "I used to come here once a month with the boys for about five years. If they were good while I got my hair done and checked the clearance racks, I treated them each to a couple dollars in here. Cole always wanted to drive. I used to race him." She bent to pick up her RadioShack bag and took up two of Charlie's as well. "But don't tell Jack that. It does him good to think I'm just more naturally talented than he is."

CHAPTER THIRTY-ONE
Trial by Firing Squad

Crowmane's trial ended faster than Byron expected, though the guilty verdict was exactly what everyone anticipated. Byron and Cole both attended, dressed in their evening coats. They each testified as character witnesses, suggesting that Crowmane had a good-natured, kind, and loyal disposition. These observations were duly written down in the court records. Unmoved, Lord Douglas Sterling wore a powdered wig, black robes, and sat with prestige in the judge's seat, higher than anyone in the room and looking down upon them all. He held a gavel in what the boys assumed was his cold, dead hand. They avoided looking at him whenever possible because he gave them chills, and because they worried that he'd found the pin buried in his flesh and done some calculating of his own.

Rochester spoke matter-of-factly as the prosecution's main witness. Their first argument was that Crowmane had been in possession of a Martini Henry rifle which belonged to The Great Mountain Army and was issued to Lance Corporal Owen Davies. Davies had gone missing in action during the campaign against the *Yulc* clan four years earlier. A second witness had last seen Davies marching to a vanguard position with his column of the 11th Devonshire Foot. The only logical assumption, the prosecutor—a middle-aged man named Migsby—argued, could be that Crowmane had killed Davies and taken his rifle. The charge, then, was at worst murder, and at best possession of illegal contraband, theft of military materials, and consorting with known lawless murderers, and enemies of the state.

It also came out during these proceedings that feelings against the *Lothka* were especially hard because of "atrocities" that they carried out against the army. When the *Yulc* warriors killed a soldier in combat, they invariably mutilated the body by beheading the corpse, and keeping the heads as trophies, a desecration that understandably outraged the British. It also meant that in areas where the *Yulc* had been victorious, they had decapitated the British wounded rather than treating them in a humane fashion.

"I bet it's not so much for trophies as it is to stop the *Danathskoti* from reanimating the dead," Cole whispered to Byron. "It's probably become a ritual to them."

"Makes sense," he nodded. "Pretty gross, though. I wonder if—"

Migsby surprised Byron by calling him to the stand at that moment. He endured a brief and blunt series of questions on the witness chair. Migsby carried a rifle up to the stand and handed it to Byron. "Do you recognize this weapon?" he asked.

"You mean, was it the one Crowmane had when he found us and that I used to fire on the gryphon?" Byron asked. "I don't know. There were a lot of Martini Henrys produced during the Victorian age. This could be any of them."

"But you admit that the accused had a Martini Henry rifle?"

"Yes," Byron said.

"And did you note whether the rifle had a crown inspection stamp and serial number?"

"I did," he replied.

"And did it?"

"It did," he admitted, "though I can't remember the number."

"No further questions," the prosecutor said. Byron returned to his seat.

The second charge brought against Crowmane was espionage. The prosecution argued that he travelled widely in British territory without permission, had observed activity, and therefore had put himself in a position to report intelligence back to the *Lothka* upon his return to *Yulc* clan lands. The arguments were made with strongly biased and emotional language, and Cole kept commenting on the use of logical fallacies by the prosecution, complaining frequently and bitterly about *ad hominem* character attacks and false equivalency.

Crowmane provided his own defense. His arguments were clear, but as the boys suspected, not of adequate legal consequence. Firstly, he said, he did not murder Lance Corporal Owen Davies, but killed him as a combatant. "Warriors fight wars," he said. He thumped his chest. "Am soldier, warrior, fighter, just like your Davies. Fight we. Victory had I. Lucky for me, sad for his family." He shrugged. "This is battle. This is war." A murmur rumbled through the courtroom after that, but whether his argument had legal ramifications was beyond both Cole and Byron. Either it made logical sense and exonerated him from the charge of murder, or it marked him out as an enemy combatant destined for execution. They couldn't tell.

"After you defeated Davies," Migsby asked, "did you remove his head from his body?"

"Yes," Crowmane answered to collective gasps from around the room. "That is the custom where the dead may be . . ." The audience had erupted in jeers and shouts, and Crowmane trailed off as it became clear that no one could hear him. A woman was crying. Douglas had to use his gavel to regain control.

When the crowd settled down, Crowmane was asked to respond to the second charge, that of espionage. He argued that he had been trapping animals for furs on his trip through the British lands. He offered his equipment and the pack of furs he carried as evidence. This was countered fairly easily by the prosecution, who asked:

"You are called *Craeka-mune* in your language, Crowmane in ours, correct?"

"Yes," he nodded.

"You are the Champion of the Illenthane, are you not?"

"Am," he agreed.

"And why would the Champion of the Illentane, a prestigious member of *Lothka* society, be fur-trapping for a living?"

Crowmane made no response.

"It is my understanding that the clans provide for the livelihood and upkeep of the Illenthane. Is that correct?"

"You speak truth," Crowmane confirmed.

"And as the Champion of the Illenthane, that includes your upkeep and livelihood, too. Correct?"

"Yes."

By the end of the trial, no one in the courtroom doubted the verdict. It was just a matter of hearing Douglas pronounce it. He hammered his gavel on the desk for silence, looked stonily down at Crowmane for a pair of heartbeats, then said, "After due consideration of the arguments made by both sides, this court finds the defendant guilty of espionage. The murder charge shall be dropped from the record because the accused is a self-professed soldier in the *Yulc* clan army. However," Douglas cleared his throat, which silenced a growing unease in the room, "as a soldier in that army, travelling in our lands, *out of uniform*, he is—by definition—a spy and therefore guilty of that offense. All that remains is to sentence him and dispense the Queen's justice. Mr. Crowmane," he said, "please rise to hear your sentence."

Crowmane stood; he gazed unflinchingly at Douglas as he spoke.

"It is the judgement of this court that the defendant is guilty of the crime of espionage and shall be executed. Traditional punishment for this crime is to be hanged by the neck until dead, but as that custom is abhorrent to the *Lothka* for religious reasons, I will commute the sentence to death by firing squad." He lifted his gavel to end the session, but Crowmane spoke up, paying careful attention to his English, as if rehearsed.

"Lord Douglas," he said, "I would make a request." Douglas stopped his hand and gave a nod.

"Go on."

"I desire trial by combat. The Champion of the Illenthane cannot be shot like a deer or a dog. This would anger the *Lothka* people. If I die in a fight, it will be accepted. Grant, then, that I shall fight."

Douglas smiled. "My dear Mr. Crowmane," he said, his tone patronizing, "I shall not modify the Queen's justice for fear of a war with the *Lothka*. Justice must be impartial to external circumstances to be considered *just* at all. And, indeed, if your people are angered enough to invade this land, they will find me and the Great Mountain Army ready for them." He smiled, then added as an afterthought, "And I find defensive wars so much easier to justify to the public than wars of aggression, don't you?" He cleared his throat and raised his voice. "I hereby find the defendant guilty of the crime of espionage and heredo sentence him to death by firing squad, a public execution to take place not later than three days, or 64.5 hours from now." The gavel came down with crisp finality.

Chapter Thirty-Two
Shooting Party

Charlie adjusted his glasses and squinted through the scope on his rifle. Even with the enhanced vision and laying down to minimize body motion, a target 600 yards away was a tough shot. He exhaled, stopped breathing, and held his arms perfectly still. Gently, he squeezed the trigger—aimed, squeezed, aimed, and squeezed a third time.

"Jesus," Jack said from beside him, staring through binoculars. "You bullseyed all three of those." He clapped his brother on the back, just as another round left the chamber. It went wild and kicked up dust. "You've still got it."

Charlie smirked. "Runner-up, 1975, New York State championship."

"The *high school* championship," Jack reminded him.

"Yeah," Charlie replied, then laughed. "Where did you rank? I forget."

"Shut up, narc" Jack answered, reverting to their high school dialect. "Why do you think I'm giving you the sniper rifle? Run a chainsaw as long as I have, and I guarantee that your hands'd shake, too."

"Shouldn't matter too much with that laser sight," Charlie nodded in the direction of Jack's rifle. "At least not within fifty yards."

"That's the idea," Jack agreed. Charlie squeezed off a few more shots. Jack returned his binoculars to his face and shook his head again in admiration. "Jeez," he repeated. "You shoulda joined up. Sniper pay-grade is better than your university salary, probably."

Charlie didn't even look up. "Hard to be a family man behind a gun," he commented between shots, "and tenure lasts until I retire."

"Some guys pull it off," Jack responded, "having a family behind a gun. Others . . . well," he looked down at his empty ring finger, "how do you share what you've seen or done with someone who's never been there or done it? When you start off with secrets, it's hard to ever feel . . . I dunno."

Silence hung between them for a moment. A cardinal singing from a nearby maple tree broke it.

"Hard to feel unconditionally loved?" Charlie said, getting up.

"I think we're done here." He wiped off his jeans.

Jack nodded, agreeing to either one or both of his brother's statements.

"Do you feel secure with me by your side?" Charlie asked.

"Oh yeah," Jack laughed. "You outshot me in everything today from handguns on up. But don't kid yourself. Target shooting and live combat are two different things. Experience matters."

"You keep assuming we'll be in combat," Charlie noted as they walked back to the Bronco. "Why?"

"In Narnia?" Jack laughed. "I guess I do. Could be just wilderness over there, I suppose. Kids camping in the tent for five months. I doubt it, though, and I like to be prepared."

"You just being prepared for a firefight, or are you *looking* for one?" Charlie asked, suddenly very serious. "Because I need to know. I avoid conflict whenever I can."

Jack held up his hands, defensively, his keys jingling. "Me too, man. Me, too. I guess I'm just edgy. Missing a whole summer's work here, you know."

"I know," Charlie looked at the ground, "and I thank you for it."

They laid the guns in the trunk, got into the Bronco, and bumped along the rutty, muddy road back toward the trailer. Jack switched on the radio. Tim McGraw's twang filled the cab.

"Since when do you like country?" Charlie asked. "You used to make fun of it, if I remember. What'd you used to call it, 'goat-ropin' music?"

Jack chuckled. "I suppose I did." He glanced over at Charlie. "So what? People change. You're a card-carrying Democrat these days, aren't ya?"

"Woah," Charlie held up his hands. "We'd better not get into politics. You know how that ends—badly. And I won't let politics be thicker than blood."

"Sure, sure," Jack waved him off. "It's just that y'all think the world owes you a living. I believe in making my own—"

"Wait, what? 'Y'all?' Did you just say 'y'all'?" Charlie laughed aloud. "So it's not only country music, and Limbaugh radio talking points—it's southern dialect, now, too? Jesus, Jack—you're from upstate New York."

"Yeah, that's true. But, you know, infantry is full of guys from the south. Most of my buddies in Iraq were from Mississippi and

Alabama. We had a guy from New Orleans whose dad was black and mom, Japanese. Weird looking fella. Intense. Named Gaston, like the guy from *Beauty and the Beast.* Strong like him, too. Called himself the Blasian Cajun—that's how PC we are in the Army—don't have time for taking offense when you could get blown up at your next step. So, when we got back stateside, Gaston took us out on Bourbon Street one night and to a Saints game . . ." He smiled, staring off into space.

The Bronco hit a mud puddle, hard. Water sprayed to all sides and the suspension jolted. It lifted them both briefly from their seats. Jack shook off the memory and winced.

"Sorry. Anyway," he concluded, "you hang around with guys like that—tough, dependable men, all of 'em—and they start to grow on you. Guess I picked up more than just country music and uncanny skills at *Contra.* Speaking of—Nashville's a nice place, too. Had a guy in the regiment from there—Danny. His name was Boucher, but we called him Boone." He sighed. "Well, you know how it is. Don't tell me your snooty college friends haven't changed you. They have. I see it."

"Fair point," Charlie nodded. "I admit, I find myself listening to G.F. Handel and Telemann on NPR sometimes. I rather enjoy Baroque harpsichord, and I like to think of King George listening to it with his courtiers while Washington froze and starved at Valley Forge. It's a nice contrast—it sets the piece, gives it ambiance. I guess I even enjoy the history of my music." He grinned, foolishly. "And a bunch of us went to a wine tasting last month—I hate to say that cabernet is growing on me. Still don't like smoky cheese, though. You know," he picked dirt from a fingernail, "it's funny how two guys who grew up the same way in the same place can turn out so different." His phone rang in his pocket. "Probably Felicity," he said, shifting his weight and digging for it.

"Sure, we're different on the outside." Jack swerved to avoid another pothole and rattled across some washboards. "Jobs. Tastes. Friends. Lifestyle. Stuff like that. But inside you're still the same guy I knew when I was ten. You still chop wood. I cut trees for a living. There are similarities. I—I've just seen some stuff that's changed me. Done some stuff I can't forgive and can't forget, but beneath all the layers, I'm still the same guy, too." He looked over. Charlie stared at the dash, his mouth open, the phone at his ear. "What?"

His brother set down the phone and looked up, his expression solemn. "She says she's finished it."

Chapter Thirty-Three
Jailbreak

Byron shoved his hands deeper into his sweatshirt pocket. The cool air cut through him, propelled by a stiff wind. He looked up at the clear sky, thankful, for the first time, for the perpetual shadow and absence of a moon in Avalon. Instead of crossing the courtyard directly to the guardhouse, he moved stealthily, hugging the wall, and trusting to his forest green sweatshirt to keep him out of view of the sentries on the tower.

Crowmane's execution would take place in about five hours, at the beginning of the first of the three daily duty shifts. Byron had silently decided that he couldn't sit by and watch that happen, so he'd created an escape plan—a bad one, even he admitted that. Cole wouldn't come with him, wouldn't help, and insisted that he'd tie Byron up—all day if he had to—to prevent some kind of half-baked rescue op. He'd been so serious about it that Byron had to give a solemn promise not to attempt what he was now attempting. He felt bad about breaking his word to Cole, but he figured his brother would forgive him, eventually.

Byron had a backpack full of supplies and carried an elaborately curved bronze sword. Their knives and hatchet had been confiscated and weren't returned with the rest of their things. He'd snuck down to Douglas' trophy room and filched this blade from the mastodon leg container. He figured he could whack the guard upside the head with the flat. If things worked like they always seemed to in movies, the guard would go down, then he could stuff his mouth with cloth—a pair of *clean* socks, he wasn't a barbarian—and zip tie his hands and feet to a chair. Easy-peasy. After that, he figured he'd use the keys to set Crowmane loose, and the two of them could sneak to the kennels to release Harald. Then Byron would go to the far side of the compound and set a fire. In the commotion, Crowmane and Harald would escape, and Byron would slink back to his room with Cole—he couldn't just abandon his brother, after all.

There were difficulties, though: 1) Byron couldn't be recognized by anyone, including the guard he had to knock unconscious; 2) The kennels were full of dogs that would probably make quite a commotion; 3) They couldn't kill anyone because if he got caught, he'd be executed as well; 4) Rochester would certainly trace the zip ties back to him, so he was hoping there might be handcuffs or shackles in the jail; 5) Well, the uncertainties just kept compounding from there, really. He didn't highly rate his chance of success. Yet, no matter how much he considered it, he hated the consequences of doing *nothing* more than those of doing *something*.

He arrived, without complication, outside the guardhouse. His back against the wall and head near the window, he whispered.

"Crowmane."

No answer.

"Pssst, Crowmane," more urgently this time.

Still no answer. A raven croaked from atop the jail building. Its wings fluttered and it landed between the bars. He flinched.

"Byron Oakes, speaking are you to me?" Crowmane's voice came, whispering through the window, so silently that at first Byron wasn't sure he heard them.

"Yeah, it's me. I'm going to set you free."

"No," Crowmane said, his voice firm. "Trading your life for mine is not a bargain that find I acceptable. Leave me here. My fate is clear."

"They'll kill you."

"Death makes all men equal—visits it everyone, eventually," he sighed.

"Look," Byron whispered, setting his jaw. "I'm coming in there. I'm going to knock out your guard, and I'm going to open that door. You can stay if you want, but I'll have done my part at least."

There was a pause, as if Crowmane deliberated. Finally, he blew air out through his nose, like an annoyed horse. "Asleep, the guard, head-down on his desk. Leans, his gun, against the wall. Be silent and come in. Put the gun to his cheek and have him open my door. The rest, will I do."

Byron nodded. "Okay. I'll see you in a sec." He slunk around the guardhouse to the front, reaching to grasp the cast-iron handle of a nail-studded, wooden door. He gently depressed the latch, hoping that it wouldn't make much noise and that the hinges were well-oiled.

The latch lifted and the door swung open, with only the slightest creaking. The room was warm from smoldering coals in the fireplace, and Byron worried about waking the guard with the temperature change. He swung the door, lifting the long iron latch to avoid making a sound. The door thumped closed, a slight sound that the quiet seemed to amplify. Byron winced and his hands shook, clanging the latch, slightly. He glanced over at the table; the guard shifted. Some coals crumbled in the fireplace. Crowmane covered the noise by rolling over on his cot and sighing loudly.

Byron stepped across the plank floor to a rifle that he saw on the wall in the glow of the dying coals. He set down his sword, hefted the gun, and looked for the safety. He couldn't find it in the gloom, but he didn't figure it mattered all that much—he didn't plan to kill the guard anyway. Pulling the drawstrings of his hood tight to conceal his face, he stepped boldly toward the desk and lay the cold steel of the muzzle against the guard's temple. The man tensed in his chair.

"Do what I tell you, and you'll live. Take the keys, unlock the door and step in with the prisoner," Byron instructed. "Make a move or say a word, and I'll blow off your head, so help me God."

The man moved his head to look at Byron. He pushed the barrel more forcefully into the man's hair and pulled back the hammer on the rifle until it made a cocking sound. "Don't look at me," he instructed.

The man nodded. He stood, carefully, the muzzle moving down to his cheek. He reached to his belt, pulled off a large key ring with a single key, and walked toward the cell door. Byron rested the gun on the spot where his skull met his neck.

The noise of the key turning in the lock and the creaking hinges felt unnaturally loud.

"Now, step inside," Byron repeated.

"But," the guard stammered, "the prisoner—"

His speech cut off as an arm went around his throat and another clamped, vice-like over his mouth.

"Remove his belt," Crowmane instructed.

A few minutes later, the guard, now both undressed and unconscious, had been tied up and belted into a sheet, laying flat, face-down on Crowmane's cot. Crowmane adjusted the buttons on the red uniform jacket, a makeshift disguise to aid his escape.

"You won't take Harald?" Byron asked again, a hint of pleading in his voice.

"No—not safe." Crowmane slid the curved sword into his belt. "Both of us would be caught. Unknown, your part in this. Go back to your brother. Can I escape, alone. The Champion of the Illenthane will owe you his life, a debt he will repay." He shouldered the rifle.

Byron nodded. "Okay. Should I go first or should you?"

"Go," Crowmane nodded, somberly.

"Okay," Byron repeated. "Well," he stood by the door, looking back at Crowmane, overcome with a sudden burst of emotion. "I hope I see you again someday."

"Again gaze, we will, upon each other," Crowmane said, his voice firm and certain. He grabbed Byron by the shoulders and leaned in, putting his forehead against the boy's. "Again will meet we, on this side of the mountains or the next, under a new horizon." He released him. "Go now."

"Is that a *Lothka* saying? A proverb or something?" Byron asked, his hand on the door latch.

"No," Crowmane chuckled. "It is *my* saying." He paused, then waved his hand at Byron, shooing him. "Now, go!" he said again.

Byron nodded and opened the door, still looking back. He took one step out and ran right into someone who grabbed him by the neck and flung him back into the room.

"I suspected as much," he heard a familiar, prim voice sigh. "Though I had rather hoped it wouldn't come to this." Byron turned his head to lock eyes with Lieutenant Rochester, who appraised him coldly and drew his revolver.

CHAPTER THIRTY-FOUR
Magneto

Back in the trailer, after an unsatisfying meal of store-brand boxed macaroni and cheese and pan-fried hotdogs, Felicity, who had been too preoccupied with final adjustments to eat anything, announced that the mirror was ready for its first official test.

Felicity's mirror looked quite similar to Cole's—she did follow his blueprint, after all. Her loops of metal and wire had the same dimensions, they were attached to a similar circuit board at the base, and two orange power cords snaked out of the back. She plugged them into a nearby outlet. "Work, baby, please," she whispered, caressing the wire-wrapped loop.

They all held their breath. The rings hummed. A screwdriver, left on the floor pointing away from the mirror, swiveled to point directly at it, drawn by the magnetism. Three screws lifted off the cheap pigeon-blue carpet and plinked onto the loop, but no portal appeared.

"What's wrong?" Charlie asked, cutting the tension.

"I don't know," Felicity admitted. She pulled off one of the screws. It took some effort. "The magnetism is pretty strong. It's just not—" she paused, thinking. "It's almost like it isn't drawing enough power."

"How can that be?" Charlie asked. "You plugged it in."

"What about the stove outlet?" Jack asked. "That thing produces what, like twice the amperage of a regular outlet?"

"It does," Felicity agreed, "but it has a different prong configuration. I'd need to replace the cords, and we only have one stove. The mirror requires two equal, harmonized currents."

"Dryer is on the same kind of outlet," Jack said. "I can run off to the store and try and get cords."

"But these are the ones Cole used," Felicity rubbed her temples. "They should work."

"Maybe the problem is that you've got them both in the same plug," Charlie offered, Going to the nearly-empty bookcase for a home repair guide he picked up at Salvation Army. "I don't know much about home electrics. Let me look it up."

Felicity pulled off the other screw and set it on the counter across the room. She went to the stove and scraped some lukewarm macaroni noodles into a bowl. The cheese powder hadn't separated very well and a granular orange clump clung to the wood spoon. She wrinkled her nose at it, returned the spoon to the pot, and went for a fork, leaving the silverware drawer open, as she often did.

"If I get it running, how soon can you two go through?" she asked Jack through a mouthful of mac.

"We're picking up Charlie's donkey tomorrow," he replied. "All our stuff's ready. We just need to organize it, pack it up, and get gone. I'd say we could be headed through in four or five hours, max."

"Says here," Charlie interrupted, "that a circuit can only provide 15 or 20 amps. So, by plugging both plugs into the same one, we're just splitting the energy."

"So we switch outlets?" Jack asked. "Simple enough."

"Not quite," Charlie corrected, "we split it across two *circuits*. We'll have to open the breaker box and figure out which circuit goes to which outlet and be sure we've got them plugged in right."

"So, where's the box?" Jack asked.

"Believe it or not, the box for the trailer is outside." Charlie went to the door. Turn on all the lights in the house. I'll flip switches to figure out which rooms are on which circuits."

Jack went around the place, flipping switches until the house blazed with light. Charlie worked on the breaker box, and the two of them hollered at each other through the open door. Felicity put her empty mac and cheese bowl in the sink and ran the water. She shivered as the cool September night invaded the house and went to the bedroom to pull on a sweater. As she slid it past her head, her eyes fell on the picture above the bed—Cole at age four, eyes twinkling with laughter, playing peekaboo with his one-year-old brother. She smiled despite herself. She'd cried when it arrived in a package from her parents.

"We're coming for you, babies," she whispered. "Hold tight." She kissed her hand and touched the glass.

"We've got it figured out," Jack stuck his head into the room. "Do you have an extension cord? It's got to go into the bathroom."

"Okay," Felicity said, dragging her gaze from the picture and collecting herself. "Okay, um, I don't know that we do have one," she admitted. "We had to buy everything new after the fire, and I cut up the ones I'd bought to make the mirror."

"You know what," Jack snapped his fingers. "I have one in the Bronco. I live out of that thing seven months out of the year. If not, I've got the one out to my tent. Let me go check." He left and she followed. As he passed out through the door, Charlie came in.

"Where's he going"

"To look for an extension cord." She closed the door and wrapped her arms around Charlie.

"Cold?" Charlie asked.

"Yeah," she admitted, "cold, sick, nervous, worried—you name it."

He kissed her forehead. "Me too, but I'm excited as well. This is going to work, I feel it."

"You're putting a lot of faith in a Maryland girl who grew up the daughter of a postman."

"Your dad was only a postman because of the prejudiced world he grew up in—the man was smart enough to have been working at NASA, as evidenced by his daughter."

"Stop with the compliments." She pushed him away. "They didn't work at that Boston bar where you tried to pick me up, and they won't work here." Her eyes were flirtatious. She swatted at a moth that had flown in through the open door. There were five for six of them circling the light fixture.

"Yeah—my compliments didn't work," he chuckled. "Whose ring is that on your finger?"

"Shut up. If it wasn't for that snowstorm, you wouldn't have had a second chance with me."

"Remember the brass band playing Christmas carols while I helped push your car onto the road? I still can't hear a brass version of 'Deck the Halls' without smiling."

"Yeah, I remember," she said.

"You're the one who moved to Boston without buying snow tires and then parked on an uphill grade in a blizzard. Don't blame me for starting this relationship," he joked. "It was entirely your fault."

"Okay," she said. "That's fair, but—" The door opened and Jack came in with an incredibly long cord around his arm.

"Found it," he said, stating the obvious.

"Jeez," Charlie exclaimed, "how long is that thing? What did you do, run a line a half mile so you could plug in your beer fridge beside your tent?"

"Heh," Jack chuckled. "It's a long way to the power sometimes. Always best to be prepared. Let's do this thing." They plugged the first cord into the wall socket, then Jack plugged the second into the extension cord and walked down to the bathroom. "It's in!" he shouted through the door.

The harmonic humming grew louder. Both Felicity and Charlie suddenly felt lightheaded and swooned, leaning into each other. The toolbox rattled and a number of loose screws and a drill bit flew up to stick to the coil. A brief cyan glow appeared at the center of the loop.

"Charlie," Felicity said, grabbing his hand. Jack stepped from the bathroom to watch. At the same moment, though, the toolbox tipped on its side, and every wrench, screwdriver, and loose bit of metal catapulted out, clanging into the coil. It collected screws, nails, hinges, L brackets—even the hammer slammed into it with a metallic clang. Then, the two screws that Felicity had moved to the counter flew by and the open silverware drawer began to disgorge its stainless steel contents.

"Down!" Charlie yelled, pulling Felicity to the carpet as forks and knives passed over their heads, followed by a pot and frying pan.

They were colliding with force now, crashing into the coils and increasing the strain on them. The cyan blue disk forming in the center winked out as the coil lost its circular shape.

"Unplug it, Jack!" Felicity yelled. "Unplug it now!"

He lunged into the bathroom and an instant later the humming stopped. The next second, all of the metal that had been magnetically stuck to the mirror fell off in a heap on the floor. Leftover macaroni splattered onto the circuit board and a wisp of smoke trailed through the air.

Felicity and Charlie stared at the mess, trembling.

Jack emerged from the bathroom. "Successful test." His face was emotionless and deadpan, making a *Ghostbusters* reference that Charlie got immediately, yet chose to ignore.

"It works," Charlie said. "You saw that glow?"

Felicity nodded.

"That was the portal. I recognize it from Cole's video."

"Yeah," she agreed. "I just hope I can fix it—" she ran a hand across the bent metal "—the shape has to be perfect for the field to form—the circle creates the harmonics."

"First we have to clean up this mess." Charlie bent to pick up the pan. "And then we'll have to move everything metal before we turn it on."

"I'll get it fixed. I just hate the delay," Felicity sighed. "It's already been so long. Every added hour is another worry on my shoulders. I hope they're okay over there."

"They're fine," Charlie said. "I have to believe that or I go crazy. I just picture them camped by a river cooking fish over a fire. Maybe Byron's cracking a joke and Cole is laughing. It's easiest to imagine them like that."

Chapter Thirty-Five
In the Jailhouse

Rochester gripped Byron by the neck and forced him back into the jailhouse, his other hand now curled around a silver revolver. Despite the panic clouding his mind and the apparent hopelessness of the situation, Byron did notice a small but important detail: Rochester's hand felt warm against his skin—he was certainly still alive.

"I'd advise you to lower that sword, or the boy dies," Rochester instructed Crowmane as they entered the room. "I would be loath to put a bullet between his young ribs, but a man must do what necessity dictates."

Crowmane lowered the curved bronze blade but did not drop it.

Rochester let go of Byron's neck and motioned to the door. "Close it." Byron complied. "Now, *native*," he addressed Crowmane with distaste, "remove that rifle from your shoulder and drop it on the ground, then both of you into the corner, if you please." He waved his weapon toward the east end of the room.

Crowmane shrugged the rifle onto the ground in a smooth motion. It made a loud clatter as it fell, but he did not relinquish his sword. He moved toward the corner, Byron with him.

"How'd you know?" Byron asked, sullen.

"It wasn't hard, really," Rochester replied, carefully bending to retrieve the rifle and laying it against the wall by the door. "You'd asked about Crowmane's fate, you went to his trial, you defended him with your testimony, and for days you've been introspective and taciturn, moping about the grounds. According to Campbell, you skipped practice with the squires, too—a first. I observed this and then I took a chance on the third-shift when most of us are asleep, and I was rewarded. My only question was whether you'd involve your brother or not—it seems not, but I've got you in here and the door closed, just in case."

"Cole wouldn't help me," Byron admitted. "In fact he forbade me from trying it."

"Smart lad," Rochester nodded. "And yet here you are. Where's the guard?"

"Tied up in the cell," Byron said. "We didn't kill him."

"That mercy may well save your life," Rochester said, "though, even that outcome is far from certain."

"I didn't have a choice," Byron began his defense, "and you don't either."

"I didn't come here to be lectured by you, young Master Oakes." He leaned against the desk, more comfortable now, his gun still pointed vaguely in their direction, and his eyes on Crowmane. "I now must decide what to do with you. Your actions, Byron Oakes, are quite easy to predict, but I'm afraid your friend's are not. He is to be killed soon, so he has nothing to lose, and such men are invariably dangerous. I doubt that I can convince him back into his cage. Logically, I should just shoot him now and be done with it—I'd be fully exonerated, a hero even—but . . ." he trailed off.

"But, as do I, place you value on your honor," Crowmane finished, never taking his eyes from Rochester's face and still holding his blade.

"Indeed," Rochester nodded, "so I will not kill you, spy though you are, in cold blood."

"Which is why you left him his sword," Byron pointed a knowing finger at Rochester, "so that if he made a move, you could kill him in self-defense." Rochester smirked and inclined his head slightly. "You're giving him his trial by combat," Byron observed.

"Perhaps," Rochester admitted.

"Crowmane, drop the blade," Byron instructed. "I didn't risk all of this to watch you die here."

With obvious hesitation Crowmane placed his sword on the plank floor. Rochester lowered his revolver, politely, so that it pointed to the ground near their feet.

"Now what?" Byron asked.

"Now," Rochester said, "as I can no longer shoot an unarmed man, I'm afraid I'll have to demand that you enter the cell and release the guard."

Crowmane nodded and moved toward the cell. Byron mimicked his behavior but steeled himself to act as he passed Rochester. He knew that he had an advantage in speed and thought if he could use those temporal powers Adhita had explained to him, he might be able to knock the gun loose before the Englishman could react. Running through the scenarios in his head, it seemed like his best—perhaps his only—chance for survival.

He'd have to flee with Crowmane, but maybe Cole would understand. And then, if they escaped, he worried, they'd be out in the wilderness with the dragons, jabberwocks, and giant centipedes. Byron shuddered, remembering the trophy room. But he fortified his nerves with the thought that Crowmane would die if he didn't help.

As he passed, he lashed out—backhanded—with his left arm. Rochester saw it and brought the muzzle up, but Byron moved fast as lightning and the lieutenant reacted too late. Byron's fiberglass cast connected with the bright steel and knocked the gun, unfired, from Rochester's grip. It bounced across the floor and slid into the glowing coals of the fireplace.

Rochester pulled back and began to draw his sword. Byron lunged across the room for the discarded blade, and Crowmane turned to face Rochester, the key-ring gripped in his clenched fist.

Rochester swung at Crowmane, but the warrior blocked the slash with a punch, deflecting the blade with the iron ring. Byron picked up the sword and Rochester shifted toward the door and the rifle that reclined against the wall beside it.

"HELP! JAILBREAK! HELP!" Rochester began to yell, his voice echoing through the room.

Byron abandoned his plan of throwing the sword to Crowmane and used the blade to swipe the handgun out of the coals. It skittered back onto the floor. He reached for it but could feel the heat radiating from the metal. The stained wood on the grip was charred. He marveled that the bullets had not yet fired.

Rochester continued to back away, hollering. Crowmane lunged at him, deflecting another sword-blow with the keys. When Rochester made a thrust to drive him back, Crowmane sidestepped and allowed the blade to pass through the center of the ring. When the sabre blade slid halfway, Crowmane twisted it, hard. The metal clanged and grinded, bending the steel and locking the sword in place. He tugged, trying to wrench it from Rochester's hand. When it wouldn't come, he punched at the soldier's head, delivering a solid left-hook.

Rochester took the fist full to the face, which stopped his yelling for a moment. He hadn't defended himself because his left hand had been groping against the wall for the rifle. Now he had it in his grasp. He let his sword fall and began to shift the gun to a firing position, but before he could Byron yelled:

"STOP! I'll shoot—I swear to God I will!" His right arm pointed outstretched and his hand held the revolver. The heat of it burned, but even as he held it, he could feel the metal cooling in his grip. Rochester opened his mouth to speak, but Byron cut him off. "You yell one more time, and I'll have no reason to keep this gun quiet."

Crowmane retrieved Rochester's sabre from the ground and then collected the rifle from the lieutenant, whom Byron had moved to the chair at the desk. They all waited, sure that Rochester's cries for assistance would be answered. Crowmane had his rifle raised to his shoulder, sighted on the door. However no alarm sounded and no footsteps could be heard outside.

After a few tense moments, Byron said, "Go. I'll keep him here until you escape."

"No. Tie him up too. Leave with me."

"I can't," Byron replied, making a fateful decision. "I've been seen, and I won't leave Cole here. Your time is running out—there's no telling how much of it you have left. Someone might've heard. He may have backup coming. Who knows?"

Crowmane nodded. "I understand." Without another word, he threw the rifle strap over his shoulder, opened the door, and disappeared into the twilight.

Rochester watched him go, then put his feet up on the desk and hands causally behind his head. "So," he smiled, "what shall we discuss?"

"Why should I even talk to you?" Byron asked, his emotion and anxiety giving way to anger.

"To pass the time," Rochester shrugged. "My chances of being shot decrease as your friend gets farther away from this room. If I raise the alarm now, you'll shoot me. However, if I give him an adequate head start, you—being a moral person—will slowly become more reluctant to do so. All I have to do is judge when your concern for your friend is no longer enough to risk putting a bullet in my brain." He cleared his throat. "Now, a few moments ago, you claimed to have something of import to tell me, and I rudely silenced you. I apologize. Would you still care to explain yourself?"

"Yeah," Byron frowned. "Yeah, I guess I would. I was saying that you'd understand why I had to let Crowmane out—that you'd do the same thing if you knew what I know—"

"And what is it that you know?"

"That Lord Douglas is a *Danath*—a necroid."

Rochester laughed out loud. "And who told you that rubbish? Crowmane?"

"No. Adhita."

"Did she?" he chuckled again. "Hogwash." He paused, gathering his thoughts. "Perhaps you are unaware that her family has a longstanding feud with Douglas? Her father and mother managed to wrest power over the government from Douglas, and they have threatened to remove and imprison him for crimes they imagine he has committed. She has every reason to poison you against him—and after the way he cares for her, too. Shameful."

"Cares for her? By that you mean he locks her in a tower and forces her to complete calculations for a portal that he hopes to build?"

"Yes, I suppose I do—but he meets her needs. She's fed, clothed, educated, living in comfort, protected from dangers. Did you know, the Lord Douglas even offered to marry her? Some would call that generous."

"Generous?! Ugh!" Byron gagged. "He's an old man and she's a teenager!"

"He's an established gentleman of rank, wealth, and power—that's not infrequently what a woman wants." Rochester rubbed his chin and sat up in the chair. "But you are not a fool, generally speaking, so you must have more evidence than the word of a woman—of a captive, female half-caste."

Byron's eyes narrowed at the pejorative. Being from a mixed family himself, he felt it as a personal insult. "Have you noticed *nothing*?" he asked, his tone taking on the patronizing sound of his mother when she explained the obvious. "Think about it for a moment."

"The lord is eccentric," Rochester said. "I admit that, but certainly not a necroid. He retains all of his flesh. He speaks. He laughs. He coughs. He enjoys music and art. He's every bit as alive as you or me." He folded his arms on his chest.

"He retains all of his flesh, you said. Well, when did you last observe him gain or lose weight?"

Rochester shrugged. "He's a man of moderate routines—established routines."

"I have proof," Byron said, biting his lower lip and looking down at his hand. It throbbed to his heartbeat, clearly burned, but he didn't dare put down the revolver.

"Enlighten me."

"Well, when did you last touch Douglas' skin?"

"I shook his hand yesterday."

"Did he wear gloves?"

"He always wears gloves."

"You don't find that strange?"

Rochester raised a blonde eyebrow. "He's a fashionable man."

"When you shook it, was his hand cold?"

"Cool, but he may have just donned the gloves," Rochester smirked. "His handshake is always firm."

"And when did you last see him eat?"

"Only his valet sees that, since the poisoning. I told you that earlier."

"Have you seen him sweat? He's large—doesn't he ever get hot?"

"Come to think of it, no . . ." Rochester trailed off.

"He likes jokes, right?"

"Sadly, yes," Rochester said. "And he always laughs at his own humor."

"When was the last time he told you a new one?"

Rochester remained silent, his brow furrowed.

"The necroids can't learn, you see," Byron explained, "so he's limited to his past understandings and sayings."

Rochester bit his knuckle in silence and stared into the coals of the fire. Finally, he looked up ". . . So you'd have me believe that my uncle is dead, a ghost or ghoul or something?"

"I think he was poisoned—assassinated by the *Danath*—and reanimated, yes. We think that. Cole, Adhita, and I."

"What about his flesh? It doesn't decay. He doesn't smell—well, no worse than usual, certainly."

"I don't know," Byron admitted, but are the other *Danathskoti*—excuse me, Necrologists—alive? Have you touched their skin, seen them eat, or seen them sweat? I haven't, and I'd bet money they're dead. Maybe they turned him into one of them."

"And where is the proof you offer? All you've provided to me is barefaced circumstance. Nothing clinches your accusation into fact."

"I stuck him with a pin."

"Douglas? A pin?"

"A sewing pin—about two inches long with a white glass

head—at the last entertainment, when the army came to town. You weren't there."

"And?"

"I stuck him in the butt—plunged it right into the fat flesh, up to the glass. Nothing." Byron shuddered and shifted his gaze to the fire, reluctant to recall the experience. "He didn't cry out, wince, or flinch. He made no indication that he felt a thing, and he didn't bleed."

An uncomfortable silence followed. Rochester lowered his voice. He leaned forward in the chair. "You swear to this?"

"Yes. Scout's honor."

"What?"

"Ah," Byron rubbed the back of his neck in embarrassment, "I'm a Boy Scout—a Star Scout, it's two ranks below Eagle—well, it's kind of like being a squire, I guess. We take an oath and have a code. We value honor."

"Tell me your code."

Byron cleared his throat. Memorizing the Oath and Law had been the hardest thing for him in Scouts, and he still occasionally skipped a line or lost his place. "On my honor," he began, "I will do my best to do my duty to God and my country, to obey the Scout Law, to help other people at all times, and to keep myself physically strong, mentally awake, and morally straight."

"A good oath," Rochester nodded. "I approve. And you swear on this?"

"I do."

"To help other people at all times," Rochester repeated and nodded introspectively. "That helps explain why you risked so much for that native. You fulfilled your vow."

"I'm not a liar," Byron said. "Not about important things. Douglas is dead. You're in danger here."

Rochester shifted in his chair. "Well," he sighed, "then I shall certainly consider your words." He took his feet down from the desk. "Who else knows about this?"

"Just Cole and Adhita."

"Not that Crowmane fellow?"

"No. We never got a chance to tell him."

"Then he's not taking this intelligence back to his people. Good."

"What will you do about it?" Byron prompted. "Who will you tell? How do we proceed?"

"Do? Tell? Proceed?" he scoffed. "*We*? My boy, I don't see how I'm in a position to *do* anything. Certainly I'm not going to change a lifetime of allegiance and familial obligations on the sworn word of a stranger."

"But I thought?"

"But nothing—in time I may conduct my own test of your theory." He slapped his thighs and stood suddenly. Byron raised the pistol, his hand shaking. "But," Rochester continued, "with the army leaving to the *Lothka* border this week, it is hardly the ripe moment to break an alliance with half our fighting force. Even if you'd convinced me down to the marrow—which I'm bound to state that you have not—now would not be the time to act." He began to step around the desk. "Now, however, I am going to walk to the door and call the guards. You will be imprisoned, and I shall report your friend's escape to Lord Douglas."

"No—you'll do none of that!" Byron advanced a faltering step.

"I'm afraid I will," Rochester said. "In my judgement, enough time has elapsed to act. Your friend has his head start, and you only stand to lose by shooting me. You've told me your great secret—perhaps I will find it to be true and become the ally you need." He shrugged. "And perhaps not. Shoot me, though, and that will never happen." He put a hand on the door latch. "Kill me and you'll be alone—you'll also be the slayer of Douglas' nephew. That will be a quick death sentence, I assure you."

Byron's arm wavered and the gun lowered in his grasp. He felt so helpless and betrayed that he struggled to hold back tears.

"Weigh your options, young Master Oakes, and I think you'll find that a bullet in my back isn't worth the consequence it would bring, especially since the sound of the shot would alert my guards far better than my actions ever could." He opened the door and stepped out. A smallish brass bell hung from the wall with a cord dangling from it. He reached up and began to ring it. Over his shoulder he said, casually, "I'd put down the gun, if I were you."

Chapter Thirty-Six
Churchill

The Bronco splashed down a muddy one-lane driveway between old cedar fence posts strung with electrified wire. They stood out, darkened by water, against the faded green of the pasture. A single red-tailed hawk hunted from the telephone line, silhouetted against the steel-gray sky. Wind shook a nearby oak, portending the changing weather. Charlie adjusted the knob-twist radio, trying to focus the staticky voice of the newsman. He was giving an update on the Oakes' investigation:

. . . local cold case . . . eight months ago . . .

Charlie finally brought it into focus.

. . . remember how they labeled it arson, and when they thought the two boys living in the house were killed, it became a murder investigation? Well, an interview out of Concord on WPXG last night raised some eyebrows. According to the local police, the boys' remains were never recovered, so it's changed again—from arson, to murder, to kidnapping. They're following leads, but nothing has turned up yet and they'll be bringing in the F.B.I. If you know the Oakes or have some thoughts on the topic, call in to the station and we'll talk, but first if you have information that could help the investigators, or lead to the recovery of the two boys, ages 14 and 17, please call the Crime Stopper's hotline at 1-800-

Charlie twisted the volume to the OFF position. They drove in silence for a full minute.

"F.B.I. huh? Well, at least they haven't caught on yet," Jack observed finally as they thumped across a cow baffle and splashed into a barnyard.

"How would they?" Charlie asked. "They're not equipped for this kind of sci-fi scenario."

"F.B.I. is a government organization. They'll be slow. It'll probably be another eight months before they arrive. We could be back by then. Have you thought about what you'll tell them when you return with the boys?"

"No, I guess I haven't. I just figured I'd tell the truth."

"Well," Jack slowed, looking for a place to park, "you may not want to do that. Government will take the technology from you. They'll probably muck it up, too. God knows what they'd do with it. I'd come up with a convincing lie. It gives you more options."

Charlie raised an eyebrow at him. "You're advising me to lie to the police? To the F.B.I.? Look, lying and stretching the truth may have worked on Mom and Dad, but it's kind of a big deal in the legal world. They'll ask the kids and get their stories, anyway. I don't see how we could bottle this up."

"I suppose," Jack said, unconvinced. "But you give this secret to the government, and we'll be sending troops and aid to Narnia inside of a year. Mark my words."

"Look, at this point I just want my boys. What happens after we get back isn't even on my radar."

"Yeah," Jack nodded. "I get that." The Bronco's brakes squealed as the truck came to a stop next to a muddied John Deere in front of a dilapidated red barn.

"This is the place, huh?"

"Yep," Jack said, opening his door.

Charlie stepped out, too. It began to drizzle. Across the rutted mud, a series of concrete bins were filled with various types of feed. An old windmill creaked above them. Mourning doves cooed, perched on an electric wire that sagged between buildings. The whole place smelled of hay, mud, and manure. "I wonder where—" he began.

"You here about the donkey?" A voice called from behind them. They squinted into the darkness of the barn to see a tall, skinny man with an orange baseball cap and work gloves.

"Yep," Charlie replied. "Seven-year male?"

The man nodded. "You gonna take him in that?" He gestured to the Bronco.

"Guess so," Jack said, sticking his hands in his pockets.

The man shook his head as if to indicate that he thought they were crazy, then said, "Whelp, follow me. I got him back here."

They entered the barn, passing stalls crammed with soft, brown Jersey cows. The man led them down a central corridor around small mounds of fresh manure to the last stall, in which stood a gray donkey, placidly chewing some hay.

"He's a seven-year-old male, alright, just like I told you on the phone. We use him for breeding—making mules. It's a sight when he goes for the ladies." He slapped his knee and smiled.

Jack returned the grin. "I bet," he mused. "Knew a short guy in the service who only liked tall girls. He was 5'-2" and never went for a girl under six foot. Funny guy. Greek heritage. Comical how often he got rejected."

"You a vet?" the man asked.

"Yeah. Panama and Iraq. Infantry."

"I thank you for your service," the farmer said, holding out his hand. "My cousin's stationed in Germany—at Ramstein. He's an airman. I used to be, too, Vietnam. Ordinance."

Jack smirked. "Chair Force," he said. When the man looked angry, Jack backtracked. "I'm just yanking your chain. Your boys won Desert Storm for us. Never had to worry about the sky while driving across the sand." He took his hand. "Thanks."

The farmer nodded.

"We said four-hundred dollars, right?" Charlie asked, taking an envelope out of his jacket pocket and thumbing through some bills.

"Yep," the man agreed, turning to him. "That was the deal." Charlie handed him the envelope and he removed his glove, pocketed it, and shook Charlie's hand. "What you want him for?"

Charlie had foreseen the question. "We're hiking and camping out west for a few months—in the mountains—he's going to come with us and carry our gear."

"And you're going to drive him out there in the back of that Bronco?" the man laughed. He went into the stall, slipped a rope around the animal's neck and led it out.

"Nah. We're borrowing a trailer," Jack lied as they passed out of the barn. "Just don't have it today is all."

The man handed the rope to Charlie, and didn't say anything else, just watched with an amused twinkle in his eye as the two brothers made fools of themselves trying to negotiate a 220-pound donkey into the back of a Bronco.

Charlie held the animal's lead while Jack swung the spare tire out and lowered the tailgate. He went in and folded down the rear bench seat.

"How do you want to do this?" Charlie asked as Jack came around.

"I dunno," Jack shrugged. "I suppose he won't just jump in like a dog."

"Nope."

"Well, why don't you take one side and I'll take the other and we'll lift him in."

"Sure," Charlie agreed, his voice uncertain. The two brothers stood on either side of the donkey, reaching under it in a kind of awkward fireman's carry.

"Lift with the knees," Jack instructed. They did, but the donkey's legs were only a foot or two off the ground, and the tailgate of Jack's lifted Bronco opened nearly four feet high. They set the donkey down. It still chewed placidly. A soft rain continued falling.

"Look," Charlie said, "you climb in through the front and take the rope. I'll push from the rear." Jack followed the instructions and Charlie handed him the rope through the tailgate. He pulled and Charlie pushed, but the donkey didn't budge. Charlie's feet slipped in the mud and he ended up on his face. Pushing up, cold and dripping, unsure how much of the 'mud' was cow poop, he grumbled. "Stubborn ass."

"Looking good, Charlie," Jack quipped, giving him two thumbs up and a smile.

"And you're a smartass," Charlie retorted.

"At least you didn't call me Jackass," Jack winked.

Charles rolled his eyes. "Dad called to approve that pun." He turned to the tall, lanky farmer who grinned broadly. "What's his name?" he pointed a thumb to the donkey.

"Churchill," the man replied.

"Like the British prime minister?"

The man shrugged. "I guess. My wife named him—she watches a lot of PBS."

"You mean BBC?"

"Same thing, Masterpiece Theatre. It don't bother me, though, gives me an excuse to read *Bowhunter.* Got a new issue yesterday."

"You going to help us with this or what?" Jack asked, climbing out of the truck, his tone belligerent.

"Just waiting for you boys to ask, is all," the man replied. "You need motivation." He went into the barn and came out with an old cottage cheese container filled with feed. "A donkey is half stomach. You two lift his forequarters onto the tailgate and I'll wave this in front of his face. When he gets interested, lift the hindquarters."

It worked. Five minutes later, the two were pulling away from the farm with a live donkey awkwardly stuffed into the rear of the Bronco. Charlie sat next to him, stroking his head to keep him calm.

"You know," Jack observed, trying to use humor to console Charlie for his soaked clothes and hurt pride, "this feels disturbingly similar to that unfortunate scene from the movie with the deer in the convertible," referencing a comedy that had come out the previous year. "Saw it in the theater."

"Thankfully this has a hardtop and Churchill here doesn't have any antlers" Charlie laughed, and rapping his knuckles on the roof.

"And we're not a couple of idiots," Jack added with a shake of his head, a smile melting from his face. He became suddenly serious and contemplative. "Charlie, as bad as this whole thing is, I'm glad to spend time with you."

"Yeah," Charlie agreed, pursing his lips. "Sorry it takes something like this to make it happen. I guess I just got lazy."

"Complacent, more like," Jack observed. "Married, fat, and happy. You're content and I'm . . ." he paused. "If I'm being honest, I suppose I'm a bit jealous and embarrassed—always feel like I'm butting in on your busy, educated, middle-class life—me a single, high-school-diploma-holdin' seasonal logger—at least, that's the excuse I use for not calling."

Charlie nodded. "I always assume you're out in the woods, away from a phone."

"You know," Jack sighed, "we let life get in the way. We don't see each other because we feel like it's inconvenient, expensive, or the timing isn't right. They're all excuses, every last goddamned one of them."

Charlie locked eyes with him for a moment in the rear view. He knew his brother well enough to tell when he needed to talk and not be interrupted.

"And," Jack continued, "we cheat ourselves out of what we need to save a few days or dollars, or because it's easier to live in past moments than make new ones. It's been what? Three years since we seen each other? And we'll do it again after this is over. We'll fall back to old ways. It's who we are. Brothers," he chuckled sadly, "brothers—we're there for each other when the chips are down, but when they aren't, we don't make the effort. We always understand each other in crisis, but we just assume everything is fine the rest of the time, and we miss out on . . ."

"On everything," Charlie finished. "Truth is," he chewed his lip, "I have the boys and I watch them and think of us. They spend every moment together, get on each other's nerves, laugh together, and grow together. They're like grafted trees—both separate and unique, but both one. We were that way, too. Spent half our lives joined, and then . . ."

"We grew up?"

"We drank the American social Kool-Aid that said growing up was about independence, freedom, and self-reliance—said growing up meant abandoning others to find yourself. Well, turns out we abandoned the bonds that made us who we were. And I've always dreaded the day that Cole and Byron would do the same."

"Grafted trees, you say? That supposed to be a metaphor?"

"Yeah."

"Well, grafted trees share common roots. Cut out the roots, and they both die. We don't see each other enough, Charlie. Life's better together. We gotta act on that. But even if we don't, our shared experiences—they don't change. They get buried, but they still feed us. Roots. Jesus," he shook his head. "Listen to me—I sound like goddamned Sigmund Freud."

"So, what's the bottom line here?" Charlie asked. "You've been thinking on something and you haven't said it all yet."

"Yeah," Jack nodded. He pulled out of the dirt lane and onto the main road. The rain picked up enough that he adjusted the wipers. The wheels hissed against the wet pavement and the exhaust rumbled. "Yeah. I guess I'm trying to say that brothers get shortchanged here. We're taught to be tough and then use toughness as a wedge and drive it between ourselves and our families and pry ourselves loose. We bleed, but we do it in proud silence and then scar over. It makes us distant. Anyway, sisters—they don't split. They stay in touch. They put in the effort." He paused. "Hell, man, I don't even know what I'm saying." He reached out and snapped the radio back on.

"Yeah," Charlie agreed. "I don't either. But," he said as *The Eagles* "Desperado" filled the air, "I do know that you're coming for Christmas *every* year from here on out. And a camping trip with the boys. No excuses."

"Agreed," Jack said. "Hey?"

"What?" Charlie asked, prepared for some kind of joke or harassment.

"Can our trip to Narnia count as this year's campout?"

"Yeah," Charlie laughed. "Sure. Why not?"

CHAPTER THIRTY-SEVEN
Justice

Byron had been pacing the cell for hours. As Crowmane must have done before him, he assessed it for weaknesses. There were none. The front face of the cell was a forged lattice of iron bars, and the walls, floor, and ceiling were made of sun-dried mud-brick, the mortar firm. The cell's thin window was barred. It was visited, from time to time, by his single companion in the cell, an old black raven that was probably looking for Crowmane.

After a nap, Byron worked to complete a second, more thorough inspection in the pale light, when the outside door opened to reveal the form of Lord Douglas. Douglas entered the building, accompanied by Aquinas Justice, who immediately dismissed the guard. Then, Justice used the jangling key ring to open the cell door, and the two entered.

Byron turned to them, composing his face into what he hoped seemed a defiant expression. He looked Douglas in the eye. Surprisingly, it was Justice who spoke.

"I hear from Douglas that you had a talk with his nephew," he said. "For now, Douglas has convinced Rochester that you're just spreading lies, but *I* do not wish those lies to go any farther, so let me be clear." He advanced on Byron, took him by the throat in a cold, steel grip, lifted him high off the ground with one arm, and thrust him against the wall, gasping for breath. His feet dangled, helplessly. Justice waited a few moments, then leaned in and repeated himself with a hint of his Jamaican accent: "Let me be clear, boy: if I hear ONE more word about your conspiracy theory—from *anyone*—I will stop your talk forever by cutting the tongue from your mouth, removing it at its root. Do you understand me, boy?"

Byron tried to reply, but only sputtered and choked. He nodded his head, fractionally. Stars swam in his vision and just as he thought he might pass out, Justice dropped him, gasping and crying, into a crumpled ball on the ground. The raven fluttered down to land between the bars of the window and rasped a throaty caw in Justice's direction before ascending again. The bodyguard paid it no mind.

"We need you alive to motivate your brother, so you will

continue to breathe—for now" he said.

"But I thought . . . Douglas?" Byron managed to croak through aching vocal cords.

Justice glanced at Douglas who stood nearby, impassive and staring blankly at the far wall. Justice laughed, a deep, cold sound. "You thought Douglas was the boss-man here? An easy error to make, and one that I encourage after my sacrifice to Syrinkeri." He gestured to Douglas. "I am his killer and I am his master. And I am immortal, and *I* hold the power here. And," he paused for a moment. "I have plans for your flesh. Take off one shoe, or I will take off the foot that it covers."

Byron wanted to ask why, but he felt certain that Justice would make good on his threat, so he hurried to comply.

Chapter Thirty-Eight
Icarus

"Why did he do it?" Cole asked Adhita for the sixteenth time. As it was an obvious rhetorical question, she offered no answer. "Why'd you do it, Byron?" he pleaded to no one.

Cole had been pacing the floor of the tower for hours, ever since he'd been awakened and escorted there by Douglas' guards. Glimpsing Byron's empty bed on his way out the door, it didn't take him more than a few seconds to reason out what must have happened.

"Fool. Idiot. Moron," he repeated, driving his fist into his palm, still pacing, his mind already producing escape plans, calculating odds of success, and rejecting them, one by one. He felt angry with Byron, certainly, but far stronger than his anger was his concern. "Do you think they'll kill him?" he asked, finally.

"They haven't yet killed me," Adhita offered, spreading her hands. "So, no, I don't think they'll kill him unless it suits their purpose. I cannot see the advantage to it at the moment."

"Okay, okay. So we get out. We rescue him. What choice do we have?"

Adhita smiled sadly and crossed to Cole, the fabric of her sapphire dress swishing. She placed a thin-fingered hand on his forearm. "That may not be possible." "I've been trying to escape for years, without the kind of scrutiny you can expect now, and without an army encamped outside." She sighed. "And I'm still right here, where Douglas wants me."

Just then the door opened and Douglas stepped in, followed by his intimidating and silent bodyguard.

"Speak of the devil," Adhita said, dryly.

"A pleasure to see you, milady, as always," Douglas quipped, then he turned to Cole. "It can be no mystery to you, why I've come." He paused. "I have your brother in my custody. He aided a known spy in his escape from my prison, so by definition, he is guilty of treason and should be put to death by firing squad."

"No!" Cole gasped.

"Yes," Douglas corrected. "But I intend to keep him in prison for a long while, ere that execution occurs—if, *if*" he repeated, "you cooperate with me fully."

"What do I need to do?" Cole asked.

"What you're already doing, my boy—make me my mirror."

"What do you want with it?" Adhita cut in. "What can you possibly want with it?"

Douglas smiled, winningly. "Why, to go home, as I have always declared, to stand once again under a noon-high sun."

"But you don't have a home. You're—"

"Justice!" Douglas interrupted. "Shut the door, if you please." The bodyguard nodded solemnly and complied. After it clicked shut, Douglas resumed his smile. "But I'm what, my dear? Dead?"

Adhita bit her lip and nodded.

"I brought you here as a political pawn, but I kept you for your brain," Douglas said. "It does not surprise me that you found me out, clever girl. How long have you known?"

"A year," she replied.

"And you've kept it a secret all that time? Brava." His left eye shifted to Cole. "I suppose I should thank these Oakes brothers for helping to reveal your deception. Perhaps you shouldn't have trusted them so fully."

"Perhaps," she agreed, averting her gaze.

"What will you do with the mirror once I make it?" Cole asked.

"The use I have for the mirror will remain my business," Douglas responded, shifting his other eye to Cole as well, "as will the nature of my existence. If either of you breathe a word of it to anyone, I will execute young Byron—painfully. Am I understood?"

"Yes," Cole nodded. He gripped the back of a chair with white-knuckled hands. "Perfectly clear, sir."

"Capital," Douglas nodded. "My boy, I appreciate the polite and compliant tack you have decided to take. It will pay you dividends." He stopped and thought for a moment. "It has been long since I lived in the old world. Tell me, do they still tell the tale of Daedalus and Icarus?"

"The Greek inventor and his son?" Cole asked.

"Exactly," he clapped his hands together. "You, Colton Oakes, are my Daedalus. I'm your King Minos, and I have you in my tower, inventing an incredible contraption in my name. Your brother, Byron, you understand, is my Icarus."

"They escaped," Adhita observed tartly.

"Indeed," agreed Douglas, "but I have an advantage that Minos did not. I am not burdened with emotion. Evil though he might have been, Minos had a daughter and out of a feeling of parental compassion, left Daedalus his son to keep him company—an act of mercy that planted the seed of his downfall. In contrast I am utterly heartless. You, Colton Oakes, will never see your brother again unless the mirror is complete and functional. What's more, Byron—my Icarus—will be your motivation to succeed."

"What do you mean?" Cole asked.

"Today," he reached into his coat pocket and withdrew a small leather bag, "I have removed a piece of his body—a token of my determination." He opened the bag and tipped it upside down. A small, brownish bit of flesh fell onto the table. A pale toenail indicated what it was.

Adhita covered her mouth with a hand but did not take her eyes off the grisly, severed toe.

In contrast, Cole's expression filled with rage—he hollered, taking up the chair he'd been holding and swinging it with all his might, intending to smash Lord Douglas where he stood.

The chair connected with Aquinas Justice's blade, mid-swing, and shattered, sending chunks of wood in all directions. Stunned, he didn't even have time to react to the bodyguard's vicious backhand.

Crack! The hand—hard as oak—hit him in the face and sent him sprawling. Adhita crouched beside him, soothing him with her outstretched fingers. Blood dripped from his lip and nose; he tasted its iron tang on his tongue. Both prisoners looked up at Douglas.

"Work as hard as you like," Douglas said, his voice now crisp and businesslike. "Stay up all hours. Burn out your life with the midnight oil. I will have my mirror, and every two weeks, if I don't get it, you will find another bit of your brother on this table." He rapped the workbench with his knuckles. "We'll take toes first, then fingers, ears, nose, lips, tongue—the unessential bits. You're both talented mathematicians. You can calculate the progression on some kind of timeline."

"But," Adhita stammered.

"And if either of you tries to escape, you'll find an arm or a leg slapped down on that table. Even after that, we can make him last a long, long time, I promise you."

Cole was openly crying now.

Douglas' expression softened. "Ah, sorrow. The beauty of having once been alive is that I recognize your primitive emotions, know when they are appropriate or inappropriate, and am able to precisely mimic them—in everything but tears. Free from emotion myself, I now use it to manipulate the living—to manipulate you." He nodded to Justice. "We're finished with them, for now. Farewell, my young Daedalus."

The door closed on Cole and Adhita. She ran her fingers through his curling hair. "It's okay," she soothed. "Everything is going to be—no." She interrupted herself. "No. It's not. I won't lie to you or delude you. I've been a prisoner here long enough to give up my delusions and accept life for what it is. It's not okay, and it never will be again."

"It will be," Cole sniffled and wiped his bleeding nose on his sleeve. "I'm not going to sit here and take this."

"What will we do, then?"

"We're breaking out. He wants a Daedalus? I'll give him a goddamn Daedalus—a genius escape artist." He stood, dipped a cloth in a water pitcher near the door, and began to daub the blood off his lip.

"You have a plan?"

"The start of a plan," Cole said, "And we have exactly thirteen days to carry it out—less, he corrected. If Byron is going to be a long-term prisoner, they won't keep him in that little jail for long. They'll move him inside to an undisclosed location, and then we'll really be screwed. So, we've got to act fast."

"What can I do?"

"Start making a list of materials. We need an iron ring with a four-foot diameter. We'll need a mile or two of thick copper wire, wire-cutters, and insulators—you don't have rubber or plastic, so we'll need clay and beeswax."

Adhita went to a slate chalkboard that covered one wall and began to write them down. "But, Cole, aren't those materials for making a mirror?"

"Yes, and we'll make one that looks real. And we'll get the materials because we're making it. I'll also need thick leather gloves. Oh, and I'll get an escort down to the powerplant to take a tour—I'll need to know how much voltage it can produce, how long it takes to start producing power, it's hours of operation—that sort of thing."

"Am I going to be privy to this secret plan?" Adhita asked.

"Of course," Cole replied. "You're going to assist me every step of the way. In fact, maybe you can help me with some of the particulars now. Do you know the train schedule by heart?

"No, I'm afraid not—well, maybe that's not true. I'll try to piece it together from memory. The *Royale* comes and goes every other week."

"Good. Get it done this afternoon, then, and we'll observe it this week. When it leaves and arrives—when the train is sitting at the station—see if it matches up. We need that train. It's our escape vehicle."

"But the telegraph line"

"We'll cut it—"

"But—" she interrupted.

He interrupted her in return.

"AND then we'll wrap it around the caboose of the train, so as we flee, we pull down all the wire between here and the next station. The wire is connected to glass fasteners. It should come down easily enough."

Adhita smiled. This determined, brilliant side of Colton was new to her, and she loved it. "How do we escape?"

"Like Daedalus," Cole smiled. "Through the window."

"Flying? It's a sixty-foot drop."

"If we have to," Cole said. "I'd rather use the wires, though." He gestured to the electrical lines leading out of their room and down to the powerplant. "Right now, however, I've got to get the power on and find a way to charge the batteries to my Walkman, and to amplify the speakers." He pulled the dead device out of his pocket and plumped it down on the table, opening the compartment and pulling out two double-As. I bet I can rig up a charger and splice it to the wires here. If I can control the current, I can juice them up. It may not be new tech, but it has a voice recorder and playback." He ejected the tape, The Counting Crows' *August and Everything After*. "I just have to fill the divots at the top of the cassette and—presto—we've got audio."

Adhita shook her head in confusion.

"Don't worry. I know what I'm doing." He returned to thinking aloud. "I wish we could get rope, but Douglas is no fool. Do you have a belt with a sturdy buckle in your wardrobe? Two would be better than one."

She raised an eyebrow at him. "A belt? Made of leather?"

"Yeah—the thicker the better."

She smirked. "I suppose women wear pants in the year nineteen-hundred and ninety-six? Well, they don't here. I have many, many things that may be termed 'belts,' but nothing as utilitarian as you men wear."

"I'll have my wardrobe transferred up here—they provided both Byron and me with some clothes. Don't put that on the list," Cole smiled, "And, yeah, women wear pants in 1996, and they work and get paid, and vote, and hold elected office."

"Is America such a paradise for women?" she asked, incredulous.

"No," Cole replied. "It's not. Trust me, equal in law isn't the same as equal in fact or equal in treatment."

Adhita nodded, surveying the chalkboard. "Will we need anything else?"

"Yeah," Cole answered, back on topic and totally focused again. "I need two long leather straps—one inch in width and at least four feet long. And a small lantern. I have to communicate with Byron down in the jail to know if they've moved him or not. I wish I knew Morse code—all the nerds in books and movies seem to know Morse code, but not me. Byron doesn't know it, anyway. If he knew binary we could work something out. At least I'll be able to wink at him out the window."

"Just so you know," Adhita said, "I followed very little of that."

"Heh," Cole chuckled. "Sorry. I get caught up sometimes." He gripped her by the shoulders and kissed her forehead. "I'm going to do this," he said, into her hair. "*We're* going to do this. We're getting out of here, or I'm not Colton Oakes." Before he could turn to begin pacing again, she folded him in a tight hug.

"You remember when Douglas said I shouldn't have trusted you?"

"Yeah."

"Well, he was wrong."

"Dead wrong," Cole agreed.

CHAPTER THIRTY-NINE
Cracked Mirror

Charlie and Jack entered the trailer, dripping. The September rain soaked the ground, and they'd been out in it for the past hour, rigging up a donkey pen out of a tarp, rope, and lashed tree branches. They'd filled it with straw bales and Churchill looked relatively comfortable as they left—at least he stood, placidly chewing on a bale of hay they brought with them.

"I know it's 51 degrees out there, but I'm freezing," Charlie said, stripping off his soaked coat and hat and shivering. "Felicity, where do you want us to unload this wet stuff."

"Uh, just hang it in the bathtub," she said, absently, as she tinkered with the mirror. It looked good enough to be in working condition.

"We going to fire her up tonight?" Jack asked.

"Hope to."

"What's for dinner?"

"Frozen pizza. You want to preheat the oven?"

"Yeah," Charlie handed his coat to Jack and crossed to the fridge.

"I hope it's supreme," Jack remarked, heading toward the bathroom. "Only box pizza worth eating is supreme."

"Nah, just pepperoni," Charlie said, his head in the freezer.

"Once you get those in the oven," Felicity instructed, "see if you can't clean up anything metal and take it to the bedroom. I don't want a repeat of the other night."

"Can do" Charlie replied. "You want a cup of tea?" He put a mug of water in the microwave and dialed in two minutes.

"No thanks."

"How about you, Jack?" Charlie hollered.

"Tea?" Jack's incredulous voice came from the bathroom. "That tree piss? That's a big ol' negative."

A cup of chai, three slices of pizza, scrubbed and dried dishes, and an iron and steel roundup later, Charlie sat on the futon with Jack, watching Felicity put the finishing touches on her repairs.

"So, it's time to nail down some of the details of how we're going to manage this," Charlie said.

"Such as?" Felicity asked.

"Well, you're staying here and keeping the portal open," Charlie pointed out. "But you can't just leave it on 24-7. That's how our house burned down. I think maybe an hour or two a day."

"Okay," she said, twisting a screw. "How will you know where the portal appears after you've left?"

"We'll build a cairn of stone, like the trail markers on Mt. Washington."

She nodded, glancing back and forth between her laptop and the circuit board. "One of these chips looks a little fried," she mumbled.

"I think we've got enough money to get by," he stayed on his subject. "Truth is, even given what's happened, I'm going to lose my job at the university any day. As it is, I've used up a decade worth of sick days."

"We've talked about this," she said, arranging the tools in the tool box. "The job doesn't matter compared to getting my boys back. I've got the disability check. It'll stretch our savings. We've still got about a quarter of the insurance check left. I'll do per diem telework to get some more, too. I'll manage."

"How will you defend yourself?" Jack cut in. "Can I leave you a handgun?"

"I don't do guns," Felicity replied, leveling a stare at him that chilled the room. She cleared her throat. "I know you guys need to take them with you—I understand that, but that doesn't mean I want one here."

"You'll be all alone," Jack persisted, "and who knows what might come through that thing." He gestured to the mirror. "Felicity, you're being foolish—"

Charlie reached out and put a hand on Jack's arm. He gave him a look that said, *I'll handle this, later*, and Jack shut his mouth.

Felicity took up the tool chest and carried it to the bedroom. She shut the door behind her when she came back out. "Charlie," she stopped outside the bathroom and bent to pick up the extension cord, "can you go plug in the other one?"

"Yep," he replied, plugging it in. The mirror hummed again, coming to resonance. Everyone felt lightheaded. Charlie leaned against the wall. Just like last time, a cyan glow appeared in the center of the circle. It began to expand, revealing a shimmering scene of fern, trees, and mountains.

"Hot damn!" Jack exclaimed from across the room. "It's working!" As if the words were a curse, though, smoke started to waft up from the circuit board. Sparks burst from it, smelling of electrical heat, and the portal winked out. Charlie pulled his cord from the wall, but too late. So did Felicity.

Checking the circuit board, she begged, "Please don't be bad. Please don't be bad," and then found where the damage had occurred. She sighed. "It's only one chip, the one I worried about. I'll call tomorrow, order two, and overnight them." She began typing into her computer.

"Looks like we've got a couple more days, Jack," Charlie sighed. "What do we need to do still?"

"Nothing," he replied. "You could still use some more physical training, but it'd take a month or two—nothing you could improve by tomorrow."

"I have an idea, but I don't know how practical it is," Charlie said. "We have walkie talkies, but the batteries will die. Batteries are heavy to pack and carry—even with a donkey. How about a solar charging apparatus and rechargeable batteries?"

"Where'd you get one of those on short notice?" Jack asked. "I doubt it's at the local RadioShack."

"Point," Charlie conceded, then snapped his fingers. "We could call tomorrow, overnight ship it, too."

Felicity sighed, her fingers typing faster.

"What's the matter?" Charlie asked.

"In all the online catalogs, it's listed as backordered," she replied, her tone desperate. "Backordered everywhere. There's a notice claiming it'll be a month—a month, Charlie!" Tears welled in her eyes.

"Why?" He asked. She typed a question into the *Mosaic* browser.

"There was a catastrophic fire at the factory that makes them, in Guangdong, China."

"Are there pictures of it?" Jack asked.

"Of the microchip? Why?"

"No, of the fire. Is there an image?"

"Um," Felicity scrolled down the screen, "no."

"Then you can bet it wasn't a fire," Jack replied, a smug look on his face. "My guess is labor strikes being hushed up by the communist party leaders. Can't trust a thing that comes out of state-run news outlets. They won't show anything that makes them look bad. Hard to hide stuff from a free press, though."

"Can you fix the chip you have?" Charlie cut in, bringing the focus back to the mirror.

"No chance," Felicity said, clicking through more search results.

"What about coming at it a different way." Charlie asked. "What else has that chip in it?"

"What do you mean?" Felicity asked.

"I mean, if it's a component in say a computer, a motherboard, or—I don't know—video game console or something, we buy the product and remove the chip for our own use."

Felicity smiled, stood, and kissed him. "Charlie Oakes, sometimes you're a genius—not often." She patted his cheek, "but occasionally. Now, if you'll excuse me boys, I have some research to do." She scooped up the laptop and carried it off into the bedroom, dragging the ethernet cable behind her. Once inside, she swung the door closed.

Charlie ran a hand through his hair. "Let's drop by RadioShack tomorrow to research solar charging stations," he said to Jack. "We may have time to order it after all."

"Sure," Jack agreed. "If we have time, I'd like to stop by Blockbuster, too. I think *Independence Day* hits video this week. We missed it in the theater. Haven't seen a movie in months."

CHAPTER FORTY
Daedalus' Flight

Nearly 130 sleep-deprived hours after the confrontation with Douglas, the train was preparing to depart, and Cole and Adhita stood ready to carry out their plan. It was dangerous—any number of things could go wrong with it, and it was elaborate (at least as convoluted as the plan to save Han Solo in *Return of the Jedi*, Cole worried), but it was the only one they had. Cole intended to make the most of it.

Wind blew into the lab through the open window, cool and humid. It was the onset of afternoon shift in the castle. The gray sky, tinged with rose, muted the shadows below as Cole looked out over the grounds. The squires practiced in the yard, their blades chiming. Cole gnawed his lip with impatience. They couldn't begin their escape until the proverbial coast was clear. He went over his preparations one more time. He'd managed to charge the Walkman batteries from the unstable current of the power line—the hardest part about the plan, but they'd done it without melting anything or setting fire to the place. After "testing the charge" by listening to the album with Adhita (it was difficult to be listening to his favorite album for what he assumed might be the last time, overwhelmed by nostalgia and regret, while she heard it for her first), he'd filled the tabs and recorded half an hour of conversation that would playback through makeshift volume amplifiers after they left, fooling the guard who stood outside the door. He'd have to leave the Walkman behind, but that'd be no big loss.

Weighing down one hip pocket of Cole's pants were wire cutters, and the other, a pair of heavy, flexible leather gloves that they'd coated with beeswax—they'd be for handling the electric wires. He hoped they'd provide enough resistance, or their plan would go belly-up in a hurry.

He looked out at the power plant. No smoke rose from the brick stack, perfect. They'd be traversing the wires, and the plant had shut down for the day, as it did every day for the second shift—they were supposed to run their electrical experiments during first and third. He shifted his gaze to the train. In contrast to the inoperative power plant, smoke rose lazily from the engine, drifting away from the mountains in the breeze. Its scheduled departure in about two hours meant they had to make their escape during a relatively busy time. They needed the train's boiler hot in order to make a fast getaway, so they were pushing their timing close to the edge.

"I hope it rains," Adhita interrupted his thoughts. "People stay inside in the rain, and they keep their heads down. They won't see our escape, or the smoke when we start the generator back up."

Cole nodded. "Only downside to rain is the water." He jangled some thin copper wire that he wore coiled around his chest. "This stuff isn't insulated with anything more than a layer of wax, and we'll be running it across the ground and into Byron's cell. I don't want the current to ground in pools or puddles before it gets there."

"Look, there they go." She pointed out the window as the squires formed up and began to tromp into the fortress. Cole stuck his hand out the window.

"And here comes your rain."

She smiled, grimly, her dark eyes glinting with determination. "Are you ready, Colton Oakes?"

"Yeah," Cole nodded. "You want to go first or me?"

"I'll go," Adhita said, pulling a chair over to the raised window. She stood on it, wrapped a loose brown belt around her shoulder like a sash and then looped a thick leather strap around the electrical wire, tying it in some form of hitch that left room for it to slide along the wire. Twisting the rest of the strap around her right hand and gripping it with her left, she readied herself to take the plunge.

"Tell me the plan one more time," Cole prompted before she could step onto the windowsill, "so I know that you know what you're going to do."

She looked annoyed for a moment then took a deep breath to center herself. "I'll slide down to the first pole. Then I'll loop this belt around it," she tapped the one over her shoulder, "and descend. I go straight toward the wall and from there through the gate to the powerplant, where I'll restart the generator and stoke the fire. Once the power's on, I go to the train depot and wait for you."

"Good." Looking up at her, he took her hand. He kissed it. "Good luck, and no matter how this fiasco ends up, I'm glad to have met you."

"Likewise, Colton Oakes," she agreed, then stepped from the chair to the windowsill, lifted her legs and began to slide down the power line, her storm-gray dress flapping behind her.

Clearly tense, Cole watched as she ziplined away from him, closer and closer to the first electrical pole. The moment when she made contact would be dangerous. If she lost her grip, she'd fall 40 feet to the ground.

He exhaled as she made it, then held his breath again as she fumbled with the leather belt, struggling to fasten it around the pole and herself while holding onto the strap. The complicated process looked far harder than he imagined—like some kind of athletic challenge on *American Gladiators* on TV. For a few agonizing seconds he felt sure she would drop the belt or fall, but then she had it secure and used the belt like a lumberjack to lower herself down the pole. It was a process, but when she stood on the ground, she turned to him, mock-saluted, and ran off toward the nearest wall.

He went to his Walkman, turned the volume up to full, and pushed PLAY. His and Adhita's voices—a bit tinny, but clear and crisp—came out of the headphones, magnified through the megaphone that he'd designed. He scribbled some final instructions on his note to Byron and stuffed it in his back pocket. He then ran a five-foot belt through the loops of his blue jeans. He shuddered imagining the descent he'd have to make.

He glanced back into the room one more time. Their mock-mirror loop sat in the center, attached to the power source. He didn't think it would fool Douglas, but if he touched it while power still flowed, he'd be rather *shocked*. Cole chuckled, appreciating his own humor; he was a regular James Bond with these puns.

He stepped to the open window and stood on the chair. Then, taking a thick leather strap, he hitched it over the line as Adhita had done, wrapped it around his hand and gripped tightly. Stepping from the chair into the windowsill and crouching there, he looked down and froze. His grip clenched onto the strap and he reached his off hand to steady himself against the wood frame.

His heart hammered in his chest. At least sixty feet up and atop the hill, the ground fell terrifyingly far away. Cold sweat broke out on his face and the palms of his hands—hands, he realized with a shiver, that he needed to grip the strap and manipulate the belt around the pole. Closing his eyes and holding his breath, he lifted his feet.

Cool air rushed by his face and raindrops peppered his skin as he slid down the line. Faster than he expected—the wire angled steeply. He felt the impact as he stopped at the pole and swung back and forth in mid-air. Hanging from his right fist, the leather strap cutting into it under his weight, he opened his eyes and used his left hand to slide the belt around the electrical pole and fasten it. Bracing his feet against the wood, he leaned back, felt the belt take his weight, and cautiously released the strap. He hung there, braced by a single leather belt, forty feet in the air atop a pole.

"So, this is what it's like to be a linesman for NEHC," he said, looking around and thinking about the hard-hatted power workers he'd seen in their cherry-picking trucks. He also thought of Uncle Jack cutting trees in Maine. They all had to master their fears. If they could, he could too. And if he failed, it'd be an arm or leg hacked off Byron. Rather than scare him, the thought braced his nerves. He wouldn't fail.

The rain fell harder now. From his high position, he watched a soldier, head down, traverse the courtyard to the fortress. A guard paced the wall far away. His gaze focused outward at the small sea of tents encamped beyond—the Great Mountain Army. Looking at it, Cole realized, with a start, that the area was alive with activity. Tents were being stowed, and some men were forming up in battalions as if preparing to march. He had no time to consider the implications—he had work to do.

Now, where Adhita had simply been able to descend, Cole had to stay up and maneuver for a few moments. He needed to remove the spool of thinner gauge copper wire from his shoulder and splice it onto the main lines. Then he'd descend and unspool them until he reached the guardhouse—maybe 100 yards away. He glanced toward the powerplant. He thought he could see wisps of smoke from the stack. Adhita was efficient—he found himself as attracted to her competence as to her looks, but if she got the power back before he made it down, her competence would fry him alive.

Still sick from the dizzying height and with shaking hands, he unwound some of the wire and reached up. Using the cutters, he scraped off what remained of the wax insulation and then began his work.

Chapter Forty-One
Electricity

Byron sat on his hard, wooden cot, nursing his throbbing foot. He aired it out, shoeless. He wiggled his toes and winced. Two toes to the right, two to the left, and a gap in the middle—a mass of clotted blood. He shuddered, remembering it, and tears came to his eyes, not for the first time.

What was a toe, anyway? he asked himself. Not a big injury, not a finger that would hamper sports, not obviously disfiguring like missing teeth or a broken nose. Plenty of hockey players had worse. The raven descended in a flurry of blustering feathers to land in the window.

"Caw!" it called, tilting its head toward him. He stood abruptly and hobbled over to it. Before he could get there, it took off again, back to the roof.

Byron looked up at Douglas' tower. For the last three days he'd grown accustomed to signals from Cole: flashes of light, a candle or something. It took him a day, but he'd been able to signal back. He waited for the sliver of sunset to be opposite his window. He'd removed his Boy Scout belt, polished the back of the buckle with spit and sand, and sent random blinks back. He couldn't say anything more than "I'm here. I'm alive," but it'd been enough. They were still connected. Crowmane hadn't reappeared, so Byron felt content about that, anyway—it seemed that the *Lothka* champion must have made good his escape.

Byron sighed, staring wistfully out into the gray clouds and through increasing rain at the tower, and drew in a sharp breath. There, suspended in midair from an electrical pole, maybe a football field away, he made out a backlit form against the sky. He couldn't tell for sure, but Byron would have bet his whole bank account that it was his brother.

He spun around to assure himself that the guard wasn't looking, then stared back out, riveted. The form descended now, a slow process. He looked like he'd fastened himself to the pole by a rope or something. Byron scanned the area, hoping that no one moved out there. The courtyard stood empty. A solid rain poured down, hissing on the clay roof and dribbling to the ground in rivulets.

The figure hit the ground, unbuckled, and hurried, crouching and unspooling what looked like wire in his direction. The movement reminded him of a film he'd watched once with his dad—a World War II movie. He couldn't remember the title. They were blowing a bridge and the wires went to a TNT box.

A minute later, Cole arrived at the window. They made eye contact. Byron smiled broadly. Cole nodded and put a finger to his lips. He slid a pair of gloves through the window, then a piece of paper, and finally two thin copper wires. He nodded, winked, and was gone. Byron pulled the wires in far enough that they wouldn't slide back out, then sat down to read the paper. He unfolded it and two pieces of spearmint gum fell out. Intrigued, he bent to pick them up and read the contents with more joy and excitement than he'd ever read anything before:

Byron,

You're a moron, I forgive you, and we're busting you out. You've got gloves and wire. Act fast. Chew the gum—both pieces. The electrical wire is dead now but will be live soon—maybe in moments. Pull both wires across your cell to the door. Keep them separate. Stick them inside the keyhole, one on each side, with chewing gum, and be sure the ends remain exposed, but don't let them touch. Wait ten minutes. DON'T TOUCH THE WIRE AFTER THAT UNLESS YOU WEAR THE GLOVES. Fake some kind of emergency. When the guard puts the key in the door, he'll complete the circuit and shock himself. He'll either be dead or unconscious. Kick the door open with your shoe. Put on the uniform and meet us at the train depot. I've gone for Harald.

You owe me for this, idiot. I get ALL your Christmas presents next year.

—Cole

A sloppy notation at the end added,

Didn't plan on this rain. We waxed the wires, but they could ground in standing water. Work fast.

Byron read it again, smiling broadly. He put the gum in his mouth and chewed—the mint reminded him painfully of home and New Hampshire. He limped to the door and looked out. The guard remained engrossed in a thick, leather-bound novel at the desk: *The Woman in White* by Wilkie Collins. He'd asked yesterday, and the guard had refused to read to him, but he heard that it was a mystery. Thankfully, the rain still drummed on the roof, which would help drown out his actions.

Back at the window, he put on the gloves—the right one fit and the left was a struggle to get on around his cast. Slowly and silently, he spooled in the wire, gathering enough to reach across the cell to the door. When he got there with the first wire, he found he had to take a glove off to retrieve the gum from his mouth. He split it and affixed half to each side of the keyhole. After putting the gloves back on, it took only a few brief seconds to attach the wires. He felt like he could feel a charge prickling through the gloves, his skin and hair standing on end. Perhaps the power was already on? He returned to his bench.

He needed to think about how he'd draw the guard to the door and make him open it without noticing the wires in the room. After a few moments' consideration, he decided he'd have to fake suicide. He took off the gloves, picked up the belt he'd been using to signal Cole, walked over to the barred window, and looped it through a bar and around his neck. He paused as he fastened it. Even playacting suicide gave him an eerie chill.

He fastened the belt. If he picked up his feet, he'd now be hanging from the bar. He figured that to make it convincing, he'd have to basically go through with it, for a few moments at least. He took the plunge and lifted his feet, lurching down. The belt immediately tightened around his neck, and he gagged, reflexively gasping for air. His arm went to his throat, but he willed it down, slapping the wall. He gagged and choked.

Through the blood suddenly pounding in his ears, he heard the chair scrape against the hard floor in the next room and the guard get up. The keys jangled.

"Hey!" the man shouted as soon as he saw Byron. "Hey! You there! No!" He rushed to the door, inserted the key, and ZAAAAP! There was a flash of white light, a frying, electric sound, and a jet of blue flame burst briefly from the lock—the gum igniting, Byron supposed. The guard landed with a thump outside the door and the gum continued to burn, a lazy yellow. Byron put his feet down and stood, unsteadily.

Removing the belt, he limped over to his cot and picked up his sock and shoe. He studied his oozing amputation wound and dug into his pocket—he still had the clean sock and zip ties he'd planned to use to gag and restrain the guard last night. Taking a minute to consider the particulars, he used them as a makeshift bandage plugging the wound and fastening it in place. Immobilizing it would reduce pain. Then he pulled his sock on and grunted as he forced the swollen foot into his shoe, wishing he'd had some ice. He slid one glove onto his right hand, his palm still tender from holding Rochester's super-heated pistol. Redness shone on his skin, but it hadn't blistered much. He still couldn't get the left one on properly over his cast. "Byron," he shook his head, "you're a mess."

Through the bars, the current had knocked the guard prone. He lay flat on his back with blood oozing from his nose and ears. Byron felt a pang of guilt. This was the first person he'd intentionally injured—injured or *killed*. He shuddered. No time for that now, he thought. First, he had to solve the problem of disconnecting the wires without ending up similarly shocked. He decided to use his wooden cot. He pulled the frame away from the wall, set it up lengthwise in front of him, and then slid it forward, sweeping the electrodes out of the socket. They sizzled in the corner.

Byron reached through the bars and turned the key, swinging the door open. He moved to the guard. He had a pulse. Byron's rudimentary first aid didn't cover electrocution. He didn't know what to do for the man, and he couldn't get him help without giving himself away. Feeling guilty about it, but afraid to get caught, Byron began to strip off the soldier's clothes. He needed the red coat, black pants, and hat. There was also a sword and a rifle. He took them all and pulled them over his jeans and sweatshirt. He hesitated before he left, walked over and pocketed *The Woman in White*. His reading was getting rusty. As a dyslexic, he knew that he had to keep grinding or he'd slip back. Reading didn't stick with him like with other kids. Besides, he shrugged, it was always nice to have something to read on the train. He smiled, considering that with cool, witty narrations like that, he sounded a bit like James Bond.

CHAPTER FORTY-TWO
The Great Train Heist

Cole had remarkably little trouble releasing Harald. The kennels were empty except for his shepherd and one young hound nursing her puppies. He figured the rest must have been out hunting Crowmane. He grabbed a leash off a pegboard, opened Harald's kennel door and got bowled over, smothered in slobber, licks, tail wags and whimpering wines.

"Okay, okay," he laughed. "I missed you too." He hugged the shepherd and rubbed his head. "Let's go meet Byron," he said, looping the leash around the dog's neck and heading off toward the train depot. The rain continued steady and hard, coming down in a constant hiss around them, now pooling in the streets. It ran down his head and dribbled between his shoulders. His clothes were soaked.

He splashed through the mud with Harald. They had to get out the palisade gate to make the train station. It shouldn't be a big deal, he thought. It was generally left open and unguarded. There were guards atop the towers, but they weren't watching for a kid and a dog, and they weren't worried about who left so much as who entered. Also, the army on the move would be a good distraction. If he walked purposefully through, chances were he'd be left alone, but he'd do better if he slipped through with some other non-military traffic, so he stopped beside a mud-brick building to observe for a few moments.

Two redcoats came through the gate, heading up the slope at a brisk trot toward the fortress. About a minute later, a soldier came from the other direction with a marked limp. Harald's tail started wagging almost immediately, but it took a few more seconds for Cole to realize that it was Byron. He waited until his brother came nearly abreast of him and then walked briskly to meet him near the gate. Byron simply nodded and the two of them matched strides, walking out of Fort Douglas together.

It was all Byron could do not to reach down and pet Harald. It took the entirety of his mental energy to maintain an aloof posture and gait.

"Thanks," he said, simply. "You sure did earn my Christmas presents."

"How'd the electrics work?" Cole asked under his breath.

"They lit him up. He's breathing, but God knows if he'll ever wake up, or what state his brain's in."

Cole nodded. "Sorry for him, but glad to have you back. We have to make for the train depot. Adhita's already there, probably." They were walking down the main road. "Oh, and you're a moron."

"Yeah, I agree," Byron said. "But Crowmane escaped. Let's turn here. We'll come at the depot from behind."

Cole nodded. "How's the foot?"

"Gruesome," Byron grimaced. "I'd rather not talk about it."

The back streets were empty in the rain, but the sucking mud got deeper. It squished under their feet and caked the fur of Harald's legs and belly.

"Do you know how to drive a train?" Byron asked. Once out of sight of the gate, his limp became very marked.

"I believe the term is *engineer* a train. No, no idea," Cole laughed, "but I think there's a lever and it gets pushed forward. There's going to be a steam gauge measuring pressure and a temperature gauge. There'll be a brake, too. Don't know what it will look like. I'll figure it out. I managed to successfully land the Space Shuttle in glide mode in the simulator that time we went to the Air and Space Museum with Nana and Tata Asante, and I was only eleven. How hard can a train be? It has a track."

"Don't derail," Byron said. "Watch your speed on turns."

"Duh."

"There it is," Byron pointed "the engine is called *Royale*." The hulking black machine sat, in front of a line of fifteen cars. Smoke rose steadily from the stack. On the far side of the train stood the depot and station, it's clay roof slick with rain.

"Do you see Adhita?" Cole asked.

"No. She's probably on the other side."

"Let's go around—the front, past the engine," Cole instructed. "And keep your eyes open. They could figure out that you've escaped at any time."

"Or that you've escaped," Byron pointed out, and the boys and their dog moved beside the shining black engine. Rain hissed to steam as it touched the hot metal of the boiler.

"No—I managed to charge my batteries and record a long conversation with Adhita. They think we're in the room—and if they listen to the conversation, we're talking about going through the mirror that we made—it's a fake, but it may mislead them for a few moments."

"Nice. I left the unconscious guard on the floor. " Byron added as they rounded the front of the engine. "I thought about locking him in the cell, but I didn't know if I'd cause him further harm by moving him. He was in a bad state." They looked down the wet platform along the train. "What are you planning to do about the engineer?"

"Threaten him with your rifle," Cole shrugged. "Gag him and tie him up in the station."

"Okay," Byron nodded, as if the idea of threatening someone hadn't occurred to him. "I can do that, I suppose." He took the rifle off his shoulder, opened a pouch that he'd taken from the guard's belt and inserted a round. "You mind if I leave the safety on?"

"Whatever." Cole seemed distracted, scanning the area carefully, obviously looking for Adhita.

"Let's get behind the building." Byron said. "I don't like being in plain sight." A sound from their left drew their attention. Adhita walked along the side of the station building, a long-handled, flat coal shovel in her hands. She motioned them to join her.

"Oakes brothers," she smiled. "I'm glad to see you together. I assume the plan went well?"

"Swimmingly, as you Brits would say," Cole replied, obviously punning off the rain. Harald sniffed Adhita and licked her hand. "Did you have any problems?"

"I had to lay a worker out with this shovel," she admitted, "but otherwise, no."

"You hit a guy with a shovel?" Byron asked.

"He was a big man and he caught me stoking the fire. I didn't have much choice. I just turned and popped him in the skull with this." She patted the handle. "I brought it with me because I figured I'd rather be armed"

"Right," Cole agreed. "Look, I love talking, especially to you," he blushed a little, "but we're running out of time. Byron, you need to tie the engineer and station attendant up. I've got to stoke the fire and figure out how to run—er, engineer—this train, and Adhita, do you think you can cut the telegraph line and attach it so we can pull it down as we leave?"

"I can do that. I kept my belt so I can scale the pole. Do you have the electric gloves?" she asked Cole.

He turned to Byron and raised his eyebrows.

"What? No." Byron stammered. "I—your note didn't say anything about bringing the gloves."

Cole sighed. "Telegraph lines are electrical. You'd get a shock touching it barehanded—not enough to kill you, certainly, but it would be unpleasant."

"Would thick gloves be enough," she asked.

"Probably. I think so—I don't know," Cole faltered.

"They'll have to be," she decided. "The engineer will have some. He handles fire, doesn't he?"

"Okay, right," Byron agreed. "Let's go." He hefted the gun, turned the corner, and stepped up onto the platform. On the other end, walking briskly in their direction was Rochester. "Every. Single. Time." Byron said between clenched teeth. He lifted the rifle to his shoulder, aimed, and Rochester stopped walking, waving his arms.

"Byron, don't!" he shouted.

Byron set his jaw, closed his eyes, and pulled the trigger. Nothing. He had the safety on. "Seriously!?" he exclaimed, lowering the gun to check it.

"Stop," Rochester shouted, advancing at a run. "Stop, I beg you! I believe you, Byron. I believe you."

Safety off, Byron lowered the rifle, suspicious.

"He believes what?" Cole asked.

"I told him about Douglas," Byron admitted. "He didn't believe me."

"Remind me never to share a secret with you again," Adhita growled. "Who *didn't* you tell?"

"He's the only one, I swear," Byron squirmed. Rochester stopped a few paces from them, his hands still in the air. By now the station attendant and engineer were at their respective doors, looking out at the platform. Harald barked at them and at Rochester.

"I believe you," Rochester said again. "I—you aroused my suspicions, so I began an investigation. The Necrologists are dead. You were correct on that point. I contrived to touch one—skin like a wax statue. And, so, I checked Douglas' personal cesspit. We don't have water closets out here." He sighed. "It hadn't been used in years—not for its intended purpose. It was full of food, rotting food, hundreds and hundreds of meals scraped into the pit, untouched. He can't have eaten in years. He's been lying to me—his own nephew—keeping up a charade."

Byron nodded. "Okay, so you're joining us?"

"Yes," Rochester said. "I'm in a bit of a scrape, myself. You see—"

"Can I help you, sir?" the Station attendant asked, interrupting Rochester's explanation.

"Why thank you, my good man," Rochester responded, not missing a beat. "Yes, certainly you may, and you, too," he said to the engineer. "Are your fellows in there too? But, never mind, we should all be out of the rain. The three of you as well," he nodded at Cole, Byron, and Adhita. "May we talk inside your station?" he asked the attendant.

"Of course." The attendant held open the door as they all entered. Grumbling, the engineer followed. As soon as they were through the door, Rochester pulled out his pistol and pointed it at the engineer, a blue-turbaned Sikh.

"Over there," he said, gesturing to the corner. "You too," he told the station attendant. "I'm very sorry about this, fellows, but I'm afraid we have to tie you up. I wouldn't advise resistance. I'm a dead shot with this at close range. Byron, Cole, if you please."

"We don't have any rope," Byron said.

"If they don't have any rope, then we'll have to shoot them," Rochester concluded.

"Sir, please," the attendant begged. "I've got a wife and daughter. I don't have any rope, but there's a closet. You could lock me in—I wouldn't move for hours; I swear to it!" he blubbered.

"And you?" Rochester turned to the engineer who glowered up at him behind thick eyebrows. "Do you make a similar promise?"

"I suppose I have no choice," he responded.

"Good, then into the closet, chaps" Rochester instructed. "If you make a peep, I shall have no choice but to shoot you both. And sorry I would be to have to do that."

The two of them moved to a closet and shut the door. Rochester braced a chair against the knob.

"How do we know you're really on our side?" Adhita asked.

"As I began to explain," Rochester responded, "I am on your side by necessity. I was discovered by a necroid servant while checking on the state of Douglas' um, internal affairs. It became aggressive. I had to smash it. On my way out, I had to deal similarly with two more." I assure you," here he spoke directly to Byron, "it is disconcerting to be attacked by something you thought of as furniture." He chewed his lip for a moment. "Headed upstairs," he continued, "I passed a Necrologist. He stared strangely at me, side eyed, a dangerous glint visible. Before I knew what I was about—I found myself seized by a wave of revulsion and hate (it was a compulsion of the blood, I suppose)—I'd whipped out my sabre and cut his head from his shoulders. That was the final push to my decision. You see," here he shuddered, "under the waxy skin of that Necrologist, his flesh had been replaced by a sort of mycelium or fungal-looking growth. No blood seeped from the wound, just white oozing as of a milkweed or dandelion plant. I hid the body in a closet. When I left, I went to rescue you, Byron, which is how I found you'd gone. In hopes to catch you, I travelled straight here."

"Okay," Cole interrupted, somber. "That's good enough for me. Let's get to the plan."

"One more thing," Rochester interrupted. "The army is moving to attack the *Lothka*. They broke camp during first shift. There will be war here before we return. I've been assigned a command. I may be missed already."

"Not much to do about that now," Cole said. He pulled the wire cutters out of his pocket and handed them to Adhita. He turned to the door, and headed back onto the platform, talking over his shoulder. "I'll get the train ready to roll. Adhita, get that telegraph line fastened. Byron—"

His speech faltered as the distant sound of a ringing alarm bell reached their ears. It came from Fort Douglas. His face froze with fear. "We've been discovered. This is going to be close." He bounded up the steps into the engine. A moment later, he leaned out the door and threw a pair of black heat gloves to Adhita. "Put these on. Byron and Rochester, guard the platform."

Within a few moments, black smoke billowed from the *Royale's* stack and Adhita clambered up the nearest telegraph pole. The wire came down, displacing a raven that cawed loudly. Steam wooshed from the engine, and Adhita descended. She took the line and dragged it to the nearest car—the fifth in line behind the engine, a boxcar—and began to bend and twist it around the coupling.

"Here they come!" Rochester shouted. Sure enough, Byron could see six red-coated soldiers advancing down the road at a trot. At their rear, clad in silver armor, but helmless, rushed Aquinas Justice.

Rochester fired a round at the soldiers and missed—it was hard to be accurate with a pistol from that range. Byron aimed for Justice and fired, too. His shot went wide but hit one of the soldiers in the shoulder. He crumpled. Rochester fired again, and this time a soldier went down.

"Drop!" Rochester yelled. He fell face-first onto the platform. Byron followed suit, only just in time. Bullets whistled over their heads simultaneous with the crack of rifle fire from the road. Byron glanced up, his cheek against the platform, to see the remaining soldiers kneeling in firing positions. Only Justice still advanced, and he'd drawn a sword.

"Get on the train!" Rochester yelled, raising his gun. "I'll handle Justice!"

"But he's—" the rest of Byron's words were drowned in the sound of gunfire as Rochester sighted and fired into Justice's chest.

"Go!" Rochester shouted. "I'll get on the train as it passes. Start it up."

Byron jumped onto the engine as another shot rang out. Pain shot up his leg from his toe and he bit his lip. Harald bounded up with him. "Go!" he shouted to Cole, echoing Rochester. "Go—start it up, now!"

"What about Adhita?"

"I'm here," she said, climbing into the engine from the opposite side, still carrying her shovel. "No one's shooting over there."

Cole jammed a lever forward and the train lurched, the pistons hissing and great wheels screaming for traction on the rails, pushed too fast from nothing.

While the train shuddered, grinding forward on sparking wheels, Byron fumbled another round out of his pouch and loaded the rifle. He leaned out the side to see Justice at a full charge, closing like an Olympic sprinter. His body was interposed between the redcoats and the train. Their guns had gone silent, yet they advanced again.

Two dark holes in Justice's silver breastplate showed where Rochester's bullets had struck home. The Lieutenant now took aim with his last shot, kneeling, holding his gun at arm's length, and sighting down the barrel.

Byron fired first—he didn't know how to kill Justice—if kill was even the right word for an undead—so he tried to stop him by taking out a leg, aiming for the knee. Unfortunately, the train made for an unstable platform, his target moved, and the range increased as the train pulled away. The shot missed, punching a hole in the wooden planks a few inches from the target. Rochester's bullet, however, hit home.

The pistol flashed and the shot struck Justice in the cheek, twisting his body, cracking the bone, and removing half his face. It didn't bleed, and the hulking warrior hardly flinched. Rochester barely had time to unsheathe his sabre. His blade connected with Justice's longsword. Byron couldn't hear the confrontation through the sounds of the steam, wheels, and pistons, but he watched in terror as the blades clashed. Once, twice, and then to his horror Justice's sword suddenly tore through Rochester's red coat, protruding at least half a foot under the lieutenant's shoulder blade.

In a rage, Byron groped in his pouch for another round. He dropped it; it bounced off the floor and off into the gravel by the tracks.

Justice paused long enough to shove Rochester off the blade. The lieutenant's body crumpled to the platform. Justice took a step toward the train, reaching to grab a handrail on a passing car.

Byron managed to load another round. He leaned out, aimed, and pulled the trigger: a hit. It struck Justice in the gut, spinning him and causing him to lose his grip. The train picked up speed, passing him by. Barely fazed by the gunshot, Justice made eye contact with Byron, then leapt between two passing cars and disappeared. The remaining soldiers ran after the train, but Byron could already tell that they wouldn't catch it.

He turned to Cole, pale and shaking.

His brother whooped, exultant. "We made it, Byron! We made it!" he shouted over the roaring fire and chugging engine. He clapped him on the shoulder and laughed. "We've escaped—they'll never catch us now!"

It was Adhita who read Byron's expression. "Cole, be quiet. Byron," she touched his hand. "Byron, what is it?" she asked.

"Rochester's dead," he replied. "And Justice is on the train."

CHAPTER FORTY-THREE
Mirror Images

Charlie, Jack, and Felicity were returning from the grocery store, this time in Charlie's Jeep. Mid-October rain misted the windshield. Nearly a month had passed since the last failed mirror test. The plan to pull a replacement chip out of another product had failed three times—it was nearly impossible to remove the frail, tiny soldered circuit without causing damage—and the new, backordered one should have arrived three days ago, but hadn't. They passed a mail truck and Charlie wondered if the microchip might be onboard or had already been delivered. He looked at Felicity, who seemed to be staring off into space. The stress and illness both showed on her face. Biting his lower lip, he pushed the knob, turning on the radio. The WPNH DJ read the weather in a jaunty tone:

> *You all thought winter was a month away—just wishful thinking. That's New Hampshire for you, and it's why my parents moved to Arizona. You folks in Lincoln, Plymouth, Dorchester, and the Waterville Valley are under a Winter Storm Warning. You can expect rain to start at noon, turning to a wintery mix and freezing rain before sunset. By 6:30 PM, that rain should have transitioned to snow, which will fall—heavily—and accumulate over the course of the evening to the tune of 12-20 inches. It's gonna be wet snow, too—good for snowmen, but sticking to the branches, and with maples and oaks still decked out in fall foliage, it'll start bringing them down—wouldn't want to be a linesman tonight. If you can get off work, do it early so you can make it home before the worst starts. I-93 may be a mess. Stay off the roads—and stay tuned as we'll keep you updated about school closures. Stick with 101.1 The Planet for your next song set, too. We've got Tom Petty, Heart, and The Who on tap.*

"Don't look now, but it's already raining," Charlie said to the radio.

"Sounds like a classic winter storm," Jack observed from the back seat. "Good thing we bought bread and milk," he winked into the mirror. An advertisement for carpet cleaners came on. Charlie turned the volume down to a whisper.

"Yeah, this snow's the kind of thing we lived for as kids," his eyes smiled, full of memory. "Remember checking Channel Seven for school closures?"

"Yeah, we'd play chess or monopoly in front of the TV all night and just wait for the announcement. Does your university ever cancel?"

"Nope. My students live on campus."

"Well," Jack waved and smiled out the window at a college girl who braved the cold rain to go for a run, "you might be over snow days, but I live for 'em still. For a lumberman in the offseason, snow means work—plowing, shoveling—I can run a skid-steer, dump truck, anything with wheels, generally. Make some bank that way."

Charlie nodded. "Remember that January back in what, '74? That time we talked Dad into letting us sleep in the igloo we made in the back yard? I was 17 and you must've been . . ."

"Nine," Jack laughed. "Mom almost had a conniption, but we did it anyway."

"It stayed surprisingly warm," Charlie reminisced. "One candle kept it livable."

"Yeah, but we cheated on that igloo. Remember, we didn't have enough snow, so we built a base from snow-bricks, then anchored crossing pine branches in it and packed sled-loads of snow onto the branch frame."

"Yeah, and it froze that night—got down below zero, became hard as rock." Charlie chuckled. "I think there was a cold-snap after we built it that lasted almost a month. We had an igloo darn near half the winter."

"Yeah, and you didn't ever pick up the branches when it melted until Dad yelled at us—there was a brown spot in the yard until the end of June."

"I don't know if he got more upset about the mess or that we'd cut the branches off his white pine."

"We never got much snow in Maryland," Felicity joined the conversation. "They'd cancel school for an inch." She wiped some condensation off the window. "Charlie knows I don't much like the weather up here—I mean, it's going to snow in October—but at least winter is *winter* in New Hampshire. In Maryland it's just cold rain for months. Outside is bleak and soggy. I don't have the kinds of memories you two do."

"Do you have siblings?" Jack asked. "I'm trying to remember if I met them at the wedding, but I can't. Sorry."

"I've got a brother," she said, "Bruce, but he's older than me—six years. We weren't close. He attended, though."

"Yeah?" Jack asked, politely. "What's he do now?"

"Bruce runs a Tech company in D.C. He started it with a couple of his college roommates. One of them just left for a job at Microsoft. Bruce's doing alright, though. Has three girls."

"And lives in a McMansion, drives a Porsche, and makes enough to send all three to private school," Charlie added with a hint of jealousy." He swung the old Jeep off of route 25 onto River Road.

"Fiona is in college now," Felicity reminded him. "Johns Hopkins. She wants to be a doctor."

Jack whistled in admiration. Charlie looked into the rear view and saw the longing expression on his brother's face. He wondered if his brother felt more upset that he didn't have a Porsche, that he'd become a lumberjack instead of a doctor, or if he wished he had a wife and daughters of his own. Charlie smiled wryly. He knew the feeling. Sure, he had a family, but he was a history professor at a small New England college. He could house, feed, and clothe his family, but at one time he'd had bigger ambitions, both in terms of money and fame. Maybe all small-town educators had to satisfy themselves with the idea of the domino-effect, he thought—that either the children he raised or some of the students he taught in school would be influenced to do good in the world, each creating his or her own chain of good deeds. By choosing education, he mused, he was paying it forward instead of taking the pay-out himself.

"What are you thinking, Charlie," Felicity asked. She'd been watching his expression as he drove.

"Oh, nothing, really—just spacing out," he replied.

"Thinking about the boys?" She rested her hand on his.

"In a manner of speaking," he nodded. They were approaching their driveway.

"Stop here," Felicity said. "I'm going to hop out and check the mail."

Charlie stopped the Jeep, its brakes squealing as they always did. The windshield wipers swiped noisily up and down. He noted that the sound of the rain had changed. It hissed against the windshield—obviously transitioning to sleet. His eyes fell on the slate sign reading

"Oakes' Oaks." One of the oak saplings next to it had been run over by a fire engine back in February.

Felicity got back into the Jeep, her face bright. She held a small, white package in her hands. "It's here! Let's go."

While Felicity worked on the mirror, Charlie and Jack packed their things. They had a lot—sleeping bags, a two man tent, coats, hats, gloves, expensive durable socks, biker shorts (Jack had suggested that change from underwear—less chafing), flashlights, freeze-dried rations, pots and pans, matches, water bottles, filters, instant coffee, caffeine packets, a first aid kit. The list went on, ending in a significant portion of weapons and ammunition. They'd separated it into two manageable loads, leaving the lion's share for Churchill to haul on a specialized harness they'd found over the internet.

Jack checked his guns, while Charlie raided the medicine cabinet for his medication, as well as plenty of antibacterial ointment, acetaminophen, and ibuprofen.

"Seriously," Charlie chided over his shoulder, "Jack, it's not like we'll be walking into a war-zone. You can cool it with the weapons checks."

"Old habits die hard," Jack grinned, blowing into the chamber of his handgun. "First order of business before a mission is the weapons check—that's how it's got to be."

Wind whistled outside. The lights dimmed for a moment and came back to life. Charlie set down an orange prescription bottle and went to the window. Snow was piling up—three inches already on top of the Jeep. Large flakes descended steadily.

"You got enough meds?" Jack asked.

"Yeah," Charlie replied, returning to his task. He drew another bottle from the cabinet. "They're just for blood-pressure and cholesterol—I'm pre-diabetic, so the doc's concerned with keeping my kidney and heart in pristine condition. I've been taking half-doses for four months. That means I have four months of half-doses to bring with me. Truth is, I don't need as much since I've lost this weight." He slapped his belly. "I should have been controlling it with diet and exercise all along, but I was lazy. I'm guessing the hiking on short rations will trim me out a bit more before it's all over."

"Yep," Jack nodded.

Felicity set down her soldering iron. "Well, it's ready, again," she sighed, caressing the wire-wrapped ring. "Shall we try it?"

"Yeah," Charlie said. "Jack?"

"Sure, sure," he said, gathering his guns. "Where can I put these?"

"In our room, just inside the door," Charlie said, moving to gather any loose metal objects. The wind whistled outside again.

Jack shut the bedroom door while Felicity and Charlie plugged in the mirror. It hummed, the coils harmonized, and the cyan glow of the portal bloomed in the middle, expanding in concentric circles like water when a pebble drops into it. The portal finished materializing and stabilized. Felicity exhaled, passing a hand over her forehead.

The three of them remained silent, as if under a spell, drawn to stand together in the glow of the mirror. The coils hummed and crackled with electrical static. Through the loop, a beautiful mountain scene wavered: tall, snow-capped mountains bathed in sunset, pine and willow trees, lilies and ferns. A breeze blew, wafting the vegetation slowly. Felicity reached over and grabbed Charlie's hand. Her flickering reflection did the same. After a few more seconds of awestruck silence, Charlie ventured to speak.

"Okay. Alright, then," he placed a hand on Jack's shoulder. "Let's get our stuff together and get through."

"Not so fast," Felicity interrupted. "Let's make a test." She pulled Jack's hat from his head and tossed it through at an angle so it wouldn't fall right back to them, like the tennis balls did in the video. It vanished.

"Hey!" he complained, rubbing his head and starting toward the portal. "I'm going to have to go get that."

"Yes," she smiled. "That was the idea. Once you're through, turn around and come right back."

"Sure," he said, stopping for a moment, on the verge of passing the portal. "This is one small step for man," he started.

"Shut up," Charlie chuckled.

Jack winked. He ducked his head beneath the level of the coil, but at the instant that his foot grazed its surface, the wind whistled again outside, and the power flickered. Jack hesitated, and the power cut off. The room went dark, the humming and crackling stopped, and the portal closed.

"Aw Hell," Jack swore. "I really loved that hat!"

CHAPTER FORTY-FOUR

Battle Royale

The steam train hurtled down the track, a black bullet whistling through gray rain, its chugging rhythmic. The wheels clacked from rail to rail. Wind blustered through the windows and curled around and into the open back of the cab. Outside, the grass blurred by. The fire crackled and hissed through the grate. They must have reached nearly forty miles per hour by now. Cole tapped a gauge.

"Looks like the ideal pressure is between 225 and 250," he shouted as Adhita shoveled in another load of coal. "The gauge goes up to 360. We're at 265-ish. I think that's enough fuel for now."

Byron stood behind them, loaded rifle in hand, looking uneasily back along the train, waiting for Justice to appear. It'd been about ten minutes and he still hadn't. The suspense was awful. He thought about Rochester, impaled on the bodyguard's longsword, how Justice had sloughed off the body, letting it thump to the platform. Byron shivered with horror then wondered if he had a right to be so affected by the death of a man whom he, himself, would have shot a half an hour ago, had the safety been released on his rifle. He chewed his lip, struggling with mixed emotions. This wasn't the time for an existential crisis. He pushed his turmoil aside.

Adhita put her head out the window and looked back, her hair flapping around her face in the rain. "The telegraph line is still coming down," she observed. "So far, so good."

"What are we going to do about Justice?" Byron asked, not for the first time.

"You said he jumped between the cars?" Cole said, moving toward his brother. Byron nodded. Cole scratched his head. "Maybe he got run over?"

"No," Byron replied. "We can't rely on that. We need to have a plan."

"I agree," Adhita said, huddling up with them. "Let's uncouple the cars."

"Brilliant!" Cole exclaimed.

"Sure," Byron agreed. "We have to climb past the coal tender and uncouple the rest. We'll need that coal to get across the plains."

"What about the telegraph line?" Cole asked suddenly. "If we uncouple the cars before that line, it will stop coming down. We've only gone about seven miles."

Adhita sighed. "Yes. It's tied on four or five cars back."

"The first is a passenger car," Byron added. "We can walk through that one, but we'd have to go over the top of the others."

"Too dangerous," Cole concluded. "We uncouple it. We can travel an hour or so and then stop, cut down the telegraph line again, and attach it to the end of the tender."

Adhita nodded. She looked down at Byron's foot and then up at his brother. "Cole, let's get to that coupling."

"Keep an eye on that pressure gauge," Cole said to Byron, "and the other on that passenger car. I don't want Justice surprising us."

"Wait," Byron pleaded. "What should I watch for?" he gestured helplessly to the gauge.

"It goes into the red at 300," Cole said, "try not to let it get there."

With that, Cole and Adhita climbed awkwardly over the mountain of black, jagged coal in the tender. As he passed, Cole noted that one whole side of the tender was hinged, able to dump the load if necessary. It latched vertically with a pair of half-inch diameter iron pins. He figured it must be how they loaded the coal.

Once over the pile and at the rear of the tender, the two of them looked down between the cars. There was a five-foot drop to the coupling, beneath which rails and crossbars sped by at dizzying speed. One false move, Cole realized, and he'd be spilled onto the tracks under the onrushing train. He began to sweat.

"The coupling looks simple enough," Adhita said from beside him, apparently unconcerned by the danger.

Looking closely, Cole agreed. Each car had thick iron couplers—they were obviously the ends of the steel beams that ran underneath and supported the weight. Each coupling had a round hole driven through it. The holes through each had been lined up, then a one-inch diameter L-shaped pin had been slid inside, its bend on top, preventing it from falling through. A chain linked the top and bottom of the pin to prevent it from popping out. They'd just have to detach the chain from the bottom and pull the pin up. 'Easy-peasy,' Cole thought, sarcastically.

"I'll do it," Adhita said, hiking up her gray skirt with one hand, and leaning over the wall of the tender to grab the end rail of the passenger car with the other. She swung one leg over, then the other, and lowered herself down toward the coupling. Cole stood open-mouthed, amazed at her bravery. "Get over here and hold my feet!" she hollered up at him.

He nodded and followed awkwardly, his heart in his throat as he shifted between the moving cars. Yet, when he stretched halfway across, perched over the rushing rails, the door to the passenger car unexpectedly opened, revealing the grinning skull of an animated skeleton. Cole recoiled in shock, almost losing his grip, and realized in horror that more—many more—skeletons filled the car behind the first.

Thinking only of the danger to Adhita, Cole pushed off the tender with his feet and launched himself across the gap at the necroid, his weight bowling it backwards into those following. "Adhita! Hurry!" he shouted, kicking and thrashing against his enemies. "We're not alone here!"

Adhita glanced back, then braced herself and lowered her body, unsecured, onto the coupling between the cars. Even though the rain had slowed to a drizzle, everything felt slick. The tracks hissed by only a foot below her. She reached down a trembling hand, fumbling with the chain which was fastened to the coupling with a cotter pin.

Byron kept a nervous watch between the steam gauge and the tender. Harald sat by his feet, his ears erect, emitting high-pitched whines, clearly affected by the tension. In the boiler, the pressure increased. Byron tapped the glass. He worried that they'd added too much coal to the fire, and as it combusted, the temperature began to spike. The pressure already rose to 290 pounds and continued climbing. Cole hadn't given any instructions for *how* to cool the engine. Byron tapped the gauge again, squinting at the needle, then glanced back to see that both Adhita and Cole had vanished over the edge of the tender. He was about to return to the instruments when he realized the car's door had opened behind them. He could discern movement inside, and something white, but couldn't see well enough to know what was happening. Fearing the worst, he picked up his rifle and abandoned the engine, leaping painfully onto the tender and scrabbling across the piled coal. The unsteady footing was murder to stand on and it avalanched beneath his feet, tumbling down and releasing black dust, despite the recent downpour. Harald followed him, then began to bark ferociously, growling from the back of his throat, the hair along his back spiked in fear and aggression.

Lifting his eyes, Byron could see skeletons advancing atop the passenger car. Doubtless, they were what had drawn Harald's attention. "Fudge sundae!" Byron whispered, raising his rifle. Taking careful aim, he fired at the nearest one, shattering its skull. The Martini-Henry kicked hard into Byron's already-bruised shoulder. The bones rattled to the roof and bounced away. He loaded another round, couched the rifle in his shoulder, aimed down the barrel, and fired, wincing, with the same result. The train, unattended, continued to pick up speed.

In the doorway of the passenger coach, Cole leapt up before the skeletons could, grabbed the car door and slammed it closed. It jammed, crunching into a femur on the ground and a skeletal arm about halfway up. The hand clenched and unclenched, grasping at air. The door, which opened into the car, jolted in his hands as the skeletons pulled at it.

"Hurry up!" he shouted again, risking a glance at Adhita.

"You're on the wrong car!" she responded. "If I detach it, you'll be left with them."

"I can't let go of this!" He gestured with his head at the door, which jolted again in his hands. Pair after pair of skeletal fingers were wrapping around the frame through the crack and he strained to keep it closed. A gunshot rang out from behind them on the tender—the fourth such they'd heard. "Pull it!" he called. "I'll jump."

She nodded, tears in her eyes, tensed her muscles and yanked on the pin with all her might. It didn't budge. Not a millimeter. She strained harder.

Nothing.

"I—I'm not strong enough," she shouted. Another shot sounded. The door lurched open six inches behind Cole. Whole skeletal arms were through it now, groping for his forearm.

"I'm not, either! They're getting through!"

"Hold on—I'm coming." Adhita deftly turned and scrambled up onto the car beside Cole. Another rifle shot rang behind them. Harald continued to bark, aggressively. With her leg still dangling over the railing, Adhita leaned to grab hold of the door handle. Using all her weight, she pulled with Cole. The door closed five inches. "Hold it there!" she shouted.

She slid the long belt over her head, the one she used to scale the telegraph pole. Unfastening the clip, she looped it through the handle and around the steel railing. The rifle fired again. A ribcage fell from above, glanced off the railing and landed at her feet.

Cole grunted, bracing his knees against the wall, and strained against the onslaught. The door almost closed. Adhita latched the belt tightly and let go, gasping for breath.

"Come on!" Byron shouted from above and behind them. "Hurry up! More are coming and I'm running low on ammo." He held out a hand, and Adhita took hold of it, climbing up into the coal tender. Cole followed, glancing back at the shuddering door. The leather strap held, for now. Skeletal hands scrabbled against the door, the hinges, and the grimy window, but so far it didn't budge.

"Where are they coming from?" Cole asked looking up at the roof. A skeleton moved along it. Byron took aim and fired. Another hit. The sound of the shot rang in Cole's ears.

"There are probably whole boxcars of the things down the line. I watched them load this train up a couple of weeks ago. There were, easy, a couple hundred skeletons. They're a major export as workers. I bet Justice is controlling them." He glanced down for a moment. "It won't uncouple?"

"Not while the train is moving," Cole answered. "Too much weight and friction on the pin. Maybe if we were going downhill, but we're on a level plain right now." Byron nodded.

"How many bullets do you have left?" Adhita asked.

"Two dozen, maybe." Byron replied, loading another round into the chamber. "And Cole, the pressure's got to be way over 300 now. I couldn't stay to watch it."

"Okay," Cole nodded, "give me a second, and I'll see what I can figure out." He started for the engine.

"What's that roof made of?" Adhita asked, pointing at the passenger car.

"Looks like tar paper," Byron answered.

"And the car is wooden. Let's burn it."

Byron put the rifle to his shoulder and blasted another skeleton. There were three crossing the roof now. He loaded another round. "It's pretty wet, and it's still misting out here. You think it would catch?" He shot the first one, emptied the chamber and fished in his pouch for another round.

"It might take a while to get going, but it should catch. With the wind, it should fan the coals, if we can get some out of the furnace up there. Tar is flammable, and the wood under it should be dry."

"We may not have time," Byron replied, shattering the second skeleton. "But any plan is better than nothing. Go." Adhita struggled off through the coal.

Byron stayed, loading and firing like a machine. He missed occasionally, and his shoulder throbbed from the kick—'great,' he thought, 'another injury'—but his steady marksmanship held back the tide. By the time Adhita came back, he had under a dozen rounds left. She hauled a black scuttle full of glowing red coals in one thick-gloved hand and held her shovel in the other. She launched a shovel-full of coals up onto the roof. Many bounced and bounded, shooting off sparks, before falling off the car onto the tracks.

"*Khota*!" she swore, apparently a term from her father's language. Then, turning to Byron, "keep them back. I'm going up there." Without waiting for an answer, she bent, scooped up some unlit coals, added them to the bucket, then moved to the end of the tender. There, she reached across to the car's iron ladder and climbed it, one handed, dragging the bucket. Byron redoubled his fire.

At the top of the ladder, Adhita emptied the scuttle gently onto the roof, then used the edge of the bucket to arrange the coals into a pile. They smoked but didn't immediately erupt into flame. She leapt from the ladder back into the tender, scraping her knees and tearing her dress. By the time she got back to Byron, he had five rounds left. Skeletons were still appearing on the roof.

"We need this to go faster," he observed. "We want kerosene or something. Is there a lantern back there?"

Unexpectedly, she leaned in and kissed his cheek. "Yes!" she laughed, "I'll be right back. Byron, your brother isn't the only Oakes genius."

'He may be a genius of careful planning,' Byron thought, 'but I'm better at improv.' Four bullets later, she returned with a glass bullseye lantern that had been hanging in the engine cab. It sloshed, more than half-full of kerosene. Three skeletons were crossing the roof.

"This is my last shot," he admitted, shouldering the rifle and taking aim.

Without responding, she passed by him and reached the ladder. He squeezed the trigger, blasting one last skeleton.

Cole met him as he lowered the rifle, a shovel in each hand—Adhita's long-handled one, and the shorter, thin-headed one that was in the engine. "How many left?"

"I'm out," Byron winced, lowering the rifle.

"I managed to drop the pressure some, released some steam. You were right; it was at 330 when I got there."

Adhita swung the lantern from the ladder, shattering the glass against the roof and splashing out the kerosene. The tar paper erupted in bright flames and she leapt back, on fire. She mistimed the jump and connected against the metal side of the tender with both her shins before flopping into it, atop the pile of coal. Her dress burned, some of her hair smoked, and she cried with pain. Cole ran to her, kneeling and patting out the flaming bits of her dress and hair with his hands. He hugged her.

"Can you move?" he asked.

Before she could answer, a skeleton leapt through the smoke and landed beside him, its grinning face and empty sockets turned down toward them. Harald had it before it could attack. The dog grabbed it by the femur, shook it, and pulled its feet out from under it. The bones fell and Byron smashed the skull with the butt of his rifle. Another followed, and this time Byron knocked it off the side of the tender with a baseball swing.

"Home-run," Cole smirked.

"That fire's not stopping them!" Byron shouted. The roof of the car was an inferno now. Flames, fed by kerosene and wind, had combusted the tar paper across its length and were burning four-feet high and leaving a cloud of curling black smoke behind. Skeletons ran right through it, as if the flames were nothing more than air.

Cole stood and hefted his shovel, swinging to connect with a skeleton, mid-leap, and sending it spilling to the side of the tracks. "It'll stop them when it loses its structural integrity," he said. "We just need to hold them for a while."

And so they did, for a while. Byron inverted his rifle and clubbed skeletons with the thick, wooden stock. Cole jabbed with the long-handled shovel, keeping enemies at bay, and Harald pounced, biting, tearing and throttling skeletons, knocking them over again and again. Adhita stood, gingerly, on bruised shins and lifted the small shovel, doing her part, but the skeletons kept coming, wave after wave, as long as the roof continued to hold their weight.

Soon, two necroids who'd lost their legs in the leap grabbed at Harald, pulling him down. He whimpered and thrashed, helplessly immobile, as they dug their fingers into his flanks and bit at him with their teeth. Adhita's shovel had been clutched by another enemy, and she competed in a tugging match with it. Cole, slipping on avalanching coal, went down on a knee—his other foot buried—jabbing at two advancing skeletons, trying to force them back. Only Byron truly held his own, having smashed at least ten skeletons or knocked them off the train with his rifle. His muscles ached from the strain, and he gasped for enough air to fill his lungs. His toe throbbed and a blister on his hand had ruptured, but he carried on. They all could see that it was a losing struggle.

The skeleton facing Adhita tore the shovel from her grip, smashed her sideways with the handle and raised it to drive the blade down, straight into her neck. Byron and Cole watched in horror. Byron swung with blinding speed, shattering the ribcage of the necroid opposing him and taking a clumsy step toward Adhita, but he already knew he'd be too late. Cole dropped his shovel and reflexively held out a hand.

"NO!" he screamed, with wild and hopeless desperation, emotion surging through him. The twilight dimmed for a split-second.

As if on command, the skeletons—all of them—halted. They stood in a trance for a handful of heartbeats, long enough for Byron to smash them all, save Adhita, and free Harald. And—even better—as Byron gave Cole his hand and helped him raise to his feet, the roof of the passenger car collapsed in a torrent of fire and smoke. No more necroids could arrive that way. All three of them looked back into the flames, exhausted.

"What was that?" Byron asked.

"What?" Cole replied.

"What you did to those skeletons. You stopped them."

"Me?" Cole's expression showed shock.

"You screamed 'No!' and they just froze, like they were under orders."

"It's true," Adhita confirmed. "You used your mind to stop the necroids—the *Danath*. Byron seems to be able to warp time—a Temporal power. What you just displayed is a true, and powerful Necrological ability. Perhaps both Oakes brothers have magical gifts."

"But why Necrological?" Cole asked. "I'm not a Necromancer. I'm not . . ." he stuttered, "not *evil*."

A loud pop, followed by a grinding noise from the flaming passenger car drew their attention. The leather belt snapped and the door ripped open. There, wreathed in flame, his skin backlit into shadow, but his silver armor reflecting the inferno of orange light, stood the hulking form of Aquinas Justice, naked longsword gripped in his clenched fist.

CHAPTER FORTY-FIVE
Down the Rabbit Hole

The power came back to Plymouth New Hampshire at 1:20 AM. Charlie had flipped the light switch to ON before going to bed so that it would wake him up. It did.

At first he felt groggy and disoriented, squinting, groaning, and feeling like he always did on Christmas morning when the kids used to burst through his door before dawn, ready to see if Santa had visited. He sat up, rubbing his eyes and scratching his rough chin. His mouth was dry. Felicity sat up next to him.

"Power's back on," she observed.

"Yeah," he replied. "Time to go." He swung his feet off the bed and sat for a moment with his hands on his knees. The air in the room was chilled. No electricity meant no heat, he reminded himself, and the trailer had inadequate insulation. On cue, the furnace hummed to life, circulating lukewarm air through the vents.

"I'll wake Jack," Felicity said, slipping out of bed and pulling on a pair of slippers.

"Already up." Jack called from the next room. "Going to fry some eggs. Want some?"

"Yeah," Charlie replied.

"No thanks," Felicity added.

"How many?"

"Four?"

"Sure." The noise of the refrigerator opening and pots and pans rattling told them Jack was busy. The coffee machine burbled.

Felicity wrapped him in a tight hug. "Bring them back" she said through tears. He kissed her hair.

"We will," he soothed, rubbing her back. "Keep the light on for us, is all."

"I'll run it every day," she said. "Come back to me, too."

"Promise." He turned and began to change, pulling on biker shorts, then tan Carhartts. He slid a thermal tee shirt over his head and took a camouflage, hooded jacket from the closet.

"Felicity," he said, turning to her. "You're not going to like this," he began, "but I think Jack's right." He patted a cardboard shoebox on the closet floor. "There's a handgun in here. It's easy to use, intuitive. It's magazine-loaded. Slap it in, turn off the safety, and it's ready to fire."

"Charlie," she began.

He held up a hand.

"No. I understand your convictions, but it's just you here, now, and you'll be tending that portal. Things could come through. You have to be ready. If something happens to you here, we're never going to be able to come back—Cole and Byron will never come back to their world. Do this for them.'"

She hesitated, then nodded. "Okay. I'll guard the mirror, keep it open."

"It's not the glamour job," Charlie said, "I know, and waiting is always worse than doing something, but it's just as important—what you'll do here—as what we're going to be doing over there."

"I know," she said, tears trailing down her cheeks.

"Look," he sighed. "I love you."

"Stop it," she said. "This isn't goodbye, and you *are* coming back to me, so don't give me the departing hero act." She was trying to sound annoyed to cover her emotions.

"Yeah. I'm going to go eat." He turned awkwardly toward the door, mumbling, "Never been good at goodbyes."

A half hour later, they'd dressed, eaten, and were packed and ready to go. The mirror shimmered in the middle of the room, and Churchill the donkey stood, dripping wet, in the living room beside Charlie, all harnessed up. Instead of eggs and coffee, of which the room had smelled pleasantly moments before, the air was now laden with the musk of mud and wet fur. Bringing Churchill through the door had been a strange moment and the donkey certainly looked out of place standing on the carpet with muddy, snow-crusted hooves, but here the mirror stood, and he had to go through it.

Their plan was to pass through, scout around a bit, build a cairn of stone, and then come back to appraise Felicity of the situation before heading off in earnest. Jack would go first as a sort of vanguard, scanning the immediate area for danger, and Charlie would follow thirty seconds later, leading the donkey.

"Ready?" Jack asked.

"Yeah," he replied. They fist-bumped.

"I'm ready to recover my hat," Jack quipped with a wink at Felicity. He hefted his AR-13, which was made heavier by the pull of the magnet and checked his watch. He flexed a bicep and winked at Charlie. "See you on the other side, *Lance*," he smiled crookedly and ducked through the portal, vanishing.

Charlie nodded at Felicity and sighed. She grimaced.

"Well," he said, "we've already been through all this. I gotta go."

She reached for his hand. "You be careful over there, Charlie Oakes."

"I will," he said. "I've got Jack, just like Cole has Byron. We'll keep each other safe."

They kissed and parted.

He hunched his shoulders and walked without hesitation into the mirror. The rope on Churchill tightened, and the animal moved forward slowly, reluctantly, but also melted into its own reflection.

"Well," Felicity said, standing in an empty, silent room staring into her own eyes in the cyan glow of the mirror. "I suppose I'd better get used to this."

CHAPTER FORTY-SIX
Dispensing Justice

Justice loomed before them, wreathed in flame and backlit into shadow. Adhita screamed, Cole grabbed her hand, and Harald began a torrent of aggressive barking and growls. In contrast, Byron leapt into action. He crossed the distance to the end of the tender in the same amount of time it took Justice to climb the railing and make a leap. Byron slammed the butt end of his rifle into Justice's armored chest, mid-leap, forcing him back and making him miss the mark. Instead of landing inside the tender, the undead bodyguard found himself hanging off the outside edge by his left hand.

He looked up at Byron, and to his horror, the young man saw Justice's damaged face. The right half, blown off by Rochester's last shot, revealed white bone and an empty eye-socket. Grinning, gaping teeth shone up from the exposed jaw. In the left socket, one eye stared fiercely up at him, bloodshot. The flesh of that half of the head actually burned with flames, combusted as Justice had crossed through the passenger car. An involuntary shudder of fear shot through Byron's limbs.

Justice pulled himself up with his left arm and swept at Byron with his longsword. The swing came blindingly fast—Byron attempted a jump, clearing the blade by a millimeter. He grinned, realizing his good fortune then landed painfully on his hurt foot.

Trying to pull his armored bulk up into the coal car, Justice then swung his sword arm over the lip of the tender wall, bringing his clenched fist down against the coal and hoisting himself up. Byron saw Justice's longsword braced at an awkward angle, between the bodyguard's firm grip and the iron wall. Taking advantage of the moment, Byron drove the rifle butt into the flat of the blade with all his strength. It clanged, snapping in two. He retreated a step as Justice pulled himself over the wall and onto the pile of coal.

Justice took one look at his broken blade and discarded it, rising to his feet. A few straggling, blackened skeletons began to climb up the rails behind him. Byron backed off further, trying to keep his extended rifle between himself and Justice. Harald, however, attacked. The dog leapt for Justice's throat. Instinctively, the bodyguard threw up an arm, which the dog took in his teeth. Justice growled, shaking his arm violently to remove him. Dislodged, Harald fell to the scattered coal, but the distraction lasted long enough for Byron to take a swing. The rifle butt came in crosswise, aimed for Justice's head—a crushing blow. Seeing it out of the corner of his good eye, though, Justice shifted his weight and took the assault on his shoulder plate, deflecting the rifle over his head. He then kicked out viciously, connecting with Harald's chest and sending the dog, yelping, over the edge of the car and into the air.

"No!" Cole screamed again, watching as his dog hit the ground hard and roll into the tall grass, disappearing from view as the train hurtled on. Cole turned to Justice and made an ill-advised rush with his shovel. Jabbing it like a spear, he missed. Justice sidestepped and used Cole's momentum against him. He flung the teen into the back corner of the tender, stripping the shovel as he went. Cole crashed painfully against the iron wall, dazedly looking up to see two soot-stained necroids advancing on him, apparently all that remained of the skeletal contingent.

Realizing his disadvantage, Byron had taken a moment to fix the sword-like bayonet to his rifle. He now stood with the weapon outstretched like a spear, facing off against the greatest fighter in Avalon, Aquinas Justice, now armed with a coal shovel. The two of them sparred. Byron used all of his reflexes to counteract his opponent's skill—retreating all the while. He was outmatched, and he knew it.

Adhita fled back to the engine, to the side of the coal tender with the hinged wall. She had an idea. She looked at the pin, then at Justice, and grinned. If she and Cole, who was at the other corner, could pull the pins simultaneously, she thought, the tender would dump its load of coal—and Justice with it—off the side of the rails. She tried to signal Cole, but he focused his attention on two skeletons standing over him. Like those before, these two seemed frozen. While she watched, Cole gestured and the two turned, scrabbling away from him toward Justice.

"Cole!" she shouted. "Colton!"

No response.

She picked up a chunk of black rock and lobbed it at him. It hit him in the shoulder.

He looked over, his mouth forming the word 'ouch.'

She pointed at the pin and mimed removing it.

He nodded, then looked back at Justice. "What about Byron?" he shouted back.

Byron ducked a sweep of Justice's shovel and retreated a pair of steps, jabbing with his bayonet. It glanced off his opponent's armor. He backed a step and blocked a counter-swing, but Justice then brought his shovel down on the gun with such force that it jarred from Byron's grip. He fell backwards, grabbing the far wall of the tender. Justice lifted his shovel for a killing blow, but was grappled, unexpectedly, by the pair of skeletons.

Reaching back, Justice ripped the skull from one, launching it out into the grass. Byron groped for his rifle, but Justice stepped on it, glaring down at him, one-eyed.

Byron stared up, his mouth agape, but got struck in the side by a piece of coal. He turned to lock eyes with Adhita.

"Hold on!" she hollered. "Grab the wall!" And without waiting for an answer, she pulled the pin from the latch on the side of the tender.

Cole did the same. The wall fell open, connecting with the ground, lurching the train on its track, and ultimately tearing from its hinges to clang to the gravel rushing by below.

The coal began to slide, cascading over the edge. It shifted under Byron and under Justice's feet. Byron clung to the wall with both hands. The undead bodyguard grabbed at his injured foot, but he kicked Justice in the face at the right moment, dislodging the fingers. He watched over his shoulder as, rumbling and emitting a cloud of fine black dust, the coal tumbled down and off the tender in a black avalanche, taking Justice and the other skeleton with it. They flew over the side, and into the grass among a tumble of black rock. And then they were gone, left behind by the rapid progress of the engine.

Cole stood, still shaking with adrenaline and fear, and carefully walked the width of the nearly empty tender to reach his brother.

"Hey, jock, you okay?" he asked, putting his hands on Byron's shoulders.

"Yeah, but Harald," Byron blurted, tears smeared the coal dust on his face.

"I know," Cole replied, holding back his own sorrow. "I know, but we can't do anything about it now. We have to plan—to get out of here."

Adhita moved near them now. "Pressure's dropping in the boiler," she said. "We're slowing. We need to feed that fire."

"Shovels are both gone," Cole replied. "We'll have to do it by hand. And we don't have the coal left to cross the steppe."

"We need a plan," Adhita said, looking at Cole, expectant.

"Well, I don't have one," he snapped, then regained his composure. "Not yet." He lifted the front of his sweatshirt, making a storage space, and started filling it with coal. "Right now, let's feed the fire and put some distance between us and Justice. In an hour or so, we'll stop the engine and search the cars. Maybe one is full of coal. That would get us there. If not, we can unhook the other cars and extend our range some. We'll figure something out." Having filled the bowl of his shirt, he trudged off toward the engine with his load.

Adhita sat heavily against the wall about a body length from Byron, who stared into the distance, his eyes uncomprehending.

"What are you thinking?" she asked.

"I'm not," he replied. "I'm trying not to, anyway. This whole thing has been a nightmare—start to finish."

A sudden rumble jarred them as more of the passenger car collapsed in on itself. A cloud of sparks erupted and was carried off by the wind. Enough of the car had disappeared now that Byron could see the boxcar behind blazed as well, flames reaching high into the air. Perhaps the whole train would burn in a domino effect, he thought.

"Nightmare or not," Adhita replied, looking back to Cole, "I'm glad to have met you two."

Cole nodded and grunted, sitting painfully between the others, his back to the wall. "If I have to be here," he sighed and reached down to take both Byron's hand and Adhita's "I'm glad it's with you."

They sat silent, listening to the chugging of the engine, the clack of the rails, and the crackle of the burning boxcar. They watched the grass blur by in the foreground against the twilit backdrop of the white-capped, jagged ridgeline, their faces smeared with coal dust and tears, and their eyes glazed with exhaustion—both physical and emotional.

"You suppose one of those mountains is the source of the *Wyrmhod*?" Cole asked, "where this whole thing started?"

"Yeah," Byron replied, "and it's fading into the distance."

Adhita stood and pushed a length of wet, dirty hair out of her face. She lifted the front of her dress into a bowl and began collecting a second load of coal, then carried it to the engine, limping on pained shins. Byron and Cole sat together for a moment longer, still holding hands.

"When we get home and I turn eighteen," Byron observed, looking down at his hand in Cole's. "Let's get matching tattoos."

"Sure," Cole replied. "What of?"

"Our hands, maybe? And just one word," Byron said, setting his jaw: "Brothers."

Cole nodded solemnly. "Done."

EPILOGUE
Hats off to Narnia

Jack and Charlie stood next to the rolling waters of a mountain stream. Behind them, the sunrise shone on a backdrop of snow-capped ridges, and a breeze blew along the water, tossing the cattails. Thin white clouds scudded across the rose-tinted sky. Raucous crows cawed in the distance and a hound bayed somewhere.

"Helluva angle to come out of the mirror," Jack complained, scanning the area in front of him from behind his shouldered rifle. "Haven't had to crawl through the mud like that since boot."

"Yeah, everything's oriented perpendicular on this side," Charlie agreed, swiping some mud from his Carhartts. He took a deep breath of fresh mountain air. "Nice place, though," he observed, pulling Churchill's lead and advancing to stand beside his brother.

"Yeah," Jack agreed, lowering his muzzle and squinting into the nearby woods, "except I can't find my goddamned hat."

"Perhaps I can be of service, chaps?" A prim, British voice sounded from over their shoulders. The brothers whirled to find a tiny, tubby man with a pointed hat, blue vest, and brown pants sitting cross-legged on a stone. He held a long-stemmed pipe in one hand, and on his lap rested Jack's camouflage baseball hat.

"You weren't here two seconds ago," Charlie said.

"Poindexter, at your service," the small man chuckled in a self-satisfied way. His eyes twinkled. "May I assume that you, also, are Oakes brothers? And that you," he pointed the end of his clay pipe at Charlie, "are the first-born? I can always tell."

"What the hell are you, some kind of leprechaun?" Jack asked from behind the lifted barrel of his AR-15.

Charlie put an arm gently up and lowered his brother's gun. "*Also* Oakes brothers . . ." he repeated. "Then you've seen my sons?"

Poindexter fixed a stony look on Jack for a pair of heartbeats, yet when he spoke his tone remained warm and cheerful. "You'd best get over that human superiority complex, my boy. So many of your kind possess the erroneous idea of human exceptionalism—especially those who cross over from your mundane world. You have no magic, and you're in our world now." He puffed out a licorice and mint scented smoke ring and tilted his head to listen to the crows. Jack's hat lifted off the little man's lap, almost—it seemed—of its own will, and floated over to Jack, rotating, and settling down upon his head.

Poindexter sniffed. "I am, properly considered, an elf, though I get various reactions from the British humans with whom I interact: leprechaun is fairly frequent, as is gnome." He turned to Charlie. "Byron and Colton—yes. I met them. They walked downstream together." He gestured, again, with the stem of his pipe. Both Charlie and Jack turned to stare down the river to where it curved in the distance. The sun shone down, and the water sparkled in its rays.

A tear came, unbidden, to Charlie's eye.

"You know, Charlie," Jack said, readjusting his hat and cracking a cocky smile. "This might be easier than we thought."

But as he said it, a large man burst from the woods, sprinting up the stream toward them, curved sword in hand. He was followed by a murder of jabbering crows. In the distance behind him, Charlie and Jack could hear the baying of hounds. A handful of seconds later, a dozen diminutive, demonic skeletal creatures broke from the trees, giving chase. They galloped up the riverbank on small hooves, grinning white skulls sprouting curved goat horns. Sharp spears glinted in their hands.

"Maybe not," Jack corrected, raising his rifle again.

"Definitely not," Charlie agreed, dropping Churchill's lead and stepping on it before drawing his own gun from the pack-saddle.

Jack fired. The skull of one demonic centaur skeleton shattered in a cloud of dust. "Welcome to Narnia," he quipped, drawing a bead on a second.

To be continued . . .

ACKNOWLEDGMENTS

A novel is indelibly associated with the name of its author, but none is ever completed in seclusion. Many folks have an invisible hand in this one, and I'd like to take a moment to thank a few of them.

Robert Scott, thank you for your continued mentorship, optimism, and enthusiasm. What you do for the writing community and the youth of northern Virginia cannot be overstated.

Bob and Elaine Kaven, I've always enjoyed our readings, visits, and conversations. I invariably leave our interactions energized and inspired to continue my writing. This alone would be enough to warrant thanks, but you also took the time and energy to beta-read the whole manuscript, and it is a much better novel because of your efforts.

Speaking of beta-readers, I want to thank Lauren Howard, Andrew Panning, and Virginia Saunders for taking the time to read the manuscript and give me feedback at various stages of its development. Your work was helpful and is appreciated. And Ginnie, double-thanks to you for the beautiful cover design. Folks, do yourselves a favor and visit her page: www.VirginiaSaunders.com.

I'd also like to acknowledge the *Poets and Writers* group and *Deja Brew Café* in Warrenton, VA. To the former, thanks for your open interest in and feedback on the manuscript over the past two years. To the latter, thank you for providing a safe and stable home to the local writing community (and for the chai tea).

And finally, Elizabeth Todd, rather than list all the myriad things that you've done for me and the boys for the past two years, I'll just continue to appreciate that you put up with my pretentions and give me time and space to write, edit, confer, publish, and publicize my writing. I love you.

Scott Davis Howard holds an MA in British literature from the University of Montana, Missoula (2008), a BS in communications from Norwich University (2000), is a *Washington Post* Teacher of the Year nominee, and is the author of two novels and sundry short stories. He spends his days regaling his 9th and 12th grade students with thrilling tales about Beowulf, Odysseus, Sir Gawain, Jim Hawkins, and Dorian Gray, and his nights ferrying his offspring between the soccer field, swimming pool, and Scout meetings. In his rare moments of quiet (when the children are eating snacks in the van, sprinkling crumbs all over the carpet), he wonders when and how he became a soccer mom. In his spare time, he writes.

Byron and Colton's adventures will continue in *The Pursuit*, Book 2 of the *Faraday's Mirror* Series.

Coming December, 2021.

Made in the USA
Middletown, DE
18 August 2020